Wilton Sankawulo

SUNDOWN AT DAWN

A Liberian Odyssey

Dusty Spark Publishing

SUNDOWN AT DAWN
A Liberian Odyssey

A Novel by

WILTON SANKAWULO

BY THE SAME AUTHOR

The Marriage of Wisdom
The Rain and the Night
Why Nobody Knows When He Will Die
Liberia and African Unity
Tolbert of Liberia
One Hundred Questions About Liberia
What My Country Needs Today
Pot of Gold
In the Cause of the People

Library of Congress Control Number: 2004116462

ISBN 0-9763565-0-3
Printed and bound in the United States of America

Dusty Spark Publishing
www.DustySpark.com

HOUSTON

DUSTY
SPARK
PUBLISHING

In memory of Data, NeSuaa, Ma Miller

NGALAKEMENI

Lightning pierced the dark sky and thunder crashed; a fierce rainstorm rustled thatched roofs and the forest, sending debris all over. Torrential waters coursed down the laterite slope to the bamboo swamp north of the village. People bustled indoors for cover, and bleating animals pressed themselves against houses. Mother hurried her cooking for us to eat and go to bed.

When *Zamai's*[1] fury reduced, I asked Father to tell me a story, for the bleak night was good only for storytelling. Wrapped in a white homespun bed sheet, he went out to the porch and slouched cross-legged in his rattan chair, staring at the grim darkness.

"Don't you see how wet and stormy it is?" he said somberly. "Wait till tomorrow night." By then the moon might be up, and I would want to play with my friends.

I watched him with entreaty and groaned. Spying my pouting lips by the glare of the center room fire, he said:

"I'll tell you a short story just to put you to sleep."

"Not about Mr. Spider, I hope," I said, laying my arm on his thigh for support. I was tired hearing about Spider and his greed.

"No!" he said, so loudly that I thought he was addressing the lightning that tore the sky and brightened the porch for a moment. "My story is about Ngalakemeni[2] who was born in his parents' old age. Not wishing to leave him a helpless, lonely orphan when they died, they sent him to school to become a *kwii.*[3]"

"Where did he go to school?" I hung my head in contemplation.

"Ducor[4] , *kwii* people's biggest town." Father scratched his beard stubble softly. "After finishing school, Ngalakemeni got whatever he wanted: money, women, wine, and servants—not to speak of cattle, rice, oil, meat, and fish. All he had to do was ask and he was given. He deserved the privilege, though, for he gave up the comfort and security of home and chose to suffer."

"Must have become a king, then."

"You could say that. The president made him Deecee[5] for Salala District. Became the mainstay of support for his family. Ngalakemeni fought his battle alone because his parents were too old to help him. His relatives said they would be dead or too old when he finished school. What would they get out of him for their troubles? But the lonely battle made him wise, brave, and determined. As they say, 'The child with too many hands to hold never learns to walk.'" After a pause, Father ended the story on a firm note: "I want you to be like Ngalakemeni."

---

1. Name given to the rainy season when it reaches its zenith.
2. "God's doing." A name given to a child whose birth occurred through the grace of God. Either parent was known to be barren or too sickly to have a child.
3. An educated person or one who is a member of the elite.
4. The native name for the city of Monrovia, the capital of Liberia; believed to originate from the Vai language.
5. Term for D. C. or District Commissioner.

Really a short story! I loved it, of course, and even wished to be like Ngalakemeni, but his story was too sketchy to be true, a pretext I believed Father had devised to send me to school. Ngalakemeni had never existed.

Adjusting the voluminous bedclothes round his broad shoulders, Father shambled into the house. As I pondered the story of the unknown boy, he returned and sprawled in the chair again, looking at the cold rainy night. If the story had touched him so deeply, I thought, it must be true.

"Don't be afraid," he said. "School is good. You'll make many friends there; learn how to send a message on paper to another school person elsewhere—even in faraway America or England. That person gets your message, exactly what you put on the paper—"

"A society?" I said.

"With members all over the world. The whole world becomes your family when you join it; so you won't grieve much over our death. You'll consider it an opportunity to show your love and respect for us."

"My friends will go there with me?"

"I don't think so." Father reflected awhile and said, "Their parents will want them to be farmers, hunters, fishermen, *kenablad*[6] —as if stuffing the belly with food were all there's to life. Of course, the Poro[7] teaches boys how to survive in this terrible world, but I don't want you to merely survive. A market[8] ago, the Land[9] chose you as this year's sacrificial lamb, but the Shrine doesn't accept an only child. They gave me two markets to find a full-grown bull and ten pounds to redeem you! From where could I have gotten all that? Luckily, last year white people asked the Land for children to put in school—one child from each town. This request had the full backing of the government. Any Chief who failed to comply with it in a year, risked a long prison term in Belle Yallah. You were chosen for Haindi. In their opinion, sending you to school amounted to killing you. That spared me the impossible redemption fees and saved your life, for boys recruited for the mission are exempt from all obligations to the tribe."

"Are you people not eating?" Mother called, her voice tinged with annoyance.

"Give mine to the child," Father said, absently scratching his leg and looking at the cold night. He usually gave me his suppers during rainy seasons when famine raged.

"Zurong[10]," Mother said, "come eat. Don't mind your father's long talks. His stories never end."

"It'd be unfair to leave him in the dark any longer," Father told her. "School will soon open."

The food had hardly gone down my throat when I returned to Father. I wanted to know more about the sacrificial lamb: what purpose it served

6. Initiates of the Poro Society.
7. A society that prepares males to be good citizens, husbands, fathers; also teaches males the history and traditional values of the tribe.
8. The weekly market is the basis for the calendar; one market equals one week.
9. When capitalized, land refers to the living, dead, and unborn members of society. It also refers to the leadership of the tribe which represents God and the Ancestors.
10. "The man." Name given to a male child.

and why it had to be a human being rather than sheep, goat, or chicken. I was afraid he might not wish to dwell further on the somber affair which involved my narrow escape. How fortunate was I to be free from a cruel death and have the honor of representing my home in the *kwii* world! And why all this talk of death? Now I understood Father's contempt for traditional life. Presently he was telling me about challenges of the *kwii* world:

"Many sons of Fuama[11] joined the *kwii* society but never came home again. Home became too poor and uncivilized for them. What a shame and sad mistake! An uncle of yours tried to join it, too, but, like most of his friends, he was expelled from the mission because of woman. The mission doesn't allow you to put your hand in woman business while in school. It's their greatest law. You can't blame the poor child, however." Father adjusted his toga and continued: "The boys we gave the white people at the time were full-grown. We'd thought matured boys would cope better with the *kwii* world.

"Unfortunately, they sneaked regularly out of the mission at night to look for women in Gargbelei, Haindi, Mauwa—even Dingshu! They had their women but at a heavy price. The mission expelled them!" Father sighed with dismay and looked in my face. "Now they were condemned to be mere farmers, hunters, fishermen, and *porlortor*[12]." He nodded his head for each word.

"I love farming, Data," I said. "No matter how many books I learn, I'll always make farm."

"*Kwii* people don't make farm, my son. It's hard to understand, but they don't."

"How do they get food to eat?"

"We provide their food," Father said. "That's why I want you to become a *kwii*." After a pause he said, "When you go to the mission, forget about girls and learn book so that people won't take advantage of you.

"School takes time, my son—plenty of time. You can be sure I won't be around when you finish it. But once you learn enough books to care for yourself, your family, and your old mother, I'll be more than happy in my grave—and you'll have my blessings." He sauntered into the house without a backward glance.

For a market after the sobering revelation, I kept at Father's side daily to learn more about school, but he had no more to say about it than what he told me that night. To take time off my hand until school opened, I chased birds from the rice shoots. Often I sat in the farm shed on many a rainy day recalling some of the lovely action-packed tales Father now told me each night at no special request. I especially loved those about brave hunters crossing large rivers and toppling tall mountains to kill lions and elephants.

One evening Bopaa, our gang leader, sent me word to accompany them on "an important mission" the following morning. If I didn't, he would "jail" me; he was tired of my boycotting their activities.

---

11. Distortion of the Kpelle word "furanma", meaning where no economy is practiced as far as food is concerned. The novel's principal setting is believed to be such a place.

12. Forced laborer. Kpelle distortion of the English word "porter."

PARTING GIFT

They came for me at sunrise. Bubbling with excitement, we jaunted along the bushy path to the riverbank, searching thickets with keen eyes for rodents. We decided not to swim, for the river was full to overflowing. Dismissing fishing in consequence, we only chattered, debated, and wrestled until Molley, who disliked rough plays, suggested that we gamble.

"With what?" Bhea asked him.

"No *kpano* here?" Molley said, starting his collection of the flat nuts littering the sandy bank.

Obviously, nobody wished to spoil the good day with a fuss or fight, so we agreed to gamble, even though hunting or gathering palm nuts would have been better for the sunny day.

Suddenly, we heard a loud rustling and a deep lowing in the thicket on the upper bank.

"Mooooo!" blared the voice.

"Woor! Woor!" sounded the rustling.

Growing sober, we abandoned the nuts and armed ourselves with clubs, watching the thicket with a fixed gaze.

"A cow," Bhea decided, his eyes challenging anyone to differ. "Let's get out of here!" he advised, crouching to run away. (Since a stampeding cow pierced Flomolon's heart a year ago, no one ever fooled with the demon-infested cows of Haindi. Senator Bheipu Loryii who owned them, sacrificed one each year to prolong his life, but only after a Zoe had exorcized the demon out of it. Overgrown and bored, these cows were dangerous.)

"Fool," Zina dismissed Bhea's claim, bracing for a punch as Bhea often forced his ideas on others with blows.

"Mooooo!" the lowing resounded. Then rasping in baritone, it declared, "You naughty boys are now caught in The Devil's net; he'll chew you raaaaw!"

"Bopaa!" Molley thought he recognized the voice.

"Bopaa!" Zina confirmed the claim.

"Let The Devil come meet his match," Dakena said as we put our clubs down.

"Were it The Devil, you sinners would have wet your pants and run away," Bopaa said, parting the thicket and walking slowly to us. "So, you boys have nothing better to do than gather nuts on this fine day!" he raged.

Bopaa had a stout build and a narrow face with large eyeballs. Like us, he was covered from head to foot with the scabs and scratches of the jungle. He carried a cutlass in his armpit, suggesting that we might cut palm nuts or clear bushes for a cassava patch. Bopaa headed the gang because he was a *kenamu*[13]. Often he scared us with the Poro Master (called Ngamui, The Big Thing, The Devil, Basai, or The Bush Thing) to ensure immediate compliance with his stern orders.

---

13. An initiate of the Poro Society.

The Bush Thing's visit to town, which usually occurred late at night, was infrequent but terrifying. He would harangue the village with his presence in a chilling, esoteric voice that sent uninitiated boys scurrying under beds for refuge, for he would threaten to bore roofs and ceilings with his talons to snatch them from their beds and eat them up. Only initiates of the Poro like Bopaa could meet him and return safely to their houses. As for women, who were not entitled to "rebirth" after he "consumed" them, it was a matter of life and death to be behind closed doors during these ominous visits. Whenever the Poro was in session, they sang their whereabouts while traveling or fishing to avoid an unexpected encounter with him.

Although he was a stern disciplinarian, we loved Bopaa because he treated us like the big brother and *kenamu* that he was. He let us have the first picks of any food he divided among us, while he took the last, usually the least. He was always the first to quit eating whenever we ate from the same dish and was fair in settling our disputes.

"Deyn is angry today," he said, glancing sourly at the swollen river. "To Willietaa road we go!"

Pocketing our *kpano*, we followed him at a trot, first to town for shirts and cutlasses, then to Willietaa road. After walking awhile in the shadows of enveloping foliage on the winding, rocky road, searching treetops and thickets for birds' nests and squirrels, Bopaa surprisingly brought the hunting party to a sudden stop on the crest of a hill. Pointing his sinewy arms at two crossed branches of adjoining *sara* trees scraping each other in the gentle breeze, he asked harshly:

"What caused that?" He searched our faces with bulging eyes. Only the screeching branches and chirping birds made a sound. We looked at the boughs and then at him with puzzled eyes.

"What do you mean?" Zina braved a query, sniffed, and wiped his nose. "The trees grew up together, and so their branches were bound to cross each other!"

"Use your head, Mister Fool!" roared Bopaa. "Many trees stand together, but their branches don't cross each other like this. Think. Your head isn't made for decoration. Do I have to draft someone?" he asked. "Well, Sepor-lor[14], it's your question." Everyone looked at me with curiosity. "You'll soon go to book house where you'll have to use your head, so we must put plenty of sense in it." The boys darted their eyes at each other and at me. "You fellows haven't heard the news yet?" Bopaa said, pointing at me. "This man has been marked for book! He'll soon leave us to go to school." I wondered how he got the news. Well, nothing was secret to a *kenamu*.

I watched the *sara* branches intensely, and then looked at the ground. All sorts of fuzzy ideas whirled in my mind, none taking on a definite shape; but I must say something quickly to avoid punishment!

"A big *lorbha*[15] and his family once lived on the upper bough," I began

---

14. Old man, name given to a male child that resembles a grandfather.

15. A big, red forest monkey.

with hesitation, looking at Bopaa for reassurance. He nodded. "Their weight pressed it down until it touched the lower one and couldn't rise again."

"You're on the way. Go on."

"So, the wind is forcing it to return to its former place—"

"Monkeys don't sleep in trees but on the ground!" Zina cut in with an ironic grin.

"Shut up!" Bopaa barked at him. "You said nothing when I first asked the question. Why laugh at someone who is trying to answer it? Seporlor, you seem to know the fact-finding game, but monkeys don't live in the same tree that long; the shotgun brings them down before you bat your eyes." Giving the "real" explanation of the puzzle, he said, "Many years ago, Mother Hornbill picked a mouthful of ripe *sara* nuts in a faraway forest for her starving children. While flying home she spied a ripe bunch of nuts on a solitary palm tree. Being too greedy she tried to pick some to carry; two of the *sara* nuts fell from her mouth. After many years, they grew into these colossal trees. Seeing none of their kind round here, they stuck together.

"'The farmer who is foolish enough to cut one of us down will surely be crushed to death!' they said. These trees are a problem for farmers. See, who can cut any of them down without endangering his life?" Looking at us with widened eyes, he said, "The next thing I want to know is what makes the rain fall. I want the answer this evening—by the way, who's hungry? Molley, take us to your farm. I'm sure your mother has plenty of food there for you, knowing how you love eating."

The road to Molley's farm wandered past ours, crossed the Waydiyea, and wended through a grassy field, the site of their old farm. We met his sensitive father sharpening cutlass on a piece of granite before the farm shed. NanSee, who was slow of speech, replied our greetings with questions:

"What have you boys been doing in town? Playing?"

Molley frantically removed lids from pots and bowls in the shed and flung them aside. All were empty.

"We're hungry!" he said with irritation, looking at his father.

"Can't you boys cook?" NanSee said.

"When too hungry can you cook?" Molley said, glancing sideways in distress.

"Shouldn't boys who idle in town all day playing do their own cooking?"

"Don't we bring plenty of spoils home at times?"

"Does your mother have a mate?"

"Is that my business?"

"You expect me to cook for you boys?"

"Can all this talk fill our bellies with food?"

"NanSee, don't mind him," I said. "We have plenty of *kpano*."

"Talk for yourself!" Molley retorted. "What can *kpano* do to the gut of a hungry person?"

The Old Man flushed, tested the edge of his large cutlass with his fingers, and walked through the burnt farm towards the forest.

We met Molley's exhausted mother planting rice under a cottonwood tree crowded with squeaking *sorya.* NeFita straightened her back, placed one hand to her hip and threw the other one bearing her small hoe over her shoulder.

"No food here," she said crisply in response to our greetings. "Go to NeSuaa." A sullen expression appeared on every face.

Once beautiful and vivacious but now prematurely old and emaciated, NeFita always carried a drawn face and complained of chronic stomach pains and breathlessness. One couldn't help concluding that her maladies were due to hard work and indifference to food. She worked from dawn to dusk every day and cooked only one meal each day, late at night in town. "One can't do much work on a loaded stomach," she was fond of saying to Molley's displeasure, whose sunken stomach and bulky build called for at least two round meals per day.

Having turned into a large crimson ball, the sun was sinking rapidly in the West when we met Mother and a large group of women singing an unruly Sande[16] song and planting rice with gusto. She said the women had vowed to complete planting a big portion of the farm before sundown. Father had already gone to the river for his evening swim.

Mother gave us a big bowl of rice and stewed cassava leaves, dry fish, and palm oil. We ate until our bellies stretched like *samkpa*[17]. To earn the rich food, we decided to catch a monkey the following day for our hardworking mothers. On the way home Bopaa changed the plan. He said each one should cut two bunches of ripe palm nuts for his family, for men should never leave the bush with empty hands.

He wandered into the forest while the rest of us went down to the swamp round Gbonkpotoli Creek where wild palms grew in abundance. We had cut only a bunch of ripe palm nuts when he summoned us with the hunter's call. The humming, nasal tone sounded urgent.

"Has caught a deer!" Molley said excitedly, his ears cocked.

"Think so?" I said. "Could be in danger!"

"Don't you understand the call? A trap of his has caught something!"

Rattling through the tangled shrubbery in the direction of the call, we saw Bopaa holding tight the tail of a huge monkey with both hands, his face contorted, his left leg stretched far behind him, the right one bent at an angle. We bludgeoned the creature frantically with clubs. Despite our brutal attack, it broke loose from Bopaa's firm grip and sprang on Zina who wielded the biggest club, biting him in the chest, savagely twisting his head sideways. Bopaa landed a powerful blow on the head of the misguided beast; it tumbled to the ground instantly, made several awkward gasps, and died.

"He thought I was a monkey," Zina said with disgust after the fierce battle, gloomily inspecting his bloody, torn shirt; panting. Bopaa took it off him. Happily, only minor scratches were on his chest; thanks to the shirt. As Bopaa applied herb juice to his wound, we laid the monkey on the grassy

16. Women's society that prepares females to be good citizens, wives, and mothers; it also educates them about the history and traditional values of the tribe.

17. Tom-tom held by the thighs and pounded with the palms, usually played by males.

roadside for butchering.

"I heard a grunt," he explained as he cut up the monkey while we held it for his convenience. "Thinking it was a boar; I dropped on all fours and crawled quietly into that thicket." He pointed vaguely with his bloody cutlass at a cluster of tangled undergrowth behind him. "But it was this fellow that came down from that *kobeley* tree to join his 'playmate'—and we really played." Bopaa giggled briefly and gave me the largest share of the meat—the head and a whole haunch—obviously as a farewell gesture. Then he wrapped up the *gaigai*[18] in fresh leaves to cook in town later, for night had fallen.

"You've become a man," Mother told me with pride when I gave her my spoils. "Mere boys catching a living monkey with their bare hands is no joke! But, you had better learn how to set *lifa*[19]. Catching a living monkey with your hands is dangerous! A monkey's bite is as fatal as a snake's."

"Don't make a woman of him," Father protested. "In these dangerous surroundings, a boy must learn to be a man as soon as he is able to stand on his feet."

---

18. Certain parts of an animal reserved for consumption by members of the Poro Society, such as the legs, heart, liver, intestine.

19. A monkey trap, usually set in a tree.

HAINDI

Christmas was only a market away. Already in a festive mood, the village was slow in wakening despite piercing rooster crows and riotous squeaking of wrens and pepper birds in kola trees on the outskirts. But when the sun exposed the three scores of black thatched roofs, scabrous wooden doors flew open, and people scampered out of their cozy houses.

"You're not playing today," Father called me as I hastened for the riverbank to enjoy the beautiful day with my friends.

He had me put on the new blue denim short pants and white drill short-sleeved shirt Mother had bought for my Christmas. He too wore new clothes: a green gown extending below his knees and covering his black short pants; and a green cap embroidered with blue, red, and black yarns adorning his head. The new outfit gave him a commanding presence, although he despised chieftaincy, something he left to "idle men who enjoy living on whirls of gossips and other people's sweat."

"But Father, this is not Christmas Day!" I said as we came down the dirt steps. In lieu of a reply, he pointed at the road to the river.

It occurred to me that he was taking me to The Big Thing. The cold morning breeze couldn't stop the sweat that poured all over me; the clothes stuck to my body. I remembered Boima making a similar trip with his father to the river to be "reborn" four years later at a Poro graduation.

Father's grave face and Mother's perpetual scowl during the week had foreshadowed the present event. To seal it all, the night before the trip, an owl had hooted ominously in the kola tree behind our house while fire still burned on hearths. Father had planted my navel cord with the seedling of that kola tree! Cold shivers ran down my spine, but I grew calm and relieved when I remembered that Zoe Matadey had secured our home from witches by planting a *towaa* horn in the yard and hanging a *pili* bark to the lintel of the front door. The loathsome creature would soon drop dead, I thought, but the hooting continued and grew more frightening. I became weak and numb, my scalp crawled, my heart swelled, my head grew heavy like a large stone. I couldn't pry myself up from bed despite all my effort. I called Father, but my voice was a mere whimper. Mother rushed to my rescue. (She later admitted that she had heard my voice in her dream.) Shaking me briskly by the shoulder, she whispered, "Who's bothering you in your sleep? Tell me! I'll deal with the person!" In reply to her query, the owl gave a prolonged, sinister cry.

Bamboo torch in hand, Mother flew out of the house, denouncing the demonic bird with a strident voice that resounded in the night:

"Go away with your dirty witchcraft, you despicable witch! Vanish! Drop dead by the power of Zoe[20] Matadey!" Coming to her aid, angry voices from neighboring houses screamed rebukes at the witch that had turned into bird. The owl flew away, its wings chopping the midnight air spitefully.

---

20. A herbalist or medicine person believed to have supernatural powers.

Having bathed, the women now returned from the river with buckets of water delicately balanced on their tousled heads, swinging their outspread arms to maintain balance and watching us with suspicion. They knew better than inquire into our mission.

I stumbled behind Father to the biggest plum tree in Haindi. It stood near the river; its massive boughs in full leaf, a tryst for witches, swayed in the gentle breeze. We descended a low incline to the bank. Squirrels squeaked and bolted up and down huge *kobeley*, *kpano*, and *bhen* trees while saucy monkeys with raised tails walked on their boughs, barking and spying us with wary glances.

"They aren't afraid because we don't have gun," Father told me what I already knew. "They come to the river to drink when the women are taking their morning bath. Women never carry weapon." Grasping my hand firmly, he heaved, "Son, you're now a man, so I can trust you."

When we reached the sloping, rocky landing stage, I looked with longing at the tall, bulky cottonwood tree showering us with fluffy wisps. A lone canoeist paddled the old dugout towards the other shore for travelers who sat by their bundles and *kenja*[21] awaiting his arrival. Suddenly a cawing crow swooped down on the rolling waves, rose steeply in the blue sky and vanished in a patch of mist drifting over Dingshu. Gripping Father's hand with all my might, I tried to contain my fears but couldn't. The unexplained appearance and disappearance of the crow spelt disaster.

Following an obscure path slithering in the thick undergrowth some hundred yards downstream, we parted a blind of dry piassava thatch on our right and entered a fresh clearing with four reed benches. Near the shore was a formation of rocks unevenly spread in the river; in the middle of the spread, tipping downstream, stood a jutting piece of rock resembling a broken pestle.

His lips compressed and a solemn expression on his bronzed face teeming with beads of sweat, Father broke four branches off a sapling and threw them to the right of the rocks where the water bubbled, foamed, and spun like a hollowed top. The fresh leaves sank at once. As if tongue-tied, he twice parted his lips and closed them without saying a word. Then his eyes suddenly lighted. He put his arm round my shoulders and smiled while looking at the rocks.

"Thank God your sacrifice has been accepted!" he said. "Not a single piece of leaf was rejected. The goddess is sorry for your poor mother! You're now ready for your journey! Let's hurry home. These hungry lions—you're lucky they spared you. Son, you're brave. A coward would have cried and consequently been thrown after the leaves."

Hardly had he spoken the last word when two thugs dressed in red caps and black- and yellow-striped skirts with black suspenders studded with cowries, amulets on their left arms, stormed the fence and knocked me flat on my back. Earnestly, I can't recall what happened next, for I was wrought

21. A backpack made from palm or piassava thatch for carrying loads.

unconscious. On awakening, I saw blood pouring from four cuts on my chest, the men nowhere in sight. Father led me away, saying:

"Don't worry. Nothing will happen. You've just taken leave of the Land."

Hitherto, I had considered the Deyn another playground and wonder to explore. Father said the copious torrential waters came all the way from Guinea, cut through the rain forest and snaked its way for a week's walk to the seacoast. I often fished and swam in it, paddled canoe across it; sometimes walked along its sandy shore, marveling at its immense size and the countless breeds of delicious fishes it contained, such as the butter-nose *bulu*, *gornzuleh*, *tounyeh*, and *fulay*.

The Elders feared that my preoccupation with the river meant I had been "sold" to water people—strange, insidious creatures who lived in the river. They sneaked into villages at night during festivals and ensnared children and fools into the depths.

I once asked Water Zoe Deynpolu Kollie of Gargbelei whether it was really true that people lived in the river. The old Zoe, who was sprawling in a wooden chair on his porch, cast an angry, sidelong glance at me and stared into space as if I had broached a forbidden subject.

"I've heard that you're fond of the river," he said coldly. "I warn you not to tamper with it, or you'll be found floating in it one of these days." He spat a lump of phlegm in the yard and looked at me up with his reddish eyes. "Do you hear me?" he declared.

"I've swum across it many times without problem," I told him.

"The top of the river looks calm and peaceful, but horrible things happen underneath!" He emphasized each word with a whisking finger and paused for his words to sink in. "Haindi boys," he shook his head with pity, "are arrant fools." Speaking with authority, he said, "The words of a Zoe are the words of God! Obey them!" Throwing his head back and looking far away, he said, quietly, "I'm sure water people have bought you. Your parents had better do something about it before it's too late."

"I've dived to the bottom of the river many times but found only fish, rock, sand—"

"Don't doubt it!" he roared. "If you doubt their existence, you'll make a fatal accident, go mad, or contract an incurable disease! Do you want to live?"

The Water Zoe's rebuke and stern warning only increased my curiosity about water people. I had learned many fascinating tales about crafty mermaids beguiling innocent lovers on the land and stealing all their money and other valuables, or enriching them overnight but shortening their lives; crocodiles emerging from the depths and playing tug-of-war with elephants, lions, or pythons; monkeys and spiders attending feasts in underwater towns, and so on. No storyteller ever claimed that these weird tales were true. They were only meant for entertainment. But the Zoe's veneration of water people and his warning against casting doubt on their existence implied that in bodies of water were real worlds inhabited by real people.

When I told Father about the Zoe's warning and threat, he said, "Don't worry about water people. The Zoe was simply teasing you. He was drunk, wasn't he?" I nodded. "Water people spirit away only those who are sold to them."

"He said they have bought me!" I cried.

"Only your mother or I can sell you—something we can't afford. Yes, real people live in the river. They hunt, fish, farm, conduct Poro and Sande—everything we do on the land. The smallest of their towns is larger and more populated than Haindi, Dingshu, and Digei put together. Long ago they used to mingle freely with people on the land, but they lost that privilege due to their own arrogance."

Father looked into space steadily as if he was piecing together a recollection that had fled to the edge of his memory. The story he told me was familiar, except that this telling was solemn as if it were a true happening:

"When Genkema put Kwesee Piyonto on The Stool, the town went wild with jubilation. Taking advantage of the happy occasion, a large group of water people, all dressed in white, descended on the town at midnight, singing and dancing with abandon. Their wonderful songs and remarkable dancing feats turned the town upside down. Everybody—from toddlers to old men and women—greeted them with bobbing heads, rocking shoulders, swinging hips, stamping feet—all to the rhythms of *samkpa* and *gbongbon*[22]. The townspeople cheered their visiting merry-makers and showered them with rum, coins, and kola nuts. Who they were or where they had come from was no concern of theirs.

"Strange to say, they carried their *samkpa* drummer shoulder-high like a hero, chortling that he could make the drum talk—and actually he could. Instead of dancing around the village first to honor its residents as was customary for visiting players, they went straight to the square where they placed the *samkpa* man on a chair. There he sat all night, beating away, accompanied by a *gbongbon* drummer. Every so often, the *posia*[23] poked a bottle of rum into his ever wide, open mouth; he would drink lustily, wipe his mouth with the back of his hand and resume his duty with verve. At dawn the players, who were mostly men, gradually reduced in number until they disappeared from the town altogether, except their *samkpa* man who slept like a baby, his head and arms hanging, his drum between his thighs, snoring loudly. Spittle dripped from his mouth. Gathering around him, the people amazingly discovered that he wasn't a true human being at all! Curled under the chair was his only leg, which was nothing but a piece of flabby flesh. A large, lidless eyeball resembling a crescent moon sat in the center of his broad, wrinkled forehead. Wiry white hair covered his cone-shaped head and plump, square face. The white short-sleeved shirt and short pants he wore resembled woven fish scales. Smoke escaped his enormous nostrils with each exhalation of breath. The people cowered away.

---

22. A large drum hung on the shoulder and tapped with sticks in accompaniment to the samkpa. It is usually played by males.

23. Kpelle distortion of the word "purser" for the treasurer of a group of players.

"Suddenly, a succession of urgent calls sounding like the desperate cry of a lost hunter shot out of the river: 'Kotokpolo paoooo! Kotokpolo paoooo!' The river roared and crashed against the shore as never before. Fear gripped the village. Half its residents fled into their houses for refuge while the rest, believing that the water people had taken over the town, ran into the forest in disarray. Eventually, the calls turned doleful and the waterman awoke with a jolt, looked right and left like a caged monkey, took one incredible leap out of the town, and plunged headlong into the Deyn, leaving his drum behind. Blood tainted the spot where he had jumped. Clearly, his fellow witches had executed him for carelessly exposing their secret. Coming from their hideouts, the people found their town safe. Indeed, they were lucky! Had the water witch not betrayed his people, they'd have all died. Since then, water people have never mixed with land people in Fuama. Only members of their society, called Gborlorkpili[24], maintain secret contacts with landsmen. So, you have nothing to fear."

The reassuring tale had dispelled my fear of water people until my encounter with the Shrine. It was now impossible to deny the danger the river posed to the innocent inquirer. Abandoning my preoccupation with it, I hoped my pending journey would take me where no river was found.

24. Millipede, adopted name for the Kpelle Water Society.

SECOND FATHER

After the planting season, Father said he was taking me to some relatives of mine in a village called Willietaa for them to help support me in the great battle I would fight for the family. I was anxious to meet my relatives, especially the young ones, and make their acquaintance. There was nothing like being with people with whom you shared the same blood and taboo. I couldn't wait for the journey to begin.

Much to my chagrin, Mother suggested that we make the trip after the rice "had taken belly"—some four months hence—for it to withstand the ravages of the avaricious *sorya* and groundhogs in our absence. Father would have us make it even later—after harvest, when the rainy season and famine would be over, making traveling convenient and sparing our hosts the embarrassment of being frugal with their hospitality. Mother argued that people usually think you're after their food when you visit them during or shortly after harvest. The debate continued until a strapping young man in frayed clothing brought us an invitation from my "second father" in Willietaa who wanted to see me before I started school. Indeed, news traveled in the jungle at incredible speed! It no longer mattered when we made the trip. However, Mother's suggestion won the day.

The birds were singing dawn when we set off for Willietaa. Mother carried a new raffia basket containing our clothes and other needed items on her head while Father carried a sheathed sword and an old leather pouch slung to his shoulder. Following the main highway north of Haindi, we branched off in Shormetaa, a short distance beyond the Waydiyea, and wandered through an ancient forest filled with birds and rodents. Midway, Mother, who headed the traveling party, stripped a sapling and placed the leaves on a black ant nest resembling a large mushroom standing on the roadside. "May darkness stay behind us and sunshine be before us," she murmured solemnly and gave us some of the leaves to place on the goddess.

By noon we saw across our path what Father said was a leopard trap. Quite an amazing feat of engineering, it comprised a large *beleh* log that might have required no less than twenty men to raise. It was fenced left and right with wattle. A passage spanning its length underneath had a trigger concealed in dry leaves. Pointing at it, Father said, "The hapless leopard or person who steps over there however slightly, will be crushed to death instantly." He led us along a narrow path round the perilous trap.

When we emerged from the cold shadows and entered the noonday sun fiercely impinging on the young bushes, Mother said her prayer had been answered. She went several yards into the bush with her basket and soon returned neatly dressed in a new *fanti*[25] lappa and a buba with streaks of blue, red, and white colors.

Except for straggling chickens scratching refuse piles on the outskirts,

---

25. A Ghanaian tribe and the calico print they often use.

there was no sign of life in town. Father led us to a round, yellow house standing on a tall foundation, wandered about and returned with a short elderly man dressed in an armless homespun yellow shirt, black- and yellow-striped short pants, and an old peaked, black cap. He was trifling with the blade of a new hoe. Soft-spoken, he regretted the absence of his family who had gone to their farm. He said we would have missed him too had he not remained in town to make hoes for women who had been harassing him for their planting tools.

"Why you people never told the messenger the exact day of your visit?" he asked.

"How could we, when witches are forever busy spoiling people's plans?" Mother replied.

"Quite true," he agreed. "Are you well?" he greeted Mother and snapped her fingers.

"God has no blame," Mother said. "He's your second father," she told me, pointing at the strange man. "Don't be shy. Greet him."

"How are you?" the strange man smiled at me and placed his hand on my head.

"He's called NanMolaa," Mother said.

Going next door, NanMolaa brought a small raffia bag of country bread about the size of a fist, strapped it to my neck, and said, "Eat this for now. Nenkpeh[26] will cook for you people this evening." Then he told Mother, "We stopped living in that house once your sister died there. Only boys live in it nowadays."

That evening he introduced us to a host of relatives. Suddenly, I had many fathers, mothers, brothers, sisters, aunts, cousins, nephews, wives, sons, and daughters who snapped our fingers with affection. My parents accompanied members of our new household to their farm each day, while I played with the boys. The boys said I was lucky to have been their relative; otherwise, I would have had to prove myself in several wrestling bouts to qualify for membership in their gang.

After a week of happy life with them, I woke up one morning and found myself alone in the house. Had they excluded me from their company, after all? I saw only NanMolaa standing in the square, watching me with a tender, reassuring face. Footprints strangely riddled the square.

"Where is everybody?" I asked him. "Why the footprints?"

Placing his hand on my shoulder tenderly, he said, "Don't worry. Nothing will happen to you." Looking in the distance with his cavernous face, he informed me that my friends had lost a battle with The Bush Thing during the night.

While I pondered the terrible news, two men, one with a scraggy neck and the other a pockmarked face, came from the blue and bombarded me with a barrage of embarrassing questions, laughing:

---

26. "Dew driver." Name given to the first child who prepares the way for others to follow. The dew driver is usually the leader of a traveling party; when he or she travels a path, others are assured that it is free from dew or danger.

"How did you spend the night, heh?"

"Your friends died in a battle with The Bush Thing last night!"

"Won't you avenge them?"

"You said the other day you'd kill Basai and give his ears to your mother to winnow rice. Ready for the battle? Basai is only a stone's throw from here."

"Need a spear or a sword? We have many here."

"This is a *kwii* man," NanMolaa intervened, leading me to his shop. "This is not his kind of war."

"Now listen," warned the man with the pockmarked face. "You're now the only boy here, so don't roam the bushes, or The Devil will steal you."

"What do you mean by 'steal you' as if he were an orphan?" NanMolaa protested bitterly. "Look, the stranger has a right to enjoy his visit!"

"Don't take a *kpolowa*[27] to the blacksmith shop!" cried the man with the scraggy neck.

"Don't listen to them," NanMolaa consoled me, holding fast to my hand. "If they touch you, I'll prick them with hot iron." Offering me a stool in the shop, he worked the bellows to heat a long piece of iron he put in the furnace.

Dressing close to him and holding my head in my hands, I tried to make a meaning of the incident. The Devil had stormed Haindi many times at night, occasionally capturing some prey but not a whole dozen in a single raid.

"Where's Data?" I asked NanMolaa.

Easing on the bellows, NanMolaa searched about the shop as if my first father had hidden in it. At length he stammered that Father had accompanied my friends' corpses to The Devil's home. "I should have accompanied them," he said, "but your first father is now the head of this house."

NanMolaa's firstborn NeYasa, a beautiful woman of beige complexion, repeatedly warned me to be with women at all times for my own safety.

"The Big Thing doesn't fool round women," she would tell me seriously, "but he appears among men at will, wherever they may be. Trust neither your first nor your second father in this matter. Men deceive! They can hand you over to The Big Thing without a second thought."

My short-lived acquaintance with the boys of Willietaa and their unexplained disappearance left me cold and perplexed. Indeed, my own fatal encounter with The Bush Thing was just a matter of time. No. I wasn't secure. NanMolaa was fighting a losing battle.

Four days later, a large crowd gathered in and around the spacious palaver house in the center of the square. Squeezing through the crowd, I stood under the eaves of the palaver house and watched twenty-four bare-breasted girls standing in a straight row at the far end of the wide hall, their heads neatly wrapped in headties, their faces painted with black and white chalks. White cloths with fringe trimmings circled their waists and extended be-

27. Anyone who is not a member of the Poro or Sande Society.

low their round buttocks, which were embedded in black- and white-striped homespun *bombor*[28]. They held wands plaited like checkerboard with black, white, and red beads. Stamping their feet at short intervals, the nutshell rattles on their ankles ringing in tune with the footsteps, they glanced sideways, brilliant smiles on their pretty faces, swung the wands gently from left to right and right to left, bent forward and sang a painful dirge in memory of the fallen "heroes":

There they carry them, the sons,
Sorry for their mothers!
Who used to set the fish traps,
Sorry for their mothers!
Trap the duiker and the python,
Sorry for their mothers!
Climb the tall palms,
Sorry for their mothers!
And fetch the firewood.
The sun has gone down!

Then they capered all over the hall, their agile feet raising a cloud of dust. A thousand fascinated eyes watched the marvelous dance while appreciative spectators showered the girls with coins, kola nuts, and rice. There came a pause in the dance, the girls only tapping the floor with their feet. Then their virile voices exploded again with a sweet melody that echoed through the town and in the surrounding forest:

Will their mothers eat meat and fish again?
Sorry for their poor mothers!
Or taste palm oil again?
Sorry for their poor mothers!
Oh, may they come as they went!
The young girls are crying!
Oh, may they come as they went!
The young girls are crying!
Crying for their sweethearts!
The sun has gone down!

Once again, they resumed the dance. To my surprise, the palaver house clamored with weeping, cheers, murmurs, laughter. Presently a towering man with solid muscles dressed in T-shirt elbowed through the crowd, stood before the girls, and shouted down their song and dance. Then slashing the air with his robust arm, he said, "My son, having fallen victim to The Big Thing, I can't speak in vain. Here is one pound." He dived into his pocket

28. Country Clothes or homespun undergarments.

and produced two silver dollars. There was a rousing cheer as the leader of the dance, a fat, middle-aged woman, smilingly received the coins and, gyrating her body, ordered the girls with a nod to resume the dance. Immediately, a short light-skinned man with a round face made a similar speech and presented a demijohn of rum, which another man was bringing on his shoulder.

I left the dance with only one desire: to go home. Father said we would go home after something important happened; regrettably, he didn't elaborate.

Before dust could settle on this development, a disturbing cloud of mystery hung over me again. Everybody warned me to be wary of a certain man called Kote "who makes food bitter in young boys' mouths." Who Kote was and why he ruined the appetites of young boys baffled me. People kept me at arm's length and only scowled whenever I spoke to them. To crown it all, my mother disappeared from the house early one morning.

While searching for her, I ran into a man in the square who claimed to know where she was. We found her on the northern outskirts strangely blowing on a fire under a pot of herb. Now and then a "sister", "niece", "cousin", or "wife" of mine would bring a bucket of water, set it by the fireside, and glance at me with pity. The man pulled me on by the wrist. Though puzzled, I felt reassured because Mother wasn't disturbed.

We passed by a boy buried chest-deep in a hole filled to the brim with steaming black mud and scrambled herb. My heart speeded when we entered a new clearing where two men, looking aside suspiciously, stood by a knotty old log lying on the edge of the clearing. Leaning against it were two sharpened, fresh *lolo* sticks emitting yellow sap that made puddles on the ground.

The man ordered me to take off my pants and sit on the log with my back turned to the bush. He held me near the armpits, quickly pressed his callused palms forcefully over my face, and, in the twinkling of an eye, someone cut my foreskin. I felt no pain. So, this was all there was to circumcision. I tried unsuccessfully to push the man's hands from my face to see the wound. When he finally removed them at his own behest, I saw streaks of blood on my thighs and the ground. The men we had met shook with suppressed laughter, holding the *lolo* sticks over the wound, their sap dripping on it.

"I'm not the one who did it," one of them said.

"Neither did I," the other one said.

"Who did it?" I asked with outrage.

It occurred to me that it was Kote's doing. I vowed revenge when I got well.

"You won't have a case by then," one of them reasoned with me. "You'll have to show the wound to justify revenge, but there won't be any."

"Look, Kote will pay doubly for his mischief! I will know him," I cried.

I grew dizzy. Mother poured a bucket of steaming, scrambled *peyeng* leaves mixed with mud in a fresh pit, looked around in a preoccupied manner and left. The men urged me to sit in the pit. I refused.

"I'll never go into a hole alive!" I cried.

"Don't you want to be healed?" they said.

"If you don't sit in the pit, the wound will eat up that thing and girls will eat your money for nothing."

"Let them eat it!" I said, taken aback by my own reckless words.

"So you're afraid of death? Ha! Ha! Haaaaa!"

"After The Devil eats you up and vomits you out, death won't mean a thing to you."

"It's foolish to fear death, for the moment you're born you begin to die!"

"But death—"

"Look, my friends," I said weakly, "tell my mother—"

A large, black wooden bowl filled with boiled *peyeng* leaves in her hands, Mother was already with us, watching me with concern. I sat in the bowl, the black water turned reddish instantly. I retched.

"It's his own fault," one of the men told Mother. "He refused to sit in the hole!"

Mother brought me a white kola and pleaded that I forgive the affront. A woman whom I only viewed with squinting eyes brought me a yard of white cloth and said they would make it into the first pair of pants I would wear when my wound healed.

"Now you're a true husband to me," she said.

The following morning Mother showed me the many gifts my relatives had brought for me while I slept: clothes, foodstuffs, money, kola nuts, and the like.

"I was afraid for you!" she sighed with relief.

"What is this, my people! Witches, what have I done? God, help me!" I said.

"Truly, you're strong and brave. You never cried or moaned all night. God is with you, Child, and will always be with you. I asked him for his mercy, and he answered my prayer. Sit up and eat. I cooked a whole chicken for you last night! A big red rooster your mother Keema[29] brought for you. You haven't eaten a thing since it happened! Sit up. Try! You can make it! The day has broken and the morning sun is up."

"But where is my father?" I asked her.

"Don't worry about your father," she said, her voice laden with anger. "As far as he is concerned, you're now a man, so you should go through such things by yourself. He doesn't know that a child needs the greatest care in times like these—We'll give Kote his white kola when he returns from his hometown in two markets. You're not to see him until then."

After my wound healed, Father said we were returning home. I was disappointed because they wouldn't give Kote his white kola and get his blessing, which they said I needed to bring healthy children into the world.

On the eve of our departure, we met with our hosts on NanMolaa's porch. Father thanked NanMolaa and his household for the hospitality we

---

29. "Rub on him or her." Name given to a child that sticks on the father or mother.

had enjoyed. We would leave with fond memories. They should expect another visit from us in the near future. They too were welcome to visit us any time.

"We're about to send your son to school for him to become the family's backbone," he told NanMolaa formally. "In this changing world, we must prepare at least one member of the family to fight for us. Let's implore God and the Ancestors to help the child know book to meet this challenge. Bring anything you people can afford to buy him clothes, pencils, and copybooks. He shouldn't suffer shame while we're still alive. School opens in two markets. This is why we came to you people."

NanMolaa shifted in his seat, grunted, and passed the matter over to his headwife.

"What can I say?" NeNenkpeh clapped her hands once, turned them up, and laid them calmly in her lap. "Your word is my word. Sending our Haindi son to school is good because none of the boys round here is going to school. If your hands are not tied up, help him."

A man with tight bearing, wine gourd in hand, entered the porch breezily and demanded a seat. NeNenkpeh offered him hers and went into the house for another. The man slumped on the stool and said he was annoyed. Why was NanMolaa holding such an important meeting without his blessing?

Everyone laughed briefly. NanMolaa apologized and said he had sent for him yesterday. "After the night was far spent and you hadn't come," he explained, "I thought we should proceed, for a Zoe's arrival in a meeting is never overdue. Not so, my people?"

"So it is!" everybody agreed.

"But who knows," NeNenkpeh said in jest, "you might have gone for herbs. They say your wine tree is pouring well. Do your duty and be quick with it; our eyes are heavy."

"Women are bold, indeed," said the new arrival. "Addressing a great Zoe in this manner! First, this is the cold water." He set the wine gourd before NanMolaa. "I Kote, the maker of life, the savior of life, hereby bless this gathering."

"Let it be so," everybody said.

"Again I've put my hand on the flesh of a man with a pure heart; fixed it to multiply life—may the offspring it brings into the world live to ripe old age and go to The Place of Truth at God's own invitation."

"Let it be so."

"Should any man or woman in our midst or elsewhere bewitch this child in order to spoil the good work we have done—may we walk over that person's grave."

"Let it be so."

"If misleading this honored gathering with sweet mouth while bearing hate or malice in my heart against the child—may the air I breathe and the water I drink turn into poison in me."

"Let it be so."

"May the man we have fixed be a true man in the house."

"Let it be so!" Hearty laughter.

The wine passed from hand to hand in a white enameled cup as the meeting lapsed into idle discussion of farming, fishing, hunting, dreams, and so on. At length NanMolaa dived into his pocket, took out a nickel, and displayed it in his palm for all to see.

"NanDougba, thank you," he said, handing Father the coin. "The way this coin is white is the same way my heart is white towards the child. May he get the needed strength and courage to carry out the great responsibility on his shoulders."

"Let it be so."

"May what brought us here end in moonlight."

"Let it be so."

"Witches abound, prowling through nights and days, ready to snatch the hapless child who hasn't seen much of life and the tired old man or woman who is no part of their deadly games. May God clothe us with darkness for us to be invisible to their eyes."

"Let it be so."

"May the trap our enemies set for us catch them instead."

"Let it be sooooo!" The prolonged reply evidently signified a desire for an end to the torrent of blessings. Mother frowned her face and looked aside.

"I need not say, NanDougba, that what you're doing is good," NanMolaa continued. "Almost on the other side of the river, we Elders must ensure that those we're leaving behind are protected. Protection in these *kwii* times is not a matter of hanging a charm to your neck or waist but knowing book. We see it when a common Deecee takes from us whatever he wants when he wants it: money, rice, chickens, goats, sheep, cows, girls to warm his bed, young men to tote his loads and make his farm—we need a redeemer. Seporlor will redeem us. Why, he'll tell the Deecee—"

"He could be a Deecee himself," someone interposed.

"He'll tell the Deecee in his face, 'Don't do that to my people!' The Deecee will pass on to some other village because he knows if he troubles us, the matter will lie before the president in Monrovia in no time. NanDougba, you're doing our own good. It's my duty to help you, but some thief has dug up every cent I've been hiding under my bed for years! Hawks have wiped out my large flock of chickens. As for my cattle, leopards have feasted on them. You people might have seen the leopard trap on the way.

"That white coin shows not only the purity of my heart, but also a promise: Let the child depend on me as he fights this great battle for us."

Well spoken, but what can you do with a nickel? The following morning we left unceremoniously for home, half the town asleep. We took a swampy, winding path to bypass the dangerous leopard trap. After we sloshed through the swamp, Father bemoaned our kinsfolk's disappointing response to his urgent appeal.

"I'd thought Molaa would give us at least a pound or two—or a goat—"

"It's not his own child," Mother cut in sharply. "Let me tell you something, NanSen. Sister Korpoh was never one of Molaa's favorites. The culprit was nobody else but Nenkpeh, that dry, ungainly woman who has taken hold of his life through witchcraft. She orders him around like puppy. She made life impossible for the poor girl: finding fault with everything she did and keeping her shabby. Molaa agreed to all that—wholeheartedly! The poor child died of heartbreak—" Mother stopped talking abruptly; she might have imagined her sister's image, which she often found too painful to endure.

Father added, "Family relation is no obligation, although we make great fuss about it. You never know your true relative until you have a problem. I'm sure Zurong's brother and nephew in Kwalakomai will help him. Sumowor Zokpooh and his son Sewor make large cane farms; and gin sells well nowadays. They'll be proud to learn that their brother and uncle is trying to become a *kwii*—and he has an uncle on your side in Gbangei—" Father sighed wearily and grew silent as if the words had choked him.

Mother said, "You get the most strangers at harvest time, not at clearing, felling, or planting time. Let the child finish book—and his family will do anything for him. Why? Because they expect much, much more in return—nothing less than all he owns." Then she wondered why all the fuss over preparation for a venture we had no clear idea about. Were they not doing the *kwii* people a good turn by giving them one more student? How many parents could do that willingly? Indeed, the *kwii* people were obliged to take care of me and reward them for their courage.

FAREWELL TO THE OLD

After the most elaborate Christmas and New Year festivals I had ever witnessed, Father said school would open shortly. In preparation for the great adventure, he taught me the alphabets and the first hundred numerals in English. I was amazed to learn that much from him because I had never heard him speak a word of English. He said he was sending me to school to live a better life, but not to turn my back on the Land.

"Book gives you power and wealth, but the Land gives you health, joy, and long life," he gave me his final advice on the eve of my departure for the mission. Then he launched upon another familiar story that showed why it was important I remembered the Land.

"During slavery time, a group of obnoxious watermen once packed all the children of Fuama in a large, white, underwater canoe in the dead of night to carry them to the seacoast for sale," he began. "Had their wicked plan succeeded, there wouldn't have been any Kpelle man or woman on earth today. But thanks to Luen[30] who rescued the children. We used to offer the Shrine two full-grown bulls and seven white roosters each year—a tradition *kwii* people have abolished. No wonder people die like flies nowadays. But always remember that you owe your life to the Land—to Luen; come home after learning all the book you can."

He cut the story short apparently for Mother to have a chance to render her own admonition. She had never commented on my schooling. I thought she would refuse to see it through. Sitting at my beside near the blazing fire, looking gloomy but tearless, she spoke mildly; admonishing, instructing, recounting stories she had kept secret over the years.

She said I should be fearless, wise, hardworking, obedient, and courageous. She warned me against climbing tall trees, swimming in deep waters, interfering in matters not concerning me. I should ignore the hostilities of my enemies and enjoy the love and companionship of my friends.

"Never feel sad or lonely even if friends turn their back on you," she whispered, "for God is always with you. And the spirit of your brother Kollie, who loved you dearly, hovers over you always." Stifling a sob, she said, "He was strong, intelligent, and strikingly handsome. He promised to care for us until he laid our tired bones to rest. Kollie gave us enough rice, oil, meat, and fish at all times. When he became a man, he never allowed his father to touch the handle of a cutlass. He said that his marriage would be the end of my handling a hoe. He fell in love with a girl in Zaraimu; she had pretty eyes and plenty of soft, black hair. Your brother died four markets before he could marry her." With the tip of her lappa she wiped trickles of tears rolling down her cheeks. "Witches didn't permit it, for ordinary fever couldn't have killed such a strong young man so suddenly. They'd thought Kiapeh was too good for him, though she had no eye for any man but him.

30. Eddy, name given to the Shrine or the rocks below Haindi on the Deyn River.

We left everything to God," she sighed deeply and slapped her thigh in despair. "We're sending you to the *kwii* world because we don't want to gamble with witches for your life—"

She stopped talking only when roosters crowed and the blue light of dawn poured through a thousand chinks in the sooty thatched roof into the center room.

Bouncing out of bed, I ran to the river and bathed, hurried back and put on my new clothes Father had bought for "the great day", and bade Mother goodbye.

"Eat something first," she said, handing me a bowl of rice and soup she had kept overnight.

"I'm not hungry!" I told her.

"You don't want to spend your first day in the mission on empty stomach, do you? How will you learn the book?" Not wishing to break her heart, I munched several spoons of the food and drank a cup of water.

Clearing his throat, Father, who was still in bed, gave me his final advice: I should be fearless, careful, polite, obedient, and so on. He said many other things I didn't hear because I was already in the square. I heard my mother cry; her piercing voice jarred on every nerve in me. My heart jolted. A metallic taste welled up in my mouth. I made the fatal mistake of looking back. Mother was sitting by Father who looked stiffly in the distance. Ashamed of appearing cowardly before my playmates who were taking me "halfway", I held back the tears and continued the journey. Surprisingly, my closest friend Molley was nowhere around.

Home tugged at my heart as never before: The morning sun spread bristling rays over the village and the surrounding, undulating greenery; birds chirped and fluttered in kola trees on the outskirts; the mighty Deyn roared with fury; swarms of flies accompanying them, mangy cattle headed for the grassy outskirts. On the northern edge of the square, by their small, round house, NeGarmei dabbed her frail, sick daughter Liikpele[31] with handfuls of herb water she scooped out of a white bucket with her left hand. I stopped by Molley's house to bid him goodbye. It was his mother who came out and embraced me.

"Your brother couldn't bear it," she drawled. "He has gone with his father to the river to check *duun*[32], saying in anger that nobody should tell him about it on his return." Her countenance fell. Holding me by the shoulders, she said, "He'll get over it. A man can overcome even death. Visit us often; don't let *kwii* people take you from us." Pressing me tight against her warm bosom once more, she blessed me. Hot tears fell on my arms and shoulders.

As I waved farewell to the crowd of well wishers, I saw my father among them. Dressed in gown and cap, sheathed dagger in hand, he was trudging towards me. Why he had decided at the last moment to escort me was surprising. Directing me to the mission a thousand times, he had said I would face the crisis alone in order to be a man. Perhaps Mother or some Elders

31. Patience.

32. Circular fence built in water as a fish trap.

had prevailed on him to accompany me.

"I'll take him to the mission but won't stay there with him," he told the crowd with a smile. Unresponsive to his raillery which they evidently considered misplaced, my well wishers made conflicting remarks about my dilemma. Some argued that it was unfair to make an only child embark on such a precarious mission, alone. Others maintained that it was a brave and wise move because it'd make a man of me. They all regretted that Father had not initiated me into the Poro before sending me away from home.

All the fuss began annoying me. Would my own father hand me over to danger deliberately? Walking with long strides from the crabby crowd, I hastened to the mission. Before taking a dozen steps, I heard a low, tremulous voice call me, many voices extending the call loudly. Turning round I saw Old Lady Yaai, a next door neighbor, wobbling through the crowd with her crooked cane until she handed me a white kola nut with a shriveled hand, saying that kola tied me to the Land. Regardless of where or how far I went in search of book knowledge or how many books I learned, I should never forget the Land. Then she blew spittle four times in my right palm for God's blessings, good luck, good health, and the love of pretty women. The crowd chuckled when she mentioned "women".

"Woman luck is no luck," someone quipped. "Should a woman be a man's first friend in a strange land, he'll flee that land in the dead of night."

In a sullen mood, the Old Lady advised me to put my head to the book and make use of my common sense. Hers was the most precious of my send-off gestures.

The wide gravel road first took us to Gargbelei, our closest neighboring village, famous for its accomplished singers, acrobats, and masks which entertained Fuama Chiefdom during funeral, Christmas, and New Year festivals. Now it was the beauty and cleanliness of the village that impressed me: the well-swept square; the well-clayed mud walls adorned with art works depicting cattle, fowls, trees, bare-breasted girls, and well-groomed young men. We saw many residents of the village on the way to their farms.

The road sloped down a hill, crossed a small creek with a corkwood bridge Father said was called Bopari, and led to a sprawling town surrounded by acanthus bushes. Except for an old two story plank building west of the town, the houses were made of mud and thatch just as those in Haindi and Gargbelei but stood farther apart with wider porches. Behind each one was a corridor enclosed in low mud walls connected to a kitchen.

"This is the mission," Father informed me as we strolled on a worn footpath wending through close-cropped lawn. "White people built it many years ago," he went on. "We used to sell them meat and fish at low prices. Not knowing how delicious rotten meat or fish could be when cooked with soda, pepper, palm oil, and vegetable, they rejected those with the slightest foul scent. A full-grown red deer's haunch earned half a pound. For fish, we demanded only soap, salt, clothes, and bread—not the parched rice your mother pounds. The white people's bread is like a roasted plantain, but much lighter; it's sweetened with honey, syrup, and half-frozen tawny oil.

You won't need that much to be filled. We also gave the white people bags of oranges, cassavas, bananas, eddoes, potatoes, and plums for the delicious food. So we named the mission Kpolopele[33]." Interrupting himself, he cast a sweeping glance at the surrounding fallow land and said, "With all this good farmland, one can't understand why healthy young men and women never make farm! Well, they're respected for their sloth. No one compels *kwii* people to work. Not even the government. They don't conduct Poro or Sande." Father chuckled mirthlessly.

Turning left, we went to the third house north of the mission; it was whitewashed, rectangular, and flanked by tall palm trees standing close together in straight rows. A lovely woman dressed in a lappa suit bedecked with red, blue, and white floral designs greeted us warmly when we knocked the door.

"You people came too early," she said, snapping our fingers. "Tama will soon come. Is this the boy?" Pointing at a long rattan chair on the porch, she gave me an appraising glance and hurried to the kitchen, saying over her shoulder, "I have a boiling pot on the fire. Be patient. Tama will take you people to Ma Miller."

"We're in no hurry," Father told her. "That's Bendu," he told me, "your brother Tama's wife."

"Who is Ma Miller?"

"The white woman who owns the mission." In preparation for what turned out to be a long narrative, Father leaned comfortably in the creaking chair. "She's kind and godly," he said. "Takes good care of children who obey. Likes things done right and quickly. I knew her husband very well." Father grinned reminiscently and continued: "We named him Flomo for his towering height and friendliness; we taught him Kpelle. His wife speaks Kpelle very well—writes it too! See her eat rice and cassava leaves stewed with dry meat or fish and red palm oil; you'd think God made her white by mistake. Flomo loved hunting, fishing, and farming—something our black *kwii* despise. Perhaps due to sheer negligence or willful disobedience—for we warned him seriously—he entered a Poro bush unlawfully! Well, the laws of the Land excuse no one; not even Senator Loryii. Flomo took sick shortly afterwards and they sent him home in a huge canoe, but he died on the way and they buried him in the sea. His wife's idea of love is unusual: she vowed never to marry again and has kept her vow since. Also vowed to spend the rest of her life teaching us about God and educating our children; she said Jesus told her to do so."

"Even though they killed her husband?"

"You could say that because death has no natural cause here. A drunkard carelessly jumps into the river and drowns, and they hold you responsible for his death once you quarreled with him before. The Land was held responsible for Flomo's death, but when soldiers started arresting people they believed to be the culprits, his wife told them to leave the poor people alone.

---

33. House of bread.

Her husband had gone to Jesus."

"Who is Jesus?"

"God's son."

"Where is he?"

"God lives in heaven. Where else will his son be?"

"Has the white woman ever been to heaven?"

"You ask too many questions!" Father said with irritation. "I hope you won't take such a bad attitude to school. Learn to listen and remember what people tell you—Jesus doesn't live only in heaven. He also lives in our hearts."

"Our hearts!" I exclaimed, placing my hand over my breast.

Father laughed, glanced at me and said, "He lives in everybody's heart. Whenever you want to do something bad and your heart says, 'Don't do that,' it's Jesus talking to you. Or it says, 'Fetch firewood and water for that poor old man or woman,' it's Jesus talking to you. Jesus guides our every step. Even when we're asleep, he is with us."

"A spirit, then," I said.

"Present everywhere. Even here on this porch—right now!"

"Let Zoe Matadey drive him from behind us."

"Jesus protects us from danger! Remember when you almost drowned as you attempted your first cross-river swim? It was Jesus who saved you. If he abandons you for a single moment, you're finished."

"It's good he is with us because death and danger are everywhere."

"He'll do much more for you if you keep his commandments."

"What are his commandments like?"

"Don't worship any other God but him. Don't steal. Don't lie. Don't kill. Don't follow any woman who isn't your wife. Obey your father and mother, and so on."

"People break his commandments round here everyday."

"Jesus is giving them plenty of time to leave their bad ways and keep his commandments. If they don't, he will punish them."

"How?"

"By striking them with sickness that has no cure, or by taking away their children and properties. Pray to Jesus to forgive you when you break any of his commandments. He will forgive you."

"How do you pray to him?"

"Bow your head, close your eyes, fold your hands, and talk to him just as you're talking to me."

A torrent of loud and angry complaints suddenly interrupted our conversation:

"You think we're here to play! My friend, you'll get exactly what you work for! In fact, you're absent for today! Be sure of that! What do you mean by coming to work after sunrise? I'll mark you absent, and you must work all day, or you'll be dismissed. You always carry on this nonsense and expect equal pay with people who work from dawn to dusk every single working day! You aren't paid with rock but money! You think money drops from the sky or grows on trees? My friend—"

The angry speaker was an imposing man dressed in old blue denim long pants, a yellow T-shirt torn in many places, and old canvas shoes plastered with dirt, his small toes sticking out of the sides. Behind one ear was a yellow stick, one end sharpened and the other fixed with a red mass encased in a gold socket. He had a flat black book in his hand. He winced and grew quiet when he saw us.

"Father, I'm sorry for greeting you people in a bad mood," he apologized and snapped our fingers. Then he slumped in a chair beside us and laid the book in his lap. He cupped his chin in his hand and pursed his lips as if he had received news of a relative's death. "I don't normally behave like this," said he. "This irresponsible boy, Marley of Mauwa, an expert dancer, wastes time at funerals while others work from dawn to dusk in the scorching sun, and he wants the same pay they get. He thinks I'm a fool—So this is the boy," he grinned and looked me over. Gazing in my face, he said, "My friend, mission life is no joke! The white woman likes only boys who are obedient and hardworking. Whenever she tells you, 'Don't do this', don't do it! Or 'Do this', do it! Boys don't mix with girls here—except in the schoolhouse or on the football field. Unless the matron calls you there, never be seen in the girls' dorm. Never fight here! When offended, report the offender to a teacher, to me, or to Ma Miller herself. Don't you ever leave the mission without permission! Whenever you want to visit your home—"

"No, no," Father cut in. "We want him to be here until he learns how to read and write."

"He might wish to see you people sometimes. Besides, the mission sends students home for vacations. The fee for a boarding student is three bags of rice and a tin of oil. Can you afford it?" He glanced at Father dubiously.

"It's only a matter of pounding," Father said. "We have plenty of rice."

"Anyway, let's hear from the white woman. I don't think she'll expect that much rice and oil from an old man like you. Bendu, I'm taking them to Ma Miller!"

Ma Miller's house, whitewashed and fronted by a rose garden, stood on the eastern fringe of the mission near a reed valley. Close to its southern eaves stood a palaver house with a hammock, a bamboo table, and four rattan chairs. South of it stood the school building, and west of it lay the football field.

A whiff of pleasant scent greeted us when we entered the screened porch. We sat on a bamboo bench neatly covered with a thick sheet of black- and white-striped homespun, our backs to the wall. Tama sat opposite us on a similar bench. I grew tense but relaxed when I viewed beautiful pictures hanging on the walls, colorful flowers in glass jars perched on windowsills, and pretty books ranged on two bamboo shelves against the northern wall above a bamboo desk. My eyes kept veering back to the picture of an exhausted, bearded, young white man with overgrown hair nailed on a roughly hewn wooden cross. A wreath of thorns encircling his head pricked his scalp; blood poured profusely down his temples. His sunken belly looked pathetic. Wrapped round his slender waist was a white lappa. The man seemed resigned to his fate despite his immense suffering. Why the white woman displayed the picture of a man in agony for public view puzzled me. Was she teaching us how to endure pain?

A preoccupied middle-aged white woman wearing plain clothes came from a narrow hall, greeted us crisply, sat in a rattan chair at the bamboo desk, and pounced away on the fingers of a popping machine with her own slim, delicate fingers. A sheet of printed white paper rolled gradually from the machine. When the paper was halfway up, she pulled it out with force, scribbled on it with a writing stick she jerked from a knot of silver hair at the nape of her neck; then laid it on the table while putting the writing stick back. Engrossed in her task, she had evidently abandoned us.

At length she assumed a relaxed posture, her beautiful face beaming with a smile. Bridging her hands in her lap, she fired us with gold-rimmed glasses. Tama spoke to her with hesitation, his face pinned to the hard, gray floor. She responded rapidly in a high-pitched voice. Looking at her briefly, Tama made another remark, which she replied quickly, leaned back in her chair and shook her head. I noted that she called him "Thomas."

"The white woman wants to know your name," Thomas told Father.

Father stroked his jaw and said with pride that "Crusoe" was his *kwii* name. After writing it in her book, the white woman spoke to Thomas again and looked at Father in suspense.

"Ma Miller wants to know your first name, Old Man," Thomas said.

"Well, if she wants to write a Kpelle name in her *kwii* book, then she may add 'Dougba'."

Again, Thomas conversed with the white woman and said, "Ma Miller wants to know the boy's name and age."

"His mother and I call him Zurong," Father said. "Other people call him Seporlor. We stopped counting a child's years after losing five children by it."

"The only way your son will be admitted to school is by telling Ma Miller his age," Thomas said firmly. "Old Man, it won't do him any harm. Ma Miller records the ages of all the students in her book. That's how she knows what medicine to give them when they're sick."

Father grew sober. He looked at me with concern, his eyes narrowed in concentration. Tipping his head far back, he gazed at the black and white checkerboard bamboo ceiling and sighed. "Well," he said, "I've stopped putting a pebble in a raffia bag each New Year Day after a child's birth since we lost the fifth one, so I have no idea of his age—but he was born round the year Hitler entered the field."

"The white woman says your son was born one thousand nine hundred and thirty-nine years after Jesus was born," Thomas said, after conferring with Ma Miller. Father smiled, probably wondering what connection Jesus' birth had with mine. This Jesus must have been quite an important man, I thought.

Thomas consulted Ma Miller again and said, "The white woman says that the boy doesn't have to live on the mission to go to school. He should come to Gargbelei each afternoon when shadows lengthen, Mondays through Fridays, beginning next month. She'll send a Primer teacher there. After completing the Primer, he'll then be qualified to attend Kpolopele."

After all, I would be right at home while going to school! Happily, it also happened that my friends would also go to school, for shortly before school opened, the government increased the number of recruits per town to ten students.

GOD LOVES US ALL

After a quick swim in the cold river in the afternoon, Bhea, Zina, Bopaa, Dakena, Shiaffa, and I dressed hurriedly, ran to Gargbelei, and joined some three dozen boys kicking green oranges before a spacious palaver house east of the village. Later, we wrestled and climbed up and down the tall breadfruit and kola trees shading the palaver house. On the sound of a gong we scampered into the palaver house. A group of goats that had been lounging there clattered down the dirt steps and ran into the bushes. Several of them refused to budge. We had to push them away, but not before they butted and kicked us in the legs.

We sat on new bamboo mats, stretched our legs full-length, clasped our hands in our laps, and hung our heads. You could hear a pin fall. Suddenly a rotund man of medium height, rattan switch in one hand and book bag in the other, entered breezily and laid the book bag at his feet, hitched up his long black pants, glanced at his shiny black leather shoes, and cleared his throat. Slashing the air with the switch, every pair of eyes watching with keen attention, terrified, he lashed out the rules of conduct for the class in Kpelle. We should always be prompt and tidy. He detested our soiled clothes, dusty feet, and unkempt hair—offenses he would forego this first time, but woe betided any pupil who came to class afterwards looking sloppy. We should pay attention in class, for failure to recall what he taught us would mean severe beating or expulsion from school. Anyone not interested in learning should leave now to avoid embarrassment and waste of time. Our parents should buy copybooks for us. The mission would supply us with pencils, slates, and chalks. When he was through talking, he taught us a song we parroted after him, clapping our hands with the rhythm:

Praise him, praise him
All ye little children
God is love, God is love
Praise him, praise him
All ye little children
God is love, God is love

Love him, love him,
All ye little children,
God is love, God is love—

Were school only a matter of song, it would have been the most exciting experience of my life. Learning to speak a new language is difficult, but singing it is easy. Though we knew not the meanings of the words, we loved the songs, if only for their rhythms. We whistled each new tune as we went about. I sang some for my parents who enjoyed them and encouraged me with all the pencils, copybooks, and clothes I needed. But school also involved writing.

We began with the alphabets. Holding the chalk correctly and writing what Teacher wrote on our wooden slates exactly as he did called for such coordination and concentration as we could scarcely command. During writing periods, eyes were squinted, lips distorted, heads conked, ears pinched, foreheads creased, armpits perspired, the switch cracked. I had problem writing "s". My "s" always looked like "z".

On one occasion, Teacher watched a boy named Sulontei with annoyance as Sulontei looked at young pigeons chirping in a kola tree behind the classroom—his eyes were so glued on the lovely birds that he forgot he was sitting under Teacher's infuriated stare, the switch hanging over his head. Sulontei had obviously given up his fruitless effort. The class grew tense. Putting our chalks and slates aside, we watched Teacher with frightened faces and the poor fellow with pity.

"Sulontei," Teacher barked, "go out and do your hunting!" Still buried in his daydream, the boy looked at Teacher with puzzled eyes as if wondering whether the man had not gone mad. The switch whizzed in the air and landed on his back with a heavy thud. Jolting to attention, Sulontei threw his slate and chalk away, bent backwards, and pursed his thick lips. "Go hunt!" Teacher roared, pointing his switch at the bushes. "You belong in the bush and not in a civilized place!" Before the switch could hit him the second time, Sulontei flew out of the class like a bird. He never returned.

On another occasion, Teacher wrote several words on a blackboard and asked us to write them on our slates exactly as he had done. Except those containing "s", the words posed no problem for me to write. When he inspected my hundredth unsuccessful attempt to write the letter correctly, he whacked my head with the switch "to beat out the mice, fish heads, and cassava leaves that have muddled your brain! A chicken can scratch better than this!" he declared. "Do you ever practice writing at home?" Yes, I practiced writing at home, not only in my copybook with a pencil but also in the sandy square and the riverbank with my fingers, and on the walls and doors of our house with charcoal. "I'm sure all you do at home is eat," he added. "By tomorrow if you don't do better then this, you'll pick pin." The following day my earnest effort seemed to have mellowed him somewhat. After a cursory look at my writing, he raised the song, *Jesus Loves Me This I Know.*

In the middle of the year, Ma Miller transferred the Primer Class to Haindi where a majority of the students lived. Perhaps my home environment would boost my morale and thus help me overcome my writing problem, I thought. Fortunately, Ma Miller published the Bible Primer, which cost only a dime. I remember flying to Mother on the farm early one morning for the dime. She was breaking dry fern stems to string for beads. "Mama, dime!" I cried breathlessly. As she fished the coin in her hair, she said, "Why are you so anxious about a task that will take all your life? I hope witches haven't sold you to book."

The first half of the Primer was written in longhand; the second half was typewritten. We were required to read and write at least the first half to qualify for promotion to the first grade. Everyday I painstakingly imitated the longhand writing and read each lesson aloud. My reading and writing improved, but I still had problem with my "s".

Father visited our classroom one afternoon to see my progress, the only parent I remember doing so. He watched me as I fought with the slate and the chalk. After inspecting my work, Teacher shook his head dismally and said I was destined for failure. He had tried his best to help me, but I couldn't learn. However, it was the white woman who would separate the sheep from the goats, not he. The sheep would go to Kpolopele for the first grade, while the goats would remain at home to plant rice and cassava. So, all Father's sacrifices to make me a book man had come to nothing at the very beginning of my school career! I felt so miserable that I didn't eat for days.

When Ma Miller came in the middle of November to administer the final exams, she first told us a story about Jesus, with Teacher interpreting. Jesus once went to a hilltop to worship God, but the devil told him to forget about God and worship him instead. He would give him all the money, rice, clothes, palm wine, and beautiful women he wanted. "Students," Ma Miller declared with emphasis, flashing her eyeglasses at us, "the devil is a liar! He owns nothing! Whenever you try to do something good, he tells you to forget it because it's too much trouble. Some of you might not qualify for Kpolopele this year. Perhaps you can't read or write that well now, but don't let the devil fool you to give up. He might tell you, 'Your parents don't know book and are living happily, so why bother with book? Relax and enjoy life.' But don't pay him any attention. The best things in life are hard to get. If you don't make it this time, keep trying and one day you'll succeed."

Encouraging! After all, I wouldn't be expelled from school if I failed, but I didn't want my classmates to leave me behind! The shame would be unbearable! My heart pounded my ribs painfully and my head swam. I might not be able to do even what I could.

The reading went well. Then Ma Miller wrote the sentence, "Father, Mother, Brother, Sister, God loves us all," on the blackboard and said we should write it on our slates. So every English sentence must contain a word or words with the letter "s"! Tense, I struggled with the chalk, perspiration coursing down my forehead, armpits, and temples. After nodding approval of several students' work, Ma Miller loomed menacingly over me and watched my furtive effort for a while. Then, stooping low, she carefully guided my trembling hand with hers until I wrote "sister", "loves", and "us" correctly. The mountain that had thwarted my progress had been removed.

When I reported my promotion to him on the porch where he had been waiting for the final exams result, Father said he had known all along that I would make it. "There's no fool in my family," he declared with pride. "But it takes time, hard work, and courage to accomplish a goal." Looking far away, he continued: "That teacher of yours once thought he couldn't learn. After spending ten years in school without getting anywhere, he told his father, 'It seems as if I'm not made for book or book isn't made for me. I'm leaving school to become a farmer like you.'" Father smiled pensively. "The fellow began tapping rubber trees in Firestone for a living. Later, he discovered his mistake and went to night school. Now he's highly respected as a book man. I don't know why he was so impatient with you.

"Now I know that you can write," he told me smilingly. "But, can you read?"

No problem. Turning to the first lesson in my Primer, I read:

> *I see my father,*
> *I see my mother,*
> *I see my brother,*
> *I see my sister,*
> *Father, Mother, Brother, Sister,*
> *God loves us all.*

"What does that mean?" he asked.

"I'll ask my teacher tomorrow," I said. "He hasn't told us the meanings of the words yet."

"That's strange," he said. "He should have told you what they mean before you learned to read them. Have you ever asked him?"

"Yes, but he always tells us that speaking Kpelle is uncivilized."

While waiting for school to reopen, I spent the summer helping Father clear bushes for the ensuing year's farm. Two nephews of mine whom I had never met came to help their grandfather with his farming. Unmarried, adventurous, and about the same age, they almost had the same name. One was called Kawor; Father said his mother Nyanka Manang was his eldest daughter who and her family lived up the fish-rich Waydiyea. Sewor's father was his eldest son Sumowor Zokpooh who lived in Kwalakomai. They had named Kawor for his eldest brother who lived in Zulotaa. As *kenablaa*, they were not so open with me. Their shyness compounded the problem, for they spoke only when addressed. Disturbed by my great mistake in life (going to school) they urged me to leave school for two "important" reasons:

I was one of only ten boys who had qualified for Kpolopele; perhaps a mermaid or double was responsible for my "remarkable achievement." If I didn't leave school right away, my secret teacher would take my life as compensation. Additionally, school took a long, long time; and when you were through with it, unless you had learned a trade like mechanic work, building work, or tailor work—none of which the mission taught—you would live and die in poverty.

Kawor decided to teach me how to farm, hunt, fish, and build a house. He was disappointed that a boy my age had no knowledge of such vital activities. Why had Father not initiated me ever since, that important passage to manhood? Would I ever be able to support a family? As for Sewor, money was the answer to all life's problems. He recommended that I join him and his father and do rum business. "A tin of gin earns ten dollars," he said. "And the average cane farm produces five to ten tins. So, the choice is yours to remain poor and helpless, depending on your old father who already has one foot in the grave; or make money to support him, your mother, and yourself."

My nephews almost made me give up schooling. When I told Father about their observations and recommendations, he said bluntly:

"Don't listen to them. People like those don't like to take risk or face unusual challenges, so they'll never encourage others to do such. See, at their age they're still unmarried, with no definite plan for the future. Consider the ordinary farming we do here. The strong and determined farmer begins his day's work at dawn and continues working long after the sun has gone. But for the lazy farmer, it's either too soon or too late to work—the axe is either too heavy or too light to wield—as for the cutlass, it's always dull."

NEW DAY

Attending Kpolopele required a new pattern of life. My day began at cockcrow when I would eat the food Mother often kept for me in a small iron pot by the hearth, dress, collect my book bag; and join my friends in a frantic race for KP. The first round of our race would take us to Bopari Creek, where we would wash our feet, faces, arms—and brush our teeth with twigs; the second round would take us to the school building.

We would stand in line with the early arrivals, usually boarding students, for inspection and flag salute. A tall, jovial Sierra Leonean man would saunter from one end of the line to the other, examining our clothes, feet, hands, fingernails, teeth, hair—ogling the girls and cracking jokes with the boys. He and the rest of the students would jeer any late comer, who would be made to cut grass for an hour or two before setting foot in a classroom. After inspection we would salute the Lone Star, singing the National Anthem, then rush to our classes.

Contrary to my hopes, the mission teachers never translated our lessons into Kpelle "because it'll hinder your learning correct English." Surprisingly, some students spoke both English and Kpelle fluently. They said the quickest way of learning to speak English was living either on the mission or in a settlement on the seacoast.

Our first teacher was a stocky, self-possessed, young woman who usually dressed in skirt and blouse; she taught what I later learned was arithmetic. She would write several figures on our slates, pronounce each one slowly, and ask us to write and pronounce them as she had done, forming our lips exactly as she formed hers.

The second teacher, who taught reading, was a tall, slim Mende man, again from Sierra Leone; he had light complexion, protruding cheekbones, and an Adam's apple. After parroting his words in a chorus up to ten o'clock, we would take a fifteen-minute recess on the sound of a gong. Then we would assemble in the school building. Ma Miller would stand before a lectern on the platform; tell us a story about Jesus in a piercing voice, illustrating it with pictures she would stick on a green board. I observed that Jesus was white and he always wore a flowing white robe. The devil, who was said to be constantly at war with him, looked black and hideous; he was always dressed in a black robe.

Ma Miller's stories were fascinating, especially those about miracles. Each one taught us how to live right. She often said that whoever disobeyed Jesus would end up in hellfire, but those who obeyed him would go to heaven. The hall would be deathly still, for none of us seemed qualified for admission into heaven because Jesus opposed nearly every traditional practice in our society such as worshiping ancestral spirits, rocks, rivers, trees, mountains; joining Poro, Sande, and other secret societies; marrying more than one wife or going to bed with a woman who wasn't your wife, and so on. We were often confused because the Elders claimed that God ordained our manner of life, but it was risky to question the white woman about such matters because your remaining in school depended on complying with the teachings of Jesus.

After devotion, a woman of disturbing beauty with a tender voice, curly black hair, and small delicate eyes concealed under bushy eyebrows, would teach us the Bible. At twelve-thirty, school would be over, followed by quiet hour. Boys who would rather not observe quiet hour played football. The girls would go to their dorm and do such chores as the matron would assign them after quiet hour. By two o'clock, Thomas would divide the boys into several work groups to cut palm nuts, bamboo thatch, sticks, grass, and the like. I was usually assigned with the grass-cutting group. We used long metal strips hewn from kerosene or lubricant drums, one end sharpened for cutting grass, the other wrapped with a piece of rag for handling. Thomas would demarcate a portion of the compound for clearing; then appoint a headman who would in turn divide it into "tasks". Unless you completed your task, no teacher would accept you in class. After roster work, I would fly to Haindi, dump my books at home, and run to the farm to eat. On spying me, Mother would say, "Why did you not wait in town once and for all? I've already cooked the soup. I'll cook the rice in no time when I get to town." I would find cassava or ripe pineapple or pawpaw to eat to gather strength while waiting for supper.

Despite the rigid schedule, hard work, and hunger pains, I loved school because I learned something new everyday and made many friends there. One who played a significant role in my life was called Caesar Augustus. As I sought wild fruits on campus one afternoon, I ran into him and two other boys, candidly engaged in a fist fight near a palm tree against which leaned a large bunch of bamboo thatch. Augustus was clearly on the defensive. His assailants, who looked alike, stabbed him on his back and temples with frantic blows. He swung to and fro like a swing, throwing wild punches with both fists but every one going into the breeze. On an impulse he leaped savagely at his rear assailant, grabbed him by the throat, knocked him down with a brutal kick in the legs, and sat on top of him, while his other assailant rained telling blows on his back. Augustus' quarry pushed him off his body and grasped both his legs, but before he could rake Augustus down, Augustus had already grabbed his neck in a headlock. He fought fiercely to break loose, applying all the fighting tactics he knew: pummeling Augustus on his back with blows, kicking him in the legs, pushing him with his shoulders, and so on. Soon he gave up the fruitless efforts; his eyes became fixed and he breathed with difficulty. Seeing his friend's life in danger, the other attacker judged that some drastic action was in place. Snatching a heavy club from the bushes, he aimed at Augustus' head. Had the club hit its target, Augustus would have died on the spot. I quickly stung the club wielder's head with an unexpected punch that sent him squirming in the grass; his club slashed the air and fell from his hand. Seizing it again, he bounced back like a bowstring and swung the deadly weapon at me. I ducked and leaped for it, but a backward stroke hit me on the head. I saw stars and staggered but didn't fall as he might have expected. Buckling under him, I pulled both legs off the ground; he fell in a heap. I grabbed his head in a headlock, pressed it hard until he choked. Dropping the club, he fought unsuccessfully to free himself. We rolled over and over until the palm tree applied brakes to us. He reached for my eyes, but I flung my head backward in time to see his friend aiming the deadly weapon at me. I broke away from him and ducked; the club hit him with a heavy thud in the stomach. Bending double and holding his stomach with both hands, he cried that he had been killed. His friend fled. Augustus vanished. Fleeing too, I met him talking with several boys with wild gestures near the football field.

"Saturday and his brother Taatee wanted to kill me and he saved my life!" he explained, pointing at me. "But they'll be in serious trouble with Ma Miller."

The boys felt my wound and bloody T-shirt gingerly. When the blood ceased to flow, they squeezed herb juice into the wound and recommended that we shouldn't report the fight to Ma Miller; she might expel us from school. To hide the wound from my parents, I made sure to go home after dark. When Mother inquired why I had gone home late, I said that we had worked overtime to complete an important task that day. Next morning I left for school while she and Father were still asleep, but the line inspector told Ma Miller about the wound and she dressed it in her office.

"Were you fighting?" she asked me.

"Fall down, Ma," I muttered.

"Are you sure it was a fall?"

"Yes, Ma Miller."

She gave me twelve tablets to take two, three times a day, for the pain. She demanded that I take two in her presence. I felt the bandage around my head with apprehension, wondering how Mother would take it.

After school, Ma Miller summoned me to her office where I met Caesar, his assailants, and Thomas. She looked very disturbed. Thomas told me that she didn't believe that I had been wounded by accident as I had told her, but she couldn't get the truth out of me because I couldn't speak English, so she had asked him to look into the case and get the facts.

"Augustus' two attackers admitted guilt," he said, "so Ma Miller only suspended them from school for one week. A repetition of such misconduct on their part will mean expulsion. As for you," he said with a heavy sigh, "—you'll stay out of school for a day to clear a portion of grass for punishment. Yes, you tried to stop the fight, but you became one of the fighters! When parting fighters, don't throw punches at them; wedge yourself between them."

I totally disagreed with him; had I not intervened in the handicapped fight in defense of Augustus, the boys would have killed him. Besides, the fury of the fight did not recommend passive involvement.

Obtaining permission from Thomas, Caesar accompanied me to our farm and explained the tragedy to my parents. He told them not to worry; henceforth, he and I would defend each other. Father congratulated me for being a hero, but Mother advised me against engaging in a handicapped fight. Next time I should run to the nearest people for help. They thanked Caesar warmly, welcomed him to our home; and gave him rice, palm oil, banana, cassava, and dry fish. Mother urged him to be a brother to me as I was her only child.

Caesar and I became thick friends—almost brothers. We shared secrets, played, and studied together. He told me that his real name was Caesar Dennis, but his friends called him Caesar Augustus, the Roman Emperor during whose reign Jesus was born. His family descended from Africans who were once slaves in America. After their ancestors obtained freedom, they returned to Liberia and established settlements along the seacoast, including Monrovia, his home and the largest of the settlements. Very brilliant, Caesar led his class in every subject, except math, which he said was confusing. "When you tell me a story," he once confided in me, "I learn something. For instance, in our Reader there is the story of a dog walking across a bridge with a bone in his mouth. Looking in the creek, he saw his own shadow but thought it was a different dog he had seen. Desiring the other dog's bone, he barked to intimidate him to drop his bone. Unfortunately, when he took a second look in the creek, the other dog no longer had a bone, and he discovered that he too had lost his. The story is saying if you want everything, you lose everything. This means something. But to add, subtract, divide, and multiply—what are you trying to prove?"

Caesar translated my lessons into Kpelle for me. In a month, I was far ahead of my class in all subjects. Much impressed by my progress, my teachers promoted me to the second grade at the end of the first semester. The honor earned me the hostility of both my former and new classmates who ostracized me from their company immediately.

The second grade cost me many a sleepless night. I was always on Father's back for money to buy kerosene for the small hurricane lantern I used for studying. He once asked me, "Don't you ever read at school? You might go blind if you continue reading like this!" Sometimes I wished I had remained in the first grade.

Until my Bible Primer teacher confirmed my claim, Father had misgivings about my promotion to the second grade.

"The boy is making remarkable progress," he told Father when he called by our house one evening. "I'm surprised!"

"There's no fool in my family," Father told him with delight. "But the beginning of everything is difficult. My son will be a great book man in this country—like you." Teacher bent his head and walked away.

WARNINGS

While Father told me a story early one evening on the porch, Water Zoe Deynpolu Kollie ambled to our house, his medicine bag slung over his shoulder, and asked Father to buy him a drink; he had news for him. The Zoe already reeked of alcohol, his speech slurred, and his movements unsteady. Even though Father offered him a chair, he elected to sit on the dusty porch and lean on a mahogany pillar, his legs dangling. He placed his medicine bag by the pillar and repeated his request.

"Tell me the news and I'll buy your drink," Father told him with impatience.

"NanDougba, your son has a mermaid companion who should be driven away from him, or he'll die," the Zoe said and spit a lump of snuff smear in the yard. I had listened to his incredible allegation, amazed.

"Deynpolu Kollie," Father said quietly, "my son knows nothing about such a thing. *Kwii* people have no time for witchcraft."

"Dougba," the Zoe said without adding the 'Nan' title, indicating the severity of the case, "You think I came here all the way from Gargbelei to joke? Such things happen! But it's an easy problem." He trifled with the bag of medicines, gazing at Father.

"Kollie, I like jokes," Father said, "but not about matters of life and death."

"How else can you explain the boy's incredible achievement in school!" the Zoe insisted, looking at me with dilated eyes. "When he began school, he couldn't learn a thing, and his teacher threatened to expel him in your very presence! Inexplicably, he becomes one of four among a hundred boys to finish book in Haindi! Then, he leaves all his friends in the first book in Kpolopele and goes to the second! You're a full-fledged *kenamu*; experienced enough to know that witches are dangerous! He'll have to pay for the mermaid's service with his life!" The Zoe knitted his brows and nodded his head vigorously as he spoke.

Father adjusted his toga about his shoulders thoughtfully, stepped down from the porch with care, stood in the yard, and cleared his throat. Looking far into the distance, he murmured, "This is a serious matter. Doubtless, someone has told this fellow about my son's progress in school and he is using that information to rob us, as he might have robbed many other families." Returning to the porch, he sat again and crossed his long legs. Beads of sweat stood on his face.

"NanDougba," the Zoe called him in a friendly tone, "I can save your boy's life if you like. It's nothing to worry about. After I treat him, he won't want to even put his foot in the river, not to speak of dealing with a witch in it."

Still reflecting, Father seemed not to have heard the Zoe. Observing Father's flexed face, Mother who was busy cooking, abandoned all culinary affairs and dressed her stool near the doorway to give the discussion her full attention.

"NanSen," she said, "let him look into it."

"Let's first make sure if there's something to look into," Father said, "and if there is, whether a drunkard like this can do anything about it." Sizing the Zoe up with a glance, he said harshly, "Let me tell you something, my friend—and get it straight in that head of yours: As of today—this very moment—you're fully responsible for my son's life."

"He's only trying to help!" Mother pleaded.

"If his head hurts, you're responsible," Father went on, paying Mother no attention. "If his stomach hurts, you're responsible. Should he die—pray that such doesn't happen—even by accident—you'll be buried with him." Father went into the house.

Grunting, the Zoe slung his medicine bag over his shoulder and shambled away. He didn't look back.

For three days Mother tried to persuade Father to reconsider his decision because "where life is involved, it's risky to be inflexible. The Zoe could be right; since his fees are next to nothing, he should see into the problem."

"If Kollie wants anything from us," Father maintained, "he should ask for it outright and not try to get it by arm-twisting."

"Son," Mother asked me one night, "if you're dealing with a mermaid, tell me! You came into this world with nothing, and you'll leave it with nothing, so it's foolish to endanger your life for the things of the world. Life is more important than book!"

"I know nothing about mermaid," I said. "I don't know how Deynpolu Kollie got his strange idea."

"Have you ever seen a strange girl in your dream?"

"Mama, I don't make a secret of any unusual experience I get. Were I dealing with such a creature, I would have told you about it long ago."

Unconvinced, she took me to the Zoe one night and implored him to protect me from water witches. He shouldn't mind my father. "Men don't bear children," she said. "That's why they don't know their importance."

"How can I get mixed up with this matter after your husband insulted me like that?" the Zoe cried bitterly. "I'm well respected for my trade and need no insult from Dougba Senfenui[34] for it!"

Mother took me to Spirit Zoe Dumelekali of Volobelai, who lived two days upcountry, for consultation. He presumably had the power to disarm evil spirits and witches, and even cure insanity. After paying him one cock, a bottle of oil, and a pound, the Spirit Zoe gave her a talisman for me to wear on my waist as protection against witches and evil spirits.

Afraid of Ma Miller's threat that anyone wearing charm would end up in hell, I kept the talisman hidden in my book bag and prayed to God for protection instead. I prayed for two round months and didn't so much as dream an unpleasant dream.

Meanwhile, Father took sick with whooping cough and became so pale

---

34. There's nothing to the human being.

that we feared for the worst. Mother applied all the herbs she knew, yet the sickness continued to worsen. As a last resort, she consulted Poro Zoe Kpakolo of Mauwa who was also a famous herbalist. I accompanied her. Believing that Zoe Deynpolu Kollie had taken his revenge, Mother decided "to give the unscrupulous witch a stern warning!"

"Why should he pick on us?" she fumed and fretted as we approached the Zoe's house. "We're not rich. We harbor no hate in our hearts against anyone! But the best medicine for a rascal Zoe is strong rebuke." She pounded the Zoe's door fiercely, but he wasn't at home. We tracked him down to his farm on the eastern bank of the Deyn where he was drinking palm wine in the farm shed. Mother screamed imprecations at him and told him that he would bear full responsibility for whatever happened to Father. The devious games he and the witches of the Deyn played should be limited to their kind. Ours was a God-fearing family. The Zoe only stared at her speechlessly with inebriated eyes, holding the large, red bowl whose contents he had just drained. The biting attack stopped only when two Elders of Gargbelei came by for a drink. They pleaded with Mother to try all the medications she knew; if they failed to heal Father, she should take the matter up with Chief Gumo and the Elders of Gargbelei.

"We have advised Kollie repeatedly to stop accusing people of witchcraft, but he doesn't listen," one of them said in anger. "Poverty is no disgrace!"

Zoe Kpakolo called for a stone with a hole naturally bored through it as the main ingredient of the medication. Our search for the peculiar stone should commence at sunrise the following morning and end before sunset. If we didn't find it by then, it meant that Father wouldn't make it.

Before dawn, Mother and I began examining stones on the gravel road to Gargbelei. Time flew at incredible speed. Before we thought of it, *corkweh* and Blue Wings were announcing dusk. We now explored the gravel with our hands and feet. Giving up, Mother looked with horror at the dying sun. Her hands were trembling. I decided to appeal to God for help. Had Ma Miller not said that he answered prayers? Bending on my knees, I closed my eyes, folded my hands, and said:

"Dear God, please help us find this hollowed stone right now. May it heal my father. I pray in Jesus' name."

"Who are you talking with?" Mother asked with anxiety. "My child, a dangerous creature is behind you and you don't want to tell me!" Tears ran down her cheeks. "Your father will soon leave me and you want a mermaid to take you from me, too?"

"I was praying to God, Mama," I told her, continuing my search. "Ma Miller said we should pray to him whenever we need help."

"Will God listen to a child like you?" she said, wiping her face with her lappa.

"Ma Miller says that God hears the smallest child who prays to him. Once some little children were going to Jesus and the people round him drove them away, but he told them to let the children go to him because only children would go to heaven."

"Keep quiet! And never say such a thing again!"

"I've found it!" I exclaimed, holding the hollowed stone in my open palm. "NeSuaa, here's it!"

Mother smiled with delight as she examined the stone.

"Thank God," she said. "You're a lucky child. Let's hurry home. The medicine man is waiting."

Poro Zoe Kpakolo put the stone in a bowl of scrambled herbs and water and told Father to drink from the bowl twice a day for one week. Exactly in a week, Father recovered.

After these experiences, I resolved never to wear the talisman. Ma Miller was right. God could do anything, anything! It was better to pray to him for help rather than consult Zoes, who were mostly mountebanks like Deynpolu Kollie. I didn't tell Mother about my resolution, however. Once when I had malaria and she helped bathe me, she became upset when she didn't see the talisman on my waist!

"Where's the medicine?" she raged. "Don't you want to live?"

"Ma Miller says we shouldn't wear such things," I said.

"Listen," she said sternly. "You're going to school to learn how to speak English and not to despise the ways of your Ancestors. When the white woman forbids you from doing this or that, she means you shouldn't do things she dislikes in her presence. What you fail to do for yourself, God will never come down from heaven to do it for you."

TO BE A MAN

Again, I had the distinction of being the only student to get a double promotion at the end of that year. To the rousing applause of teachers, parents, guardians, and students, Ma Miller presented me a red-edged Holy Bible as a prize. Zina, Shiaffa, and Bhea failed; Bopaa and Dakena passed on condition. They told everybody in town that there had been mass failure on campus. They couldn't understand how I had managed to get another double promotion. Was my head better than theirs? Did we not come from the same village, play in the same square, rove in the same forest, and swim in the same river? Definitely something was wrong. Father became concerned when Elders he respected shared the boys' opinion and advised him to apologize to the Water Zoe for him to take his curse from me.

"Go to Willietaa, away from this nest of witches, to rest and have some peace of mind," Father decided. "Your relatives will appreciate rather than envy your achievement."

I was happy for the trip, not only because it would put a long distance between me and the corrupt Water Zoe and his unfounded allegation; it would give me an opportunity to make another attempt to get financial aid from NanMolaa. Now on the battlefield, I believed that he would give me the needed support.

Arriving in Willietaa next morning, I met Sister Yasa on NanMolla's porch, a sad expression on her face. She began crying on seeing me. My heart missed a beat. Who had died? Recovering quickly, she told me that our father was very sick and could die any moment. Her brief wailing drew a crowd that inquired whether the Old Man had died. On seeing me with her, they understood.

Sitting by her, I searched in my Bible for the story of the Roman Centurion's servant whom Jesus healed. In my haste I couldn't find the story, so I read that of Nicodemus, a favorite of mine, though not appropriate for the occasion. All eyes trained on me in wonder and surprise as I performed the miracle. I told my audience that it was the word of God I had read. It had the power to heal.

When Sister Yasa announced me to NanMolaa who had been listening, I sat by his bed in a stifled room near the porch. A column of light filled with motes poured into the room

"What is God saying, Son?" he asked me.

"The story I read is about a Jewish Chief who wanted to know how to go to heaven."

"Who has ever been to heaven and back?" The Old Man rose on an elbow and watched me with puzzled eyes. "Who did he ask such an embarrassing question?"

"The son of God," I said. "His name is Jesus Christ. He came down on earth as a man, saved us from our sins, and went back to heaven."

"He must have been a great Zoe, like those of Malawu who claim to have come from the sky. But how did he save us from sins? We still commit sins!"

"Once God destroyed the whole world with water because of sins, but people continued sinning. They couldn't help themselves. Feeling sorry for the world, he sent his only son on earth to die on a cross so that he will forgive us when we sin."

"Hmm," NanMolaa grunted. "How could God's son—supposing he has one—possibly die? With all the power he has, will he let such a thing happen?"

"Jesus agreed to die for us because he loves us. All these matters are written in this book." I raised the Bible in the air.

"Why should someone die for sins others committed? Are you saying then that God is unjust?"

"Love sometimes demands life."

"That's true." The old man lay back in bed, looking meditatively at the bamboo ceiling, batting his eyes. "A Bandi man gave up his life to save his people long ago. But how does this story happen to be the word of God?"

"Everything written in this book came from God." I raised the Bible in the air again.

"That too could be true, because God speaks to people in dreams and visions. If I could write, I too would have written many things God has told me. But to say that God has a son is completely untrue."

"God himself declared in this book that Jesus is his son. People believe it because Jesus did what nobody else could do—or has ever done."

"For example?"

"Opened the eyes of blind people."

"We have Zoes who do that, but we don't call them sons of God," the Old Man said with an ironic grin.

"Made the lame walk."

"Many Zoes I know can do the same thing."

"Made the dead to rise again."

"Don't lie to me! Such a thing doesn't happen! Whoever saw him raise people from the dead? And where did he do it?"

"Jesus did his miracles in Israel before crowds of people. He simply told blind people to see and they could see, and the dead to get up and they got up."

"You're lying. If such a thing had happened anywhere in the world I'd have heard about it before you were born."

"People who saw him do these things wrote everything in this book." Again, I raised the Bible.

"The witnesses of liars are never accessible," the Old Man said. "Since Jesus and your witnesses are all dead and buried, there's no way of verifying your claim."

"Jesus did not remain in the grave. On the third day after his burial, the grave burst open and he arose."

"Where is he now?"

"He went to heaven as I told you."

"You've proved again that you're a liar, for there's no way I can go to heaven and see him."

"Jesus is present everywhere but in spirit. He is even here with us; only you can't see him. If you believe in him, anything you ask him to do for you he will do it."

"I don't see how we'll profit by your education," the Old Man said quietly. "Now I believe what they've been telling me, that you're not learning book in school but witchcraft. They say you learned two books in one year, while your friends couldn't cope with even one. Son, why are you throwing your life away?" NanMolaa watched me with troubled eyes.

"Some people believe that a mermaid teaches me, but I have no dealing with such a creature."

"Do you sometimes dream of a lovely white girl?"

"Not white girl, though she has light skin."

"Does she give you book, paper, or pencil?"

"No."

"She tells you strange tales?"

"No. We only joke and play."

"You've ever fallen in love with a girl in Haindi?"

"I once had a girl friend, but I no longer play with her because I have too many lessons to study."

"You sometimes feel an invisible presence while studying?"

"Data, were I dealing with a water woman—I don't even play in the river anymore."

"You're normal!" The Old Man's face brightened. "It's that playmate of yours appearing to you in your dream. I hope you won't put school business one side because of her."

"The mission doesn't allow boys to tamper with girls."

"What happens when they're matured?"

"They must finish school before marrying. Any violator of this law is expelled from school."

"Foolish law," the Old Man sneered, sat up, and looked at me askance. "It's dangerous to keep boys and girls apart when they're matured! Dangerous for their health and sanity!" As an afterthought he said, "Son, the mission is not preparing you for life. Anyway, maybe the *kwii* people know what they're doing."

"I'm sorry you're sick," I changed the subject.

"Don't worry about my sickness, my son. I'll live to walk over the graves of my enemies. They put me to bed so that I might not rejoice over the safe return of my children from the stomach of The Big Thing. But they're wasting their time. God doesn't sleep. Go to the people for them to enjoy your company, too."

I wondered why the Old Man refused to talk about his illness. Perhaps the treatment he was receiving forbade it, or he wasn't really sick. No sick person could talk in such a clear, sustained voice. He might simply be avoiding disturbance to rest. The festive mood and flurry of activities prevailing in his quarters, as in all quarters, in preparation for the Poro graduation, supported my belief. All faces were radiant, all movements buoyant, and all conversations humorous. Indeed, Willietaa bubbled with joy and happy expectations.

I helped the men hoe grass in town, lop bushes on the outskirts, gather firewood and palm nuts; women pounded rice, fished in Gorlorpaya Creek, and recoated houses with clay; girls pounded country bread for prospective lovers—bought new clothes, trinkets, necklaces, earrings, perfumes, and hair lotions from peddlers.

Members of the Poro constantly warned me to avoid direct contact with the new initiates when they arrived because The Devil hovered about them. Unsatisfied with the warning, they had NanMolaa offer him a large sum of money, a white sheep, eight white hens, and a goat as a token of peace. Chagrined by the humiliation, I wondered why I had been excluded from the honored event.

Early one cold, misty morning, deafening musket blasts, rhythmic foot thuds, and a stormy victory song announced the commencement of the great day. Rubbing sleep out of my eyes, I rushed outside and joined the joyous crowd who pounded roofs with sticks and kicked chickens and animals out of the way.

There was a massive sweeping campaign at sunrise. The men decorated the palaver house with fresh palm fronds, new lappa, and blankets; then they spread new bamboo mats on the floor. By noon, a dance troupe, similar to that which had "mourned" the "death" of the initiates a year ago, waited on the eastern outskirts for the "newborn" who had "killed" Basai and had returned with victory. On the blast of a musket, they started dancing with suavity, swinging white headties sideways with their hands and moving slowly towards the palaver house, singing:

> *I'm dying to lay my eyes on you,*
> *My love, you plague my heart.*
> *What should I do—more?*
> *Or cook a delicious dish?*
> *Wear a chain of gold?*
> *Beauty is not shining teeth or skin,*
> *Nor charming eye.*
> *Caress dear love, the new thing!*
> *Beguile—the hidden parts.*
> *When beleh falls, corkwood takes its place.*

A long, convoluted mass covered with white shirting eventually emerged from the bushes and trudged behind the girls. Musket blasts boomed all over the town, shaking the very ground on which we walked. Magnificently attired in medical regalia, Zoes marched around the covered mass, swishing black cow tails and cheering at the top of their voices. When the maidens entered the palaver house, the Zoes shoved the shirting off the mass, revealing "the white chalks" who entered with great care, sat and stretched their legs on the mats, bowed their heads, clasped their hands in their laps. Baggy homespun hats covered their heads, the tops lying on the napes of their necks.

The maidens spun their beautiful bodies before them, shook their hips and heads coquettishly—all to the rhythm of their sweet song. Cheering mothers showered them with coins, kola nuts, and clean rice. Gunfire boomed. Here and there a parent fell to the ground, rolled over, rose and raised both palms in supplication to the Ancestors, marching with the rhythm of the girls' song. Never before had I seen men and women let themselves go with so much relish and abandon.

Though I enjoyed the celebration, I left the vicinity of the graduates in compliance with the warning I had received and went to see how NanMolaa was faring.

"Enjoying yourself?" he asked me.

"Yes," I said. "This celebration is the biggest of its kind I've ever witnessed. How are you feeling?"

"Don't worry. This sickness is nothing but a test. We Zoes often test one another this way—only the strong and the brave survive. I'll survive. What you're doing is more important, Son. When you know book, those boys will all be your servants."

"Why are Zoes cruel to each other?" I wanted to know.

The Old Man's answer was laconic:

"Wickedness! Jealousy!" After a short pause, he said slowly, "You *kwii* people love one another because you're in contact with God and even carry his words around in your hands. We Kpelle deal with the devil."

"If you believe in the Son of God, he will protect you from the devil."

"Tell me more about this Jesus. You keep talking about him and God in the same breath! He might have had strange powers, but it doesn't mean that he is God! All power comes from God alone."

Opening the Bible to St. John's Gospel where Jesus said that he and God are one, I read Jesus' own words for him.

"A man can say anything," cried he. "You told me the other day that it wasn't Jesus who wrote the Bible?"

"Most of the Bible was written before Jesus was born. People who followed him as he did his preaching, teaching, and healing also wrote part of it."

NanMolaa said in a voice that seemed to put the matter to rest, "Son, whenever they teach you something in school, think plenty about it and ask the opinion of your Elders before believing it. Books don't lie, but the person who tells you what is in them may lie. Someone writes a fine story for you to enjoy and learn a lesson from it. Somebody else tells you that it's the word of God. The liar is not the person who wrote the story, but the person who told you about it. To say that God has a son is not only ridiculous but senseless. Are the white people telling us, then, that God is a human being like us?"

My elbows planted on my knees and my folded hands bracing my chin, I pondered the Old Man's discerning opinion, which seemed to make a mockery of all I had been taught in school.

"What else have you learned in school?" he saved me the confusion.

"Hygiene," I said.

"What's that?" The lines on his cheeks deepened.

"How to care for our bodies to stay well."

Laughing, he said, "So your teachers think we don't do a good job of taking care of ourselves? That's an insult, you know. Look, evil spirits cause sickness and we have plenty of them in Kpelleland. No matter what you do you can't avoid sickness."

"Our teachers say small, small animals cause sickness; they live in the water we drink, the spittle of the mosquitoes that bite us, and the ground we walk on."

"Small, small animals," NanMolaa said, looking puzzled.

"You can't see them with the naked eye, but they get into your body and make you sick."

"Are they not the same as evil spirits? If the naked eye can't see them—"

"No. They're not spirits. Our teachers say we can stop them making us sick by wearing shoes, killing mosquitoes in our houses, and boiling our drinking water."

"Interesting! But one thing I know; I've never done such things and yet I've been living since Arthur Barclay was President of Liberia. The white people get sick, don't they?" I nodded. "They die, too?" I nodded again. "Look, you can't avoid sickness and death. Think about these things—I see a group of women coming this way. I don't want them to meet me here. It was good talking with you. I feel much better. Go enjoy yourself. Only don't let a girl get hold of you. If they tempt you, tell them you'll marry a *kwii* woman." I walked away wondering which was correct: what my teachers taught or what the Chiefs and the Elders taught?

After a grand feast in the afternoon, the Zoes took the new initiates to a fresh clearing beyond the outskirts where they bathed and dressed, then marched to the palaver house to witness more dances until far into the night. The ritual continued for three days. On the fourth day, the boys, dressed in their best, were turned over to their parents amidst elaborate feasting and spectacular singing and dancing feats.

All my efforts to renew acquaintance with my friends failed. Whenever they were engaged in a heart-to-heart conversation and spied me coming, they would keep quiet and stare at me with eyes that asked, "What do you want?" They answered my queries with curt replies only. After I prodded them persistently to know the cause of their unfriendly attitude, they said it was because I was raw and they were cooked; I was a sinner and they were saints; I was a boy and they were men; I was stupid and they were wise. Further, they couldn't keep conversation with me because, through a slip of tongue, they could tell me secrets of the Poro or mention incidents that occurred before their initiation—offenses that carried the death penalty.

THE BIDDING

I never bothered NanMolaa with my problems because of his illness, which the raucous songs and reiterated shouts of celebrants of the Poro graduation aggravated. My initial estimation of his illness had been wholly incorrect. A hardworking man, it wasn't like him to take to his bed for so many weeks simply to rest. He would rebel against the boredom by going to his shop to make some implement or by going into the bush to set a trap or gather palm nuts. Indeed, the Old Man was losing ground despite his admirable courage.

I stopped visiting him when he couldn't sustain a conversation more than a moment. His voice had weakened considerably; half the words he spoke were unintelligible. What was sad about the desolate affair was that nobody could help him but a colleague. Unfortunately, as he had said, Zoes were only concerned with each other's undoing. When I bade him farewell on the morning of my departure, he craned his lean neck laboriously, turned his head to me, and said feebly, "I hope you enjoyed your stay. Continue the good work. Visit us often. Some of your relatives will join you," his speech was interrupted by heavy coughing. "But later; you're only just beginning." Rummaging with effort in the palm thatch mattress, he took out two dimes and handed them to me, saying, "Buy a pencil or two with this. Remember—" Assailed by sudden pain, he twitched uneasily, winced, and lay calm on his left side, facing the wall. Meanwhile, a group of players stormed the porch to pay him the morning homage, an attitude I considered indiscreet. They should have done what I was about to do: leave the Old Man alone for him to die in peace.

"Why did the white woman not keep you on the mission?" Father complained when I told him about my fruitless visit to Willietta. "That would have solved your problem. Anyway, ask your brother Tama for a job. I'm sure he'll give you one."

Brother Thomas was apportioning tasks to the workers when I called on to him the following morning.

"How much work can a child like you do?" he told me when I asked him for a job. "You think you're a qualified worker just because you can cut grass? That's a boy's work. When you work for pay, you do a grown man's job: cut no less than one hundred and fifty pieces of thatch, fifty poles, or ten bunches of palm nuts—in one day!"

"I can do it," I said, hoping my courage would impress him.

"So you think you're a man, heh? But who will let a small boy like you work in the bush?" he said irrefutably. "Suppose you get hurt? Or are bitten by snake?" Then he looked straight in my face and said, "I might as well tell you the truth. Remember what you did to Sianeh? Sianeh Zepe? You were lucky you weren't expelled from the mission." Continuing with a whisking finger, he said, "I warned you of this danger when you first set foot on this campus! Now you have a bad record here! You'll have to find a job elsewhere. Go to Teacher Moana in Haindi. He'll give you a vacation job."

As I returned home, disappointed, I thought of the trivial incident which had occurred between Sianeh and me several months ago—an episode that would have aroused only laughter in Haindi at the most.

I had completed my roster work an hour early. Instead of going home, I elected to stroll about campus. Reaching Teacher Josephine's house, which stood near the girl's dorm, I saw a beautiful girl sweeping the yard; she was dressed in a red blouse and a black skirt. Her round, full breasts stood stiff in the blouse; her long, black hair, plaited in three perpendicular rows, sparkled in the afternoon sun. Bushy brows overshadowed her bright eyes. Her beautifully carved lips, firm nose, and plump hairy limbs sent a fiery tremor through me. Never before had the mere appearance of a girl moved me with so much delight and desire. Not even the bare-breasted girls I played with in Haindi. I wanted to touch the girl's lovely arm to relieve my aching heart of its pain. Walking towards her with confident steps, smiling, I beckoned to her. She only gave me a taunting grin and continued with her sweeping. When I was about to grab her arm she dropped the broom and fled into the screened porch.

Now in safety, she absently stroked the wire screen with her lips, spying me smilingly as I shifted my weight. "Thinks I want to whisper a secret in her ear," I said in my mind. "Simply want to touch your lovely arm—and hear you complain. I won't hurt you. "When I walked to the screen, she stopped stroking it and watched me with sober eyes. I stood still and beckoned to her again. Grinning, she again pressed her lips on the screen, her eyes intent on me. The temptation was too much. I slapped her face and ran away, my ears pricked to hear her complain.

Sianeh didn't take the matter lightly. She screamed and reeled fitfully as if snake had bitten her. Then she ran to Teacher Josephine behind the house, where a curious crowd of girls soon gathered, asking her what had happened. I hid in a hedge on the outskirts, from where I overheard the most unpleasant comments ever made about my character. I was a shameless woman-lappa, a mad man, etc., etc.

The teacher called me loudly, the girls extending her call all over the mission and looking for me. Judging it prudent to take care of the problem before Ma Miller heard of it, I decided to honor the call.

"What you did to Sianeh?" Teacher Josephine asked, eyeing me reproachfully. "What you did to Sianeh, heh? What you did to Sianeh?" Tears streaming down her fat cheeks, Sianeh writhed in agony as never before. "You not talking?"

"I—I only played with her," I faltered in Kpelle.

"He telling story," Sianeh whined, spying me with disdain. "He wasn't playing."

"Who told you girls were your playmates, anyhow?" The woman's harsh voice and fiery eyes unnerved me. I wanted to run away, but I was rooted on the spot like a tree. "Martha, bring me switch!" she said. My blood congealed, I watched the girls in anger as they laughed at me. A short, fat one with a bulbous nose stripped a branch of guava tree and brought it to the teacher who whipped me most severely. I jumped up and down, twisted my pursed lips one side, and moaned. Sianeh's eyes lighted. Wiping her face dry with the back of her hand, she joined her friends to revel in my misery. The teacher released me only after the switch had burst a boil on my left buttock and red pus ran down my leg. "Go bathe," she said, releasing me. "And never again put your hand on a girl on this campus. Understand!"

Teacher Moana's round, white house stood outside the eastern fringe of Haindi. His son Momolu, a classmate of mine, who had grayed prematurely, said his father was out when I called by in the evening and inquired for him. Momolu was hoeing grass behind his father's house.

"Come tomorrow morning," he advised me, leaning on the handle of his hoe and scratching his head. "Come soon in the morning. What you want? Job?"

"You think your father will give me one?"

"We have plenty work here. You like hard work? Come in the morning if you want see Papa."

The following morning I met Teacher Moana lounging in a rattan chair on his porch, helping himself to a bowl of cassava and chicken gravy.

"So you want work—huh?" he mumbled as he buried yet another chicken thigh in his mouth.

"Yes, sir," I said.

"You strong?" He chewed roughly, swallowed noisily, and washed the food down with a pint of fresh palm wine he poured into a calabash from a foaming gourd.

Momolu winked at me and bobbed his head towards a large, yellow house nearby. We sat on a bench on its wide porch spanning the entire length of the house. Discussing our varied experiences, we eventually dwelled on a subject of mutual interest.

"Let's live here and study together," Momolu suggested. "The lessons are tough! Pa won't mind. Great help for your poor parents. They won't worry about your food, clothes, and school fees."

I wondered whether such arrangement would be in my interest. Notoriously dull, Momolu was absent from school too often. I would spend most of my time tutoring him. I asked him what kept him from school and if his father helped him with his studies. Taken aback by the blunt queries, he yawned, looked at my face absently as if he had not heard me, but my insistent search in his weary eyes was inescapable.

"Why are you answering my question with questions?" he said, scratching his craw-craw arm. "Let's talk about the most important thing first. Don't you think it'll be good for you to live here and save your old parents much trouble and expense?"

"Will I go to school regularly?" I asked.

"Will you live with your own teacher and don't go to school? Have you ever seen me fail? I know your problem: you want to be with your mother to get your gut full everyday."

"Once I go to school regularly, I can live anywhere. What is hard work or food? But my father doesn't want me to miss a single school day."

"Look, you'll get promotion without problem. Just do Papa's work. If you want even double promotion, you'll get it."

"Well, we go to school for promotion. I'm sure my father will agree for me to live here."

"Your Old Man might want you to stay at his side since you're his baby."

"My friend, Father once turned me over to Ma Miller for her to send me to school! He believes that I'll learn faster if I go away from home to attend school."

"Will he not oppose your living with Mende people?"

"Why should he? We're black and you people are black. What's the matter?"

"Some people don't think so. Once you're not a member of their tribe, they think you aren't a human being."

"Nonsense. The world would be a dull place if everybody had the same color and tribe."

"You saw what I was doing? We work hard here-o! If you're scared of hard work, stay home."

"Who says I don't work hard? I once made a large cassava patch for my sister. What brought you people to Liberia? Don't you feel homesick?"

Piqued by the rude query that had taken him by surprise, Momolu blushed, then sobered and returned to the previous topic:

"Working for your mother is different from working for somebody else. At home, you do what you like, but elsewhere you do what you're assigned. You'll see what I mean when you come."

"You haven't answered my question."

"Look, my man, I've plenty of work to do. Let's see whether the Old Man is through eating."

"I want to know about your country, Momolu," I said politely.

"What do you want to know about Sierra Leone?" Momolu frowned darkly. He went to his father, returned, and told me, "It's a long story." He spoke with caution as if the story were a secret he was afraid to divulge. "Let me tell you the most important part. Back home, there's no limit to family members. Every day dozens of cousins, uncles, nephews, brothers, sisters, aunts, mothers, and fathers asked Pa for money, even when they had no need for it. Pa couldn't support us. Mind you, he made good money. Teachers in Sierra Leone get good pay—not like here where they must make farm or do business to survive. When Sister Tenneh died and Father had to pawn his sewing machine and bicycle to bury her, he said we should come to Liberia." Momolu shook with laughter. "We met Mende people here, anyway. Life is something."

"Do you mean to say that all Mende people are your relatives?"

"Surely, you haven't traveled, my friend. When you travel, you'll note that once you meet a Kpelle man or woman, you've met a member of your family." Momolu stretched and yawned. "What else you want to know?"

"How come you're struggling with your lessons? Your father doesn't help you with them?"

Glancing at me with squinting eyes, he scratched his craw-craw again and said angrily, "You're too inquisitive!" Regarding me with a sneer, he added, "You want to know everything, don't you? And your questions are always rude! My man, book isn't the most important thing in life."

"What is the most important thing in life?"

"Trade. I go to school simply to learn how to read and write. When I'm through with, say, the eighth grade, I'll go after my trade."

"What trade?"

"I want to be a tailor."

"If you get good education, you'll become a better tailor."

"I know many good tailors who don't know book."

"I said better tailor—Does your father ever help you with your studies?"

"Why should he? The man has many other things to do! Why are you concerned about studies, anyway? Did I not say you'll get all the promotion you want once you do a good job for Father?"

"And why are you always absent from school?"

"Not always, my man! Let me tell you the truth. I've tried to avoid telling it, but I must," Momolu said with asperity. "I hope you won't mind. You Liberians don't believe in business or trade, but we Sierra Leoneans do. Every Liberian man wants to be a professor, a politician, a pastor, a lawyer—to sit idly in an air-conditioned office all day, gossiping. That's why foreigners have taken over your country. When I complete the eighth grade by God's grace, my father will buy me a sewing machine so that I may learn tailor work. With all the book in your head, if you don't know trade, you're nothing."

"Ma Miller says we'll understand our trades better when we go through school. Why the big rush after money, Momolu? Your life is still before you!"

"Do you know when you'll die?"

"No."

"The future belongs to no one, my friend. Whatever you want to do in life, you have only today to do it. Young people die too, Joe."

"If you live by such idea, you'll accomplish nothing in life. It takes time to develop your skills and use them. We have to live by faith, Momolu."

"Look, I'm not putting all my eggs in one basket. You're welcome to stay in school until you grow old. Do you know that book can't be finished?"

"Momolu," I said, "the white people who made the T-shirts and shoes we wear have never laid their eyes on us. Once you know your correct size in shoes and clothes, you have no problem finding them. But let Vanii sew for you! He takes your measurement himself, but after he sews your pants, the waist is either too wide or too narrow—the seat either too long or too short. Why? Because he never went to school."

"Don't white people make mistakes?"

"Had Vanii gone to school—"

"The book has already gone to your head and you're nowhere yet. I know when you finish KP, you'll have no equal round here. Let Vanii hear you talk about him like that; he'll never sew for you again."

"Let's see if the Old Man has finished eating," I said.

Having completed his dinner, Teacher Moana was picking his teeth. He smiled as we approached him.

"Joe," he said, snapping my fingers, "you're welcome here. Don't think all we do here is sit round and talk. I wanted you boys to get acquainted. That's why I let you keep a little company. If you work hard, I'll take care of all your school expenses and grades."

"Thank you, sir," I said. "My parents will be happy to hear this."

Baring his white teeth, he said, "You don't expect a student to work hard for his teacher and fails in school, do you? How does it sound: 'The farmer's son died of hunger!' I'll take care of you once you do good work."

"Thank you, sir," I said again. "I'll tell my father that you've given me a job."

"Tell him too that you've found a home where you'll learn to speak correct English. I'm told you're worried about your inability to speak English correctly. No problem. You'll be compelled to speak English fluently here, for speaking Kpelle or Mende is forbidden in this house."

Life in Teacher Moana's house was tedious but organized as life on the mission, and we had plenty to eat. Early each morning Momolu and I prepared warm baths for him and his wife, a slim, delicate woman called Ma Famata. Then we swept the houses and the yards and dug cassava from a patch several minutes away in the bush. Our Ma would then prepare a breakfast of cassava and chicken gravy, which Teacher would eat voraciously and wash down with palm wine or water if wine wasn't available. Lunch would follow at noon and supper at six in the evening. They usually consisted of rice and stewed cassava leaves and meat or fish. In the evening, we would prepare warm baths for them again, do a number of chores, and go to bed in our dark, dingy room, which was really a shop with a long counter behind the double door. Our bed stood against a rough mud wall with shelves ranged with lappa, blankets, shotgun shells, candies, tobacco leaves, cigarettes, beads, farming and cooking utensils, and bags of salt.

Momolu told me that his father also ran a shop deep inside the Western Province. "How else will he support us if he doesn't do business? Be sure to make several trips up there before school opens." The words were hardly out of his mouth when Teacher Moana called us.

"They say the salt supply in the Twalataa shop has run out. I want you boys to carry some up there this weekend," he said. "Joe, ask your parents' permission tomorrow for the trip."

SOLDIER'S FATE

My parents considered the trip an opportunity for me to gain more experience. Mother told me to find her younger brother Yakpalo Gonoh in Gbangei, which was on the road to Twalataa. "He'll be happy and proud to learn that his nephew is attending school." Uncle Gonoh owed her a big debt his conscience would compel him to repay in part by helping me. She had nursed him after their mother had died mysteriously in Muanlakwelle when he was a toddler. She indulged his every whim and caprice until he was fifteen, when she told him the truth about their relationship, but he never believed that she was only his sister.

"Those were the good and happy days," Mother reminisced. "Then, I was the wife of a Deecee. I rode hammock carried on the heads of men! What clothes could I not wear? I didn't have to make a farm. A single patrol in the District with my husband raised no less than a hundred *kenja* of rice, a dozen head of cattle, countless baskets of chickens, and more than five hundred pounds cash. I was a queen in the family; nearly all my relatives flocked on me—I'm sure Brother Gonoh will give you money to buy your school supplies."

The journey to Gbangei took us a full day. Momolu (whom I now called Momo) and I carried a hundred pounds of salt, each, on our heads on the tortuous, swampy, hilly road cutting through endless virgin forests—the heaviest load I had ever carried and the longest distance I had ever walked in a day. Whenever I reached points of exhaustion, I asked Momo that we rest; my request was frequent.

"If we rest too often we'll get sick," he would warn me each time I made the request. Then he would tell me from experience, "Whenever you're carrying a heavy load over a long distance, don't rest frequently; walk fast to reach your destination quickly."

At sundown we reached the outskirts of Gbangei with its kola orchard and vaulted bridge under which flowed a wide, beautiful creek. A cluster of the usual mud and thatched houses, the ancient town was surrounded by giant *beleh* and cottonwood trees, which stood like vigilant sentries ready to challenge intruders.

Momo took me to a round, yellow house standing near the beginning of the road to Twalataa. After we placed our burdens on the porch, I sat wearily on a stool and leaned against the wall while he strolled about the town, looking for what only the Ancestors knew. Entering the yard at nightfall were a man, hopping under a large bunch of firewood he carried on his shoulder, and a woman with a large basket of cooking utensils and foodstuffs on her head. Behind the woman walked a lean, black dog; naked toddlers with swollen stomachs shambled at her feet. After we exchanged greetings, the man laid his wood by our bags of salt, and the woman trifled with a small padlock on the door until it clicked open. Soon fire blazed in the center room.

When Momo came from his excursion, he introduced me to our hosts who welcomed us warmly and presented their house to us with white kola. We went straight to bed after bathing and eating, and slept without waking through the cold, windy night.

Early in the morning, I saw a man matching the description Mother had given of my uncle, standing in the yard. He was dressed in a ragged shirt and brown short pants, an affectionate smile on his face.

"Good morning, my Master!" he greeted me heartily. As we snapped fingers, he said, "I'm your Uncle Yakpalo Gonoh! I hope you had a restful night. Let's go to your house for you to meet your wife and children. They're anxious to see you! Momo told me all about you last night. So you're going to school! And doing very well! I'm not surprised at all! That's how they're—the Senfenui clan. I'm sure you'll know book from top to bottom. You must, because you're our only hope. You have a large family looking up to you for support and protection! Do you know that? You can't afford to fail. Is Sister well? I hope so. I know she's old now. The backbreaking farm work! The menace of witches!" He wrinkled his nose disdainfully. "A long time since I saw her. She still makes farm? On your return, tell her that she hasn't seen me so long because of sickness. I'm not well, Nephew. I'm sick! Seriously sick! You see me on my feet because a poor man can't afford to lie down with sickness. I don't breathe well, Nephew. That's my problem. I sleep standing up most nights, for when I lie down, great weakness attacks me! My head swims! My breath cuts off! Can you imagine that? In other words I die! Gormah has to shake me vigorously and set me up erect before life comes back to me. I don't know what sickness treats a full-grown man like that, and what wrong I've done to deserve it. We've consulted every available Zoe in Bokomu Chiefdom. No way! A man ought to die instantly when his allotted time on earth expires. No pain. No suffering. Sickness is shameful! Unfair! Unpleasant! And dangerous if you don't know the cause—You could carry one or two of your children to tote your book bag, sharpen your pencil, wash your clothes, tie your shoestrings. They wander here doing nothing but only eat, cry, and cause trouble. You're a King! You know that? A King with countless subjects! I know Sister is vexed with me because I haven't visited her for years! Tell her to forgive me. It's not my fault. This stupid sickness—"

"She's well," I cut in quickly.

"How long you'll be in Gbangei?" he asked as we jumped across a ravine. "A week or two?"

"We're leaving for Twalataa this morning to return home tomorrow," I said.

"Why the big hurry!" he said with mock anger. "A long-distance trip should never be done in one stroke! It's dangerous for your health! When young, your body stands any strain or stress, but when you get a strand of gray hair on your head, you realize how dangerous you have lived." We were now in his yard. "Here is your family," he said.

Watching me with curious eyes were a woman and five children: four boys and a girl. Three of the boys were small and completely naked; the oldest boy and the girl were teenagers; they were scantily dressed—the girl with a red-, blue-, and white-striped towel round her waist and the boy wearing only a pair of brown short pants. They embraced me excitedly.

"This is your wife," Uncle told me as his wife shook my hand, "and your children." He pointed at the children.

"Welcome to Gbangei," the woman said with delight. "This is your home. My name is Gormah."

"He's already on his way to Twalataa and returns to Haindi tomorrow," Uncle informed her. "Don't disturb your father!" he chided the small children who clutched my hands and legs. "He's weary from the long journey. The distance from Haindi to Gbangei is far!"

"I'm not disturbed," I said, stroking the kids' heads.

"One day you'll carry them with you to put training in their heads. They trouble us too much."

"I want to go with him now!" cried the smallest, who was about four years old. He held my hand tight and stamped one foot with impatience. I gathered him in my arms. Uncle went into the house and brought me a small raffia bag of country bread.

"Eat this on the way," he said, looking abashed. "Sorry, I can't do better than this because your trip is too quick! *Kwii* people are always in a hurry. Hope you won't tell Sister that all I gave you was a pint of country bread. Let's go down the road for something to drink. Good for the hills. Twalataa is not far from here but the hills! You'll reach there before noon. Follow us," he told his wife and children. I handed the baby to Gormah.

On the way, I told Uncle it'd be unfair to take his bad name to his sister because he hadn't expected me. "I'll pay you a special visit," I said. "Then, you'll have a chance to do something for me."

"You must spend some time with us really! Long enough to know each other better. Perhaps a month or two. You drink? Schoolboys don't drink of course. Whenever you're with your Uncle, put school business aside. You become a man like me."

"It's good to drink something for the road," I said, though I had never drunk before and didn't feel like drinking.

"That's the only way to conquer the hills! Animals are plenty here. On your next trip, bring shells for me to get you some meat. I know you people suffer for want of meat in Haindi. River people—all they eat is fish. Of course, some people consider fish the best of foods. A year ago, a soldier died for fish here."

"Stole somebody's fish?" I said.

"No and yes," Uncle drawled. "Do you see that spot?" he pointed casually at a dark, wide, stagnant portion of the creek as we climbed the log bridge with care. "It's full of catfish. This creek is called MaDeyn. Mother of the Deyn! Funny, isn't it?" He glanced at me smilingly.

"How come the soldier—"

"I'm coming to it. Be patient. This story has to do with life and death, so we don't tell it hurriedly because we don't want any stranger to say tomorrow, 'I didn't know', or 'I didn't understand.' Barren women get children from MaDeyn," he said as we came down from the bridge. "If a barren woman wants a child, all she has to do is take a bowl of rice powder, three red kola nuts, and a black hen (if she wants a girl)—or a bowl of rice powder, four white kola nuts, and a red rooster (if she wants a boy)—to that spot by herself, weeping. Real tears must flow down her cheeks, you see. For many women the tears come easily because barrenness is most unbearable for women. Then she sprinkles the rice powder on the bank, cuts the chicken's neck, showers the powder with its blood, throws it with the kola nuts into the creek, lies flat on her back, and closes her eyes. A catfish would turn into a baby and enter her belly, if she wants to bear her own child; or she lies on her side if she wants a baby already born—and a catfish would turn into a three-month old baby and lie beside her. A mystery, isn't it? I know you don't believe it." Uncle looked at me skeptically and giggled. "*Kwii* people doubt everything except what they see with their own eyes and touch with their own hands. But life isn't always like that. Nobody is allowed to fish in MaDeyn, or even be seen round it with a net, stick, hook, cutlass, or spear. That creek is purely for drinking, bathing, and washing." Uncle was completely engrossed in the story as if it were a dream he had the night before.

"Once a soldier came here and said he wanted catfish from MaDeyn to cook soup! We told him that it was dangerous to tamper with the catfish in that creek. We offered him rice, chickens, meat, money, palm wine—and put the town in his hand with white kola. But our kindness meant nothing to the doomed man. 'Why, you people have plenty of good fish right here but refuse to eat some!' He stamped the ground with his gun butt and marched to MaDeyn.

Angry but impotent we watched him bait a hook he demanded of the Chief. Of course, the fish came to the surface of the creek as soon as the fellow set his foot on the bank. He didn't need a hook. He pierced a catfish with his soldier knife! The first time such a thing ever happened in Gbangei! The sun disappeared behind a thick, black cloud; it grew immensely dark. Fear descended upon the town." Uncle paused, looking disturbed as if the irreverent act were occurring presently. He resumed his story after we had walked for a long time in silence. "He cut the fish into pieces and asked Yaa Kolleh's wife Kpanaah to cook it for him, but she refused. He beat the woman with his soldier belt—cursed her—but even beating and cursing couldn't make her put a finger on the fish, much less cook it. He stuffed an iron pot with the catfish, set it on a fire he built in the square, and seasoned it with palm oil, salt, and pepper, like a house-wife. Thinking that it was done, he put it in a big, black pan, but it was too bloody to eat. 'Maybe it didn't cook long enough,' he said. Putting it back into the pot, he set it on the fire again; it boiled long enough to make dry elephant skin pulpy, yet the fish was bloody. He salvaged some bloodless flesh with a spoon and ate it. His stomach swelled all of a sudden, his eyes turned bloodshot; he complained of headache and stomach pains. There came the most powerful crash of thunder in known memory. We became blind and deaf, but everything quickly returned to normal as if nothing had happened. The soldier lay in a pool of blood by the bowl of fish. His head and arms were blown off; his gun lay at his side like a bed mate. What a pity! The Chief ordered that nobody touch him because the deadly power of the lightning was still active in him. Only The Bush Thing could bury such a corpse.

"So, whenever you're here, we can catch you plenty of fish in other creeks. Never ever tamper with the fish of MaDeyn. Tribal laws excuse no one. Any questions?"

I had questions, but I made no query. From my experience with lore about water people, I had learned that the most you could do with such a story was ignore it. Uncle climbed a tall wine tree off the farm road and brought down a large gourd of wine. After drinking to my fill due to his insistence, I bade him farewell and hurried back to Momo. My head swam as I ran on the narrow, bushy path. I bade Gormah goodbye as she walked at a snail's pace with the children on the way.

I stopped briefly by the sacred spot in MaDeyn; pieces of kola nuts were scattered all around there. The catfish wriggled to the surface of the water on the sound of my footsteps.

We made the last leg of our journey to Twalataa with haste, Momo much impressed by my speed. It was his turn to trail behind me by some hundred yards. We reached Twalataa before noon as Uncle had predicted.

"You'll note," Momo told me when we placed our burdens on the shop porch, "that palm wine gives you strength but leaves you broken. I've tried it before; many times. Do you drink often? You're too young for that."

"Perhaps the wine has something to do with it," I said, "but I'm hurrying to return home and find shotgun shells for Uncle Gonoh. He promised to hunt for me."

"Good luck to you!" Momo said. "Maybe Gonoh will help you since he's your uncle, but I've never seen a faithful hunter round here."

Momo was right. When I gave Uncle Gonoh a whole pack of cartridges on our second trip to Twalataa—now we carried bales of *fanti*—he advised me to return home and wait; he would spend at least a week or two in the deep forest to do the hunting. I never saw him again.

My only hope now was whatever Teacher Moana would pay me. We had carried enough merchandise to Twalataa to last for a year, a project which had taken ten round trips and delayed our return to school by a month. My parents were concerned about the delay but hoped that the pay would worth the sacrifice.

"What did Teacher Moana pay you?" Father asked me as I sat with him and Mother on the porch discussing my late return to school.

"He gave me one dollar to buy soap to wash my clothes," I said. "He promised to give me more pay later."

"Why later?" Father asked, ostensibly angry. "After all, you're not asking for favor."

"The pay is not money, Data. He'll give it to me in school."

"Must be something special, then," he observed, looking away reflectively.

"Does it not have a name?"

"Grade." I spoke "grade" in English for want of a Kpelle equivalent.

"Grade!" Father said, baffled.

"Number you get for the work you do in school," I informed him.

"Number," he sighed and said, "I don't understand. Paying someone with number rather than money for their sweat is something I've never heard of." He searched my eyes for an explanation.

"The importance of the number is this," I said. "Whether I go to school or not—study my lessons or not—I'll pass to the fifth book."

"Look," Father said in anger, "tell Moana I say he should pay you with money to buy your pencils, copybooks, and clothes. People are not paid with number for their sweat."

"Suppose Moana doesn't pay him?" Mother observed, placing an elbow on her knee and cupping her cheek in her hand. "NanSen, fighting a losing battle is useless. Let's see to the child's school supplies."

"He has worked for money to buy them!" Father said. "If Moana doesn't pay him, I'll take the matter up with the white woman."

"A bad and sad mistake," Mother reasoned. "The white woman might dismiss Moana when she learns that he used one of her good students through the vacation, caused him to be late for school, and failed to pay him on top of all that."

"That'll be fine," Father said, laughing. "It won't bother me at all. If you do good, you do it for yourself. If you do bad—"

"I know," Mother cut in sharply. "Not every drop of water in your bath bucket touches your skin. Let's thank God our boy is alive. His life is still before him. Revenge will only make matters worse; Moana could poison the minds of the other teachers against him in case he is dismissed."

"Well, Son," Father sighed with resignation, "let's forget that tricky man. We'll pray to God for money to buy your school materials."

The morning was cold, gray, and drizzling, for the harmattan had not yet released its grip on the land. Vainly but persistently I tried to catch a glimpse of Bo Mountain, which was a pleasure to view in the morning. Crowned with primeval forest and looming against the blue skyline, it dominated the western horizon. Now it was completely buried in mist. However, I cherished in my heart the joy of having toppled it many times on the way to Twalataa.

I wondered what credible excuse to give Ma Miller for my lateness as I picked flower for her on the roadside. As usual she was pecking at the keys of her typewriter, completely lost in thought, when I knocked the screen door. After a time she hastened to the door, her shoes clicking on the concrete floor. A bright smile on her thin, red lips, she invited me into the office and received the bouquet of flowers. Carefully placing it in a jar half-filled with water, she rummaged through stacks of brown files on the shelves, pulled out one and sat at her desk. "Sit down," she told me, opening the file and putting a pencil point in it.

"You must have enjoyed the vacation a lot!" she said with a smile.

"Yes, Ma Miller," I said.

"Ready for school?"

"Yes, Ma Miller."

"You're now in grade—"

"Four."

Filling the form quickly, she went into a room across the hall, and brought me a heap of books and a plastic bag stacked against her bosom.

"Wish you good luck. Study hard. May God bless you," she said.

"Thank you, Ma Miller," I said with relief.

When I entered the classroom, my classmates snickered but grew quiet when Teacher Moana held his switch at the ready, daring anyone to make another sound. The students were standing in a straight row reciting various portions of a small, blue book called *Luther's Small Catechism*. Amazingly, Momo wasn't in class. As I skimmed the Catechism, I wondered which was important: what Martin Luther said about the Bible or what the Bible had to say? The students were holding their own very well. With time, I too would cope with the Catechism, I thought.

A strange drama suddenly unfolded before me: Mary Soonaah failed to recite correctly a portion of the Catechism, which Seelar recited without a single mistake. Teacher Moana gave him the switch "to teach the idiot how to quote Luther correctly." The boy tapped the girl only lightly in the palm with the rattan. Annoyed because of his insincere performance, Teacher grabbed the switch and told him gruffly, "Show me your hand!" The beating was so severe that the boy jumped up and down, shaking his hand frantically and groaning piteously. "That's how to teach someone how to quote Luther," Teacher Moana said. Fear gripped the class. The students whispered to one another, apparently to fill gaps in their recollection of the Catechism. I grew frightened because I have a poor memory, which hardly recalls dreams or the names of casual acquaintances. Fortunately, Teacher Moana didn't ask me to quote. I discovered later that he employed the same method in teaching spelling.

To avoid the rod I memorized not only the Catechism and spelling but any text which aroused my interest or curiosity such as poems, Bible verses, European folktales, and the like. However, I took beatings for skipping an article here, mispronouncing a word there, or confusing one quotation with another.

But I had my days of wielding the switch. On one such day, Dougbawor Leipor, a tall, brawny fellow from Gargbelei who stood next to me, failed to spell "catechism". Even though the word wasn't in our Spelling, Teacher Moana said we ought to have known how to spell it because it was the title of a textbook of ours. A newly converted Lutheran, he almost put Dougbawor out of class for misspelling the word. "Joe, you try," he told me. I spelled it correctly and he handed me the switch to "teach the bushman an unforgettable lesson in spelling." I shuddered with fear because the fellow was older and bigger than I, perhaps stronger, and vengeance glared in his brown eyes. When I raised the switch, he watched me with entreaty. I would have beaten him lightly had Teacher Moana not raged, "Do your duty properly or I'll show you how!" I brought the switch down with all the force I could command. Teacher Moana nodded approval. "Good. Two more times," he said. Dougbawor shook his hand, pursed his lips, and stamped his foot in agony. Tears stood in his eyes. The class was deathly still.

After school, I made sure to be with people for protection just in case the fellow decided to revenge. Perhaps knowing that fighting on campus was risky, he postponed his attack until I had done my roster work and left for home.

Bhea and I walked together with our book bags on our heads. In the middle of the hill below Gargbelei, Dougbawor and his brother Gbanjah mysteriously jumped out of the thicket and approached me with a clear intention to fight. Bhea inquired what the matter was.

"You have nothing to do with it!" Dougbawor growled, pushing him aside.

"If you touch the people's child, I'll tell," Bhea said, ducking a blow and running to Gargbelei.

"Who were you beating?" Dougbawor asked me, his eyes bulging.

"I have no time for questions," I said and attempted to walk away, but the boys blocked every direction I took with outstretched arms.

"Don't bother with him," Gbanjah told his elder brother who stood so close to me that a fly couldn't pass between us. "Leave him to me. Who's he for you to spoil your name fighting? Won't you answer my brother's question?" Gbanjah demanded with widened eyes.

"I say who were you beating?" Dougbawor asked me again, paying his brother no attention. Remembering the injury and punishment I had borne for fighting, I thought it advisable to go home, although fear of engaging in a handicapped fight influenced my decision. The confrontation would have ended had I denied beating Dougbawor, but a denial would have convinced the boys that I was afraid of them, making me a laughingstock on campus and a target for future attacks.

I told Dougbawor, "Get out of my way! I want to go home. I don't like fighting."

"Say you hope to go home, because you aren't going an inch from here unless you answer my question." He drew a line across the path with a crooked stick and dared me to put a foot across it.

"Had you known your spelling, I wouldn't have beaten you," I said.

"Oho! So you actually beat my brother!" Gbanjah said, bobbing his head and raising his clenched fist to strike.

"I too get beaten for spelling mistakes," I said. "I didn't beat your brother because I wanted to. I was only obeying order." I thought that my putting up of no resistance would make the boys ashamed of fighting me, for you fought only the enemy who fought back.

"Whether you were obeying order or not—the fact is you beat my brother." Gbanjah pushed me violently. I staggered but regained balance and placed my foot across the line. Dougbawor sent a stinging blow between my shoulder blades. I fell instantly; my books scattered. Inexplicably, it was Gbanjah who and I were hooked together, rolling over and over in the gravel, bruising our knees and elbows. I managed to pin the fellow down, sit on top of him, and hit him furiously with heavy blows. Another sharp blow landed on the back of my head. Then another. Dazed, I fell over, rolled and staggered up. Another came but I ducked. It went wild, sending Dougbawor tumbling to the ground with a heavy thud. He rolled downhill several yards and struggled to his feet. His bloodshot eyes glared with anger. No need pretending I could fight two boys at the same time. I started gathering my books with haste to run away, but it was a sad mistake. The boys rushed at me and knocked me down. Making one last effort, I stood up and hit Dougbawor on the chin with an uppercut to put him out of the fight, but he returned the blow. I sent another with all my might. Coming to the aid of his brother, Gbanjah raked me down. After some moments, I only saw the boys dimly as they ran away, their toes sending gravel flying behind them. Then I heard the faint voice of a man shouting at them reproachfully:

"I'll tell your parents what you boys have done! You'll surely get good beating for your mischief!"

The man pulled me up by the hand, staring aghast at blood pouring from my nose and numerous cuts and bruises all over my face, knees, and elbows. I was plastered with yellow dust. As he helped me collect my books, he said with disgust:

"What is this, my people? Have Gbiyaminling's boys become murderers?"

Bhea ran to us breathlessly on the outskirts of Gargbelei, his eyes glazed with anger. "Nobody in town," he panted. Inspecting my bloody clothes and bruises, he said, "I'll tell your parents if you don't; I know you'll want to protect those boys as you once did on campus."

"And I'll be the eyewitness," said my helper.

"Somebody has to stop the mad boys of Gargbelei from menacing us," Bhea said. I wondered why he hadn't stayed to help me. If the fellows had killed me, what would his reporting of it have done?

When Bhea informed my parents about the fight, Mother vowed to draw blood from "the wicked, heartless brutes," but Father calmed her down with words of prudence: "Our son will run into many such problems," he said. "He must learn how to fight."

Chief Gumo found the boys guilty of unprovoked assault for which each received twenty-five lashes on his bare back. However, their menace persisted, and I wasn't their only victim but also other boys from Haindi and Dingshu, whose only crime was passing through Gargbelei to go home. We had to practice wrestling on the riverbank and travel in groups to and from school. That was the only solution to the problem.

After Father's dramatic clash with Water Zoe Deynpolu Kollie and my fight with Leipur and his brother Gbanjah, my school career proceeded without distraction. As a result, I made rapid progress. When I passed to the fifth grade, Father would have handed me the moon as a present had it been possible. Only lack of clothes sometimes interrupted my schooling. I remember going to him in tears several times after failing the morning inspection because of patched pants and torn T-shirt.

"I'll take you to Brother Zokpooh this vacation," he told me when school closed. "I'm sure he'll give you all the money you need for your schooling,"

"We've sought help from many relatives but nobody is willing to help. So we must find some other means."

"What do you propose?"

"Make palm oil for sale."

"Good. Now you're behaving like a man, but let's visit your brother first. Kwalakomai is but a day away. If Zokpooh fails us, you'll have time enough to cut all the palm nuts you can to make oil."

On arriving in Kwalakomai, we grew sober when Brother's two wives, who were winnowing rice behind his house, greeted us with uncontrolled wailing. The women rushed into the house, fell on the dusty floor, and rolled over, crying and beating their breasts. At length they sat up and stroked their legs in despair, chanting disgust at Sewor's "betrayal":

Sewor, why have you deceived us?
Sewor, what wrong we did?
You promised to bury us!
Why didn't you take us along, then?
For, what's the use of living,
When life has lost its luster?

We stood transfixed in the yard, father fidgeting with his small leather pouch while I hugged our bundle of clothes. The news was shocking. I could remember Sewor just the other day in Haindi, young, plump, vital. I couldn't believe that he had died and been buried weeks ago.

Bolting out of the house, Brother Zokpooh grasped Father by the shoulders, buried his face in his chest, and cried bitterly. He almost threw the Old Man off his feet with his robust arms.

"Sewor has deceived me, Data!" he said when he grew calm. He wiped the tears and offered us seats on the porch. "I was just about to go to Haindi and inform you people about it. It's good you have come."

"Son, you weren't fair to us," Father protested with a sigh. "You should have let us know about it when it happened. Now I see the reason for our many misfortunes. Zurong couldn't get a job on his own mission during the last vacation, even though he is hardworking and good in school. He worked for one of his teachers through the entire three-month vacation but didn't get a cent; he gave a whole pack of cartridges to his uncle in Gbangei to hunt for him, but Gonoh was too crazy and dishonest to be of any help. A member of the family could have died! That's bad, Son. Very bad."

"Data, the witches have had their way," Brother said. "Now I'll end up poor and helpless because Sewor was my hands and feet and backbone. I've become a crippled man."

Father hushed the women whose wailing drowned the conversation.

"Keep quiet, my people!" he said. "You're only making it impossible for Sewor to cross the river! Sewor didn't leave you without a caretaker! Think of how to help his uncle with his schooling. He's now your only hope!" The women grew silent and wiped their faces.

Sewor's mother, a short, skinny woman with tousled hair, came over to the porch and sat on the floor by us, stretched one leg flat, raised the other at an angle, placed an elbow on her raised knee, cupped her cheek in her hand, and said with distress:

"Why he ended up like this a mystery. The child surprisingly took to excessive drinking! Often went without food for days! Witches made liquor very sweet in his mouth!"

"Witches can do that," Father agreed.

"I don't drink," the woman maintained, raising her upturned palms to heaven. "His father doesn't drink. Why he became fond of drinking, only God knows."

"But Data shouldn't be surprised," Brother said. "He knows of the hate behind us. We wrong no one, envy no one—but witches don't let us live in peace. A strong, ambitious son helping his father and himself is a crime! I hope this brother of mine will live long enough to finish school and help us. I heard that he's doing well in school." He glanced at me with a smirk.

"Extremely well," Father said. "Has already completed four books and is fighting with the fifth one."

"I heard that you'll soon finish book in Fuama!" Brother told me. "Where will you go from there?"

"I don't know," I said.

"I hope the witches will spare you until you're out of your homeland. Once in a strange land you're safe."

"Quite correct," Father agreed. "The bug that kills *kumung* lives nowhere else but in its stem."

"Sorry," Brother sighed, averting his face, "I'm in no position to help my little brother in his struggle." He scratched his head absently. A wave of disappointment swept through me. "I stopped the gin business when the child died four months ago. One tree can't make a forest no matter how big it may be. But if you own nothing, you lose nothing. Nobody envies or betrays you."

"Resume your business and never be discouraged," Father advised him. "How will you become a man if you don't triumph over great obstacles?"

"I want to take the rest of the family to Haindi, away from this nest of witches."

"You can't run away from witches, my son," Father said. "They're everywhere, so wherever you find yourself is the best place to be." Speaking with a scowl on his face, he said, "If conditions round you are bad, change them. If you can't change them, bear them. You have my blessings even here in Kwalakomai."

We left for home early the following morning, contrary to our plan to spend at least a week with Brother Zokpooh. Before leaving, we visited Sewor's grave to pay our respects. It was the usual mound of red earth surrounded with rocks, covered with white sand, and sprinkled with rice powder; it lay on the crest of a hill just outside the town.

"Everybody must end up like this," Father remarked, looking grimly at the grave and then at the sunrise. When he began chanting the traditional incantation, I could no longer contain my grief. I burst into tears and clung desperately to his arm.

Putting his hands around me, Brother said, "Why do you weep? I expect you to make me forget." He too burst into tears, holding onto Father.

"It's true what you told me yesterday," Father said as we crossed Kwalakomai Creek on a corkwood bridge. "You're engaged in a lonely battle—but heroes fight alone. Try again to find a job on the mission. You're now old enough to do a man's job. Tell Tama about the work you did for Teacher Moana. He shouldn't take you by your looks."

As fortune would have it, I didn't have to look for job. A schoolmate of mine called Amos Sinatuai told me one evening that Teacher Josiah Lorkula had jobs for two boys. Could I join him to do it? We went to the teacher immediately.

SWINDLED

Teacher Lorkula was sitting at a table reading a book on the porch of his isolated house fronting a newly planted rubber farm behind Kwentaa. Dressed in his customary white shirt with the sleeves rolled up to his elbows and a pair of brown leather shoes matching a pair of brown long pants, the teacher was completely absorbed in the book. He often recited in class memorable quotations he picked up from his readings, notable for their adoration of courage and common sense. His favorite character in literature was Julius Caesar "who lived and died like a man." A graduate of the Lutheran Training Institute (LTI), he often said that a grade of seventy percent in LTI equaled one hundred percent in any other school of the kind in Liberia, if not in all West Africa, a claim his colleagues strongly rejected. "Has this fellow ever heard of Fourah Bay College?" they often asked. But Teacher Lorkula impressed us students as the most educated of our teachers.

Students also admired and respected him because he lived by principle. He had no respect for people who believe that success is attainable through magic or idolatry. He never consulted a Zoe or joined a secret society except the Poro, which is compulsory for all males. For him, what you couldn't get through hard work wasn't worth pursuing. Although the country folk disliked his contempt for their culture, they respected him for being bold and having the courage to live by his convictions. Indeed, he was one man you could trust.

Closing the book and pushing it towards a small, portable radio which sang a gospel song on ELWA, Teacher Lorkula leaned back in his rattan chair and crossed his long legs, watched us studiously with squinting eyes, and pointed to a long bench.

"This is the boy I found," Amos told him.

Tipping his head one side, he now joined us from his mental excursion, which had obviously taken him afar.

"Oho, the book man! I too love books! You may borrow some of mine to read. That's how to become well educated. Don't depend on textbooks alone. Do you like hard work?" He stretched his hand to me; we snapped fingers warmly.

"Yes, sir," I said, wondering how I had acquired the reputation of a book man.

"Don't tell me 'Yes, sir' if you feel otherwise. 'Yes, sir' won't get you anywhere. Are you really interested in hard work? Be frank."

"We work hard on the mission, sir," I said.

Adjusting himself more comfortably in his chair, he said he wanted to open a liquor shop in Zulotaa which he wanted me to manage. He already had one up in Digei, which his headwife Gwanya was running. Amos would only supply it with gin.

"Because Digei is well populated," he informed Amos, "the longest a demijohn of gin lasts up there is two to three days. So, be prepared to take gin up there at least twice a week." Turning to me, he said, "I'm sure you can run the Zulotaa shop, for you're good in math. Since this is a new shop, I can't say how the business will fare up there. But it all depends on you. If you work hard, you'll make a lot of money for yourself. A demijohn of gin earns eleven dollars and fifty cents if you don't spill the liquor while measuring it. You're entitled to two dollars for each demijohn you sell. Well, give me only eight dollars. Now you have an opportunity to make enough money to take care of all your school expenses. The liquor business fares well upcountry, especially during the Christmas and New Year seasons. My uncle Kolibhaa will give you food and lodgings without charge, so you have nothing to worry about but your job."

When we rose to go, he told us, "One more thing. Don't you ever tell Ma Miller that you sold gin for me. Should you burst my secret to her, I'll deny it and you'll get into trouble." Defending his business, he said with a sweep of his long arms while pacing up and down the porch, "The missionaries give us the best education but very little pay when they employ us. What should we do? Starve to death? Why do we go to school if not to live a decent life?" The temperamental monologue continued in a loud voice as if the teacher were addressing a large audience: "The salary I get is nothing but chicken feed, which can't meet a fraction of my expenses. Take good care of my money because I need every cent of it. Your only problem will be girls, because you boys don't drink or smoke, and you look a trifle handsome. Girls will flock on you. Boys who don't drink or smoke are womanizers." He chuckled slightly. I thought his fears were baseless as far as I was concerned, for since my trouble with Sianeh, I abhorred girls. "But don't mind girls," he continued. "You met them in the world, and you'll leave them here when you die. See to your education before bothering with them." He ended his remarks with a firm opinion: "Girls are traps—boys are the prey! Never let any of these traps catch you. Have I made myself clear?"

To save time we slept in Teacher Lorkula's house and began our journey at dawn. We carried two demijohns of rum, each weighing a hundred pounds and plaited with rattan for safe handling. Placing our burdens atop bundles of dry banana leaves on our heads in the misty morning, we walked with vigor, crossing the Deyn at Genkema before sunrise in a small, unwieldy canoe, which rocked precariously. Remembering Father's horrifying tale about the water people of Genkema which Amos confirmed, I feared for my life. The river was exceptionally wide at this crossing. I was happy when our canoe safely touched the opposite shore.

Our road cut through a rugged terrain cluttered up with bamboo swamps, high forests, steep hills and deep valleys. My experience in carrying heavy loads over long distances and the cold, refreshing shadows of the forests took much of the strain out of the journey. When we crossed a large swamp behind Zuakpoisu, we placed our loads down and sat on an old log that had accommodated many a weary traveler. I asked Amos to tell me what he knew about Zulotaa. His knowledge of the town was scanty, but the little he told me was quite interesting.

"It's large, breezy town sitting on top of a tall mountain," he said. "*Kwii* people call it Zulo Hill. From there you see the whole of Fuama—and that Bo Mountain you often talk about. The great problem there is water, for the nearest creek is an hour away. The people of Zulotaa usually ask strangers whether they want to eat or bathe. If they choose to eat, their hosts use what little water they find for cooking. If they'd rather bathe, they might as well forget about eating. So, you had better decide now whether to eat tonight and go without a bath, or to bathe and sleep on empty stomach." Amos laughed softly.

"Really a problem, especially for someone who grew up by a river," I said. "What traveler won't need a meal and a bath after a long day walk?"

"Most travelers solve the problem by bathing on the way," Amos said.

"Quite sensible," I said. "But the towns I know are built near a creek or river. Why was Zulotaa built on a hill?"

"Tribal war is the reason," Amos informed me. "On a hilltop you can spy the enemy while they're far away, giving you time enough to run for cover or prepare to meet them like a man. You'll also notice that nearly all the houses in Zulotaa are round. It's easy to defend a round house from within—well, that's all I know about the old town. Let's hurry on. Our road is long and hilly."

By mid-afternoon we arrived in Gbalala, a sprawling town lying on an alluvial plain. Dodo and Blue Wings were announcing sunset as we rested in the town's palaver house. I told Amos that we should spend the night in Gbalala to refresh our aching bodies. He argued that since nobody expected us there, we might not get accommodation. In addition, if we postponed the trip, our burdens would be twice as heavy. Finally, Zulotaa was now within a shouting distance. Having consumed the rat, it'd be a shame if we failed to eat the tail.

"Travelers are always welcomed and accommodated in every town, Amos," I corrected his mistake. "True, a job long delayed is difficult to do. If Zulotaa is that close to us," I placed my load on my head, "we might as well eat this rat tail."

Amos had obviously understated the distance between Gbalala and Zulotaa to encourage me because it was quite a jump. We had to race with the sun to reach Zulotaa before dusk; we couldn't even afford the time to bathe on the way. Below the tall mountain on which the town sat, goats and sheep grazed leisurely. As if curious to know what we wanted in their town, they cast suspicious glances at us as we struggled up the steep mountain.

We took a break after every fifty yards of progress. When we placed our heavy burdens under a tall cottonwood tree on the edge of the town, the final break, I forgot my pains on viewing the golden sunrays over the vast expanse of turquoise forest stretching far into the distance. Birds of all kinds and colors cried and hovered over the forest, while monkeys barked frenziedly in the rolling hills. Amos saved me from the oppressive beauty with a tap on my shoulder.

"What you looking at?" he asked. "Let's go to our stranger house to find food to eat."

On the fenced porch of a yellow house, we met an old man of beige complexion wrapped snugly in a wide homespun sitting in a rattan chair and looking drowsily on the dusty floor like an invalid. He didn't stir even when we entered the porch and placed our demijohns at his feet.

"NanBhaa, good evening!" Amos greeted him in a loud voice, shaking him by the shoulder. "It's me Sinatuai, NanBhaa! Good evening!"

NanBhaa crawled out of his stupor with a drawn-out stretch and an elaborate yawn, spat a snuff smear in the dust, gave a wan smile, and shook our hands.

"Is this the boy Sulontei talked about?" he asked Amos, looking in my face with narrow eyes.

"Yes," Amos replied.

"What is your father's name?" he asked me.

"Dougba Senfenui," I said.

"Why, this is Senfenui's town!" he exclaimed, rising with grotesque and straightening his sluggish physique. "Too bad—Senfenui's only surviving brother Kawor Gonkpai died six months ago," he said. "His funeral drew a large crowd—generated plenty of drinks and food. Poor Dougba might not know about his brother's death. The bad luck! I'll show you your uncle's quarters later." He never did. "The people will soon come from the farm to give you boys something to eat. For a month now, I spend my days in town due to illness. I'm the host of a living creature that crawls back and forth between my stomach and my head. The bloodthirsty witches here want to kill someone in my quarters. Nobody else they see but me! But I'll live to walk over their graves. Follow me."

NanBhaa led us with wobbling legs to a small, dilapidated round house. Moss ranged the bottom of the wall, indicating that it hadn't received a new coating for years. A roughly hewn wooden door hung loosely at the entrance. One could see the evening sun through innumerable holes in the thatched roof; termite nests festooned the *lolo* rafters; geckoes raced all over the wall and rustled the roof.

Scratching his white head with apparent remorse, NanBhaa said, "The girls will clean it up for you boys in the morning." Then he added half-heartedly, "Schoolboys should be able to withstand hardship, anyway." The shabby accommodation was unendurable even for schoolboys. Fortunately, it was the dry season.

His large family came late in the evening, trudging up the rocky mountain in the twilight. After presenting us to them, NanBhaa instructed them to give us food and furnish our lodgings with bed and bedclothes. "You fellows bathed on the way?" he asked, staring at us with a smirk. We nodded though we hadn't. One of his sons took an old bamboo bed and a mat to our single-room house. Another hung a rusty hurricane lantern to a raffia rope tied to a crooked beam termites had all but consumed. NanBhaa gave me an old brass funnel and empty schnapps and liniment bottles for measuring the liquor. A schnapps bottle sold for ten cents, he said, while a liniment bottle sold for five.

Running the only liquor shop in town, I hosted crowds of customers from all over the town and even from neighboring villages. They puffed up my ego with flattering comments on my ability to read and write; they showered me with gifts; above all, they bought the liquor rapidly. I had to travel to Kwentaa twice a week for new gin supplies. For their generosity and friendship, I often offered them half a schnapps of liquor and permitted them to drink on credit.

I was especially fond of the girls who brought me food; amused me with jokes, tales, and riddles far into the night; and permitted me to fondle their beads and hair. Because they didn't drink, I only gave them a quarter or two at the end of each visit. Propped with love and kindness, I often thought of quitting school, marrying, and settling in Zulotaa, but my pact with Father always chased such thoughts out of my mind.

After living in Zulotaa more than a month without impregnating a girl, rumor circulated around that I was impotent. Parents who expressly hoped to become my in-laws admonished me to seek help; they said the malady affected men of all ages and the cure was simple. Why should I let it deny me the only real pleasure a healthy young man could get out of life? Those who knew of mission life tried to diffuse the rumor by saying that mission students were trained to avoid sex until they completed school. In the *kwii* world, maturity didn't mean automatic marriage. So I was normal. But the rumor soon compelled even people who understood "the dilemma" to advise me to get a girl friend to put it to rest.

Falling in love would make me vulnerable to unlimited demands for favors I couldn't afford, I thought. Everybody was related in the average town. Consequently, I would have too many in-laws whose needs would call for everything I owned and much, much more besides. Additionally, I had a long way to go in school before thinking of raising a family, and I was under no obligation to prove my sexual prowess.

But the rumor gathered momentum every day, making me literally an outcast in the village. One night six elderly customers—all men as usual—decided to throw everything in my face. As they staggered out of my house after drinking six schnapps of the fiery spirit, they grumbled about the inconvenience of a young man sleeping alone. They stood in the yard as they spoke, apparently for me to get their message:

"Suppose sudden illness or nightmare attacks him, who will help him?" a hoarse, cracked voice declared, followed by low, approving murmurs.

"*Kwii* people have a society that forbids them to marry young," came an absurd observation. "Many of them don't even bother with marriage. That's why this ugly rumor means nothing to this young man."

"And they tell us that God wants life to multiply. Paseh Noah himself said so," another voice commented.

"Since you never know how many children you'll have, the sooner you begin having them the better. If you get, say, ten or fifteen, and five die, you'll still have enough to extend the family line."

Ignoring the familiar comments to which I had grown accustomed, I closed the door, lowered the lantern, and went to bed, determined not to surrender to pressure no matter what. Father had told me that death wasn't as prevalent in the *kwii* world; I wanted no more than five children, and I was sure they would all live. Ten years from now, I would have them when my schooling was over.

Just before I dropped off to sleep, there was a soft knock on the door—and whispers. These old men and their drinking! Turning up the lantern and opening the door, Kulubah and her younger sister Yanka rushed into the house as if a wild animal was chasing them. Yanka carried in her hands bowls of rice and soup neatly tied in a headtie. She placed them on the floor carefully, hooting with laughter. She and Kulubah sat on both sides of me on the bed. Yanka inquired about my health, a smile on her lovely lips, revealing impeccably white teeth with an opening between the upper incisors, while Kulubah looked steadily on the floor, her arms crossed in her lap. The surprise visit and gift caught me unawares because these girls had never visited me before, nor had they ever enjoyed my generosity. Clearly, one of them was in love with me. It couldn't be ebullient Yanka who overwhelmed you with unrestrained sallies.

"I was just about to sleep when you people came," I told them. "Thanks for the food." Kulubah clasped her hands around her knees, bent over, and placed her chin on her folded hands. I put my hand on her shoulder but avoided asking her a question.

"What makes you so tired?" Yanka asked me, shaking with suppressed laughter. "Idling in town all day without sweat? Or you don't appreciate our presence in your house?"

"The night is made for sleeping, isn't it?" I said, pulling the headtie off her head and feeling her braided hair. "Who plaited it for you?" I asked.

"You like it?" she said, compressing her lips and shaking her legs. "My sister," she said, indifferent to my fumbling fingers.

"Staying in one place all day and night can be tiresome. It's like being in prison."

Yanka turned towards me with her full breasts bulging in her yellow blouse. I placed my arms on her shoulder. Her smooth skin and warmth sent a fiery tremor through me. I thought of Teacher Lorkula's warning. But what was wrong with keeping girls' company? As if she suspected a foul play, Yanka cast a questioning stare at me, dressed away politely, and took my hand off her shoulder. Tapping the floor with her restless feet, she bent over her lap, perhaps to hide her tempting breasts from my restive hands.

"You haven't even touched our food!" Kulubah complained with a faint smile.

"I'm sure it's delicious," I said. "Young girls like you certainly know how to cook. This food will be my breakfast tomorrow morning."

"Some girls don't know how to cook something as simple as clear water soup," Kulubah said.

"We did the fishing ourselves!" Yanka said, loosening the headtie off the bowls. Taking a pinch of rice from the large rice bowl in which the small bowl of soup sat, she dipped it in the soup, poked it in her mouth, and smacked her lips. I had no appetite even though the food smelled delicious.

"You didn't have to do that," I told her. "If you girls didn't love me you wouldn't have cooked for me."

"It's not your enemy you should fear but your friend," she said solemnly, looking in my face.

"True, but I'm in good hands! The people of this town are good to me!"

"Should something happen to you, they'll want to know who cooked the last meal you ate," Kulubah defended her sister.

I scooped a spoon of rice, dipped it in the cassava leaves stewed with dry fish and palm oil, and ate, the girls watching me delightfully. Teacher Lorkula's warning reoccurred to me, but I dismissed it. After all, boys and girls must marry eventually, I thought; the sooner they got used to each other the better. Besides, I didn't want Kulubah and her sister to believe that I was impotent as people were saying. Although I was under no obligation to prove my potency, once I was challenged to do so, I had to meet the challenge halfway at least.

"Delicious!" I said. "But this is tomorrow's food as I said. My stomach is full."

"A girl has already fed him," Kulubah said, glancing at her sister. They blushed.

"Not at all," I said. "How long have I been here to have a girl friend?"

"A good-looking young man like you? Don't lie to us," Yanka said, watching me from the corner of her eyes.

"I swear by the food I just ate. I have no girl friend in this town."

"We'll see," Kulubah said, bobbing her head. "Pregnancy doesn't grow on a woman's back but on her front."

Springing to her feet, Yanka said she wanted "to go behind house[35]", a droll excuse to leave her sister to me. Now I knew who was in love with me.

"You seem to be in love with my sister," Kulubah said when Yanka left. "But she's married. "She retied the food in the headtie and placed it in a corner.

Hugging her warmly, I said, "You're beautiful, Kulubah. I want to marry you. Yanka is only a child."

"I'm glad you know that," Kulubah said thoughtfully. "Flirts with every man—and her husband is jealous! She works hard though—such a girl—hmm." A smile on her pretty lips, Kulubah searched my face curiously and asked, "Do you have another woman?"

"We aren't married yet," I lied because a negative answer might have made her take my love for granted. "Her family likes me—and I love her, but—"

35. Kpelle phrase meaning "to urinate", used only by women.

"Now you have two. A man with more than one wife must be strong and wise. You'll have to satisfy both of us—build my own house and hers—make my own farm and hers." Kulubah grabbed me hungrily and snuggled her face in my bosom. I patted the small of her back gently.

"I want to marry you, but my schooling!" I said.

"What does schooling have to do with it?" she said, looking at me with sober eyes.

"School takes a long time, Kulubah. It's not fair—"

"You had better have your children while you're young. That's what most schoolboys do. Should you get them in your old age, they'll suffer. I could be here in your name—" She stopped speaking abruptly and looked aside moodily. I stroked her abundant hair, my head hanging. Spying my gloomy face, she said, "Nothing to worry about. Yanka's husband goes to school in Monrovia and comes over during vacations. This vacation he went to his headwife in Saamai. Well, find out whether I'm the kind of woman you want. It could help you decide. Did you lock the door?"

The early birds and tiny spears of dull light pouring through openings in the shabby thatched roof awakened us prematurely. It was the most restful night of my life, though we spent much of it conversing, caressing, and embracing until sleep overtook us. Kulubah bounced out of bed with a frowned face and slipped out of the house. Perhaps it was all over before it began. I understood her grievance. Admonished constantly to avoid woman until I attained manhood to protect my sanity and complete school, I had slept with her like one boy sleeping with another. So, her sullen mood was understandable, for who can withstand the pang of unrequited love? No excuse could abate the blow dealt to her feminine pride. A woman wanted to be admired, loved, and enjoyed.

Going outdoors, I stared blandly at the town; only a few runty chickens, goats, and sheep wandered about. Hastening to a luxuriant *peyeng* bush behind NanBhaa's house, I broke and stripped a piece of stem and brushed my teeth vigorously. Presently Kulubah brought a bucket of hot water for my bath. My fears were baseless, I thought. Kulubah was still a friend.

"You're not going to the farm?" I asked her as I bathed in the bath fence behind NanBhaa's house while she waited outside.

"A decent girl doesn't spend a night with a man and fails to fix warm bath for him in the morning," she said dryly. "Harvest is over; there isn't much to do on the farm. Only to pound rice and sell to buy my Christmas things."

"I'll buy your Christmas things."

"You don't have money, so don't bother. I'm not like your *kwii* women who give themselves to men for money. I would rather starve to death or go naked than do such a thing. I want to redeem your manhood. The people here think you're not a man. I want to prove them wrong, for such a reputation is dangerous for a fine young man like you. If they continue accusing you of being impotent, their words might come true. Don't worry over your schooling—or the other girl. With me behind you, you'll do your school work with a single mind. One day you'll settle down with me or with the other girl—or with both of us. You've reached the age of exploring women. Do that before choosing a wife. If we happen not to marry, don't worry. It's nothing strange to me. For each woman there is a man."

Kulubah's moving speech made me ashamed of myself. Obviously, she had rehearsed it well to produce the desired effect. If I would ever be a man, I must take charge of my own affairs now! Some lover might have either mistreated or disappointed her, and she wanted me to put him to shame. I must redeem her honor and restore her pride.

With death staring you in the eye every day, how sure are you you'll live to complete school, anyway? Or find the right woman at the right time? Who is the right woman, and what is the right time? Were you not matured a woman wouldn't want you to be her man.

Before the week's end I was "initiated into life", the most wonderful experience for a man. You feel exulted, integrated, and equal to other men—life takes on a new meaning. Daily I visited Kulubah on her father's farm and helped with her fishing and farming. Her parents welcomed me with open arms and promised to preserve her for me until I finished school.

My honeymoon turned sour when I checked the gin money one morning and found that it was twenty-five dollars short. How would I explain the tragedy to Teacher Lorkula? I dodged the issue when I made my first report to him by saying that people owed me much money, which they were slow in repaying, but I would collect every cent from them before the vacation was over.

"This is a lot of money to owe, Joe!" the teacher said with concern. "You have two more months; no, only a month and a half; to collect this large sum of money! Make extra effort to get it, for business without profit is no business."

My indebtedness soon climbed to the alarming sum of fifty dollars, and I had only one month of business left! Definitely, business couldn't continue as usual. I put a stop to credit and, before leaving town hence, made sure to lock my door with a big padlock I purchased in Haindi. I made many enemies for taking these stern precautions. The Chief and Elders called me one evening to the palaver house and demanded an explanation.

"By locking your door when leaving town," Chief Dakpaanah told me angrily, "you're indirectly accusing us of being thieves. The spirits of the Ancestors watch over this town. If you continue acting like that, they'll stop protecting it, and no matter what we do, our lives and properties will never be secure. So, I advise you in the presence of the Elders to do as we do here: lock your door only when you go to sleep!"

I walked out of the palaver house politely, resolved to maintain the stiff precautionary measures I had taken, come what may. I would never do things their way because I had no confidence in the protection of dead people.

In a matter of days, the town struck back. The people refused to buy my liquor. They sent to Gbalala, Konikaonga, Ngweei, and Digei for their drink. My debtors refused to pay their debts and challenged me to do something about it. I would only get myself deeper into trouble because they were prepared to defend themselves.

"We know the woman who is eating Lorkula's gin money," they would say. "And we can prove it, even in the presence of the Land in Gbekei."

The matter became more serious when no one offered me food any longer. I lived on cassava, pawpaw, and pineapple.

"If they think I'll go on my knees begging them for food, they're mistaken," I talked to myself one night as I figured out what to do about the problem. "After all I can cook. Am I not a student? I only need the foodstuffs."

Yes, hunting was the solution—the inevitable idea flashed in my mind. It could make up for all my losses and even generate extra cash, not to speak of food money. A shotgun shell cost only fifteen cents and could kill a deer that could earn me twenty dollars or more.

At daybreak the following morning, I borrowed NanBhaa's old single-barrel shotgun, which had long been gathering dust, bought five shells, and commenced the hunting.

Meanwhile, I used some of the gin money to buy foodstuffs to do my own cooking. Though they no longer offered me food, NanBhaa's family let me use their cooking utensils and dishes. Cooking, which I had taken for granted, wasn't easy. Frequently, fire burned my fingers or the hair on my wrists, or hot oil flashed dangerously in my face while I fried fish or meat. When very hungry, I cooked in a hurry and the food would remain half done. Women scoffed at me whenever I joined them to fetch water. Life couldn't continue like this. Once I asked Kulubah why she had thrown me away. Had she found some other man? Her reply was forthright:

"My father and uncle say I shouldn't have anymore dealing with you because you don't respect the people of this town."

"In what way?" I asked.

"By taking them to be thieves!"

Before I could defend myself, Kulubah had gone. I tried to rationalize my disappointment by concluding that she wasn't the only woman in Fuama, anyway. I had gotten what I wanted from her. Sometimes I imagined her dead, lying in state in the palaver house, players dancing around her—or pallbearers accompanied by players convoying her to the graveyard. The idea of someone who had been so close to me being a corpse would frighten me. Kulubah must continue living in my thoughts. Sometimes I wanted to cast aside all pretense of pride and apologize to her. But for what? We had never quarreled. My problem was with the Chief and the Elders. Teacher Lorkula was right: girls are traps. But avoiding these traps was another way of saying, "I'm a tree or a rock."

I wandered in the forest for three weeks; not even a mouse did I get. I decided to abandon hunting, for time was now against me. The day I made the decision I shot at a big hornbill in a piassava tree and missed. Certainly, luck was on the way. At least I could shoot at something.

An old man I met in a secluded village on my way home observed my unkempt famished condition and asked me how the hunting was going.

"Bad," I told him.

Blowing on a smoldering fire under a dryer loaded with hog meat, he said, "Hunting requires patience. How long have you been at it?"

"A month."

"That's long enough for you to become a professional. Perhaps your wife has a lover. Have you asked her to confess his name?" He looked at me in suspense.

"I'm not married," I told him.

"Then, let an experienced hunter help you. Ask Kpakolo the Lion Killer of Zulotaa. He's the best hunter round here, but you must be brave because he lives up to his name. Give him ten shells, and you're lucky if he gives you a rodent. Try him anyway. Some people are lucky with him." The old fellow gave me a large chunk of well seasoned dry meat, which I devoured immediately and washed down with a cup of water.

Fahn Kpakolo, the most popular hunter in the entire clan, brought a game home nearly everyday. He gladly accepted my four remaining shells but kept them for a week with no result. Whenever he brought a game to town, it was for somebody else.

"I still have your shells intact," he would tell me whenever I asked him how the hunting was going. "You may have them if you like."

"Had I needed them I wouldn't have given them to you," I would fire back.

"Success in hunting depends on good luck and plenty of it," he would say. "I could get you a deer tomorrow, or the day after tomorrow, or next week. Keep hoping and praying."

"Look," I told him one Saturday morning after growing tired of his tricks, "I'll accompany you to the bush today, and only my shells you'll fire. Understand! I can't wait any longer. School is about to open."

"Good," he replied affably enough. "You'll see for yourself what a hunter goes through."

We left at once for Gbiyansu Forest. Kpakolo warned that I shouldn't scrunch the brittle twigs and crisp leaves covering the forest floor while walking.

"Walk on tiptoe," he advised.

He walked without making the slightest noise. So, noisy walking was responsible for my failure in hunting! Despite our careful walking, however, we couldn't hear a single monkey cough or a deer bark. As we hurried back home at sunset, we heard monkeys howling and jumping from tree to tree on a hill near the town.

"Pray for good luck," Kpakolo whispered, bending double and signing to me to wait under a *bhasi* tree.

Treading through the shrubs noiselessly, almost on his knees, his gun cocked, Kpakolo disappeared in the tangled undergrowth. In a moment there was a loud report followed by a heavy fall. Running to him, I was delighted to see him stabbing a big *lorbha* with his hunting knife.

"I wanted to get two with one shot," he told me. "That's why it took me so long to shoot, but these things are very clever nowadays. They no longer sit close together."

Skinning the monkey's tail from where it joined the body to an inch of the end, Kpakolo partly pulled off the skin, making a loop in which he poked the monkey's head. Weighing it by the arched tail, he asked if I could carry it.

"Of course I can! Is it one of my shells?" I asked him casually. "Sorry," he said. "It's for somebody else."

The appalling words stung me like poisoned arrows. Despondent, I resolved to abandon all hunting activity and get ready for school. Kpakolo tried to palliate my mounting anger and distress with another trick. After we had walked awhile, he told me to sit down for he had seen an antelope, but I saw no deer in the dark undergrowth. Well, a professional hunter could see an animal in the darkest thicket. I obediently sat on the ground and laid the huge, stinking monkey by me. Kpakolo fired. Searching around, we saw only shell marks on trees and the ground.

"Was it really a deer you shot?" I asked him.

"Yes," he said. "A deer I saw clearly with my own eyes! But a hunter can miss, no matter how experienced he may be. Sorry, it was one of your shells."

Giving Kpakolo his monkey corpse in town, I thanked him for his "good turn" and hurried home. When I went to NanBhaa's house to light my lantern, I met him drooping as usual in a chair on the porch but roused at my approach.

"How did the hunting go?" he asked me.

"Bad," I said.

"From what I see and smell, it must have been a success! Are you afraid I'll ask you for some of your meat?"

"The blood you see and smell on me is the blood of a monkey Kpakolo killed for somebody else!"

"Why did he treat you like that?" the Old Man cried with parted lips. "I'll talk it over with him tonight!"

Knowing that his outburst was insincere, I hurried to my lodgings, hung the lantern, and anxiously checked the gin money, which I always tied up in a piece of cloth and kept under the bed. Twenty dollars was missing. I also discovered that all the gin had vanished. I grew cold and creepy. The hunger pains left me at once. I reported the burglary to NanBhaa immediately; he only stared away apathetically and shrugged. It was only when I threatened to enlist the help of a Horn Zoe to find the culprit that he grunted, "I don't know a thing about your gin money. The Crier could announce the theft tonight if you like." It was a perfect crime; somebody had removed the hinges and nailed them back without a scratch on the door.

I hardly slept that night. At dawn, I took what remained of the money to run over to Teacher Lorkula and give him a full report of the crime. NanBhaa was washing his face behind his house when I told him my plan.

"Wait a moment," he said. Staggering into his house and back, he gave me a fifty-cent piece. "This is some of the stolen money," he said.

"It was twenty dollars that was stolen!" I said.

NanBhaa went into the house without comment and shut the door. Clearly, he was the thief. I regretted receiving money from him because the Horn Zoe's medicine would have no effect on him once he had given me some of the stolen money. But I needed no Horn Zoe; the fifty-cent piece was adequate proof that he was responsible for all the stolen money.

When I reported the burglary and gave him the "fruit of crime", Teacher Lorkula agreed that the senile old man was guilty of the theft, but he only sighed and said blandly, "Since he's a relative of mine, he owns whatever I own. Nothing can I do to him. I'll only close down the shop in Zulotaa and reward you for your effort."

STRINGS OF BEADS

My misadventure in Zulotaa disturbed my parents to no small measure, for stealing is an unforgivable crime in Kpelle country. Anyone found guilty of it deserves the worst punishment conceivable, including execution. Mother blew spittle in my right palm twice to invoke the blessings of God and the Ancestors upon me. She was certain that I was an innocent victim of the wicked designs of some miscreant. Father considered the tragedy an earnest mistake. As I accompanied him to the Waydiyea one morning, he told me that I shouldn't fret over the matter. Everybody makes mistake. We would cross the bridge if we exercised patience.

"The case hasn't been taken to court yet," he said, "which alone can determine your guilt or innocence. Besides, the Land doesn't condemn people who are robbed but people who rob." The reassuring words dispelled my fears and anxieties.

"Teacher Lorkula promised to reward me for my effort," I told him. "Had he wanted his money, he wouldn't have made such a promise."

"He could still demand it due to family pressure," Father said. "It's no small money you owe."

"This is one man who stands by his word."

"His wives and relatives could prevail on him to press us for the money. Since you're doing well in school, they're prepared to go to any extreme to stop you. Why? Because they're afraid when you become a *kwii*, their children, who have failed to keep up with you, will be your servants. Adding everything up, they'll stop at nothing short of keeping you in your place. I learned that Dakpaanah and the Elders of Zulotaa told Lorkula on two different occasions to demand his money from us because you once insulted them. What was wrong with protecting Lorkula's money? Kolibhaa who stole it is behind this demand. Son, I'm beginning to feel that you don't belong here, for anyone who makes a difference here for the better is in danger of elimination. But where to send you is the problem."

"Ma Miller says Jesus protects those who believe in him. I'm not afraid because I pray to Jesus every day for protection."

"For the moment we should let the matter drop and await developments. There's no use trying to cross a bridge you haven't reached."

I wanted to tell him about my interest in Kulubah, but I knew he wouldn't approve my tampering with woman while I was in school, especially one who was in league with my enemies to destroy me.

We caught plenty of fish, which Mother started cooking at once. I went to the Deyn for a swim. It was relieving to see, once again, fishermen casting nets in the Small Cataract while others mended theirs on shore; bats streaming like a cloud over Tinkayan some five miles downstream; the Deyn roaring in the ancient forest. Tossing off my clothes, I plunged in a wide pool naturally carved with slabs of red rocks in the middle of the river. There the water stopped at my midriff, and the sand sparkled brilliantly at noonday.

After swimming with brisk overhead strokes awhile, I felt restored. I sat on a rock until I dried off, then dressed and returned to the farm to have my fill of the delicious meal Mother had cooked.

A week before school opened, I went to Zulotaa for my few belongings. On the way, I tried to assess my business performance. What had gone wrong? I couldn't handle money; that was my problem. I should have given the gin money to a trusted person for safekeeping. No. The person would have used it up and claimed that it had been stolen. I should have hidden it in a hole in the house as most people did. But customers would want change, and it'd have been a holiday for thieves if I dug up the money in their presence. Business wasn't for everybody. Yes. Anyone could do business. My problem was girls, as Teacher Lorkula had feared. No. How much money did I give girls? Father was right: making it in the tribe was risky.

I met Amos in Gbalala late in the afternoon. Thoroughly spent, he was sitting slouched in a rattan chair in the town's palaver house, his elbows planted on his knees and his cheeks cupped in his hands, sound asleep. A demijohn of gin with a banana leaf cushion hanging askew its neck stood by his feet. I shook him briskly; he woke up with a grunt, stared at me dully, yawned, and stretched.

"Going for liquor?" he queried me. "But you have no container!"

"I'm going to Zulotaa for my things," I said, sitting in a chair beside him.

"They say the girls of Zulotaa messed you up, my man. You haven't learned the rule of the game yet? Whenever you go to a new town, choose your own girl; otherwise, the wrong one sticks on you."

"I was robbed," I said. "That was my problem."

"Had you chosen your own girl as soon as you got to Zulotaa, you wouldn't have run into problem. Girls take advantage of single men. I got a girl friend the first day I set foot in Digei. Fiikpeeh is expecting our first baby."

"My problem in Zulotaa had to do with robbers, not girls," I told Amos again. To disabuse his mind, I gave him a full rundown of my activities in Zulotaa without sparing myself. I mentioned the incidents with Kulubah and Yanka, NanBhaa, and Kpakolo. Sighing deeply he said that Teacher Lorkula's best bet was putting one of his wives in charge of the Zulotaa shop as he had done for the one in Digei. Women, he said, knew how to do business better than men.

"Kulubah is in love with me despite everything," I told him.

"With your education, you need a mission girl," he said.

"Love is the most important thing where marriage is concerned, Amos. I haven't found a mission girl who loves me."

"Have you tried to find one?"

"No."

"It's risky for you to go after Kulubah. She could harm you. You know a girl in Zuakpoisu called Sianeh? I think her *kwii* name is Alice. I once met her on my way to Digei, and she asked me about you in a special way. She told me that she carried country bread to your mother for you. Why have you been hiding the secret from me? Or you're too dumb to notice the girl's love for you?"

"I once slapped that girl out of sheer boredom on the mission. That's how much I know about her. I owe her an outright apology."

"What does it take to settle a problem between a man and a woman? The girl got the cue! You wanted her but you were afraid of her. That's why you slapped her. Approach her now like a man. Don't be afraid. You have a golden opportunity: her aunt just died—a good pretext for you to visit her." Glancing at my moody face, he said, "You look disturbed! Sianeh will put you back together. Don't mind all the talk about girls being traps. Look, boys are the traps, and girls are the prey."

"I've decided to get my education before marrying."

"Joe, life comes first. I'm leaving school to live with Fiikpeh. We start school late. By the time you complete high school, you're too old to raise a family. I'm sure you want to go to college."

"Of course! You can't put your hand on the hoe and look back, Amos. Remember what Ma Miller often told us: education is the best thing you can get out of life. You're taking woman to be more important than education. You might regret your decision tomorrow."

"You and your Ma Miller! Joe, I'm twenty-two. How old are you?"

"You're not telling me that you're too old to learn, are you?"

"I want to grow up with my children," Amos said, looking at the dirt floor. "I want to be around until they stand on their own feet. This decision is not voluntary."

By undeclared mutual consent, we abandoned all conversation and redoubled our walking pace to get to Zulotaa before dusk. I wasn't surprised when I saw the door of the little round house wide open with nothing inside.

Lighting a bamboo torch, I returned to Gbalala to be as close as possible to Zuakpoisu. Leaving before dawn and running most of the way, I was fortunate to meet Sianeh and her family setting off for their farm. The family kindly left us to ourselves and went on ahead. My heart speeded as I sat with Sianeh on the porch because I was uncertain what her reaction would be. At a loss for words, we only stared at each other. Then I broke the impasse by expressing my sympathy for the death of her aunt.

"Thank you," she said.

"Thanks for the bread," I said.

"I kept that bread for weeks, thinking I would see you on your way to Zulotaa. It was Amos I saw and asked him to tell you hello for me. After attending the funeral, I returned home by way of Haindi. Your mother was good to me. I left the bread with her. How is she?"

"Quite well. Thank you."

Trifling with her neck beads, she said, "Auntie was too old to even walk. Life is precious, so it's always a pity whenever someone dies, but she lived her days in full."

"Sianeh, I also came to apologize for being rude to you on the mission."

"You haven't forgotten about that yet?" she said, blinking her seductive eyes and smiling. "I'm sorry for putting you in trouble. The slap was playful. I should have taken it like a woman. I myself was in love with you, but, as you know, women don't make the first move in love affairs. Forgive me, too, Joe."

"May I accompany you to the farm?" I said.

"You have your job to do!" she said.

"The business failed, Sianeh"

"Girls!" Sianeh stared at me with sparkling eyes.

"Not girls but the Chief and the Elders of Zulotaa. They stole the gin money."

"You don't say!"

"That's what really happened! They stole the money while I was hunting—Let's follow the people. I'll tell you everything tonight."

Her curiosity stirred, she asked for a full account of my life in Zulotaa on the way to the farm. Except my involvement with Kulubah, I told her everything.

"Next time you'll know how to deal with the country people," she said. "They want everything from you including the very blood in your veins. You were lucky they didn't hook a girl on you."

Sianeh's family received me graciously, though her father expressed misgivings because, as he said, another boy wanted her.

"I haven't given him my word yet," Sianeh was quick to say.

"You're old enough to see after your own affairs, anyway," Old Man Zepe said. "Should you knock two men's heads together, we won't be responsible for what happens to you."

"Sianeh is my schoolmate," I told him. "I only came to sympathize with her for the death of her aunt."

"This is your home," Sianeh's mother told me warmly. "Even though we're bereaved, don't let it bother you. All living things must die. My daughter is not married to any man, so she can have a visitor."

I spent the rest of the week with Sianeh and her family, helping them with their farming.

"How come a *kwii* like you works so hard?" Old Man Zepe asked me on the first day I helped with the clearing.

"Don't you understand?" said his wife, Yata, who strikingly resembled Sianeh. "The young man is working for a young girl!"

The Old Man laughed and said, "Most of his friends would never touch the handle of a cutlass no matter what. My son, continue working with your hands. God gave us hands to use. Don't let book stop you from using yours." He told me that he had sent his daughter to the mission because he felt that it was better for girls to go to school rather than boys. "I can't imagine my boys living in town all day. Women can afford to because they're men's burdens."

For the first two nights, I slept with Sianeh's eldest brother Borkpalon. A boy my age, he disagreed with his father and would rather replace his sister on the mission, but his mother had engaged a wife for him; he was cutting sticks and thatch to build their own house before bringing her home. "If I go to school," he told me, "they'll say I'm running away from the girl, something a *kenamu* can't afford to do. When will you marry Sianeh?"

"When I finish school." So Sianeh's family considered our marriage a foregone conclusion!

"And when will that be? My friend, you're now a man. Don't run away from responsibility."

"She too is going to school!"

"Brother, we can't go on any further with this conversation," Borkpalon said bluntly and rose. "Why haven't your parents made you a man? Look," he whispered as if taken aback by his own impudence, "Sianeh has no man, if that's what you're afraid of. Man-sleeping-with-man is alien to our way of life."

During the first night I slept with Sianeh, we only conversed and embraced each other until the wee hours of the morning. Sianeh assured me that she would wait for me until I completed school; it didn't matter how long a girl waited for the man she loved. I took her promise in good faith. My mind shifted between continuing with school and marrying her. The arguments my nephews and Amos had made against schooling began making sense to me. School, with its uncertain benefits, could take half my lifetime, and when it was all over, there'd be very little time left to raise a family. But Father would be fatally disturbed should I leave school. Sianeh must wait as she had happily suggested.

I felt obliged to tell her about Kulubah since we were now close friends. It'd be risky should she learn about my affair with her from somebody else.

"Why didn't you come to me?" she upbraided me when the story was over. "Am I not a woman? What did you find so special on that girl? Gold or diamond?"

"I had no idea you'd befriend me after what I did to you. But since you're now mine, I'll never have anything to do with any other girl."

"Do men ever learn a lesson when it comes to woman?" she fired back. "Only be honest and frank with me."

Sianeh's parents slaughtered a red rooster in my honor on the farm the next day and gave me a gourd of palm wine and three red kola nuts as a token of welcome into their family—generosities I found embarrassing because such honor had never been conferred on me before.

On the day of my departure, she gave me a big raffia bag of country bread while her parents gave me another red rooster and four white kola nuts, hoping our two families would soon unite. Sianeh took me halfway over my protest—all the way to the Deyn. She carried the chicken while I carried the bread. I hugged her repeatedly on the way, vainly urging her to return, for she had work to do.

"I'll return only when I see you in the canoe," she told me with each urging. On the outskirts of Genkema, she gave me three strings of her waist beads as keepsake.

While boarding the old, scary canoe, I spied her over my shoulder four times. After taking my place among my fellow squatting passengers who advised me to keep steady in the old dugout, I managed to turn my head round and wave to her; she returned the farewell gesture, a brilliant smile on her pretty face. As we plowed through the river waves, there was no doubt in my mind that I was leaving my heart behind. I clutched the beads in my pocket when we hit the other shore.

DANCE OF THE INITIATES

For a whole week my parents looked worried, an attitude I considered surprising for it wasn't like them to be so cold, reserved, and downcast. When he wasn't sitting quietly before the farm shed staring at the sky, Father was reclining on a bamboo bench or going into the bush to see after traps. In town he seldom sat on the porch, his evening preserve; he went to bed before dusk and left for his *kporlong*[36] at dawn. On the farm Mother pounded rice, fetched water, and cooked without even a grunt; she displayed the same attitude in town. The pantomime was profound. Not knowing what to make of it, I read my Bible at night and roamed the bushes during the day for ripe palm nuts I never found. I often went to bed without eating my supper. Were my parents afraid that Teacher Lorkula would sue us for his money? To put their minds at ease on that score, I ran to the teacher one evening to find out where we stood in the matter.

"Teacher Lorkula was good to me," I told them on my return, hoping the good news would lift the intolerable depression. "He said we have nothing to worry about. He promised—"

"Zurong," Father interrupted with anxiety, leaning towards me, "we have something important to tell you before going into that. And don't worry or cry about it. It's forbidden for a child to shed a tear or grieve over such a thing." After a long, agonizing pause, he blurted, "Your second father has died."

Assailed by a spell of sobs, I started, my eyes flitting from him to Mother, then from Mother to him. My stomach turned over; my mouth surged with a bitter taste; a debilitating shudder ran through me. I managed to tell them brokenly, "I'm going to the funeral."

"The Bush Thing has already buried him," Father said. "It's forbidden to mention his death. He has gone to look for herbs. A Zoe never dies. Understand? The punishment for infringing this Poro law is execution in an Evil Forest!"

"And as of now call him The Poor One," Mother cut in fearfully. "His spirit will meddle with your life if you mention his name."

"Should you go to Willietaa without us," Father warned, "you'll run into serious trouble. They say you insulted the people there during your last visit by saying that they're stupid, unclean, and devilish. What angered you? Your circumcision? No, don't take it to heart. You had to pay that price to be a man. The young men of Willietaa vowed to beat you up should you put your foot back in their village. The old people advised them to forego the offense for Molaa's sake—and ours. You were simply teaching them what you had learned in school. They should be proud to learn something from the *kwii* world—something to help them live better. They refused to listen. Molaa had to implore them with white kola: four pounds cash and a white sheep. I

36. A long fish basket, usually set in a waterfall.

don't know if that allayed their anger."

Mother said, "Let your father go to Willietaa first and apologize on your behalf before you go there."

"No, no, no!" Father declared, shaking his head vigorously. "Apologize for telling them to eat with clean hands? It'd make a mockery of all the trouble we're going through to school the child! Knowing book is not only a matter of reading and writing but learning new ideas, new ways of living. Why do we become old and feeble so soon? Why is everybody sick and helpless here? Because of the very things Zurong told the people of Willietaa, which angered them: wash your hands before eating; boil your drinking water; use footwear; kill mosquitoes; clean your surroundings. My only advice is that he limit his discussion of such matters to the mission people who understand." When the storm subsided, Father said, "We'll go to Willietaa next month to sympathize with The Poor One's family. By then you'll have gotten over the shock and the people's anger will have cooled down."

"Data, I'm going to Willietaa tomorrow morning," I insisted.

Laughing quietly and looking at Mother, Father said, "He's fearless as I used to be when I was young. Be patient, my son. The task ahead of you is great. You can't afford to waste your time fighting people who don't understand."

"I'm sure you can hold your own in a fight with any boy your age," Mother said. "But fighting gets you nowhere. As your father has said, wait until we talk this matter over with the people of Willietaa—What did Teacher Lorkula pay you for your hard work during the vacation?"

"NeSuaa," I said, wiping the tears from my face, "we'll talk about that later." Mother sighed in despair and pursed her lips.

I walked all over the town in the bleak darkness, bumping into cattle, occasionally running into a fisherman who would inquire what I was doing in the dark by myself. "Don't tell me girls have captured you so soon."

On spying the first rays of the morning sun, I ran to Willietaa. The crowded town was so busy with the funeral festival to bother with me. I went to NanMolaa's porch where Sister Yasa and two other women sat solemnly. Sister cried hoarsely when she saw me. One of the women tried to hush her while the other brought me a stool.

Contrary to Father's admission, it wasn't The Bush Thing that had buried NanMolaa. A founder and pillar of a reputable town, his body couldn't be spirited away into the forest and simply dumped in an unmarked grave. Circled with slabs of red rocks and covered with white sand, his grave lay before his house. Wiping her face, Sister spoke in a clear voice:

"Brother, I can't cry—not only because I'm hoarse, but because the Ancestors made crying unnecessary: they let Father attain a ripe, old age before dying, and he died with love. The night he died he staged a play, spent lavishly, and got drunk. It was a miracle for one whom sickness had ravaged so thoroughly; who could hardly twitch a limb, to rouse, dress, and dance in the happiest mood ever. A large crowd of singers accompanying him, he danced from house to house until midnight, bidding everyone farewell, thanking

God and the Ancestors for his long life, appealing to them to prepare a decent home for him in The Place of Truth, and ordering that we shouldn't let the sun set on his remains. Oh yes! He never died in sorrow but joy. After the dance, he showed us where his money and other important properties were hidden. He instructed us to divide them among his children equally. Especially concerned about you his *kwii* son, he directed us to give you ten pounds, one sheep, and two goats to help you with your schooling.

"On short notice all sorts of plays including *geeh*[37] and drum plays accompanying Gbetu, Nafa, and Joba, converged on the town for the funeral. You'd think it was a royal funeral. Father's many years of making hoes, cutlasses, knives, swords, and spears—repairing pots, buckets, and pans—had not gone in vain. How could I cry when joy swallowed up my grief like that? Brother, I danced the dance of the initiates, although tears kept running down my cheeks.

"At noon, and this was the most moving part of the festival, the players gathered around the palaver house where The Poor One's remains lay, sang his praises, bade him farewell, wished him sunshine on his way, and commanded him to God's care. As if suddenly convinced that Data was merely asleep, the women raised and shook their *geeh* heartily, told him to rise and account for their hoes, for the planting season had come. They wanted to cook—had he mended their pots and pans? The warriors were about to fight; were their spears and swords ready? At this point my heart cut. Had it not been for these women, they'd have buried me with Father.

"I don't see with our Haindi parents. Why did they hide news of Father's death from you? He won't harm anyone because he departed with plenty of love and joy."

Sister wiped her face, went into the house, and brought me twenty silver dollars. "Father left seven kola trees," she told me. "Whenever they bear, you may come for your share. As for the rice, any time you need food, come to me. I'll take care of your animals—Oh! I forgot. He gave the town your sheep to atone for some offense you reportedly committed here; what offense, I don't know and don't want to know. All I have to tell you is be careful with the people of Willietaa. Your own people are your worst enemies! Eat only from me whenever you come to this town! And mention nothing to anyone about what you learn in school!"

Resuming her story, she said, "Some people think only those who share the same mother are true relatives, but we the children of Mulbah Forwor don't believe in such petty thinking. Once an auntie of yours was a friend of our father's, no matter how far back, we're one family. So feel free to visit us any time. This is your real home!"

I felt consoled and greatly reassured as I returned home because Sister Yasa's intimate explanation of the circumstances surrounding NanMolaa's death and burial had made grief superfluous; what he had failed to give me in life he had given in death. Now I had two pacts to honor.

---

37. A gourd plaited with strings of beads, used by women as a musical instrument.

I recalled the lore Father often told me about life after death.

"People don't really die," he said. "They only shed off their bodies and become spirits to be free of hunger, pain, sickness, desire, restriction to time and place, aging, and death. The body we carry around is a burden. Or they rise from their graves after their burial and go to other towns where they live until former acquaintances of theirs meet them. Then they move to some other towns. This goes on forever."

I believed that NanMolaa had gone to another town because he loved people; he wouldn't want to be a spirit hovering invisibly in thin air. I wished I knew his new home.

My parents were happy for the initiative I had taken. "You're now a man," Father told me when I gave him the cash inheritance. "As of now I'll never again withhold important information from you: your uncle Yakpalo Gonoh has died. As soon as we see about your return to school, your mother and I will visit the two bereaved families to sympathize with them.

"They say you messed up the vacation job in Zulotaa by spending Lorkula's gin money on women. To cover up your misdeed, you falsely accused Kolibhaa of stealing it. Son—"

"I knew that's what Kolibhaa would say," I said with outrage. "That crusty old crocodile is a congenital thief!" I gave them the true account of the burglary.

"What did Teacher Lorkula pay you?" Mother asked.

"He promised to buy me two pairs of short pants, two short-sleeved shirts, pencils, and copybooks."

"It's just a promise," Father said, making a wry face. "See him first thing in the morning for your pay."

Teacher Lorkula kept his promise. He bought me four yards of gray cloth, which made exactly two pairs of short pants and two short-sleeved shirts. The shirts were a neat fit, but the pants were so tight I couldn't squat without risking tearing them apart.

"Vanii will pay for your cloth," Father said when he inspected a pair of the pants on me. After a second thought, he said with a sigh, "What's the use? Should we make him pay for it, people will say we're a hard-hearted lot. Poor though we are; we love our good name. Besides, God has seen to your needs. You have enough money to buy all the clothes and school supplies you want."

Relieved of the problem of school materials, I concentrated on my studies. Augustus, my classmate now, studied with me during "quiet hour" each afternoon. At the beginning of the year, we were twenty-five in the fifth grade, but in a month's time we were only two. The boys left mostly for lack of financial support. I remember a classmate of mine Joseph Tengey telling me bluntly, "I'm leaving school because my father failed to give me fifty dollars to buy clothes and copybooks! Am I going to school for my own benefit alone?"

Augustus left because he couldn't withstand the demanding mission life much longer. "I'm sorry to leave you but I must," he told me during one of our study sessions. "Cutting grass, cutting wood, cutting palm nuts, and toting water are not my kind of life. Look at my blistered hands. After all, a grandfather of mine was once a cabinet minister in this country. You learn a lot on the mission but the hard work takes everything out of you. I'll tell my mother to get you out of here. You're clever—and could be somebody tomorrow, but not if you stayed in this bush."

The girls left because of pregnancy. I had the shock of my life when a friend of Sianeh's told me one recess time, "The girl says goodbye. She has gone home to see after her aging parents."

"But she hasn't completed the third grade!" I cried.

"She's helping you!"

"She confessed my name?" I asked with anxiety.

"She put it on someone in her town. Someone who doesn't exist. So don't worry, but please visit her often at this difficult time in her life."

My parents were happy to hear "the good news." My possible expulsion from school should the affair reach the ears of the authorities meant nothing. Sianeh delivered with a bouncing baby boy. Mother named him Guladia[38]. To be a father at eighteen was no joke, but I enjoyed the miracle of having brought another human being into the world.

The fifth grade was the loneliest and most challenging class I ever attended. My only classmate was called Sarah Nuufee; we had a new team of teachers whose teaching methods were not only different but difficult. I missed Teachers Moana and Lorkula who quit teaching to do business and farming, respectively. Sarah was on probation in three subjects and I in two; we were determined to win the battle at all cost.

Ma Miller kindly permitted us to study in her palaver house during quiet hour, a privilege she granted only seniors. This helpful arrangement ended when Sarah, who had been following up my activities, attacked me with disturbing questions during one of our study sessions. I first considered her inquisitiveness a genuine concern about my welfare even though I wished she could be a little more discreet.

"You headed your class up to the fourth grade," she began on a mild note, "and even had the distinction of getting double promotion twice. How come you're struggling with the fifth grade?" I thought of my own embarrassing questions to Momo. Though disturbing, such questions made you take stock of your progress, so I took no offense at Sarah's intrusion.

"I don't know why," I told her frankly. "I study hard as usual. Probably I'll have to study harder than usual."

"I don't think it will help," Sarah said. "True, the higher you go in school the more difficult the subjects become, but that's not your problem. You have lost the teachers who used to give you free grades for your services. And you have lost your girl friend." I sat unruffled, my eyes trained on a poem in our Reader. Observing that her stinging attack had failed to disturb me, she went on to elaborate: "You and Momolu harmed yourselves by

38. Surprise, name given to a child whose birth was not expected.

trading services for grades. Now you have teachers who don't need your services! And, having lost your sweetheart, you can't concentrate on your lessons! That's why the studies are giving you hell. Momolu has left school because he couldn't cope with the difficult studies. He and his father are now sugar cane farmers."

"What brought up this talk, Sarah?" I said, staring at the slim, voluptuous girl in anger. Her face darkened slightly, and she bowed her head with what I thought was remorse. "I used to go to school regularly and take my tests and exams," I said in self-defense. "So I deserved all the grades those teachers gave me. As for Sianeh, we were mere friends."

"Then why are you struggling with the fifth grade?"

"You have given the reason. The higher you go in school, the more difficult the lessons become."

"But not so difficult that a grown man like you can't pass a single test! You're supposed to help me with my lessons, but, as I see it, I must depend on myself."

"I'm sure we'll make it if we work hard; two heads are better than one."

"You expect me to help you with your lessons?"

"Learning has nothing to do with being a man or woman."

"Who says so?"

"I say so! Whatever a man does a woman can do—sometimes better."

Sarah smiled and turned to a subject that was even more distracting.

"Why did you let another man take your girl friend from you? You didn't even put up a fight. What a shame! Now you're disowning the girl!"

"Recite Thor's war song for me," I said.

"My man, don't dodge my question."

"I told you that Sianeh and I were mere friends."

"Don't lie to me! I watch your movements on this mission, my friend. We girls know all the secrets of every one of you boys. Your way of getting a girl friend is terrible. You slap the girl!"

"Please let's go back to our studies. Recite Thor's war song and the *Psalm of Life*."

"Who cares about that reckless European god who thinks of nothing but war? 'Force rules the world, Has ruled it, Shall rule it—' Europe is too far away for me to worry about its gods. And who told Longfellow that life is real?"

"If you fail to recite these poems in class next week, you'll be beaten."

"The time for beating is over, my man! Wake up! Ma Miller has put a stop to it! You're avoiding my question." Sarah closed her book and looked in my face with a fixed gaze. Obviously, she wanted to make much of my embarrassment. I fretted over my affair with Sianeh. Perhaps Ma Miller already knew about it.

"We're here to study," I said.

"So what? Life is more important than reading. Let's marry and settle down."

"Sarah, it's no time for joke. The exams are round the corner!"

"You're afraid of women. What's so frightening about marriage?"

"I'm in no position to support a family."

"I now believe what people always say about you Haindi men. Your women are in the river."

"You don't believe such a thing, do you?"

"Why not? Human beings are capable of anything! They say the single men of Haindi become married at night. Where else would their women come from if not the river?" Sarah searched my eyes with a derisive grin.

"How are you coming on with math?"

"You're scared of women. Admit the fact! Joe, you're a coward!"

"Sarah, stop it! Ma Miller could hear you!"

"So what? She never married?"

I opened the math book and read aloud.

"Math isn't for women, my man," Sarah said. "So, close that book and answer my question."

"What do you find difficult about math?" I said. "Addition, subtraction, division, or multiplication?"

"Everything." After a brief reflection: "If the problem deals with subtraction alone, I can solve it. If with division, multiplication, or addition only, I can try. But when you mix these operations, I get confused."

Pressing my advantage, I said, "Sometimes you get money and sometimes spend it. Right?"

"Yes. But my man, you're avoiding—"

"Suppose you have ten cups of rice for sale at five cents a cup; before selling it, your uncle who has nothing to eat asks you for two cups; how much money will you get for the remaining rice?"

"This means I must add and subtract." Sarah hung her head and said, "My man, you're a crook." She laughed nervously. "You're tricking me into doing what I hate."

"It's no trick. It's something you must learn. You'll be happy you did."

Sarah said, "If I sell my ten cups of rice at five cents per cup, I should earn fifty cents because five times ten equals fifty."

"Right," I said, regarding her with an approving smile.

Looking at the bamboo ceiling, she said, "But this lazy uncle of mine takes two cups, leaving me with eight."

"Correct."

"So I'll end up with only forty cents because five times eight makes forty."

"Correct! If you put your mind to it, you can conquer math. What about fraction?"

"Joe, how many times must I tell you I don't like math? It's most unfortunate I have to take it in school."

"But you must pass it to get promotion!"

"All you like is book, book, book! When one is telling you something important—"

"Your parents won't permit you to marry unless you finish school!"

"Not if you make me pregnant."

"Don't put us in trouble. Ma Miller might be listening."

"Ma Miller knows that boys and girls must marry, not so?"

"Time is up! Hear the bell? Time for roster work! Next time let's pay more attention to our lessons. The fourth grade children will laugh at us should they catch up with us."

"Let them laugh," Sarah sneered, pushing her books aside. "They have mouths, don't they? Let them laugh! It won't make me crack my head to put book inside! My responsibilities belong to somebody else, my friend. All I need is have a child for a man and my troubles fall on his head for life. It's you who must crack your head."

"You might not be lucky to find a man who is ready to bear your troubles for life. Some men leave the children with their mothers."

"The government compels such men to support their children."

That was my last day of studying with Sarah. Henceforth, I avoided being alone with her. Happily, she left the mission shortly before school closed. A friend of hers told me one morning as we gathered flowers for Ma Miller, "Your classmate says goodbye. She became tired of school. The only way she could be done with it was getting belly for a man. I won't tell you the man's name because you boys' mouths don't sit down."

When I graduated as the only senior of the school, Ma Miller presented me another Bible as a prize. Mother held a party for me at Pastor Gbada's home. A week later, she and Father appealed to Ma Miller to send me to another school to continue my education. Ma Miller recommended Sanoyea Lutheran Mission and said I needed fifteen dollars for tuition and four dollars for transport fare; I also needed two blankets, two pairs of short pants, three short-sleeved shirts, and extra cash to buy bath and washing soap.

Dismayed by the increasing cost of education, Father suggested that I teach and save money before continuing with school.

"One must complete the eighth grade before teaching in this country," I informed him.

THICK FRIENDS

A week before my departure for Sanoyea, Bhono of Gargbelei informed me that somebody in KP wanted to see me. Perhaps it was Ma Miller who wanted to know if I was ready for my Sanoyea trip, I thought. Proceeds from the sale of thirty gallons of oil Mother helped me make during the vacation, and ten *kru*[39] of kola nuts Father gathered from his kola orchard, adequately took care of all my expenses. While hurrying to the mission next morning to give Ma Miller the assurance, I surprisingly met Caesar at Bopari Creek.

"Caesar!" I exclaimed as we embraced warmly. "What brought you back to the bush, Mr. Civilized?"

"To take you out of here as I once told you," Caesar said. "I knew you'd want to continue with your schooling after completing KP."

"You're fat and well dressed, my man! Really enjoying Monrovia!"

"You too will soon be a Monrovia man," Caesar said as we strolled to the campus. "You don't want to end up as a mere farmer. Mother agreed to take you in our family if your parents agree."

"Once I go to school, they'll agree."

"Mother came with me."

"Makes everything easy. I don't know how to thank you."

"What is a friend if not someone who cares? You think I'll ever forget what you did for me that afternoon? Those boys would have killed me!"

"I only happened to have been around; you'd have done the same thing for me."

My new mother was chatting with girls on the porch of their dorm. Some girls were cooking in the kitchen, some washing clothes in tubs in the yard, while others were sweeping the yard. On our approach, those on the porch scuttled away, leaving my new mother alone on a bench. Her copious, black hair neatly fixed like a cap, the short plump woman wore a pleated blue dress. At her feet was a shiny black bag. She welcomed us with a broad smile.

After Caesar's brief introduction, she hugged me warmly; then looking smilingly in my face, she said in a high-pitched voice:

"Thank you for saving Caesar's life! He's the only son I have! He says you're clever and hardworking! Exactly the kind of boy I want! Do you want to stay with me?"

"Yes," I said.

"You like hard work?"

"Yes."

"You're one of the few country boys I've seen who want to be somebody. You think your parents will agree?"

"Yes. Once I go to school."

"Let's go see them."

---

39. A unit of measurement, usually one bucketful of dry goods.

"I can call them, Ma. They've gone to the farm."

"I can walk! I'm a raw country woman, you know." She laughed. "See me scratch farm and you won't believe it!

"A good mind like yours shouldn't be wasted in the bush," she told me as we walked to Haindi. "It'd be a shame should you end up as a mere farmer after going through much trouble to get a good education." She went on to say that I wouldn't get more than a high school education upcountry, which was a mere drop in the bucket. Even college education didn't worth much in Liberia those days. Further, the only employer in the interior was the church, which paid nothing more than starvation wages. Above all, the interior lacked opportunity for exposure to modern civilization, which country students knew so well but only in textbooks. Thus, to be well educated, respected, and gainfully employed, it was advisable that I established roots in the city; the sooner the better.

Abandoning the idea of going further into the bush, I decided to go to Monrovia.

We met Mother sweeping the farm shed. Father had just come from his fish traps with a bucket of fish. I introduced my guest of honor to them and explained the purpose of her visit. They snapped fingers. Though Mother offered her a stool, Mrs. Dennis sat with Father on the front wall log of the shed, viewing the rice shoots with admiration.

"I'm all right," she told Mother in Kpelle, much to our surprise.

"This is your farm," Mother told her.

"Sit down, boys," Mrs. Dennis ordered Caesar and me.

"What do boys care?" Father said, glancing at us.

"They're not supposed to stand before us," Mrs. Dennis insisted. "It's no respect." We obediently sat on a log near the western wing of the shed.

"When did you people come?" Mother asked Mrs. Dennis.

"Yesterday evening. I'm not used to walking, so I suffered from the sun and the hills. Caesar could stand them for he's young."

Mother smiled and said, "That's why we want our boy to become a *kwii* man. The tough country life makes you old before your time."

"Life is tough everywhere, Mother," Mrs. Dennis said. "Many thanks for the farm! It's large!" She again viewed the rice with a sweep of her delicate eyes.

"Our boy helped us make it," Mother said. "We'll miss him, but his education is more important to us. What is food?"

"We made a pact, he and I," Father said with a chuckle. "He has to pay me for all my suffering in rearing him by going to school and knowing all the books he can."

Mrs. Dennis laughed and said, "What child can pay such a debt?"

"I only want him to do his best in school"

"We're happy you agreed to take in our child, Sister," Mother told Mrs. Dennis. Correcting herself, she added, "—and your child. Never hesitate to punish him for misconduct because we want him to get good training. Our only concern is his life—and schooling."

ing such choice ingredients as a *bulu* head, crawfish, and turtle eggs, Mother blessed me constantly, commanding me to God's care, and vowing never to shed a drop of tears again for the trip to be safe and fruitful.

At bedtime, Father told me of his own misadventure in the *kwii* world. He said he had attended a mission school called Muhlenburg somewhere down the Deyn in a Congo town called Harrisburg. He had lived with a Congo family in an isolated zinc house shaded by plum trees near the mission. "The man was kind, his name was Crusoe, he took me as his own son," Father said. "He paid all my school expenses, but his wife wouldn't let me put my foot in a classroom. The woman was impossible to please! You never did anything right for her, and you dared go to school once your job wasn't done to her satisfaction. The slightest offense made her boil over with rage, and she was dangerous when angry. She once gave me a nasty slap for refusing to empty her chimon. That slap sent me out of her house. Yes, I preferred running away than handling grown people's waste. So this Congo woman's glib talk means very little. Be on your guard in Monrovia. You're old and sensible enough to judge things for yourself and take the right action. Use your head and make friends with the right people.

"Before mission came to this country, only those country boys who lived with Congo families got education. If you could withstand hard work, curses, and brutal beatings, you went as far as the eighth grade, qualifying as a clerk for some rubber plantation, a revenue collector, an elementary school teacher, or a Deecee's clerk. Many of us would rather stay blind than suffer like that, but things have improved nowadays. People with good education get decent pay and plenty of respect for whatever job they do. When I see teachers from Sierra Leone in our schools, I feel that we're throwing our chances away. Do your best, my son, because you'll get a lot more for your suffering. Pray to God every day and night; he'll take care of you. Your mother and I will always pray for you, too."

When Caesar and his mother called on us early the following morning in thick mist, Mrs. Dennis gave final reassurances to my parents for my safety and schooling. My parents gave her my clothes and money for safekeeping; she took the money and told me to keep the clothes in my wooden box until we arrived in Monrovia. Placing the box on my head, I walked away swiftly without looking back, Caesar following me.

"That's how to take leave of your parents, Joe?" Mrs. Dennis said. "Come right back and tell them goodbye!"

INSTEAD OF "GO RIGHT BACK"

STRANGE ENGLISH

On a narrow, double-trailed road roughly hewn on a hill, high embankments soaring up on either side, stood an old contrivance on wheels, two pairs of which faced us; another pair faced the other side of the hill. As we strained up the rocky hill under the scorching sun, Caesar said in a strange English:

"Dade moto car we goin' in," pointing at a huge monster of a hut.

"Dey calley truck," Mrs. Dennis said in the same English. Confused, I wondered if the *kwii* world had its own English apart from what we learned in school.

"It can move?" I asked Caesar.

"Wa you talkin'?" Caesar said. "A alway brin' us here and carry us back. You way see."

I had seen pictures of vehicles of many kinds such as cars, buses, pickups, trucks, and trains in books and magazines, carrying people and goods from place to place, but it was something else to see a real one.

Standing with his arms akimbo beside the truck was a huge man smoking a cigarette. Dressed in a black shirt, long dungaree trousers, black leather shoes in dire need of repair, a gold chain dangling on his wrinkled neck, he looked with pleasure in the truck at passengers sitting on two parallel benches facing each other, their loads cramped between them. The loads comprised bags of palm kernels, rice, coffee; tins of palm oil, baskets of chickens, and two goats. The man bobbed his head twice with apparent satisfaction, sucked the cigarette lustily, exhaled a cloud of white smoke, and shook our Ma's hand hard, baring his yellow teeth.

"Welcome back on board!" he shouted. "My duazeh in top shape na! We way soon fly to Kakata!"

"How much I ma pay for ma two boy?" Mrs. Dennis asked, looking in his face with a faint smile.

"Your bill is twenty-five thousand bucks!"

Mrs. Dennis laughed and said, "Jackson, you helluva man. Where I gan geh da kinda money?"

What was "duazeh"and "kinda"? I wondered.

Two boys in ragged clothes saturated with yellow dust welcomed us on board with hilarious laughter. One was tall and the other was stout. A silver whistle attached to a silver chain hung on the tall one's neck. The short one whisked the box off my head as if it were feather, and dashed it among the loads in the truck. My neck stretched out with relief. I couldn't understand why, with all my experience in carrying heavy loads over long distances, I found the little box, which contained nothing but a few pieces of clothes, difficult to carry. I remember getting so exhausted as we crossed Lu Creek, a little distance beyond Nganyai, that I appealed to Caesar for help, but he failed to lend aid, though he carried nothing.

"My man, geh insye! Wa you stanin' lookin' ah?" the short truck boy shouted at me. "You neva seen truck before? He, he, heeeee!"

"Dis buguman way take us to de moon before landin' in Kakata," the tall truck boy said. The passengers giggled.

"It has no wings, my man! It not airplane! You think I fool?" cried I.

Caesar, who had climbed in, beckoned to me. Holding a rail of the old vehicle firmly, my toes gripping the iron rod ladder at the gate, I climbed in.

As she entered the front seat, Mrs. Dennis told me, "Don' mine dem. Sit down and hol' sometin', you hear?"

Many of the women passengers carried babies in their laps and arms. The babies sucked their floppy breasts greedily, waving their puny legs in the air. Jackson jumped in the front seat, banged the door hard and struggled with a piece of rod until it fastened the door. Next to him sat an old man wearing a black felt hat. Mrs. Dennis spied us repeatedly through the glass window behind her.

"Dasin, take time how you run!" a plump, beautiful girl sitting next to Caesar yelled excitedly in Kpelle. "I have a young belly!"

"Holley tighe," someone recommended in the strange English. "Dasin, my back is already broken. Don't finish me up!" an old man, ensconced in the corner opposite us, coughed in Kpelle.

"Dasin, I'm short of five cents. I hope you'll understand," a nursing mother said in Kpelle as she readjusted her naked baby in her lap. The baby urinated in an elderly woman's face. The poor mother attempted to wipe the wrinkled face with a rag, but the woman wiped her own face with the tip of her old lappa and smiled, leaning her head back and looking smilingly at the child.

"It's nothing," she said. "I too have children."

"That's good luck," someone said. "You'll have many more."

"Are you serious?" the woman said. "Don't you see me halfway across the river?"

The engine whined, rattled, and backfired, spurting voluminous, pungent, black smoke at us. I grew breathless. The babies coughed, sneezed, whimpered. Surprisingly nobody else was disturbed. The screeching monster jerked away, leaning sideways precariously and bouncing in potholes in rapid successions. A cloud of dust soon enveloped us. After awhile, the truck stopped abruptly and crawled across a sagging wooden bridge. My heart beating wild, I wondered how long the nerve-racking ride would last. "My people, your come for me-o!" a woman howled. "Nex' tine, leh geh down before you cross bridge! Dasin, you hear?" A heavy bounce. "Dasin, you ain' know de road?" The road now rushed away incredibly fast. My head swam. Without any provocation whatsoever, one of the goats jumped up and down, stepping on someone's toes. "Uh! Who goat! I tink you wan' makey way pepper soup tonai. You betta hold you goat!"

After a long while the tall truck boy crowed, "Kakata! Kakata! Kakata!" happily blowing his whistle and swinging on the top planking of the truck. Being a truck boy must be fun, I thought; you worried about nothing and you had control of a truck and its passengers.

Suddenly the truck jerked to a stop before a shop on the right shoulder of a crowded street. A young white man standing behind the shop counter watched us curiously—so white people did business, too! Lappa, blankets, and headties hung all over the shop and lay on shelves in large bundles. Stacked before, behind, and under the counter were hurricane lanterns, spades, shovels, hoes, cutlasses, buckets, bottles of perfume, hair lotion, trinkets, tins of powder, radios, and the like.

Mrs. Dennis was the first to step down; she asked how we were feeling.

"Fine," Caesar and I replied together.

The passengers disembarked and paid their fares with laughter, grumble, and comment. The truck boys took their loads down and asked them to examine the loads to ensure that nothing was missing. I placed my box far from the truck, dusted myself, and looked at the two rows of large buildings stretching far into the distance, a narrow street lying between them. Except the story house in KP, these buildings were completely different from the mud and thatched houses upcountry. I watched crowds of people, many of them carrying bags and packages wrapped in brown paper, streaming down both shoulders of the endless street, inspecting merchandise on the sidewalks, laughing, screaming, shouting. Cars, pickups, and trucks moved in opposite directions on the street, people dangerously wending their way among them.

Dusting himself also, Caesar walked over to his mother who was handing money to the driver.

"You hungry?" she asked, looking at me from the corner of her eyes.

"N-no," I said with hesitation, wondering if "yes" would have been the right answer. Hunger pain nudged my stomach, but it wasn't significant to arouse concern, the new excitements having taken my full attention.

"Say, 'No or yes, Ma'am,' whenever I ask you sometin', you hear?"

"No, Ma'am," I said.

"You was suppose to say, 'Yes, Ma'am,'" Caesar said, laughing.

"You wan' go back?" Mrs. Dennis asked me.

"No, Ma'am," I said.

"Mine our tins, yaah? Don' worry. Natin' way happen to you. I comin' jesna."

"Yes, Ma'am."

Caesar and his mother soon disappeared in the milling crowd to return presently with a brown cap in Mrs. Dennis' hand. Handing it to me, she said:

"Try a on you hay." It was a neat fit. "A for you. Take good caruf a, yaah?"

"Yes, Ma'am," I said. "Thank you." Again, they disappeared in the crowd.

Having discharged its passengers and cargoes, the huge truck pulled off, the truck boys shouting and waving, calling passengers destined for Dingshu road.

Before the dust of Jackson's truck could settle, Caesar and his mother returned sitting in the front seat of a red pickup with a metal top and a green tarpaulin curtain. Inscribed on the driver's door in bold, black letters were the words, "DIE BE DIE." Two boys about the same age, and just as dusty, as Jackson's truck boys jumped down from the pickup. Mrs. Dennis pointed at my box. One of them forced it into the pickup already filled to capacity with passengers and loads. The well-dressed young driver carefully supervised the packing.

"Man geh insye," one of the boys told me brusquely.

"Where I will sit?" I asked him, looking for a seat in the cramped vehicle.

"You wan chata taxi?" the fellow asked sarcastically.

"Geh insye man lego," the passengers ordered me in a chorus. "Don' ways our tine. We ga far way to go."

I squeezed myself between a little boy and his father.

"Papa! Papaaa!" the boy cried, holding up his arms.

"How will I take you in this cramped place?" the father said in Kpelle. "Stay where you are. Nothing will happen to you."

The pickup boys sat on the tailgate of the vehicle; one of them blew a whistle, and the pickup pulled away without the noisy sound of Jackson's truck and its cloud of smoke. The fellows called for more Monrovia passengers even though the pickup was overloaded. Several passengers managed to squeeze among us despite our protest.

Although the dust was overwhelming on the Kakata-Monrovia road, the ride was relatively smooth and fast. In half an hour, we entered a thick forest with low-trimmed undergrowth Caesar said was Firestone Rubber Plantations Company. Along the road, I saw men in tatters hopping under buckets of milky liquid hooked to split reeds on their shoulders. The rubber trees stood in straight rows and tipped in the same direction. Their thick foliage hid the summer cloud. I grew frightened because my break with everything familiar was now complete; and here was I with people speaking different English! Mother's warning about the *kwii* world, which I had never taken seriously, now occurred to me as significant: "The secret societies in the *kwii* world are far more dangerous than ours," she had told me many times. "Don't you ever let the sun set on you outdoors over there!" She said that members of these societies always dressed in black and spirited children and even full-grown adults to secluded places, killed them, and extracted parts of their bodies for *juju*.

After racing through the darkness for some time, the pickup flashed large beams of light ahead of us. The breeze, now cold, froze the blood in my veins. I gathered myself close together to keep warm. It didn't help. Occasionally another vehicle, often a car, passed us at a terrific speed, blowing its horn wild and burying us in a cloud of dust despite the frantic effort the pickup boys made to keep the tarpaulin spread around us. Strangely enough, the sound of the horn would be high-pitched as the vehicle approached us but would drop sharply after passing.

Shortly after emerging from the rubber farm, the pickup halted abruptly;

several passengers went down and paid their fares.

"Dis Careysburg," Caesar informed me. "Our nestop is Monrovia."

An hour later the pickup hit what Caesar said was "coal tar". No need asking where we were; the pickup boys shouted, "Monrovia! Monrovia! Monrovia!" Free from the dust at last, we disembarked, dusted ourselves, and resumed our trip through columns of well-lighted buildings painted red, blue, and yellow. Scores of cars ran up and down the streets, frenziedly blowing their horns. Crowds of people streamed up and down the sidewalks, laughing, calling, and shouting. After stopping for red lights and taking left and right turns on green lights at several intersections, our pickup stopped before a two-story framed house. Again, Mrs. Dennis was the first to alight, calling us in a tender voice. Caesar was sound asleep, his head resting on a metal railing, his lips parted. I shook him briskly.

"We in Monrovia you sleeping?" I said. He woke up with a jolt, yawned, and wiped his face.

"Yes-what-how-Monrovia!" he babbled and smiled.

When we got down, one of the pickup boys handed me my box. Some dozen members of the family warmly embraced Mrs. Dennis and Caesar, spying me with curious eyes. Mrs. Dennis paid the fares and hugged the greeting party one by one.

"Pa gone White Plain for church conference," a tall, brawny boy in sport shirt said. "He comin' nesweek."

"Granny sleeping!" a teenage girl in a red dress said.

"Bessie bin cryin' for you business," said a girl carrying a frail baby in her arms.

"Poor child," Mrs. Dennis said, raising Bessie before her face and smiling. "See how she dirty. You people din treat my sweetheart right. Any so?" The baby was nearly unresponsive. Even when Mrs. Dennis wiped her lean, narrow face with a handkerchief and kissed her cheeks, she gave only a wan smile and rubbed her eyes wearily.

Caesar and the other children went into the house. A stocky man with red eyes who stood near Mrs. Dennis examined me from head to foot. He reeked of cane juice[40].

"Dis de boy?" he asked Mrs. Dennis huskily.

"Yes, Bobber Joe," Mrs. Dennis said. "Tell hin you name," she told me.

"My name Joseph Crusoe," I said.

"I be damn!" Bobber Joe exclaimed. "Joseph what? Crusoe? You mean Joseph Dennis! How in hell you gan live on we sweat and carry different name?"

"Don' talk to hin like da, Bobbor Joe," Mrs. Dennis said with a smile and hastened into the house. "You way scare hin. He raw yet," she said over her shoulder.

"He betta know from de first beginin' da I de barkin' deer in dis house. My man, go to Jimmy dem. Jimmy! Jacob!"

---

40. Literally, the juice of sugar cane; name for gin locally brewed from cane juice.

"Saah!" came a strident reply. In a moment a barefoot boy, dressed only in a pair of ragged short pants, came out of the house, limping.

"Dis Joe Dennis," the barking deer told him, pointing at me. "He for us."

"Ha you do?" the fellow said, a trifle shy, scratching his bushy hair. "My name Jacob."

"He Kpelle," the barking deer told Jacob. "Your talk Kpelle."

"Anytin to carry?" Jacob asked me.

"Only my box," I replied.

"You what?" the barking deer asked. "You betta talk 'bout findin' place to sleep, da box plava you gan talk."

"My clothes inside!" I cried.

"Ma man, do what I say, you hear? You mouf sharp pass de Prophey Jeremaya. A you know what I know, you betta obey." Presently a boy looking like Jacob came forth.

"Jimmy, take dis bak insye Ma Mae room," the barking deer told him and led me upstairs, Jimmy ahead of us with the box on his head.

We entered an impressive lounge so well furnished I wondered why it was used for sitting. Mrs. Dennis, her children, and her old, gray-headed mother sat around a large wooden table, conversing and eating rich food by a bright lamp sitting at the center of the table. The barking deer sat with them and started eating.

"Where you cap?" Mrs. Dennis asked me, staring at my head with widened eyes.

Touching my bare head, I shuddered with fear. "I going for it," I said and ran outside.

"Get it quick or I gan skin you!" Mrs. Dennis shrilled after me.

I danced all over the dark yard but couldn't find the cap. Trouble, my first day in the *kwii* world! When I told Mrs. Dennis the problem, my heart in my mouth, she looked at me with the same angry face.

"Maybe he forgaley in de pickup," her mother said understandably, tearing flesh off a chicken wing with her teeth. "He bin wearin' cap before?" The Old Lady chewed roughly and swallowed.

"Comin' from where?" Mrs. Dennis said with disgust, holding her spoon at an angle. "Dey know 'bout cap plava dasye?" Batting her eyes while jabbing the spoon at me, she frowned darkly and said, "A dis wasin you firs' day here, I gan lick you! Betta go fine da cap quick!"

"Dose carboy will brinkey," her mother said softly. "Dey fool? Jimmy, go down Watersye tomorror mornin' and geh da cap." The Old Lady had hardly finished talking when one of the pickup boys handed Mrs. Dennis the cap.

The dreadful frown left her face. Handing it to me, she said, "A you loss a 'gain, you gan know who born dog." Changing her mind, she took it back, saying, "I gan keep a till you nee' a."

Crowning her anthill of rice in a white plate with potato greens stewed with bush meat, chicken, and red palm oil, she buried the food in her mouth with a silver spoon in quick successions.

"You taken baf?" she asked me after a deep swallow. I shook my head. "Jimmy, show hin de bafroom."

"Lego," Jimmy ordered, already descending the stairs.

"Goodnight, Ma'am," I told her.

"Goodnai," she replied. "See you in de mornin'. Tell my Ma goodnai, too," she said with something like a smile.

"Goodnight, Ma'am," I said.

"Goodnai, Son," the old woman replied. "A you behave youself, dis house way be for you. You won' even wan' go upcountry 'gain. But if you don', you finish!" She stroked her throat with her forefinger. I winced. "He good in school?" she asked her daughter.

"Caesar say he good. Country people ain' ga natin' to worry 'bout. Ha dey kian know book quick? Caesar say he tough and ga sense."

"Good, my son. But we Congo people don' believe in book wan. We work har'! Way all de book in you hay, a you don' work har' a natin. So expec' to work har', yaah? All kinda work, you hear?"

"Yes, Ma'am. I'll try."

"You ga to do better den try. When dey give you work to do, do a! Na try to do a, you hear?"

"Yes, Ma'am."

"Tankey for Caesar. You do good for you people. A sometin' ha' happen to hin we gan cut everybady hay in you home for his plava. Da water business your insye—your betta mine! Go na; Jimmy waitin' for you. Your takey easy."

Caesar, who had bathed and changed his clothes, stared at me dully.

"Goodnight, Caesar," I said.

"You gan tell everybady goodnai before goin' to bay?" Jimmy raged halfway down the stairs, looking at me with disdain over his shoulder. "I tink you gan sleep dirty. Stan' dare sayin' goodnai, goodnai."

"Wha' mara way you, Jimmy!" cried Mrs. Dennis' mother, waving her spoon in the air, her face looking grim. She was panting. "You gettin' wings 'gain! I way soon clip dem."

"Mama, don' leh dose boy make you heart trouber gerup 'gain," Mrs. Dennis said, pushing back her empty plate. "Lee dem way me. Dey and myself in for a."

"Dey cut we lai, but Pa lookin' for money to brinkey back," Jimmy informed me as we entered a dark room downstairs. "Take tine before you fall." Mosquitoes buzzed all over the room.

"No lantern here?" I asked.

"My man, you hay straight? Where money comin' from to put food in you gut dey comin' buy lantern for you?'

"What about candle?"

"Your know 'bout candle plava upcountry, you native man? Stop da kinda talk a you ain' wan geh in trouber, you hear? Trouber na good. Boy don' ask for natin here. Tell God tankey a you geh sometin' to eat."

"Jimmy, I hungry."

"You see rice kitchen here?"

"My man, we bin on the road whole day and I ain' eat nothing."

"Ma Mae say she ask you hundred tine a you hungry and you say no. So, geruf my ear."

"But I wasn't hungry then!"

"My man, you betta mine! You like you own way, any? We don' act like da here-o. Leh peepee and go to bay."

"I should eat when I ain' hungry?"

"I say you betta mine! You hay har', any? You tink you upcountry?" He spoke in a loud voice, apparently for the benefit of the people upstairs.

"What you mean?"

"I ma talk Greek?"

"I want bathe."

"Lego to de well. Jacob drawin' water."

Jacob was standing on the well's concrete ledge, scratching his head.

"We call dis well Jacob Well," Jimmy said. "A you tell Jacob draw water whole day he won' mine. He take baf two tine everyday. A he ain' take baf he kian sleep, he kian laugh. Kpelle people like water for true. Dea parde Nigi business ain' natin small. So my man," he addressed me cordially, "we ga plenty water here for you. You like you kian take baf all day and all nai."

"Who say we ga Nigi society in Kpelle country?" Jacob said, laughing. "Da you Bassa people ga da society."

"Oh, I forga," Jimmy said. "Your pade water society dey calley Gborlork-pili." He laughed heartily.

Jacob pulled up a bucketful, set it beside a tub on top of the ledge, and told me, "Takey and bave."

"I need my clean clothes," I said.

"Jacob, talk to dis man for me," Jimmy said, scratching his head in frustration. "I don' know wa kinda hay he ga. Talk Kpelle." Jacob stood with his arms akimbo, staring at me reproachfully.

Surrounded and roofed with rusty, corrugated zinc sheets, the well had a wooden rod with a spoked circular board, a bucket attached to a long twine tied to the rod.

"My man, wa mara way you?" Jacob chided me. "You hay har', any? You ain' make one moon here and you makin' trouber?"

"What trouble I making?"

"You ain' hear wa Jimmy talkin'?"

"I stranger here. If I want something I must ask for it, any so?"

"You neva stay with *kwii* people for true. You goin' round askin' for dis and da. How you gan wear all you clothes one tine? Dade first trouber you ga in, askin' for you clean clothes. When you take baf, wash de clothes on you and hangey in our room. A way be dry when day break. Our room hot."

Jacob emptied the bucket in the tub.

"You told me to bathe with it," I said.

"You ain' wan bave," he said. "Go to bay."

"If I don't bathe, I won't sleep."

"Da you business." Then he had a second thought: "Jimmy, hepin for me," he said. "When you bave," he told me, "go to bay and sheh you mouf, you hear?"

Jimmy and I struggled with the tub to a circular corrugated zinc enclosure several yards away under a plum tree.

"Any soap?" I asked him.

"Jacob, you hear da?" Jimmy said and laughed gutturally.

"Wa he sayin' 'gain?" Jacob asked.

"He wan' soap!"

"My man, wa mara way you?" Jacob said, holding a spoke and looking at me in anger. "Dey way soon pepper you a you ain' lookor."

Undressing, I splashed water all over me and rubbed my skin. Not sure if my clothes would be dry by the morning if I washed them, and not used to sleeping naked, I simply shook them and put them back on.

Jacob was still drawing water. Jimmy had just answered a call upstairs. Going over to Jacob I asked him in Kpelle:

"Where you're from?"

"Gbanoimu," he said. "Not far from here. The *kwii* people call it Bensonville."

"What grade you're in?"

"Well, my father brought me here to go to school, but I only work for the family. When I grow up, I'll find a job and go to school."

"Your father knows that you're not going to school?"

"Even if he knew, what could he do?" Jacob clapped his hands and turned them up to heaven.

"Carry you to some other family to send you to school!"

"Stop that kind of talk! They'll say you're bringing politics into this house. Every piece of stone and stick round here has ears! Watch your words."

"What is politics?" I whispered. He had spoken the word in English.

"Causing people to have sense," he said. "I don't care about politics myself. You have to be a fool to get something from life."

"Maybe you're right, but you must go after what you want. If you wait for it to come to you—"

"Don't put me in trouble," Jacob whispered. "Keep your voice down—Why, you want to go back? Learn to cope with whatever situation you find yourself in, my friend. If you miss this opportunity you'll regret it tomorrow."

"Will I go to school?" I said anxiously.

"Most native boys serve some civilized family for a year or two, or until their masters are satisfied—then they send them to school. That's the only sensible thing to do if you want education. You seem to be in a hurry! My friend, there's always another tomorrow!"

"Time waits for no man, my friend."

"A fifth grade friend of mine called Musa who lives on Mamba Point with the Coopers, a rich family, taught me how to read. Mr. Cooper was once Secretary of the Treasury. That's how he got rich. Do you know that I can read some of Musa's books? I assure you I'll get better education than Jimmy and all the Dennis children. They're too soft, too careless, and too dull. They get promotion only because their father pays their teachers much money."

"They're lucky."

"You call that luck? Their father is killing them, but they don't know it!"

"Look, let's find another family to send us to school. I didn't come here all the way from Haindi just to draw water and wash clothes for people."

"My man, you're dreaming. If you leave one Congo family for another, however justified your reason, you won't be accepted. Many friends of mine ruined their own future by going from place to place. The best place to be is wherever you find yourself. Perhaps one day God will get into the heart of this family to send me to school. If they don't, I'll find my own way. It's never too late to learn."

"But I want to go to school now!"

"Take it easy, my friend," Jacob admonished me. Speaking in English, he said, "Congo man say, 'Haste make ways.' The best days are always ahead."

Jimmy hurried from the house and said harshly, "Your stanin' here talkin' Kpelle? I gan tell Ma-o. We ga to full de big drum before goin' to bay. Your know da?"

"We restin' small," Jacob said. "I bin drawin' water all afternoon, and de boy jes comin'; he ain' eat natin yet. He iron?"

"Stan' dare talkin' law," Jimmy said, emptying a bucket of water in a black drum near the house. Returning to the well, he told Jacob, "My man, daha you gan show de new man de life here? Wa work he bin doin' he taya and hungry? Riding truck?"

"Why you talkin' like you neva travel before?"

"Jacob, come down," Jimmy ordered. "My man, come up," he beckoned to me with a nod and we climbed to the top of the well. "Take de buckey and dropey insye."

The bucket hit the water on the side and floated.

"You raw yet," Jimmy said. "Look." He pulled up the bucket and let it go while shaking the twine deftly. It landed on the mouth and sank. "You see?" he said, looking at me. "Come pulley up." I pulled the spokes towards me, the rope winding on the rod, the bucket coming up slowly.

"It not hard for true," I said, laughing. "It fun!"

"Jacob, you friend say we makin' fun," Jimmy giggled. "My man," he said, whisking his finger at me, "we don' play here-o."

"Jimmy, Ma call you!" someone shouted upstairs.

"I comin'!" Jimmy said and left.

"You ga hay," Jacob told me. "A na har' for natin!"

"Continue showin' hin ha," Jimmy said over his shoulder.

"That Bassa boy is hell!" Jacob said in Kpelle. "He's been with this family from baby. He lost his mother when he was born. So his father sold him to the family for a good sum of money. They trust him with everything. If you want to live here in peace, be careful with him."

"What d'you mean? It's against the law of this country to buy or sell people! Slavery was outlawed in Liberia from the day the nation was founded!"

"They call it 'white heart'. But what's the difference?" Jacob said. "Once they spend one cent on you, you're bought."

I grew sober. Probably I too had been bought!

"Is he going to school?" I asked.

"Coming from where? He doesn't know the difference between A and B, but hard work has made him wise and tough. Such a boy can live anywhere on his own. Isn't that the most important thing in life?"

"But Mrs. Dennis told my parents that she sends all the children here to school!" I said. "That's what she actually said!"

"She means her own children," Jacob said. "The children she born. Not those staying with her. Maybe you'll be lucky to go to school this year since she herself brought you here."

"Jacob, you're joking!"

"You'll see. He's coming. Let's stop talking, even in Kpelle. Otherwise, he'll tell the people that we're backbiting them. When the people here get vexed, they kill!"

Jimmy didn't go to the well this time but to a nearby makeshift rusty zinc shack.

"Ma say we ma cook," he said with delight.

Bending on his knees, Jimmy lit a pile of twigs on the hearth and blew on them until the fire blazed. He half-filled a small iron pot with water and set it on an iron tripod over the fire. Going into the house, he brought a cup of rice, washed it in a bucket and put it in the pot. When the rice was done, we ate it with a bit of palm oil and salt, and went to bed.

Our room was ominously stifled, hot, and dark. I looked through a crack in the plank wall, but there was neither moonlight to spy nor a puff of cold air to breathe. Mosquitoes buzzed in my ears menacingly. I clapped my hands round my ears repeatedly.

"You na goin' to bay?" Jimmy said.

Groping in the dark for the bed, I stomped my toes against Jacob's shoulder.

"Don' stepon me 'gain," Jacob protested. "You crazy?"

"No bed here?" I asked.

"Jacob, you hear da?" Jimmy said. "You betta geh dis empty bag and put youself insye! You tink you king?" Jimmy yelled at me.

Following the direction of his voice, I felt for the empty sack. It was coarse, stink, and itchy.

"Put you feet insye; hauley up you hay and lay down," Jimmy said. "We ga to gerup soon mornin'."

Sleeping in a sack was not to my liking, but when I asked Mrs. Dennis the following day for my blankets, she said angrily:

"De other boy dem sleepin' in sack, how you gan sleep in blankey? Leme tell you sometin': Behave youself in dis house a you like youself."

Later I discovered that she had given my blankets and most of my clothes to Caesar. I never bothered to ask for the cash.

FLIGHT

Jimmy pushed the creaking, dilapidated plank door and rushed into the room breezily.

"You betta gerup," he warned me. "Daha you sleep? Dey gan beat you-o." He hurried back, shoving the door closed with his foot.

I stretched, inhaled the musty air, and stared about the dingy room with its black plank walls and sagging floor, then at the sunrays filtering through cracks in the walls. Going outside, I found Jacob building a fire in the zinc shack of a kitchen; Jimmy was hurrying from the house with a white enameled bucket and heading towards the latrine. For something to say I asked Jacob what he was carrying.

"Buckey," he said, smiling. "You ain' ga eye? Da chimon."

"What inside?"

"My man, you like ask too much question, any? You parde tine comin'." Jacob flung his small, kinky head back with a jerk, then leaned it one side and grinned. "Wait—you way see."

My curiosity stirred, I pursued the matter.

"What is chimon, Jacob?"

"I say wait," Jacob said. Squatting, he fed the fire with wood and bamboo splinters, blew on it twice and said, "Da pupu and peepee he goin' throw way." I couldn't believe my ears.

Painful smoke from the smoldering fire made my eyes water. Jacob, who had no problem with the smoke, snickered when he saw me wipe my eyes with the back of my hand.

"You eye still whie like bigshot eye," he said. "Dey way soon geh ray."

"Who say I'm not used to smoke? You've forgotten that we make farm upcountry. Why don't the family use the toilet at night?"

"You here to serve people or for them to serve you?"

"I like serving people, but I hate doing for them what they ought to do for themselves."

"Ma man, you frisky, any? Sometin' wrong way you for true."

"Why you said that?"

"Look, listen—sheh you mouf and do wa we do here! You hear me! Dis my las' tine avisin' you."

"The toilet is not far from the house!"

"You won' do de same tin a you geh boy dem stayin' way you?" Jacob said.

"You know very well nobody dallies with human wastes in Kpelle country except those of babies. I thought the *kwii* people knew better."

"Ma man, you know wa?" Jacob said fearfully. "You Kpelle—I Kpelle. I tort you keem here to be ma friend. From wa I see, a I follow you, you way put bofor us in trouber! I taya avising you. Goodbye." He walked away.

A week later, my turn to empty the chimon came. The sun was up. Granny who was busy with needlework in her lounge, called me. She held the needle up, closed one eye shut and made several grotesque attempts to thread it. "Victoria! Mary! Who outsye dare? Your come thread dis needle for me!" Laying her hands in her lap, she looked at me curiously and said, "We use chimon for heart man plava. You play outsye ah nai, dey gan cut *you tin.* When you wan' peepee ah nai, use chimon. Go na and empty de chimon. A behine de door insye da room." She pointed to a door, her eyes intent on the cloth in her lap.

Instead of a bucket with a lid like what Jimmy had carried before, my chimon was a wide, lidless pan. I couldn't help seeing and smelling the rancid wastes—the most irksome job I ever did in the *kwii* world. Dazed and disgusted, I felt like leaving the house that very day. Quickly emptying the mess into the toilet, I rinsed the pan roughly and took it back upstairs in a rush. The entire household became enraged when the house reeked of bad smell. Granny whipped me most severely.

"You demn country fool, you ga no sense in you big, ugly hay," she cursed as she whipped me. "When dey say Kpelle people stupey, a na lie. I gan repor' you to Ma Mae when she come from White Plain."

Her daughter, who had gone to White Plains to the church conference her husband was still attending, returned the following day with her husband. Granny didn't let her take a seat before making her report:

"Guess what?" she said.

"Bobbor George na come back from de States," Mrs. Dennis said.

"You tink da wineworm comin' back jesna?"

"Sombady day?"

"It concerns your son, Joe. You can take the man from the country but you can't take the country from the man. The boy refused to empty the chimon! He had the whole house smelling. So I whipped him. He's lucky you brought him here; otherwise, he would get lost today! Lost without a trace!"

So, the *kwii* people spoke exotic English when things were all right but spoke the right one when things went wrong? My heart jolted.

"Jimmy, where's Joe?" Mrs. Dennis demanded.

"Behine de kitchen," Jimmy said. "He bin sittin' dare whole day cryin' like dey cut his troat."

"Call him here and bring me a switch quick!" Mrs. Dennis said.

"He already been whipped," Mr. Dennis said, hopping down the plank stairs.

"So what?" Mrs. Dennis said. "When these country asses come newly to civilized society, you have to beat the devil out of them! This boy has been talking plenty of nonsense in this house! What does he take himself to be? The King of England or the President of America? Bring yourself here!" she ordered me as Jimmy and I walked over to her. She was sitting in a rattan chair before the kitchen, every member of the family standing around her and looking at me in anger. Jimmy stripped a guava branch and gave it to her. Thoroughly inflamed, the woman whipped me until the switch broke to pieces.

A week later Jacob woke me up late at night while Jimmy was dead asleep and whispered that we go outside. We squatted under the house, close to one of its rock pillars.

"What happened, my man?" I asked him, trembling with fear.

"Joe, leave this house right away," Jacob whispered in Kpelle. "The other night I overheard Pa and Ma bargaining with one bigshot over your price. I've been looking for a chance to tell you about it. Do you remember the limping, potbelly, old man who came here last Sunday night? He's running for the House, the place where they make laws for the country. The bigshots kill people all over the country and make *juju* with parts of their bodies to win elections. The more people that see their victims' corpses the more votes they believe they'll get. Sunday before last, Pa told the bigshot in church that a bad boy lived in his house whom he may buy if he wished. The bigshot offered Pa and Ma good money for your heart, but Ma said that you were your mother's only child. If such a thing happened to her, she would die of heartbreak, and Ma would never forgive herself because she had promised your parents faithfully that she would take good care of you and carry you back to them, safe and sound. Pa said he didn't care what happened to 'a bad, country sonofabitch.' They could tell your parents that you got lost in Monrovia because you were strange to the city. Pa vowed to see to it that you died because you question and criticize everything we do here; you don't like to serve. You have brought politics into the house. Therefore, the bigshot may have your heart if he wanted it. God himself won't mind if a bad boy is killed. Joe, run away now! Your trouble started the very day you came here. While we conversed at the well that day, Jimmy had one of his Kpelle friends eavesdrop on us. The fellow told him everything we said, and Jimmy told the family everything. I'm scared, Joe. The people hold me responsible for your misbehavior because we're always together and are members of the same tribe. Let's go to my uncle at the landing stage. He's a watchman for the boat company. He'll put you on the boat tomorrow morning. It will take you upriver as far as White Plains. And please don't talk with anyone on board. In White Plains, ask for the road to Mount Coffee. It's Kpelle country. Whenever you miss your way, follow the river. It's the Deyn which *kwii* people call St. Paul River. If you ever come back to Monrovia, don't foot in this house! Let's go. Monrovia is already awake. Listen! Somebody's coming downstairs!"

Shoes clattered on the plank stairs. My heart beat like a throbbing *sam-kpa*.

"Da Jimmy," Jacob whispered.

"Jimmy doesn't have shoes," I whispered. "And what is he doing upstairs time like this?"

"God help us! It's the people! Lie on your belly."

A door creaked and the sonorous voice of Mr. Dennis rang:

"Jimmy! Jimmy! Tell that country ass to come here quick!"

Something snapped in me. My head grew heavy like a hundred-pound bag of rice. Paralyzed with fright I grew blind.

"Henah here, Pa! Henah here! I swear!" Jimmy cried frenziedly, slammed our door, and went outside.

"Don't move, whatever happens," Jacob whispered.

"What?" Mr. Dennis yelled.

"Henah here for true! Henah here, sah!" Jimmy cried again.

"Tell Jacob to come quick," Mr. Dennis raged. "He knows where that ass is hiding."

"He too na here," Jimmy cried.

"Then it's you we will kill!" Mr. Dennis said. "Bobbor Joe, catch Jimmy. If we don't get those bitches, we will cut his throat."

Jacob crawled noiselessly in the dust among piles of junk: rusty buckets, pans, tubs, shovels, broken blocks, rocks—and went to the yard. Now alone, I imagined myself poised in midair, thinking of my parents, Sianeh, and Guladia. *In school you only listen and remember what you're taught.* Closing my eyes tight, I tried to control my breathing. A shot rang.

"I got him!" cried Mr. Dennis.

"Da me-o, Pa! Da me Jacob!"

I wanted to die with him.

"Da gun!" someone howled in the street.

"Da pistor!"

"Da Bobbor Joe 'gain!"

"Look like he day drunk."

"Dey wan' blood 'gain for sacrifice. Election here!"

"Where's Joe?" Mr. Dennis asked Jacob.

"I don' know, Pa. Da hin I lookin' for. De boy na put me in trouber, my people!" Jacob cried.

Another shot. Surely, Jacob was finished. I felt disgusted with myself. *Why be in hiding while he dies for you, coward? You always avoid risk and danger. Why not prove for once that you're a man?*

I crawled on my belly toward the steps near the entrance and hitched myself against a huge rock pillar. A beam of light flashed over my head, powerful and blinding, then surveyed the yard. I made myself as small as possible, feeling now trapped, now relieved, now sad, now happy, now creepy. The light flashed over my shoulder two more times.

"The sonofabitch is hiding under there," Mr. Dennis said.

"He ain' dare," Jacob said. "I look dare proper!"

"Shut up, you damn liar!" Mr. Dennis said. "Jacob, you sonofabitch! You know that? You damn sonofabitch! One more word from you, you're dead. I won' shoot to scare you again but to kill the hell out of you!"

The gun popped loud. The bullet ricocheted on a pillar and whizzed back an inch of me. Another one. It went into the dust, or something soft.

"You damn Kpelle goat, come out!" Mr. Dennis said. "If you don't, I will shoot! Jacob, Jimmy, if you don't find that boy, you're finished! I give you one minute! One more minute! You hear?"

"A look like de boy run away, Pa!" Jacob said.

"Shut your mouth, you damn liar! You think we don't' know what you boys talked when the boy first came here? If we don't get him, you won' live. You hear?" The huge gorilla of a man, wearing only leather slippers and black trousers with suspenders, attempted to put one foot on the first step but staggered.

"Mr. Dennis, wa happen?" a horrified voice screamed in the street.

"Mind your damn business!" Mr. Dennis said.

Another round. A terrific scream. Then a pathetic cry: "Wa I do, my people?"

Feet stampeded into the yard; shrieking inquisitive questions and remarks fired.

"Wa happen?"

"He na kill de police man!"

"No. He ain' die yea. Only shot in de belly. He way makey."

"But wa he war doin' dare?"

"And natin way comof a."

"Maybe he stranger in Monrovia."

"He ain' know dade man a big governmen' man? Big mason man? Big church man? He kill someone self, wa way happen to hin? Natin."

Swinging the hand bearing the gun with an all-inclusive sweep, Mr. Dennis said:

"Your damn asses better get the hell out my yaaard! What happens here is none of your damn business!"

The crowd stampeded back to the street with hissing voices, exclamations, shouts, angry comments.

Again, Mr. Dennis staggered to the steps, close to me, placed one foot on the first one and urinated. He must have had a large bladder, for the ritual took no less than two full minutes. My night vision now active, I surveyed the yard with my eyes. Jimmy and Jacob were nowhere around. I pulled the leg on the ground with force. The gorilla tipped over and fell in a heap; his head crashed on a rock. The gun fired. I felt a weakness in the left arm. Jacob pulled me by the shirt, whispering, "We had better run away. Bobber Joe has gone for a soldier!"

We crawled on our bellies to the backyard. A large crowd swarmed the front one. Dawn came rapidly but was soon attacked by a deep, black cloud the ocean wind swept onto the mainland. I followed Jacob amidst market women and *yana*[41] boys with bundles of goods on their heads and bales of cloth on their shoulders, calling customers. Jacob first headed for the landing stage. On second thought, he switched completely around and walked down the muddy street, limping on his wounded leg trickling with blood. He looked back frequently, signing to me with his arm to follow. We weaved through the crowd towards a narrow, concrete bridge connecting the city to Vai Town.

Ruffians cried "Rogue! Rogue!" after us, but we paid no attention. After

41. Petty trader who carries merchandise on the head.

crossing the bridge, several of them surrounded us, their arms poised to strike. We stood still, the right thing to do in such a situation.

"We're not rogues," Jacob told them politely. "My brother and I had accident on our way from upcountry last night. We're returning home."

The explanation cooled them down somewhat; they only grimaced at our wounded limbs and walked away, murmuring.

We resumed walking with redoubled effort. Up to now, I felt no pain, though my left arm had swollen markedly. Each time I spied the thick blood clots covering the sores, I wondered why the slight circumcision wound had been so debilitating.

Jacob's thigh had also swollen out of proportion. We reached Gbanoimu by noon. Jacob's six-year-old sister was dancing *nafo*[42] in front of their small square house. She first watched us with curious eyes, her lips agape, then, terrified by our bizarre looks, ran behind the house, calling their mother who ran to us with open mouth and puzzled eyes. Flinging away pieces of cassava sticks she had in her hands, she asked:

"Son, what happened?" embracing Jacob with outstretched arms while gazing at me. As his sister stood dumbfounded, Jacob buried his face in his mother's bosom, wept quietly, disengaged himself and wiped the tears away.

"Yaai, I'll tell you everything later," he told his mother, "but first find someone to take out the bullets."

Gravely astonished, the woman cried, "Bullets! So you boys were shot?" Shaking all over, she slapped her thighs with desolation, her tear-strewn eyes flitting from Jacob to me and from me to Jacob.

"Yaai, be happy to see us alive," Jacob said. "We could have been killed."

"For what?" the woman cried.

Without waiting for a reply, she ran to a nearby village and came back two hours later with a Zoe. A towering man dressed in full medical regalia, the Zoe had us follow him to his village for proper care.

He put Jacob's leg and my arm in bamboo casts after applying herb to our wounds. The following day a bullet came out of Jacob's thigh while he dressed his wound. He said that my arm was bullet free, but the bone had a small crack, which was no problem.

Towards evening the next day, Jacob's father came to us. A small man with a scarred face, he met us lying on a mat behind the Zoe's house. The Old Man stood over us with his arms akimbo.

"Son, tell me the truth," he told Jacob.

"Data, we did no wrong," Jacob said weakly. "Pa sold this boy to one big-shot who paid good money for him. We were shot as I helped him escape."

"What's your name, Son?" the Old Man asked me.

"Joseph Dennis."

Too shocked to comment on the matter, the Old Man said that he was

42. A Nigerian dance, usually done by a single person.

happy to see us alive. We would discuss the problem in detail when our wounds healed. After the healing, he only advised us not to go to Monrovia for the time being. Giving me a white rooster, he suggested that I go home to my parents. Monrovia wasn't good for us.

PLEASANT SURPRISE

On the second and last day of my journey, I reached Mauwa by noon. Now a mere hour to Haindi, I lingered on the road until dark to avoid my unexpected return home causing a stir. Walking quickly past the square where children played *gbai*[43] in the moonlight, I entered our house. Father, who stood in the yard gazing at the moonlit sky, was piqued by the impudence.

"How dare you enter my house without saying hello?" he raged.

"Data, it's me," I said.

"Zurong! How were you—did you—what happened?"

"I'm all right, Data. I'll explain everything later." Placing the chicken in a corner of the center room, I sat on my bed.

Father came in and pointed at the small pot by the fireside in which Mother often kept food for unexpected guests. "Eat and tell me what happened. I'm going for your mother."

Hardly had I put the first spoon of rice in my mouth when Mother fell on the porch and cried hysterically. The town soon gathered at our house. Some people murmured that Father had probably died or Mother might have been told that I had either been killed or kidnapped in the *kwii* world. On seeing Father trying to console her, they focused on me:

"Seporlor, why did you pursue book learning without compromise as if it's all there is to life?"

"All your friends have left school and married. Since you knew how to read and write, what more you wanted from the *kwii* world?"

"We don't know book. Are we not living happily?"

"Why did the Old Man ignore the Water Zoe's warning?"

"Oh! There he is! And why is NeSuaa killing herself with weeping? He looks well!"

"Seporlor, what problem have you put on your poor parents' heads that's making your mother cry like this? Come down here and explain!"

Squeezed up in an overcrowded pickup I boarded in Haindi, where the motor road had reached through the effort of a large workforce Senator Loryii himself had assembled (only because the President would visit the area), I reflected on my chaotic reception at home.

My parents had cornered me that night and demanded the whole truth about my hasty and unexpected return from Monrovia, but I refused to tell them the truth because it could have ended my schooling and probably caused Mother's death. I told them the following story instead:

After service one Sunday, we boys discovered that all our clothes were missing. Since I was the last person to leave the room, everybody held me responsible for the clothes. Mrs. Dennis said I must produce them or else

---

43. A dance done in a circle in which people dance by turn and point at the person to succeed them.

she would kill me. The scar on my arm was a result of car accident.

"You expect me to believe that?"Father had asked, staring at me with incredulous eyes.

"You weren't there," I said. "So you have to believe whatever I tell you."

"Even if it doesn't make sense, heh?"

"You've been in a *kwii* family before, Data. You know how it is."

Father cleared his throat and said, "No guardian sends a child home for losing things. A child given to a guardian no longer belongs to its parents. So whatever you did or failed to do in Monrovia doesn't concern us but your new mother who could have beaten or starved you for your negligence or disobedience. The last thing she'd have done was send you home, alone."

"I myself decided to come home for help."

"Zurong, speak up! Something went wrong!"

"Whatever the case, the boy is here," Mother put in. "Let's thank God for that. What help do you need from us?" she asked me.

"I've already said I needed clothes."

"I want to meet that Congo woman and give her a piece of my mind for sending my son through the terrible Gola forest by himself," Father said. "A twoday trek at that! Anything could have happened!"

"NanSen, don't worry about what might have happened," Mother admonished. "Let's do what we can for the child."

"I don't want the boy to go back to Monrovia," Father said. "Let's implore Ma Miller to let him go to Sanoyea."

The long delay disturbed Ma Miller. Why did we not go by her instruction? Now, I had missed a whole month of school again! I really had no liking for school even though I seemed eager to learn. She ordered my parents to find my tuition and the transport fare to Sanoyea. Father pawned his kola trees to a Mandingo trader for five dollars. Mother searched all over the house and found one dollar and fifty cents; she pawned two of her lappa to a Vai woman for another dollar and fifty cents.

We took the money to Ma Miller who put it in an envelope and wrote the name, Rev. Paul Slifer, on it.

"He needs two more dollars for transport," she told my parents who looked depressed.

Addressing a letter to Rev. Slifer and putting it in another envelope, Ma Miller gave me both envelopes and said, "Hand these to Rev. Slifer when you get to Sanoyea. Ask for a Totota pickup in Kakata. In Totota, they'll show you the road to Sanoyea. Safe journey. May God bless you." Hurrying into her warehouse, she brought me a sport shirt with alternating blue and white stripes.

"I had thought the white woman would do more than that," Father complained as we walked back to Haindi. "Pay the balance of Zurong's school fees, for instance."

"I've never seen missionaries give away something for nothing, though they claim to be godly," Mother said.

The ride to Kakata was smooth and swift because government graders had torn down the hills, filled in the valleys, and leveled the road. I wondered what Haindi looked like when the first vehicle arrived there. Was it Jackson's truck?

"My man, come down. We reach," a carboy shook me by the shoulder. I instantly roused from my reverie. "Where you money?" he said, holding his dusty palm before me. Taking the envelope with the money from my bundle, I gave him one dollar. He tossed a quarter at me and asked where I was going.

"Totota," I said.

"Totota pickup dasye," he pointed vaguely at a gas station across the highway.

I boarded an old green pickup overloaded with passengers and loads. Again, I became engrossed in my own thoughts as we drove away: I had refused to tell my parents the truth about my narrow escape from Monrovia because I didn't simply have the mouth to relate the chilling experience. How could a civilized, God-fearing Christian demand someone's heart as a matter of course? Was there anything to Christianity or civilization? I also didn't want to horrify them with the story of my miraculous escape from the claws of a crocodile in the Gola forest at sunset.

Standing on the bank of a muddy creek in the middle of the dense forest, I shouted for a small canoe leashed to an outcropped root on the other shore. There was no reply. After repeating the call the hundredth time, I tied my clothes and chicken on my head with *memeh* and engaged the squalid creek that posed no challenge to the laziest swimmer. Halfway across, I heard someone else fall into the creek upstream. With company, the swimming should be fun, I thought. No! A crocodile! Its mouth wide open, the beast shot towards me like arrow. In the winking of an eye, I found myself ashore, running naked with all my might on the rutted, overgrown path, my load and chicken still tied to my head—

The pickup bumped in a pothole, leaned sideways dangerously, and stopped. A heavy cloud of dust blew at us. I couldn't breathe.

"Everybady down," the carboy announced, blowing his whistle.

"This is Gbakoryee," a passenger told me as we jostled down. With an agitated look on his face, he took a charm from his pocket and hung it to his neck, mumbling incantation. "If our pickup makes it to the top of this mountain," he said, "then the journey is over. If not, we'll have to carry our loads all the way to Totota. A two-hour journey!"

The mountain was extremely tall and rocky. Only a miracle would see the pickup on its summit, I thought.

"Your walk up," the carboy cried again. "All de way on top." He blew his whistle again.

The passengers grumbled, especially mothers with babies strapped to their backs. "Do we pay fares to walk or to ride?" they asked. When we commenced the uphill struggle, there was no more comment. The passengers now told tales of horror about the mountain, centering round two monsters northern tribesmen had reportedly planted east and west of it to ward off invasion from the south. For many generations these monsters destroyed invading forces by making them insane with magic spell or by killing them with invisible, lethal blows.

This false security crumbled in the early forties when a group of black and white *kwii* started building a road between Monrovia and the border with Guinea, using heavy equipment. Though the monsters killed dozens of them and drove just as many more insane, their mishaps only made them more determined. The brave invaders dug out boulders, knocked down huge trees, and cut the mountain down. At night, the monsters would secretly put everything back in place. If death couldn't stop them, what could mystery do? After each setback, the *kwii* people worked harder than before. The monsters enjoyed "the fun", but, one day, they surprisingly found themselves locked up in huge jars on a ship bound for America, and the road was finally built.

An interesting story, but the mountain was still a danger to travelers from the south. Wooden block in hand, the carboy jogged beside the vehicle as it crawled up at a snail's pace. He would place the block under a back tire after several yards of progress. The engine would give a stifled groan, then a loud squeal; the pickup would advance a yard or two. The carboy would block it again. Then the process would be repeated. A dangerous game! It was good the vehicle carried no passenger.

I arrived in Sanoyea at dusk and went over to the mission located east of the town. The principal's residence, a large framed house with a screened porch, stood on concrete pillars, an electric bulb hanging at the front door. A generator supplying the old house with electricity roared behind it. Climbing the sagging stairs, I knocked the door. A short, stocky white man carrying an open writing pad in his hand came and stared at me with flashy spectacles.

"Where you're from?" he asked.

"Kpolopele," I said.

"So you're the boy Ma Miller told me about?"

"Yes, sir."

"Name?"

"Joe Dennis?"

"Grade?"

"Sixth."

He wrote hurriedly in the pad and directed me to the boys' dorm. I gave him Ma Miller's letters and the remaining tuition and left.

Several groups of boys, who stood before the long building conversing and cracking jokes, scrutinized me carefully before replying my greetings in a chorus and shaking my hand.

"You student?" one of them asked me.

"From Kpolopele Mission. The Principal sent me to the dorm manager."

A tall, sturdy fellow peeled off a group and took me to a large room cramped with double-decker bamboo beds. Two hurricane lanterns hanging to the bamboo ceiling lit the room. Surveying the beds with a sweeping glance, the manager pointed at an under-bed with loose, dry grass and said, "This you bay. You got bayclothes?" I nodded.

I wrapped the grass in one of two lappa Mother had given me, folded the other one and placed it at the head of the bed. Putting my short pants under the folded lappa, I watched the other beds with envy. They sparkled with new blankets and pillows embellished with romantic epigrams skillfully knitted on the pillow cases: *Forget me not. Sweet dreams. Love is all I ask of you, but if you find it a burden, forget me. I love you for sentimental reasons—*

"What you doing? Dreaming?" a fellow student tapped my shoulder. "You better makey and find you parde girl friend to make you parde pillow case. Dese tings nothing!"

Waking up on the sound of a gong at five-thirty in the morning, I made up my bed and ran behind the dorm with the other boys to a creek, where we scrubbed our teeth with twigs, washed our faces, and scrubbed our legs and feet with pieces of soaped sack. A great deal of dirt came off my legs and feet. I hadn't done a good job of bathing the night before.

Dressing quickly, we marched to our classrooms, which stood in the center of the campus. Generally older than I, the boys wore long pants, white, long-sleeved shirts, and shiny leather shoes. Only a few of them wore short pants and went barefoot like myself.

My classroom experience was extremely disappointing. I couldn't understand a thing! Every grade I made was below passing. I remember the head of the school who hailed from Kpotoloma, a nearby village, reading the story of a winged horse called Pegasus during my first day in class. The language sounded strange. Was it English? Could it be that I had learned nothing in school? Failure stared me in the face. I recalled with remorse Sarah's biting attacks in Kpolopele.

During recess one morning, Pastor Slifer asked me for the rest of my first semester tuition, failure to pay which meant expulsion from school. Penniless, I stood worried before him in his office. From where would I find nine dollars?

"What will you do, Joe?" he asked me.

"Write to my parents," I said.

"Good. Write them today. Time flies."

In their reply, which came a month later, my parents said I should find a job and help myself. A full-grown man now, I should learn to shoulder my own responsibilities. I took the disappointing reply to Pastor Slifer who read it quickly, thought for a moment, and said:

"You could join other boys each Saturday to bring school supplies from Yanekwelle." He searched my face. I nodded. "You get twenty-five cents per trip. If you're strong, you could make two trips."

By seven o'clock each Saturday morning, I joined a dozen other boys to make the trip. At Yanekwelle, a Kpelle-writing missionary would assign loads to us, carefully weighing each one to ensure it wasn't more than sixty pounds. The loads were paper boxes containing canned foods for the missionaries, pencils, copybooks, textbooks, chalks, dusters, bundles of zinc, tins of fuel for the generator, and so on. After my first trip, I was too tired to make another one.

"Don't be discouraged," the pastor told me. "You'll be able to keep up with those tough guys after two or three more Saturdays. Here we are," he tossed a nickel to me and said the balance twenty cents would go towards my tuition. I thanked him for making it possible for me to continue school; he said he was simply doing his duty. He had done the same thing for many other boys.

Pastor Slifer frequented our dorm, not only for the routine night inspection but also to crack jokes with us, eat with us, play basketball with us. He was one of the few Lutheran missionaries I recall who took personal interest in African students. We always anticipated his inspection tour with delight because it was then that we had the most fun with him.

On returning from a trip to Yanekwelle one Saturday afternoon, I saw a large parcel wrapped in brown paper on my bed, my name written on it. Who could have sent it to me? Opening it avidly, I was shocked to find all my clothes I had left in Monrovia. A short boy with red hair rushed into the room and told me that the mission plane had dropped the parcel on the football field at noon, and he had taken it to my bed.

"Who sent you these plenty clothes?" he inquired as I loosened the package.

"My parents."

"Your parents love you very much! I never get anything from mine." The fellow examined the clothes piece by piece. When he raised a T-shirt in the air for thorough inspection, a letter dropped from it. I read it anxiously:

Kpolopele Lutheran Mission
Central Province
March 5, 1953
Dear Joe:

This comes as a pleasant surprise from your dear parents. They said a brother of yours called Jacob, whom you visited in Monrovia during the vacation, brought these clothes of yours. You had forgotten them when you left Monrovia in a hurry to come home for school. Your parents said Jacob told them everything that led to your hasty departure from Monrovia. All is well back home. Everybody sends you greetings and best wishes. Study hard and keep praying.

May God bless you,
IN HIS FELLOWSHIP
Sincerely yours,
Miriam T. Miller

I wondered how Jacob managed to get hold of my clothes. Was he brave enough to foot back at the Dennises'? Perhaps the family had sent him to my parents with the trumped up accusation that I had run away due to truancy. To rise above suspicion, they had given him my clothes. My parents were certainly relieved after knowing the true account of my flight from Monrovia; I wished I had told them the truth to maintain their trust. They must have showered Jacob with many gifts for risking his life to save mine. Would I ever see him again, that godsend?

"What happened, my man?" the red headed boy queried me inappropriately. "Somebody sick back home, or dead?"

"Nothing happened," I replied with a sigh. "I just thinking."

For some unexplained reason, which worked in the students' favor, the school authorities transferred the sixth and seventh grades to Belefanai and Zorzor Missions, respectively, for the second semester. The Church assumed full responsibility for our second semester tuition and all other fees we owed. This pleasant surprise kept many poor students in school. For the first time in my school career, I failed the semester.

My parents were delighted to know that I didn't have to pay school fees for the second semester, although they were sorry about my failure. Father said the setback was normal: "You can't fight a battle without being wounded." He and Mother managed to find the three dollar transport fare for my trip to Belefanai.

It was a difficult trip because it came in the middle of the rainy season when the downpour was the heaviest. Our pickup failed to climb Gbakoryee, so we had to carry our own loads to Totota where I boarded a pickup for Gbarnga, the Capital of the Central Province. Almost as large as Kakata, Gbarnga had strings of Lebanese shops; milling marketers spanned both shoulders of its business thoroughfare.

I waited for a Belefanai pickup until the evening sun turned scarlet. Because I knew no one in Gbarnga to accommodate me for the night, I set off for Belefanai on foot. I ran into the darkness after passing Waynsue, a small village west of Gbarnga. Much to my surprise, I wasn't afraid of the night even though I was in a strange land and vulnerable to predatory animals and ghosts. As if coming to my rescue, the early stars lighted the countryside. I reached Belefanai after midnight. A headlight hunter with a baby antelope corpse dangling at his side directed me to the campus and warned me against traveling at night. "An inexperienced hunter could mistake you for a black deer!" he cried.

I met four of my Sanoyea classmates in the dorm. They had arrived several days earlier. They said most of our classmates had gone to Monrovia, Firestone, and Bomi Hills "to acquire the things of the modern world." Aboard the same canoe, we felt kinship to one another. Since I was the youngest in the group, they constantly advised me to behave myself in our new world.

Life in Belefanai Mission centered round Teacher Paul Gayflor, a slender, handsome Loma man from Zorzor who was always well dressed in the latest style in fashion. A womanizer but strong disciplinarian, he levied the severest punishment on students for the slightest infraction of mission rule. A graduate of LTI, which he often talked about with pride and affection, he challenged us constantly to study hard to qualify for admission into the reputable institute. Teacher Gayflor settled disputes on campus, assigned roster work, inspected our foods and clothes, and checked the boys' dorm at bedtime. In short, he ran the mission single-handed.

If he exercised this much authority, it was because the principal Ma Keller, a German national, who had spent some forty years in the Lutheran mission field in Liberia, was too old. She lived in a red brick building on the western edge of the mission with some dozen orphans whom she had salvaged from death and was educating. At times, I studied with her boys in her well-lighted lounge at night. She recommended that while studying we timed ourselves with a little watch she always placed on our study table. This improved my reading speed but not my comprehension. Sometimes I took the watch to school.

The activities on campus were the same as those in Kpolopele and Sanoyea: rise before dawn, make up your bed, sweep your room and the yard, get ready for school, do roster work in the afternoon, and so forth. Because we received little nourishment from our scanty, ill-prepared diet, I lacked the needed energy to cope with these odd jobs in the cold rainy season. I lost weight considerably and looked frail. Other students brought food from their homes to supplement the diet.

A fifth grade student called John Kolimiling, a citizen of Belefanai, whom I used to help with his lessons, proved helpful to me at this point. He introduced me to his mother, a slim, short woman who still retained remnants of the beautiful contours of youth, though now weather-beaten. Whenever John and I visited her, she would cook the best meal we would eat for the week. Literally, she became my second mother.

One night I grew very hungry because they had reduced our ration that day. My stomach rumbled constantly, and I grew so restless in bed that I couldn't sleep. I decided to go to John's mother for food even though it wasn't Saturday, the only day of the week we were permitted to leave the campus. Even on Saturday, all students must be on campus before bedtime. Well, I either obeyed the mission rule and died of hunger or saved my life and be punished or possibly expelled. Because she had not expected me, the woman had no cooked food to offer; she only gave me two ripe plantains, which I gobbled and washed down with two cups of water. Life began flowing back into my veins. I thanked her and hurried outside to run into the outstretched arms of Teacher Gayflor. A group of boys accompanied him, evidently his informants.

"Oho!" cried he. "You're now in my net! Where is the girl friend?" Fear descended upon me, but I shrugged it off. After all, I wasn't the first, nor would I be the last, victim of that net—life came first. "Bring me twenty-five bunches of wood by Saturday," Teacher Gayflor told me coldly as we walked back to campus. It was Wednesday, so I had only three days tó fetch such a large quantity of firewood.

Despite the hardship, I made good progress in school. Not one red mark was on my report card. As conditions worsened, however, I wrote my parents for financial assistance. Knowing their reluctance in honoring financial requests of mine, I stated in my letter that I needed the money to buy a uniform for drilling because I had been conscripted into the militia; all conscripts were required to provide their own uniforms. Failure to do so meant a long prison term. I took my letter to Ma Keller for dispatch to Kpolopele. Unfortunately, one of her orphans called Elizabeth Yekelo intercepted it and circulated its contents round the campus. I became a laughingstock. I was a liar, a thief, a sinner, and so forth. When I discovered that Elizabeth's carelessness accounted for my disgrace, I confronted her on the football field one evening and demanded an apology. I almost slapped the girl but controlled myself for fear of the consequences of fighting on campus. I cursed her instead. She reported me to Ma Keller. The old woman sent for Teacher Gayflor and me immediately.

"What happened?" Teacher Gayflor asked Elizabeth.

"Joseph stole Ma Keller's little watch; when I told him about it, he cursed me," the girl whimpered.

The room swam in my eyes and I grew blind. I had only borrowed the watch!

"The girl lied!" I exclaimed. Extremely angry, the Old Lady wobbled to me and slapped me in both ears with her trembling, bony hands.

Teacher Gayflor said, "Well, Joe, you're guilty in this matter. Do you know that it's forbidden to utter the word 'lie' on campus?"

"Teacher, please let me explain," I pleaded. "I wrote a letter to my parents which this wicked girl read without my permission and told everybody on campus the message inside. I often borrowed Ma Keller's watch—"

"We're not talking about watch or letter," Teacher Gayflor said. "Had you stolen the watch, it wouldn't have been lying here on the table. Did you curse Elizabeth?"

"No, sir. I only denounced her for interfering in my private affairs."

"Had you reported her to me, I would have punished her. Never take matters in your own hands, my friend. Bring me forty bunches of wood by Saturday."

"But Teacher—"

"Another word from you and you're expelled from the mission! Am I clear? Should I put it in Kpelle?" His *fala* Kpelle would have been as good as Greek. Later, I discovered that Elizabeth was his girl friend.

Even though I failed in math (I made 20% in the final exam, which appeared on my report card), I passed to the seventh grade. Contrary to my fears, my unkempt bleak experience didn't disturb my parents. Mother saw it as an opportunity to get me a barber, new clothes, and all the delicacies I had missed. Father was now convinced that I would keep my side of the pact. But when I told them that my next school would be Zorzor Lutheran Mission, they expressed profound misgivings. If I could encounter bad treatment in Kpelleland, what would I not encounter in Lomaland?

POOR KEWALAI

After earning a total of fifty dollars from the sale of rice, coffee, and palm oil, I began the journey to Zorzor. Again failing to find a Belefanai pickup in Gbarnga, I continued my journey on foot, arriving in Belefanai round midnight. I slept with Ma Keller's boys and left for Zorzor early the following morning. For breakfast I ate five ripe bananas I bought in Belefanai. I met the ubiquitous Deyn by mid-morning; it roared fiercely through jutting rocks in the primeval forest. A rattan hammock bridge hung dangerously some five hundred feet over it. The other shore was some half a quarter mile away. With a palpitating heart and trembling legs, I climbed up the stick ladder and into the bridge, sighed deeply, prayed, and took one uncertain step after the other, holding the ropes with one hand and the box on my head with the other. The bridge swung and creaked dangerously. After crossing it, I prayed never to face such an ordeal again.

I caught up with a fellow traveler doggedly climbing a steep mountain with a large, black trunk on his head. His blue T-shirt and khaki short pants thoroughly soaked with sweat, he was sticking his toes in the footholds carefully and propelling himself up with force. We sat on a log on the mountain's summit to rest; fresh breeze fanned us delightfully.

"You're really strong!" I told the fellow. "Climbing this tall mountain with such a big load!"

"Your first time coming this way?" he said as we snapped fingers.

"Yes," I replied.

"The Western Province is mountainous. Where you're going?"

"Zorzor."

"You have many mountains to climb. Student?"

"Yes."

"Tribe?"

"Kpelle. Yours?"

"Same."

"You think I can make it to Zorzor today?"

"Zorzor? No. You can't reach Zorzor one day from Belefanai. Any you coming from Belefanai?"

"Yes."

"I too sleep there last night from Firestone. Went to my sister to help me with school fee; bought only clothes with the little money she gave me. No—you can't makey to Zorzor today."

"We might get a pickup," I said, looking at the double-trailed motor road stretching into the distance.

My traveling mate informed me in a strange Kpelle that vehicles seldom risked a trip to the river because the road was hilly and bumpy, the log bridges poorly constructed. Even if they fought their way to the river, it was impossible to convey their cargoes across via the monkey bridge.

"The only solution I see to the problem is building a concrete bridge over the river," he said. "But it won't happen in our lifetime. I can bet on it." He looked away disdainfully as if the subject were a bitter pill.

"This bridge will link the Western Province to the rest of the country," I said. "Remember, it's our largest province and rice bowl. These are reasons enough to make the government build the bridge in the shortest time possible."

"My friend, what is your name?"

"Joseph Dennis. And yours?"

"John Flomo. Joe, your confidence in the government is misplaced."

"Why?"

"Government officials in this country seldom think of development. They buy big cars and build big mansions for themselves and their families, travel abroad, support hordes of girl friends—while the country languishes in poverty. Had it not been for missionaries, you and I wouldn't have learned ABC. Watch my word. One day there will be a big war in this country."

"Johnny, you'll be a great politician and an uncommonly cynical one."

"See this nonsense!" Johnny was fuming. "Vehicles from Monrovia must go through Guinea before getting to our Province. Suppose Guinea closes its border with Liberia, how will we get goods in our shops? The more I talk about our selfish politicians, the more I become vexed. Well, I too on my way to Zorzor for school, but I'll spend a day or two in Salayea to look for tuition. You may sleep with me in my town tonight and continue your trip tomorrow."

"Thanks," I said. "What is your town's name?"

"Gorlu. We're Gbaleng. You speak Seghai Kpelle. The people along the Deyn all the way to Guinea are Kpelle. It's really true that the Kpelle are the largest tribe in Liberia. Where're you from?"

"Haindi, Fuama Chiefdom, Central Province."

"We'll reach Gorlu round five o'clock this evening. You'll reach Zorzor tomorrow afternoon if you walk fast. My brother is a tax collector. Makes plenty money but spends it mostly on women. Forgets he has children and relatives."

"You're lucky. My relatives don't help me with school fees. And my parents are too old and poor. Only a second father of mine helped me once, but he had to die before I got the money."

"I'll have to pay back everything double when I finish school, you know. How much money do they give me? Two or three hundred dollars for the most."

"But that's a lot of money, Johnny! Your relatives are very kind to you! Family members back home expect everything from you but never help you fight for something. But get it, and they're at your door every day asking for it."

"That's bad. We don't act like that in the Western Province."

"What grade you're in?"

We shouldered our loads before he answered my question.

"Fifth. And you?"

"Seventh."

"You lucky. I old pass you and you ahead of me in school!"

"Had my father not forced me to go to school—were the decision left solely to me—perhaps I might have never seen the inside of a classroom. My being ahead of you by two grades means nothing. The Bible says, 'The race is not to the swift but to him who endures to the end.'"

"You'll be a pastor some day."

"Knowing one Bible verse doesn't make you a pastor, Johnny. I don't even know which book of the Bible contains that verse."

"A thousand-mile trek begins with the first step. Do you have your tuition?"

"Yes."

"Your people are good to you, too. My parents always let me down, and half the small money Brother and Sister often give me I leave with my wife and children. Sometimes I give them all and stay out of school altogether."

"I cut palm nuts, gather coffee, and do odd jobs to find tuition. My girl's family takes care of her and our son."

"Why do your people refuse to help you with your schooling when you're going to school mostly for their benefit?" Johnny said.

"My mother helps me make palm oil and pound coffee to sell. My father sells kola nuts and gives me the earnings. Nothing much, but enough to get me a pair of short pants and a shirt. How many children have you?"

"Two—a boy and a girl. My girl is pregnant again; she lives with my parents. I'm not doing this because I want to. We start school late, Joe. Now I'm twenty-five. When I finish school, I'll be thirty-five or forty. I want to live to see my children grow up and be on their own. The missionaries expect us to finish school before raising a family. When their children attain my age, they've already finished college."

"Johnny, you're right. We have to use our heads in this matter because whatever becomes of us tomorrow is our responsibility."

We grew silent as we struggled up yet another steep hill. The luxuriant vegetation and refreshing, cool, light air considerably reduced the strain of the journey. Perspiration was moderate, hunger pains tolerable. Seldom did we stop to rest, and whenever we did so, it was to drink some of the iced water of a stream rolling down a mountain and crossing our path. I had learned from travelers that the mountainous north, though engulfed by the ever-encroaching rain forest, had a temperate weather in contrast to the sultry, enervating climate of the central and southern regions. But only a visit there enabled one to appreciate the contrast. The daylong trek was strenuous but not exhausting.

We met no other traveler on the way but isolated uninhabited villages whose residents had gone to their farms. Only a few straggling goats and sheep, grazing on the roadsides near these villages and the piquant, concerted cries of birds in the dense forest certified to the presence of life on the deserted countryside.

We reached Gorlu at sundown. Placing our burdens on the porch of

Johnny's house, furnished with hammock and rattan chairs, Johnny took a chair and offered me the hammock. Soon I fell asleep and awoke to note that his parents, brothers, sisters, wife, and children had already arrived from the farm and had built a fire in the center room. Johnny's mother offered us a delicious dish of rice and *torborgee*[44] she had cooked on the farm. After bathing, we slept comfortably in a small room and resumed our journey early the following morning, reaching Salayea before noon. Johnny showed me the road to Zorzor and left for his brother's house.

The mission was located south of the populous town where I arrived late in the afternoon. Weedy and abandoned, it consisted of half a dozen yellow concrete buildings scattered over some sixty acres. The largest, doubtless, the administrative and classroom building, was centrally located and dominated all the others. A flagpole of galvanized pipe with a pair of white strings spanning its length stood in front of it. The principal's residence was at the western extremity of the mission. The only evidence of life on campus was chattering coveys of wrens and pepper birds darting about in flower bushes. Far in the distant forest, Dodo and palm birds ushered in sundown with droning cries. A thick, black cloud tinged with the fading glow of sunset floated at the horizon. As I watched the breathtaking view, a wave of renewed vigor sprang in me.

When I knocked the principal's door, a girl in a red dress answered my call. She retraced her steps through a narrow hallway, and, in a moment, a short, delicate white woman with a preoccupied look, wearing a blue dress, her lips painted red, came to the door with clipped steps and inquired what I wanted, flashing her gold-rimmed glasses at me. I suspected that eyeglasses were an important symbol of being a *kwii*, but strangely enough, mostly the white ones wore them.

"I student from Belefanai mission," I told the woman who seemed impatient to go back.

"Oh," she said and made a negligent gesture, pointing vaguely to one of two long buildings across a wide field, "go over there and ask for a teacher. Okay?"

"Yes, Ma'am," I said. "Thank you, but—" The woman was gone!

A short, plump, bald-headed, middle-aged man with a surly expression on his face, sat on the porch of one of the dormitories, whistling and looking moodily at chickens chasing insects in the green grass. His clasped hands poked out of the wide neck of his short homespun gown. I introduced myself and told him that the principal had sent me to him. He looked at me coldly, and, collecting a bunch of keys from his room, said curtly:

"Follow me." He opened the door to the building, exposing two rows of aluminum double-decker beds. "Choose any bay you like," he told me, then measured a cup of rice out of a bag in a corner and gave it to me for my supper. "No oil here," he said morosely. "No salt. The kitchen over there,"

44. Staple diet of Lofa County, comprising red palm oil, soda, dry meat or fish, and vegetables.

he pointed casually behind the house and made off.

My cold reception brought home to me my parents' fears for my safety in Loma country, but I had dealt with only three persons there so far, one of whom, John Flomo, had been kind to me. My apathetic reception on the mission could be due to my early arrival. The kitchen lacked cooking utensils, and as it seemed risky to tamper with the depressive teacher any further, I simply went to bed and slept until the roaring engine of a truck and a rumpus awoke me in the morning.

A slim, self-possessed missionary, making wild gestures with his arms and head, was instructing some men to pack the teacher's things in the truck. The teacher sat unruffled on the porch as if what was happening did not concern him. When his things were all packed in the truck, the missionary told him deferentially:

"Teacher Kewalai, we're ready to go."

"Where are we going?" the teacher said blandly, staring at the missionary. He was shaking all over. The men who had packed his personal effects in the truck watched the drama with anxiety.

"Why, to your home!" the missionary told him.

"Where is home?" Teacher Kewalai insisted, rising.

"Look, my friend, don't waste our time; we have many other things to do. Get on board let's go. Are you not from Konia?" The missionary removed his eyeglasses, wiped them carefully with a white handkerchief he pulled out of his side pocket, and put them back on.

"When you talk of home, you're talking about a house in which people sleep, aren't you?" Teacher Kewalai asked. "Where will I sleep in Konia?"

"You know very well that it's against the Church's rules for a retired employee to live in a Church house," the missionary said, his voice rising steadily.

"I know all that," Teacher Kewalai maintained, looking aside. "But you haven't answered my question. I say, where will I sleep in Konia?"

"You tell me."

"No! You tell me! Talk! Don't stand looking at me speechlessly like Jesus Christ before Ponte Palley!" The teacher advanced several steps to the missionary, jabbing his finger at him. Then continuing in the same peremptory voice, he said, "I used to mention this problem in staff meetings and at conventions, but you missionaries said I was playing politics! You educate us but pay us little or nothing when we work for you! What can you do with a monthly salary of twenty-five dollars? I'm seventy-five years old, with seven children and ten grandchildren to support! What do I own? Nothing! My pension is only fifteen dollars per month! It'll be a shame should I return to my village with my large family, poor and penniless! My people would wonder why I had gone through the trouble of getting an education! Many times I asked the Church for loan to build a house, but you missionaries told me not to bother building a house because Jesus Christ had nowhere to lay his head. Look, let me tell you something. Only my dead body will leave this house, for death is better than disgrace!"

"What kind of talk is that, Kewalai?" the missionary said amiably. "It's no time for bad jokes. It wasn't I who made the rule. I'm simply ordered to enforce it. So don't blame me. Your many children could help you build a house in no time; you won't pay a cent to build it because there are plenty of dirt, sticks, thatch—"

Interrupting, Teacher Kewalai went on to say that his parents were all dead and he had no friend or relative to turn to for accommodation. The secretary of the Church should please give him a place where he would spend his remaining days in peace. There were many empty houses on campus. But the missionary said he didn't have the authority to do that.

The argument went on and on until the two men almost came to blows; or until Kewalai almost assaulted the missionary. The workers had to restrain him. Teacher Kewalai sat on the porch, held his head in his hands, looking at the concrete floor with a frowned face. A crooked vein on his fat neck protruded dangerously. On an impulse, he pounded his thighs with clenched fists and, to everybody's surprise, flew at the missionary. He would have hit him had the men not caught his arms in time, warning him of the danger of fighting at his age. He could die of heart failure and cause his fellow old man to suffer a similar fate. Besides, it wasn't fair to fight someone whose only reason for being in Liberia was to help Liberians. But the words fell on deaf ears. Distraught and breathless, Kewalai struggled to free himself from his restrainers to fight the missionary.

"You want to fight the wrong man, Teacher Kewalai," the missionary told him. "Who am I to change the Church's rule? If I had the power, I could help you. Whenever you're ready, we're ready. Paul, cut off the engine."

Meanwhile, a barefoot old woman dressed in faded lappa, two grownup boys in shredded short pants and T-shirts accompanying her, walked slowly to Kewalai. Their faces looked sulky, their eyes red, doubtless from weeping.

"Kewalai, my brother says we may live with him until we build our own house," the woman said in Loma, a variety of Kpelle I understood.

"Where will we find the money to build a house? Do you know the price of a bundle of zinc?" Kewalai said.

His face beaded with perspiration, his hands trembling violently, Kewalai went into the kitchen, returned to the porch, sat down, and looked at the concrete floor steadily again, one arm in his baggy gown.

"I'll make market," the woman continued to plead. "We can make a farm; we have many children and relatives to help us scratch it. That's what Yakpazuo and his family did when they retired him."

"Look, I'm not Yakpazuo!" he told his wife, whisking a finger at her, one arm still in the gown. Turning somewhat calm and collected, he told the missionary quietly, "I'm ready to go; but wait a moment to let me relieve myself."

"Whenever you're ready, we're ready," the missionary repeated.

The men boarded the truck; the missionary and the driver climbed into the front seat, leaving the door ajar for Kewalai. The engine screamed to a start. Teacher Kewalai stayed so long in the pit latrine behind the dorm that everyone became concerned. The driver cut off the engine and came down, holding the door. After a long, agonizing suspense, Mrs. Kewalai went to the latrine and, knocking the door, told her husband to make haste; everybody was waiting for him. There was no response. After waiting for a long time, she forced the door open and burst into tears, raised her hands to the sky, contorted her body, and collapsed in the grass.

Several men went to her aid, while others went to the latrine to find to their amazement that Kewalai had cut his own throat. They stared at one another with consternation.

"Oh God, what is this? God, why?" they cried.

I was so shocked that I couldn't bear to lay my eyes on the poor dead man as they wrapped his body up in country clothes and put it on the truck, in fulfillment of his own prophesy. The gruesome experience almost caused me to return home. Fortunately, many students came that evening and said they were not surprised to learn that Kewalai had killed himself. With his keen mind, he should have sought employment in Monrovia or in some concession after graduating.

"The missionaries are like parents who care for you when you're a child," the dorm manager remarked, "but expect you to stand on your own feet when you grow up. Who cares for the child that doesn't grow up?"

I pondered over the advice Mrs. Dennis had given me about trusting my future to the Church, but there you got the best education in the country at little cost. I resolved to continue attending mission schools, for what you make of circumstances is what matters, not the circumstances themselves.

GOOD NEWS

"I have good news for you!" Father said as we sat on the porch watching children playing in the moonlight.

"What?" I asked.

"Guess."

Hanging my head, I said, "You've got my tuition for next year."

"Not exactly. Try again."

"You've bought new clothes for me."

"No. Think."

Perhaps Brother Zokpooh had come over from Kwalakomai on a visit, or some relative in Willietaa or Gbangei had sent me a gift. The Dennis family? My mind went blank.

"For years I've been telling you about the benefits of education," Father said. "Now you can see them for yourself. A son of Fuama Chiefdom who went to school and became head of God's house in Liberia has taken over Kpolopele from Ma Miller who has gone home to rest. I knew this man from baby. I told you about him some time ago. I called him Ngalakemeni then, but his real name is Isaac Gbada. He carries his father's surname as you can see. Keikurah Gbada who settled in Tinkayan near Gordi taught his son the importance of hard work. The boy went to the seacoast where he fought his way through school and became God's messenger. I'm proud you're working hard like him. One day you too will become very important.

"Isaac is rich and powerful. Everyone respects him, including white people who call on him for advice. He goes to and from their country at will." Father paused, watched me delightfully, and continued: "We appealed to him to help with your schooling; he said we should take you to him when you came from Zorzor. After learning that your school fees had risen to one hundred dollars, we concluded that your schooling was over. But God said, 'No! I won't permit it!' Then he sent your own brother to help you."

Father said he couldn't handle the fish traps anymore. Once he had almost drowned in the strong current, and Mother had advised him to forget them. She would fight with her fishing net and baskets in Gbonkpotoli Creek. The strands of black hair on his head were now few and the lines on his face had deepened.

With Mother in possession of a *kru* of rice and a cock for the pastor, we went to Kpolopele to meet the great man who was surprisingly hoeing grass in front of a new, modern house located on the western tip of the mission near a palm grove. He cut a lovely figure in his brown leather slippers, khaki short pants, a singlet, a gold watch, and spectacles with a sparkling gold frame. He had solid muscles and a close-cropped, conical head. His face looked severe but benign.

Welcoming us warmly, he took us to his elegant living room where impressive framed pictures of him in company with white people hung on the walls, as well as Jesus on the cross and at prayer in the Garden of Gethsemane. After thanking Mother for the rice and "soup", he addressed Father with the enraptured voice of a long-time friend:

"Old Man Senfenui, thank you for what you're doing for this young man." He looked me over, bobbing his head. "Tomorrow, he'll be of great help not only to himself but also to his people."

"What you've agreed to do for us is a debt we'll never be able to pay," Father said. "As far as we were concerned, his schooling was over."

"Why do we go to school if not to help our people? My man, what's your name?" he asked me.

"Joseph," I said, mindful not to mention "Dennis", for he might expect me to carry my father's surname, too.

"The name of the father of our Lord and Savior Jesus Christ. Who chose it for you?"

"Myself."

"Joseph cared for our Lord until he began his ministry. So, you should be a man who loves and cares for people. Let us pray." After praying, he asked if I had been baptized.

"No, Pastor," I said.

"You're acquainted with *Luther's Small Catechism*?"

"I took it in school."

"Come to church this Sunday. I'll baptize you."

"Then he'll no longer be a part of us," Father said.

"You too could be baptized. You know God and the Lord Jesus Christ. Joe, bring your parents along on Sunday. God loves everybody—young, old, man, woman, black, white, rich, poor—everybody."

"God will bless you, my son," Mother told the pastor.

"Members of the Church pay only a part of their children's school fees in LTI," the pastor explained. "How much they pay depends on the children themselves. If a student gets eighty points at the end of the school year, his parents pay only twenty dollars for school fee. If ninety points, they pay only ten. If his behavior is good, the Church gives him a vacation job to earn his tuition." Looking at me he said, "I have a job for you this vacation. A building job—hard work but good money! Twenty-five dollars per month! Ten dollars more than what other students get!"

"Thank you very much, sir," I said.

"You'll start tomorrow morning. Never shun hard work, my son. What I'm today is due to hard work—and the grace of God. My father was Bandi—we don't see these things in our history books. We only read about the coming of the Congo people and their doings, but we have a history. Long ago, people from Guinea tried to take this country by force. They attacked the Bandi in the north. Had they defeated the Bandi, they'd have added the Western and Central Provinces to Guinea, but my people put up stiff resistance. When the war overwhelmed them, some fled to Sierra Leone, while others fled south. That's how my father settled in Kpelle country. The invaders were defeated only after a brave Bandi man called Seimavile Halingi offered himself as a living sacrifice for the Land. Halingi became a folk hero and Oracle of the Bandi. So, the idea of someone redeeming others with his blood is nothing new to us. My son, the war we must fight now is opening our people's eyes. I passed through fire and storm to prepare for it: emptied chimons for Congo people; made rice, potato, and cassava farms; scrubbed plank floors, hewed wood, fetched water—Look at the top of my head," he bowed his head for me to take a better look. "Do you see a strand of hair there?"

"No, sir," I replied.

"It's because I carried too many buckets of water and bunches of wood on it. Do you smell excreta on me?"

"No, sir."

"Did all the hard work kill me?"

"No, sir."

"Take courage, boy! Work hard everyday."

Pastor Gbada disclosed that while fighting for education in Monrovia, he had many narrow escapes there, but he never ran away. On one occasion they placed the knife to his throat. When he completed the eighth grade, he became a pastoral apprentice under one Dietrich Wedemeyer, a German pastor, who taught him all he knew about the Bible. Now the entire Lutheran Church in Liberia was in his care. The President of Liberia once asked him to join his Cabinet, but he would rather serve God than man.

"Did the white man love me because of good looks?" he asked. "No," he replied. "Or because I'm Bandi? No. Hardworking people are always in great demand everywhere."

After baptizing my parents and me the following Sunday, the pastor invited us to a sumptuous dinner at his modern home. His beautiful Congo wife was most hospitable.

With more than sixty dollars on hand as well as used clothing, shoes, and a letter of recommendation Pastor Gbada gave me, I left for LTI at the end of the vacation. Although I was anxious to see the reputable institute, I decided to spend several days with Jacob before going there.

At Waterside I inquired for Jacob's uncle so that he may show me where Jacob lived, but nobody knew his whereabouts. I learned that the Boat Company was no longer in business. Against my best judgment, I went to the Dennises'. On seeing me, the children clattered downstairs, shouting my name and calling their mother. Jimmy who was splitting wood ambled to me and smilingly slapped his callused hand in mine. Shabby, his toes riddled with jiggers, he was no different from a slave. I felt sorry for him, not that drudgery was bad but because his suffering held no promise. Well, he might be perfectly contented with the life he led and would have considered it a betrayal were he to alter it. Placing my box down I asked him for Jacob.

"Ma man, you ain' ask for you Ma da Jacob plava you worry 'bout?" He reproached me, glancing at my canvassed feet as we snapped fingers. "Jacob fool you and you believey? Who say dey eat human heart here?"

Before I could reply, Mrs. Dennis, dressed in black from head to foot, came to us, a quizzical smile on her thin lips, which still maintained their luster. Her eyes were gleaming. She shook my hand and said, "Da you countryman is a damn liar! Jacob finish runnin' away! He kun look ah ma face after tellin' you da dirty lie. His trouber was he din like to see new face in de house. He hated Jimmy. And Jimmy came here long before him—Welcome home, prodigal son!"

Forcing a smile, I told her, "I on my way to LTI, Ma'am."

"So you high school man na!"

"Yes, Ma'am."

"One tin 'bout Kpelle man: he ga hay but quick to run away." She laughed softly and returned upstairs.

"You ain' wan' stay way us 'gain?" the children cried in a chorus, clutching my hands and staring in my face with curious eyes. "Wa we do you?"

"Nothing," I said. "I still your brother."

When the children followed their mother, Jimmy told me the many tragedies the family had sustained in my absence.

"Granny day," he said, scratching his head roughly. "Pa day also. He die da very nai you and Jacob run away. We ain' know wa ga in his hay he started shootin'. He neva act like da before. Caesar gone America. Dey say he gone school, but I say he gone enjoy. De government ga money to ways—Jacob Watersye near Happy Corner."

"Please take me to him."

"You stranger in Monrovia? Ma man, jes go down Watersye and say 'Happy Corner'. Somebady way show you de place. Everybady in Monrovia go dare: some for woman, some for de big sikalay[45], some for cane jew[46], some to steal! A I wasin busy I gan take you dare. See you 'gain."

Jimmy knew that I knew he was lying. Had the Old Man gone crazy, he would have shot someone upstairs before coming downstairs. His reluctance to accompany me to Jacob and Mrs. Dennis' quick departure with her clan obviously meant that they didn't expect me to believe their account of Jacob's absence.

At Waterside a *yana* boy roughly directed me to Happy Corner. I wandered in vain among clusters of zinc shacks for an hour. I had to get directions from a girl who displayed her full breasts for me to admire. I wasn't so impressed, for the female breasts were nothing strange to me; they were constantly on display upcountry. Only a mad man would consider them a sexual symbol; but this girl's unusual invitation warmed my heart. I felt love and pity for her.

"You wan' me?" she asked, baring her shiny white teeth. Without waiting for an answer, she added, "One dollar. I ga place." I swallowed a knot in my throat. "Come," she beckoned to me.

As we squeezed among the shacks, lore of distresses men suffered in the hands of girls in Monrovia occurred to me. Some were said to be agents of bandits to whom they took you in broad daylight and had you robbed,

45. Distortion of "big cigarette"or opium.

46. Cane juice—local gin brewed from sugar cane.

stripped, and beaten to death. Some were said to be spirits in disguise who beguiled you to sleep with them only to rouse in the morning and find yourself lying naked in a graveyard.

"My friend," I called the girl as she rocked her buttocks before me, "I want you for true, but I new here. I looking for my friend they call Jacob Dennis."

"Oh, da rascal?" she said. "He livin' by Happy Corner because he wan' all de women in Monrovia. And dey givin' hin' hell! One Vai girl wan' kill hin. He alway go home drunk."

"Please take me to his place."

"Leh do de tin before going dare. How long a way take? You scare? No stranger in Monrovia."

"Let me put my load down first. It not good to walk about with load on your head."

"I way take caruf you load."

"You play with my woman palava? Let find my friend first. My Pa say, if you stranger, find sleeping place before looking for woman."

"I ain' ga man, a dawa you scaruf. De man I wor havin' one Kru girl takey from me. Maybe her tin' ga gold and diamon'."

"What your name?"

"Miatta. Why, you scare?" Pursing her lips, she declared, "Any man who talk 'bor bin stranger—his Pa say so, his Ma say so—a na man."

"People are known by their names, any so?"

"Yah my place," Miatta pointed at a small, rusty zinc shack surrounded by filth. "Any tine you wan' me, come here and ask for Miatta."

We met Jacob at dusk sitting at a table on the porch of a shack, his head clasped in his hands, the elbows resting on the table. A lighted candle in a small, white plate sat on the table. Sound asleep and snoring, he reeked of cane juice. Miatta shook him briskly and said:

"You ga stranger you sleepin'? Man wake up!" Jacob babbled, stretched, and jolted.

"What I do 'gain, heh?" he cried. "What—who deh? Joseph! What wind blow you disye, my man?" He yawned lengthily, his face glowing with a smile. We held hands for a long time, staring at each other.

"You takin' me to be da Vai girl, heh?" Miatta told him in a mean voice, whisking her finger at him. "She comin' for you!"

Jacob watched the girl with squinting eyes and looked at me.

"Jacob, you too dry," I told him.

"Malaria wan' kill me-o," he said. "De Freeport job I ga a hell. Who de girl behine you? She you who?" He scrutinized Miatta again.

"She directed me here. I just met her."

"Jacob, you gan loka my face and say you don' know me?" Miatta said.

"A you ga sometin' for her, givey to her and leh her go!" Jacob advised me.

"Wa you drivin' me for?" Miatta protested. "You tink I gan ask you for money? Jacob, you too cheap! Da why da Vai girl givin' you hell. A I war her,

I gan cut you tin."

"You be doin' bad to youself!" Jacob laughed.

"You na de only man."

"A you do da to me, wa man way wan' you?"

I gave Miatta one dollar, thanked her for her help, and told her to go and come back later.

"Jacob, you see?" Miatta held the money in her open palm before Jacob, smiling. "I ain' do natin for de man and he gime money. But you par' a you sleep whole nai way woman you won' give her wan cent. You de first Kpelle man I see so mean."

"Go na and don' come back here," Jacob told her. "You know dis man?"

"I ain' ga to know hin," Miatta said. "I ga sometin' for hin, and he ga sometin' for me."

"Da people husband, you hear? Leave hin lone!"

"Daha to talk to woman? You ain' ga sister? You ain' ga shame?"

"De man taya! He comin' from far way; he ain' eat natin yeh and you wan' sleep way hin? You wan' kill?"

"Da you business?"

"I know your place, any?" I told Miatta. "I'll come there."

I placed my box under the table. Jacob offered me his chair and hunted another one in a room down the dark hall.

"What news, my man?" he asked in Kpelle.

"You don't like Miatta really," I said.

"That Vai girl's money business is hell. It's good she has gone. If you make mistake and get between her legs, you're finished. She and one boy had it out here the other day; the matter ended up in court!"

"What d'you mean? She looks friendly!"

"Don't be surprised if she steals your box. She sees that you're a stranger and all you own is in that box."

"You swear, Jacob? The girl's too beautiful to act like that! Her round breasts, her glossy black hair—"

"My man, I say what news?" Jacob smiled wanly.

"You're the one to tell the news. How come you've left the Dennises? I thought you said you'd never leave them?"

"The people jailed me because they said I burst their secret and caused you to run away," Jacob said, looking into the night. "After my release, I had to bribe Jimmy with five dollars to get your clothes."

"Jacob, you're more than a brother to me."

"Your people treated me as their own son. They gave me chickens, rice, palm oil, and many other things. I brought only the chickens and the rice because I didn't have enough car fare."

"Were they to give you everything they had, it wouldn't have been enough to pay you for what you did for me."

"It's God's doing. Thank him."

"I thought the police would hold us responsible for Old Man Dennis' death because we were the only ones in the yard when he fell. It wasn't even mentioned on police report."

"After he killed the patrolman, shot me in the leg and you in the arm, no one in his right mind would say we killed him. Besides, everybody knew that the surly old man drank too much and suffered from high blood pressure and diabetes, the bigshots' great sickness. Had I not pulled you away, he'd have killed you. What made you so bold? Joe, let's drop that subject."

"I went back to my mission people. I'm on my way to LTI for high school."

"Well done! One thing you should remember, though; if you know all the books and no one knows you in Monrovia, you won't get anywhere."

"One thing I know," I retorted, "once I'm well educated I'll find a job. A good player doesn't look for jersey."

"My man, education without experience is no education."

"What is experience? Knowing people in Monrovia?"

"No need arguing with you, my friend. Time will tell."

"Miatta told me that one Vai girl is giving you hell," I changed the subject. "If you're going to live with a woman, get the right one."

"And where will you find such a woman? My friend, you're dreaming." Jacob smiled faintly and killed a mosquito on his leg. "I used to hide myself to visit Moima when I was staying with the Dennis family. Gave her every cent I could put my hand on. I didn't know I was playing with fire. Congo man says, 'Kind heart gave nanny goat short tail.'" He told the proverb in English. "But let her go. I'm still young."

"What really happened between you people?"

"First, she doesn't sit down. Lies with every man in Monrovia, if not in all Liberia. Has made me enemy to even my best friends. I should have looked for a girl at home. We leave the best girls upcountry and go round the world looking for trouble." Jacob smiled broadly.

"A home-mate might not take you seriously."

"Many boys I know married their home-mates and are doing fine. Their girls make market to support them in school. But girls down here bleed men to death."

"If you bring a girl to Monrovia, don't you think she'll behave like girls here?"

"Before her eyes are opened, I'll have put my own training in her head."

"They say boys here use illiterate girls to get their education, but drop them when they're through with school and marry educated ones. What girl can stand such treatment? Perhaps your Vai girl—what's her name?"

"Moima."

"Has Moima been to school?"

"It's no reason why she should be so violent. She can leave any time she wants. We're not married!"

"That's the problem! You're not married! The girl feels insecure! You're taking away the fruit of her life, and you might drop her some day!"

"The missionaries are certainly putting strange ideas in your head. I wonder how you'll confront real life. Look, Moima wants me to go to bed with her, but she's six months gone! Imagine that! I don't want to be charged with murder."

I slapped a mosquito on my thigh and shook my body.

"You're fat," Jacob told me, laughing. "Plenty food for the mosquitoes! You really enjoyed the country—We're sleeping out here tonight. We'll find bread to eat tomorrow morning. That wicked girl took everything I own out of the room and went where I don't know. It's better we sleep in chairs outside here rather than on the cold cement floor. We could catch pneumonia, and she could set this shack on fire while we're sleeping."

"Why does she treat you like this, Jacob?"

"Because I have a girl friend. What to do? Cassava leaf isn't for goat alone."

"Jacob, I comin' for you! Kafili[47] like you joking way Vai blood! A I kill you self who way question me? Jacob you kafili!"

"That's her," Jacob said." Bend your head." We ducked. A heavy stone flew over us and crashed into the zinc wall.

"Moima, I ga stranger!" Jacob pleaded. "Don' brin' plava to hin."

"Stranger no stranger, me and you for a tonai! You either kill me or I kill you!"

I put out the candle and hid myself in a dark corner of the porch. Jacob ran into their room and locked the door.

"My friend, I beg you," I pleaded with the girl. "Please leave him for my sake!"

"I ain' gan leave hin for God sake," Moima screamed at me. "You betta go where you comin' from!"

She was tall—clearly older and bigger than Jacob. How she could muster the strength to fight with her belly so big was amazing. She burst the door open with a nasty kick, and one of the noisiest fights I had ever witnessed occurred in the room. The couple crashed into the zinc walls repeatedly, Moima screamed hysterically. You would think the house was tumbling down. Apparently, nobody else lived in it. Jacob asked me to find him a police, but the fight had already drawn a crowd that included one. Bustling into the room, the police stopped the racket and brought the couple outside, holding them apart. Their clothes shredded up and their faces bloody, they traded insults, jabbing fingers at each other. Several women said that Moima would deliver that night.

Jacob told me over his shoulder to wait for him on the porch. He would soon be back.

"Natin will happen to you," he assured me. "Dis Happy Corner."

"Who's he?" inquired the police.

"My brother from upcountry. He was here when dis demon jumpon me."

"Da your mammy de demon!" Moima howled.

---

47. A slave, word derived from the Vai language.

"Shut up!" cried the policeman. "Not so, bofor you way sleep insye."

Dejected, I sat on the porch in the fetid warm breeze, slapping my arms, thighs, legs, and body to fight off mosquitoes. I lit the candle, placed my elbows on the table, and clasped my head in my hands. When I was about to take a nap, a group of boys between the ages of five and ten suddenly appeared before the porch, singing and dancing by the rhythm of an empty milk can one of them was tapping with a stick:

Good luck way follow you,
Good luck way follow you.
God way bless you,
God way bless you.

Good luck way follow you,
Good luck way follow you.
God way bless you,
God way bless you.

After a few minutes, the tallest of the boys stepped forward and saluted with his left hand.

"Stranger," he said, "we come to make you happy. De boys dem wan' twenty-fie cen' to buy bread."

I told him that I had no money, and that police had just arrested my stranger father for fighting his wife. I might help them some other time. One of them flashed a light at my box and said:

"My man, a look like you ain' ga hay. De man ga money insye da bak. Brinkey here!" His friends echoed the command.

Quickly pulling my box from under the table, I sat on it and shouted at the boys, "Get out of my sight, or I'll tear you to pieces! See my fist?" I shook my clenched fist in the air. They fled but promised to return shortly, bringing their older brothers along.

"We gan see wa you ga in da bak," they said with one voice and resumed their song with a slight change in the wording:

Bad luck way follow you,
Bad luck way follow you.
God way curse you,
God way curse you.

Bad luck way follow you,
Bad luck way follow you.
God way curse you,
God way curse you.

I ran to the Dennises' with my box under my arm. It was bedtime; only Jimmy lingered in the yard, carrying cooking utensils and other adjuncts into the house.

"You seen Jacob?" he asked me.

"Yes, but he in jail," I said.

"'Gain? Wa for?"

"Fighting his wife."

"Jacob ain' lokor da Vai girl way killim," Jimmy said, interlacing his fingers behind his neck, his head pinned to the ground. He paced up and down for a moment and said, "Kpelle man woman plava ain' natin small. I ain' know wa Jacob see on da Vai girl."

"They to the police station. I want go there."

"To do wa?" Jimmy looked at me gravely. "My man, a you sit down, your trouber sit down."

"I have to see him."

"You wan' go dare, go! Da you *kpoimeni*." He giggled, looking at me with the satisfaction of having given good advice. "No way for me to take you dare," he went on, "but everybady in Monrovia know de place. A disye," he pointed north of the city.

At the police station I found out that they had released Moima but Jacob was still in jail. The case would be taken to court the following day.

"Your friend is charged with attempted homicide and infraction of the peace," a police officer told me upon my query. "That's the charges we put on a man for fighting a pregnant woman. You'll see him tomorrow but not tonight."

"May I sit here until tomorrow morning?" I pointed at a bench in the long, narrow hall.

"Sure! But why not go home? Your friend is perfectly safe. Nothing will happen to him."

"I prefer sleeping here," I told the police. "I stranger in town, and Jacob is my stranger father. I know nobody else who can lodge me. The best place for a homeless man is the police station."

"Sure! You're in good hands," said the policeman.

Meanwhile, a group of agitated Fanti fishermen trooped to the Sergeant's desk with a man who had a large head wound covered with a thick blood clot.

"We pickup dis man on de beach," a huge thug among them explained to the Sergeant whose head was bowed on his folded arms, sleeping. He didn't budge even though the fisherman spoke loudly. "Dey war sacrificin' hin for fish! De people dare right now! Dey dare offisa! I can take you dare!"

"My man, hold you peace," the Sergeant said dully, raising his sleek head and trying to focus his eyes. "Why you people didn't take the man to hospital before coming here? He has lost much blood and could drop dead any time!" The police yawned prodigiously and sighed.

Having had my full share of the day's problems, I placed my box under the bench, sat directly above it, leaned against the unpainted concrete wall, and went to sleep with the assurance of being in good hands.

The following morning, I discovered to my amazement that my box had vanished. Paralyzed with fright, my heart in my mouth, I asked the Desk

Sergeant whether he had not kept it somewhere for safety. He said I should ask the night-shift commander.

"Who is he? Where is he?" I asked with alarm.

"How do I know?" he said crisply. "Don't bother me!"

I reported the theft to the secretary of the police director who listened sympathetically and promised to inform her boss about it when he rang the bell. In half an hour, the bell rang.

"The Chief said, "the girl told me on returning from the director's office, "that you have hidden your box and falsely accused the Liberian National Police of theft of property. Leave the Headquarters at once; otherwise, you'll be detained for insubordination to constituted authority and assassination of character."

Leaving the police station downcast, confused, and numb, I wandered about the city with no idea of what to do with myself. For the first time I noted that Monrovia was probably the most neglected city on earth. The countless chores and errands that had claimed all my time and attention at the Dennises', never permitted me to survey the sights, sounds, and scents of "the capital of the *kwii* world" which I had idolized in childhood. Walking now from Buzzie Quarters through Soniwen to Mamba Point, I was disillusioned by the array of congested, makeshift zinc shacks infested with swarms of flies, mosquitoes, cockroaches, and mice bearing the most contagious and deadly diseases imaginable—and overcrowded with a mass of poverty-stricken humanity engaged in the interminable search for the almighty daily bread.

Rocky Mamba Point, considered the most prestigious residential area of the city, had only two streets; its narrow alleys were impassable because of sharp-edged boulders posing grave danger to the hapless pedestrian who fell on them by accident. From this elevation, the city was one big conglomeration of brown corrugated zinc roofs cluttered along Broad Street and extending all the way to Bushrod Island and Sinkor. Ironically, isolated mansions dazzling with radiant colors, clearly unrelated to their mean surroundings, mottled the city.

Strangely enough, the most enterprising traders in Monrovia were Lebanese who ran shops stocked with imported goods such as clothing, electronics, canned foods, building materials, and so on. Nigerians, Ghanaians, and Guineans dominated the petty trade; the fishing industry, and public transport. Liberian traders engaged in subsistence business mainly, selling meager supplies of vegetables, rice, farina, peanuts, kola nuts, roasted meat, and fish on sidewalks and at General Market.

At Waterside streaming crowds of hawkers, pickpockets, and idlers amazingly reveled in their indigence. They laughed, joked, shrieked obscenities, trampled each other's toes in the cramped, narrow streets reeking with huge piles of refuse in which destitute kids scrounged foodstuffs.

Petty traders, squawking a thousand tongues, regarded my haggard appearance with a mixture of anger, indifference, hate, curiosity, and pity. My sluggish crossing of streets miffed taxi drivers who recklessly steered their smoking engines at my heels, screaming curses behind my back:

"You ain' wan' live, go lay in you bay and die!" shrilled a driver who fiercely pounded his steering wheel behind me at the intersection of Mechlin and Water Streets.

"You wan' put me in trouble, sonofabitch!" another yelled as I jumped across Water Street, heedless of traffic flow.

"A look like dey swear hin for stealin'."

"Somor dese boy take de big sikalay."

Completely absorbed in myself, I paid no attention to the verbal onslaughts. While passing by a Fanti woman who was selling dried bony near General Market and nursing a baby, I heard her say:

"Somebady pickin, my people, some woman child."

After a push and a slap from a peddler who claimed that I had almost thrown his tray of merchandise off his head, I bent to the woman and begged her for a bony. She wrapped several in cement paper and handed them to me, watching me with pity.

Munching the thorny dry fish, I merged with the streaming crowds, which had become thicker, impersonal, and unruly. The disinterested milieu kindled no feeling of guilt or shame; it swallowed you up when all the attention suddenly turns to some unexpected excitement: thugs are mugging a thief, or a crazy man in sacks is standing amidst traffic, harassing drivers and pedestrians for money. The cry "Rogue! Rogue! Rogue!" resounds and takes on a reiterated rhythm; the thief is pummeled with fists until police intervene. The crazy man is stoned, knocked about or given a nickel or dime by a beneficent shopper who shouts at his assailants to stop the racket.

At midnight the streets were abandoned, except for knots of thugs and prostitutes who slipped in the clusters of zinc shacks round Water Street when a police van careened to a stop by Salami Brothers, and a dozen uniformed men with side arms hustled out and chased them.

As I stood by the shop, watching the scene with interest, a puny police officer, gold badges glittering on his shirt and cap, swaggered to me and panted:

"You under arrest for vagrancy." He grinned maliciously. I had thought the fellow wanted my help in tracking his quarry.

"What is vagrancy?" I asked him as he furtively applied cuffs to my wrists. No match for my fists, he was lucky he carried a gun and I was thoroughly spent.

Before replying, he pushed back the peak of his cap and raked perspiration off his forehead with the air of a hard worker. Pulling a white handkerchief from a side pocket, he wiped his face and the nape of his neck. "Geh insye," he shoved me into the van. "You way know wa dey call vagrancy ah de police station."

Two huge policemen gave me twenty-five lashes on my bare back at the prison gate. As they administered the whipping, I told them that I had been in the street because they had jailed my stranger father for fighting his wife. With nowhere to put up for the night and having lost all my possessions at this very police station, all I could do was wander about town until daybreak. The inmates scoffed at my elaborate explanation, which, they said, would do me no good.

"He ain' geh work to do but steal! Killim!" one of them shouted.

"He lie on de police. Gay hin hell!" another quipped.

"He ga mouf for true! Naa a ga hin in jail! Hee heeeee!"

"Make his medicine proper, offisa!"

"Gay hin pepper!"

After the beating, I was pushed into one of the cramped cells as they placed another "vagrant" under the whip. The stifled cell reeked of urine, feces, and vomit. Blood oozed from my wounds. My fellow inmates continued laughing and giggling:

"Naa you member of de society!" one of them remarked with pity.

"Ma son in Monrovia! Da a! Heee! Heeeee!"

I was silent throughout the ordeal; hardly did I sleep. Perhaps they had freed Jacob, I thought, or he would have said or done something during the beating. Much to my surprise, he crawled out of a corner early in the morning and tapped my shoulder as I sat on the cold, cement floor, my arms wrapped around my knees, my head bowed.

"Dey way soon free you," he told me. "You din steal! You din kill! Dey bring you here to keep you from de streets till daytine. When dey free you, go to my Pa and stay way hin till you geh betta and go home. And tell hin to come geh me from dis nasty place."

"Who say you leavin' here jesna?" a voice shrilled at Jacob. "You ain' hear de girl you beat born day baby?"

"Murderer!" the inmates cried.

"Witchcraft!"

"Dey way kill you! Hang you by you neck!"

Going back to his corner, Jacob sat down, wrapped his arms round his knees and bowed his head as if the provocation did not concern him. A succession of heavy blows accompanying piercing screams and shuffling feet suddenly broke the silence. Looking over my shoulder from the iron-barred window where I tried to catch some fresh air, I saw Jacob and a ruffian hooked together and twisting from side to side. Rushing to them, some prisoners held Jacob by the arms while others struggled with the ruffian. The husky ruffian pulled his right arm free and threw a blow that landed on the wrong temple. The cell lapsed into commotion. Voices screamed, heads crashed against the concrete walls, indiscriminate blows thudded torsos, feet rasped the floor, the iron gate gritted. Boiling with impotent rage, I danced around with clenched fists, watching Jacob who now fought somebody else while his assailant rained blows on a different man he had pinned to the floor. The fighting ceased abruptly when the only police on duty roused from his nap, tottered to the door of the cell, and said, "Hey! You're crazy! Your don' stop fightin' your way not live to tell de story!" He was fumbling for his gun.

"Da Jacob!" diverse voices proclaimed, everybody watching the police with anxiety.

"No, dana me!" Jacob tried to say, pointing at the ruffian who sidled up to me. I fired the fellow with a savage blow; someone held the second one behind me. Turning round I caught the neck of the meddler in a headlock and sent a sharp blow into his mouth just before he bit my chest. Blood poured from his mouth and from my hand and chest.

No more in doubt as to the culprit of the row, the police opened the door, seized my arm, and said, "Ma man, you gettin' twenty-five lashay way governmen' dash jesna. Everybady stop fightin' but you! What kinda head you ga?" Before he could mete out the punishment, he landed flat on his belly and the prisoners stampeded out. Several pistol shots popped outside. A prisoner had made off with his gun! I flew past Buzzie Quarters and up Camp Johnson Road, looking over my shoulder for Jacob, but nobody was following. Perhaps the other prisoners, using better judgment, had disappeared in the raveled alleys of Buzzie Quarters and Soniwen. I stopped running and began walking slowly decently to avoid suspicion. Only a stray dog barked at me.

I decided to go to Gbanoimu as Jacob had suggested. He had enough sense to avoid the claws of the police and go home. After I had crossed Vai Town Bridge, he mysteriously appeared at my side.

"Joe," he called me breathlessly. I turned to him, greatly relieved. "You ga sense," he said. "I tort dey ga you; a we walk fast we gan reach Gbanoimu before twelve. Where you box?"

"They stole it at the police station."

"My God, what kindoff country a dis?"

"Jacob, I have my life. Once you have life, you have everything."

Speaking Kpelle, Jacob said, "We were trying to break jail—and you took it seriously. Were you hurt?"

"Only slight hand and chest wounds. I'm sure the police man was shot."

Jacob laughed and said, "Were he killed, he looked for it. Why did he get drunk on duty?"

We reached Gbanoimu before noon. Jacob's father, who lay in a hammock on the porch, watched our wretched condition with concern and sat up.

"What have you boys been doing? Fighting?" he asked, wrinkling his nose.

Jacob did all the talking.

"I don't think it's in your interest to go back to Monrovia for now," said Old Man Sensireh after Jacob narrated the story of our second narrow escape from Monrovia. "You boys should spend the rest of the year away from there."

Jacob made an on-the-spot decision:

"Data," he said, "I'm going to Weasua to dig diamond. Once you have enough money, you get everything you need in this world. Monrovia is full of too much trouble and confusion."

I went home the following morning.

GOD CAN TALK FOR HIMSELF

My parents and I decided that I find a job and earn some money before going back to school. Experience was a great teacher. I needed acquaintance with life outside of the classroom to learn how to survive the chaos and hostility of the world and put into practical use the knowledge I had gained in school. Of course, the decision derived mostly from lack of funds. The prospect of my parents' raising half my tuition and transport fare to LTI was just unthinkable.

I settled for a tapping job in Firestone, which posed no problem to obtain, for the company needed all the tappers it could get. In addition, Firestone provided food and lodgings for its workers, so I would save enough money for the following school year.

I got employment in Camp Forty-Five, the capital of Firestone, where its manager gave me one of the countless red brick two-room houses standing in straight rows. My "task" comprised four hundred rubber trees to tap each morning and convey the latex to the factory. After a week of intensive training, I could handle the tapping knife expertly and carry the latex in zinc buckets hooked to a split reed on my shoulder, one bucket before me and another behind, careful not to spill a drop of latex.

I thought of going for Sianeh and Guladia for Sianeh to do the housekeeping and the baby to get used to me, but another baby would come, making me abandon school to see after the growing family. I must continue with the struggle, alone.

My headman, called Charlie Mano from the Central Province, was delighted to know that I could read and write. He requested my help in keeping the workers' record of production. At times he gave me a dollar or two for my service and permitted me to eat at his house. I gave his wife my monthly ration of thirty cups of rice and a gallon of palm oil.

Curious as usual, I once asked him why he was named for his tribe. He said his Mano name wasn't only difficult to pronounce but petrifying: "Gor Klebo Mi," or "The man who can circumcise leopard."

"Whenever people learn the meaning of my name, they fear me," he said. "I'd rather be respected."

The demanding job didn't permit me to visit home throughout the year. We worked every day of the week, rain or shine, Sunday or holiday. With savings totaling one hundred dollars, sufficient to defray my school expenses for a year, I quit the job after Christmas to spend a month with my parents before going to LTI. Afraid that I had forfeited the privilege of attending the mission, I appealed to Pastor Gbada for another letter of recommendation. He was disturbed because I had wasted a whole year in Firestone. Why had I elected to work for money after sustaining robbery in Monrovia instead of asking his help?

"Maybe you thought you had made it," he said. "You need college education to make it in Liberia today. I'm happy you've decided to continue with your schooling."

Again, he gave me used clothing, shoes, and a letter of recommendation for the principal of LTI. Not a minute I wasted in Monrovia. Upon arriving at Waterside, I immediately boarded a pickup for Harrisburg. Located on the eastern bank of the Deyn, the century-old campus was small but self-contained. The Deyn spread out to a gigantic size here; its roaring waves, which dashed without respite against jutting boulders and the rugged shores, dominated the mission's atmosphere.

Shaded by huge plum trees, the boys' dorm stood in the middle of the campus. West of it, looming on a grassy hill, was a two-story building, the largest on campus; it contained the girls' dorm, all five classrooms, the dining room, and the chapel. Scattered on the twenty-acre campus were homes for the missionaries, teachers, and married students. A football field lay directly behind the boys' dorm.

With the assistance of seniors, teachers ensured that all students observed all rules and regulations of the school, especially those concerning good behavior and study. Small wonder the institute enjoyed a reputation for discipline and academic excellence. Our day began at five-thirty in the morning and ended at nine-thirty at night, when all students were supposed to be in bed. Every hour of the day was carefully programmed as on the other missions.

The teachers were predominantly white American missionaries who mastered their subjects. They kept us extremely busy and took great interest in us and our future. I especially enjoyed the physics and chemistry teacher who also taught music. Witty, astute, strikingly beautiful and skillful in teaching, she commanded the love and admiration of the students. Her husband was also popular with the students; he taught Christian Ethics and sports. The principal, whom we fondly called Daddy, was widely read; he always dressed in the latest style in fashion. The learned pastor taught the New Testament and African History. He encouraged students to absorb as much knowledge as possible and always answered their questions, not only on subjects he taught, but also on any matter of interest—something our Liberian teachers found disturbing. I often borrowed books from his library to read.

Like most rural male students, I partly supported myself in LTI by cutting logs and conducting evangelism upcountry. Kpelle students carried on their evangelistic mission among the Kpelle in Bong and lower Lofa Counties, while Loma students carried on theirs among the Loma of Lofa County. Why the Church confined its works to these two tribes in exclusion of fourteen others in the country was incomprehensible. They used the logs to cook for the students and heat missionary homes during the cold rainy season. Each log had to be no less than four inches in diameter and twelve feet in length—and sold for two cents. We cut logs during quiet hour each weekday and all of Saturday. On the average, I cut about a hundred pieces per week. Older students sometimes cut up to two hundred and fifty pieces per week.

A veteran missionary, who served briefly as our principal, turned down my first application for an evangelism job because "the faculty recommends you with reservation on account of bad disposition." The "bad disposition" phrase derived from several fights I had on campus. Fighting in LTI always carried a penalty for both parties, although the guilty party carried a heavier sentence.

Evangelism gave us an opportunity to share with our people what we learned in school—especially Christian education—and gain experience. Sometimes it was an uphill struggle. I remember a blind old man in Kologbanei turning down my first invitation to service. "My friend," he told me, "have you ever seen me in your church?"

"God loves you," I assured him. "He wants you to be his friend."

"If God loves me, why am I blind?" the old man shouted at me. "Look, my friend, God lives in heaven and not in that little thatched hut where you meet every night to prattle with your girl friends."

However, most villagers attended service, and we taught them the Bible and gospel songs. We were dispatched in pairs, and members of our congregations provided us with food and lodgings. Although I loved evangelism and even wanted to become a pastor, I discovered that preaching in tribal society was risky. The villagers never took kindly to the unassuming young man who posed as "God's messenger" and idled in town all day living on their sweat. To them, only a lazy person would want to live by word of mouth alone. What was worse, many evangelists left behind pregnant girl friends at the end of their missions, broke up marriages, and viciously attacked the well-favored traditional practices of the tribes. Heads of parishes usually recommended the dismissal of evangelists found guilty of sexual offense; the institute implemented such recommendations without hesitation. But the missionaries ignored the villagers' complaints about evangelists' disrespect for aspects of their cultures that conflicted with Christian teachings.

I tried my utmost to win the people's confidence at my preaching points by befriending them. I didn't bother their women, nor permit education to be a barrier between us. I helped them with their farming, drank palm wine with them, hunted and fished with them, and shared with them what little assets I had such as money, bath soaps, and clothes. However, they bitterly resented my attack on such "unchristian" practices as ancestral worship, sand cutting, witch-hunting, dealing in fetishes, and conducting secret societies. They could even tolerate sexual offense once it involved consenting adults, but they found it impossible to forgive any attack on their culture. I often preached against the Poro and Sande Societies for using fear and intimidation as their instruments of operation. It was in the village of Zamei in the Western Province that my attack on these core institutions put me in trouble. One Sunday I told the congregation the reasons why the Church opposed the Poro and Sande Societies.

"Before *kwii* people came here," I began, curious eyes trained on me, "we conducted the Poro and Sande to teach our children how to cope with the demands of everyday living and be good citizens and parents. Now we have modern schools to teach us everything about life and a government to see to our security—"

The sermon wasn't half-complete when everybody but little children left the palaver house in anger. The following morning my partner Benda Folokula (nicknamed General because of his interest in the military) said the village had decided at a meeting during the night to expel me. He had asked their forgiveness on my behalf. The Zoes and the Elders agreed to rescind their decision if I refrained from preaching against their sacred institutions and beliefs. Knowing that it was impossible for me to make such a concession, General told me to preach the gospel only.

"God can talk for himself," he said.

Even though I heeded his advice, the villagers continued to abhor my preaching and even my presence. Only children attended service whenever I preached, but the palaver house was always full to capacity with adults whenever General preached. People scarcely responded to my greetings and wouldn't have me visit their farms, homes, or wine trees anymore. I told General that I was afraid my mission had ended. I wanted to go home and find something else to do.

"Be patient," he advised me. "Their anger will cool down. Conduct Kpelle classes for them. They consider reading and writing their own language a miracle. I'll go to Sanoyea for Kpelle books."

Shortly after his departure for Sanoyea, fever struck me. I didn't know whether it was due to anxiety over my estrangement or to malaria. I lay trembling in bed long after sunrise one morning, wrapped up in all my clothes. My head ached and cold spasms ran through my body. A decrepit old man who no longer farmed, knocked at my door early that morning.

"Tiseh, Tiseh, what happened to you?" he croaked. There was a hint of irony in his voice. I knew that he wasn't concerned about my welfare. For several weeks now, nobody in Zamei really cared whether I lived or died. "This is not the time of day for a young man to be sleeping. Everybody has gone to their farms."

Forcing myself out of bed and opening the door, I told the old fellow, "I'm not well. I don't own a farm. Why are you bothering me?"

He looked me over briefly and smiled as if my affliction amused him. I regarded the incident a premonition of danger. I had either been bewitched or served with poisoned food or drink—and this wretched antediluvian had me under observation to see if the wicked design was working. With a painful chill running down my spine, I sauntered to the outskirts and collected *koyorokpo*, the most potent malaria herb I knew; but where would I boil it?

The men of Zamei wasted no time to quarantine me, though sickness was an ordinary feature of village life. Accusing me of being a witch, they hastily constructed a thatched blind on the western outskirts, built a fire in it, and placed me on a bamboo mat there, demanding that I confess my witchcraft activity or I would die.

"Have you ever eaten human flesh in your dream?" a Zoe dressed in full medical outfit asked me. Too sick and annoyed to talk, I only shook my head. "Don't you want to live?" he said harshly, raising his black cowtail and bringing it down with force. "The only way the witch medicine will leave you is by confessing your witchcraft activity."

"Ha! Haa! Haaaaa!" someone laughed. "Now he's helpless! About to die! Every night he tells us to throw our charms and spirit stones away and depend on God alone. Let God come down from heaven and save him."

"When these kids smell the *kwii* life, they turn against their own people. But nothing under the sun can change the sacred customs we got from the Ancestors."

"If God didn't want us to wear charms, would he have given us the sense to make them?"

"This fellow's attacks are especially ruthless: 'Don't worship the Ancestors' spirits,'—how will we enjoy their blessings and protection? 'Don't wear charm or talisman,'—how will we be protected from our enemies? 'Don't cut sand,'—how will we foretell the future? 'Don't make sacrifice, for Jesus made it all,'—how will we be cleansed of evil and bad luck?"

"Stop wasting your breath, my friend. The man will soon die!"

"What!" the Zoe exclaimed after inspecting my body without seeing a single tribal mark. "Women, leave us!" His command was unnecessary, for no woman was around. "The fellow is a sinner! The Devil must kill him right now!"

"Don't put us in trouble with the government," someone advised. "There's a law against initiating schoolboys without their consent. Besides, the women are in charge of the land."

After languishing in the deplorable shed for four days, I improved somewhat and was transferred to my house. When I informed General about my humiliation on his return from Sanoyea, he said it was something to expect. "Did Jesus not say his followers would suffer all sorts of persecution including death on his account?" he reminded me.

"We can change their hate into love," I told him.

"Have you ever seen such a thing happen?" cried he. "Listen, my friend. We came here to work for school fees, not to change the people's way of life. Only God can do that."

"Let's persuade them to build an airstrip so that the missionaries may construct a school and a dispensary here," I told him. "Whenever a village builds an airstrip, the Church carries on much development there. This will win the people's love for us."

"Don't be misled, my friend," General snapped. "Such a project takes no less than a year to complete. School opens in two months; starting a project you can't complete is bad."

"There's nothing wrong with trying, General."

Admitting the great progress airstrips had wrought in Parakwelle, Sanoyea, Totota, Belefanai, Zorzor, and Kpolopele, the people approved the project without reservation and commenced work on it immediately, their only request being exemption from *porlortor* work for its duration. Paramount Chief Korro, who was more than anxious to see development in his Chiefdom, made that concession. All able-bodied men and women in Zamei wielded spades, axes, cutlasses, and hoes with verve; maidens encouraged men with cheers and songs. Not even "the day of rest" interfered with the work. Most regrettably, the workers' meal comprised only dry rice and palm oil. They needed protein. Early one sunny morning I borrowed a shotgun "to look for soup" since the project prevented them from hunting or fishing.

Unacquainted with the forest round Zamei, I followed the road to Parakwelle, painstakingly searching in trees along the road for birds and monkeys, but the excursion yielded no more result than one pitiful, young hornbill.

On my way home late in the afternoon, the sky grew ominously dark and stormy. Branches of trees broke in the fury of the wind. Walking hurriedly to get out of danger, I heard guttural voices behind me. Turning round I saw two soldiers dressed in khaki uniforms; one carrying a heavy gun on his shoulder; the other carrying a sheathed dagger in his hand; and a *porlortor* boy with a large bundle on his head, emerge from a bend of the road. Soaked to the skin with perspiration, they walked with wide strides and swinging arms, the short, bow-legged *porlortor* hopping along. When they came abreast of me, I noted with misgivings that their eyes were bloodshot and they reeked of cane juice.

"Hello, Old Man," they said together, staring at me with arrogance. At twenty-one, I was already an old man! "Where're you going?" they crowed.

Replying their greetings cordially, I informed them that I was looking for soup for people constructing an airstrip in Zamei.

The soldier with the gun said rudely, "They say you men in this town don't do *porlortor* work. Who made you people kings? You had better get that idea out of your head. Give me the gun!" I decided to cooperate. He took out the shell and said, "So you wanted to kill the Corporal?" He watched me in anger and threw the empty gun to me.

"I hunt birds and animals and not people," I said fearlessly, waving the hornbill in his face. "Why did you take my shell?"

"This is a government road," he said gruffly. "You have no right traveling on it with loaded firearm."

As they strutted away, the corporal said in English, "Country man, you ga to hoe hin tighe. He like turtle; you ain' put fire on hin back, he kian move."

"Lee dem," the gun-toting soldier said. "We way ray hell way dem."

"Who authorized you people to rage hell with us?" I asked in English. Growing speechless, they looked at me briefly with unsteady eyes and resumed their trek. "If you fellows cause any trouble in this town, General will have you arrested and taken to Belle Yallah."

They stopped in their track and looked at each other with suspicion.

"The man is speaking book English," the Corporal told the Private in Kpelle. "Maybe he's a government official. Private, give him his shell."

"But nobody arrested him," the Private said, giving me the Remington shell. "Do your hunting and have it out with the rainstorm. See the cloud?" He pointed at the dark sky, his eyes widened, his forehead creased. "We were doing your own good."

The words were hardly out of his mouth when the cloud burst open and the heavy tropical showers poured down without restraint. The Private craned his neck and told me over his shoulder:

"See what I meant? Do your hunting and have it out with the rain and the storm."

Shivering with cold, I wondered what the fellows would do in town. Clearly, my mentioning a general had mellowed them; should they learn that he was but a student they might turn hostile again. Indeed, we were in for trouble, and Camp Belle Yallah, the nearest army barracks, was half a day away. But the fellows seemed reasonable; they had given me my gun and shell without incident. Better not draw a conclusion which might be wrong. As they bundled their load in green leaves, I walked past them. General was asleep when I entered the house and shook him by the shoulder. He jolted awake and yawned.

"How was the hunting?" he inquired sleepily. "The rain has spoiled the work."

"I got a young hornbill," I said, dashing the bird on the floor and placing the gun in a corner. Putting on dry clothes, I said, "Two soldiers raged hell with me on the road. They're coming here."

General started, sat up, and watched me grimly, his hands planted on the bed as if he was about to rise and fight the soldiers.

"Beat you?" he asked.

I opened the bamboo window and looked at the heavy downpour. Light and fresh air poured into the room.

"No," I said, "but they looked hostile."

"Soldiers are expected to look like that," General informed me. "Relax. it's nothing but posturing."

"They carry a gun."

"Afraid of gun?" General chuckled.

"I don't want to die a foolish death. I prefer dying in defense of my country. They're drunk."

"They might be heading for Gheu. The lovely girls of Gheu!" General smiled reminiscently.

"I hope you're right."

"You've become an expert hunter!" he said, looking at the bird. Then: "The Liberian soldier is no fool. Those fellows know better than cause us trouble. How far is Belle Yallah from here?"

The night passed without incident, so we assumed that the soldiers had gone to some other town. Everybody went to work on the airstrip at sunrise. By midmorning they appeared there, all dressed in resplendent uniforms, dancing to the rhythm of a belly harp Gborlui, the chief musician of the town, was playing. His head tilted to the left shoulder, Gborlui sang the soldiers' praises: They were more glorious than kings; how beautiful they looked in their new uniforms! The town should slaughter all available chickens and animals in their honor. We watched the fellows with trepidation, for their movements were unsteady, their eyes dim, their speech fuzzy. All of a sudden, the Private hit Gborlui with the butt of his gun. Flinging the harp away, Gborlui collapsed on a grassy knoll, screamed, and wriggled helplessly like a dying chicken. The private hit him repeatedly as if to finish off a game he had shot. Blood trickled down the battered head. Terrified, women and children ran away. The men felt obliged to stay. Chief Gbeenge and the Elders implored the soldier to stop brutalizing Gborlui. He now held his gun at the ready and warned everyone to get out of the way for he was about to shoot.

Fortunately, he only fumbled with the gun for a time, watched it aghast and flung it away. The gun had no bolt. With his unruly handling of the weapon, he had dropped it.

Meanwhile the Land had the soldiers arrested and taken to Belle Yallah. We resumed work once again. That evening General reiterated his fears.

"You have seen for yourself the danger of living and working in the bush among our people. Had those soldiers killed us, who would have known about it or cared? If you want to enjoy your education and profit from it, don't worry about the country people and their problems."

SOURCES OF STRENGTH

During the fifties the Evangelical Lutheran Church in Liberia decided to relocate its highest learning institution far deep in the interior to facilitate the easy dispatch of student evangelists to the remotest Loma and Kpelle villages and minimize transport costs for rural students who were in the majority. They chose Salayea, a large Kpelle town in Lofa County, as the institute's ideal location because of its proximity to Lomaland.

Rural students considered the transfer a stratagem the missionaries devised to keep them in perpetual darkness and avoid unhappy competition with other denominations that maintained vibrant missions on the coast. Indeed, they felt they would never cope with the demands of modern civilization if their education depended on textbooks alone. They read about cars, airplanes, televisions, telephones, radios, and the like but had no access to any of these modern amenities. In consequence they would never play a meaningful role in running the affairs of their country. The government needed civil servants imbued with Christian ethics to instill honesty and discipline in public administration, which was plagued by corruption and incompetence. LTI should therefore remain in Harrisburg, which was within a stone's throw of Monrovia, where its graduates had access to modern civilization, job opportunities, and further education. All these and many other arguments went into the breeze and the construction of the institute began. Be that as it may, I looked forward with pleasure to being a pioneer of the new LTI.

It was with mixed emotions that I set off for Salayea: Zamei Airstrip was incomplete and General, who was an eleventh grade student, opted to continue his education in Monrovia "so that I may not be overlooked." I felt that my future lay in the interior where my people needed my services most.

"Tell the white *kwii* that the airfield will soon be ready," Chief Gbeenge told us after General and I had thanked the workers and bidden them farewell on the eve of our departure. "We'll never be able to repay the kindness you boys have rendered us. This is what we expect of our children who go to school."

Unexpectedly, a single Cessna propeller plane, looking like an enormous eagle, flew low over us as if it was about to land; then shot back into the clear, blue sky and quickly faded beyond the forest.

"You see!" the Chief said with great excitement after the awe-inspiring event. "Something good is in store for us! The plane came to inspect the field!"

My road ran through Gheu, Gbansu, and Gbalatuai near the Deyn. Now the river had a concrete bridge at this crossing. John Flomo had lost the bet. I wondered where he was. I felt chagrined while crossing the modern bridge in a pickup. The monkey bridge should have remained for future generations to see that remarkable feat of engineering of our traditional society.

The new campus comprised a dozen buildings scattered on a plain north of Salayea. The administration and classroom building, which looked like an airplane with the offices and classrooms located in the wings, stood in the center of the campus. Still in progress, the construction was proceeding with speed. Workers busily climbed up and down scaffolding, shouting and gesticulating in the din of concrete mixing machines. Buzzing trucks, puffing columns of black smoke, carried cement, sand, and timbers around. Tankers brought in water, diesel, and gasoline. A bulldozer graded an airstrip south of the mission. It was clear, however, that time had run out. The school would have to proceed in the commotion.

A worker directed me to two long buildings which he said were the boys' dorms. I found the dorm manager sleeping in the upper bed of a steel double-decker in the second dorm. He was a classmate of mine, nicknamed DM—short for David Mulbah. I woke him up and we shook hands briskly.

"Where you did your vacation job?" he yawned.

"Zamei," I said. "And yours?"

"Borgeza. Good to see you. Take any bed you want in any room," he said.

I drew a chair and looked at the well-painted walls and ceiling.

"This place looks like America!" I said. "But—you think students will want to live this far upcountry?"

"If they have sense, they'll want to," DM replied. "Good place for studying. Monrovia overflows with robbers, confusion, noise, and filth. The bigshots will want to send their children up here to get good education and training while enjoying good health—Make haste and bathe. Supper is at seven. We eat with the workers—And the weather here is mild—This is the Church's highest learning institution, so they have to make it the best. We may not have the things of modern civilization, but after getting a good education, how long will it take us to get them?"

"This campus reminds me of Zorzor; probably you people in the Western Province bewitched the white people to build modern schools for you. Nearly all the schools they built in the Central Province are mud and thatched structures."

"It's not witchcraft but God, my friend! Whoever thought they'd bring LTI this way? All developments in this country takes place in Monrovia. But you have Totota—with modern buildings!"

"Nothing like what you have in Zorzor and here. Well, I don't think it matters where LTI is built once it's available to us all. Building this country depends on us and not on missionaries, anyway."

"I'm glad you know that," DM said. "We've been sitting on our butts more than a century waiting for white people to develop our country. It hasn't happened, and is unlikely to happen unless we roll up our sleeves."

"You're perfectly correct," I said. "What makes me upset whenever I think of development is the attitude of our so-called leaders who are forever busy hoarding and shipping our money abroad for themselves. They don't know that nobody's interest can be served once the interest of the nation as a whole is not served. Look at our capital city—it's an eyesore."

"Joe, I don't think we can settle Liberia's many problems at this sitting. It's time for supper." DM came down from the bed and put on his clothes.

"We're in trouble, DM."

"Town trap isn't for rat alone," he said, "and a baby that makes its mother stay awake, also stays awake. We're all in the same boat, Joe—we and our leaders. When the boat sinks, we all go down with it."

"You're sure they'll go down with it? They own fabulous homes in Europe and America!"

"The rebels might not wait for them to board an aircraft or a ship and leave the country before launching an attack."

"Were they to listen to us—but they don't even let us express ourselves. DM, you're right. We can't settle our country's problems now, especially while we're hungry. Let me put water on my skin and go with you to supper."

At bedtime, DM handed me a letter, which, he said, Daddy had given him for me. The writing on the envelope was hurried. I could scarcely make out my own name. More than a month old, the letter said that Father was on the point of death and wanted to tell me some last words before dying. I should hurry home. Perhaps Father had already died and been buried, I thought, for it was customary to conceal death news from family members who were afar. No doubt, Mother had not wanted me to get the distressing news while school was open.

Daddy was kind enough to give me ten dollars for transport fare when I asked him for a week's leave to make the trip. He expressed shock and dismay about my misfortune and hoped Father had recovered.

After a hazardous ride in rickety pickups, I reached home at sundown and met Father lying in a *zorbha*[48] friendly neighbors had constructed for him. Mother, who sat at the entrance of the *zorbha*, looking disheartened, raised her upturned palms and wept bitterly when she spied me.

As I took my box into the house, I heard someone tell her angrily, "Why are you giving the Old Man bad luck? He's still breathing! Keep quiet and let him give his son the last words!"

Several women held fast to Mother, remarking that the Old Man had lived his days fully and deserved his rest; she shouldn't spoil his journey home with weeping.

Surprisingly Molley walked up to me, held my arm, and said, "Seporlor, leave crying to the women." He said he had come home from Suehn on a brief visit but couldn't leave Father on his dying bed and return, especially while I was absent.

He brought me a chair, poked the smoldering fire with bamboo splinters and blew on it. The painful smoke burned my eyes and nostrils, but I didn't sneeze; neither did my eyes water. Coughing and twitching uneasily on the *gbegbeh*[49], Father asked weakly, "Is that Zurong?"

---

48. A makeshift room made of wattle and palm thatch and attached to a house.

49. A bedstead, made of bamboo, wattle, and mat.

"Yes, Data," I said. The fire blazed.

"Are you well?"

"Yes, Data. It's you I'm worried about."

"Worried? Be grateful to Kunuunamui and the Ancestors it's no lingering sickness to burden the family needlessly. And why all the turmoil? Don't I have a son?"

Rising with great strain—refusing my proffer of help—Father leaned his lean figure wearily against the bamboo wall, cleared his throat, folded his arms carefully around his knees, stared gravely in my face, and spoke in an amazingly clear and resonant voice:

"There's an end to every story," he said. The words hit me like burning pebbles. "Be thankful Kununamui let me live long enough to get gray hair. Now you can be sure of growing old. May this be the will of the Ancestors."

"Let it be so," I said furtively.

"You're a true son of the soil," he went on, "for your navel cord is planted in this Land. Let Senator Loryii give you a place to certify to it; otherwise, you'll be considered a stranger here. See to this quickly because the land is being bought and sold nowadays." He sighed and continued: "You come from a respectable tribe—honest, hard-working, hospitable, simple-hearted. Why they're called Kpelle, a distortion of 'Gbeleh[50]', is surprising, for there's no mystery about us. We were once herdsmen living on a vast, grassy plane. The land unaccountably grew barren. We had no choice but move down to the rain forest to fall victim to human eating tribesmen who killed us indiscriminately and took away our cattle, all we knew of livelihood.

"I never laid my eyes on any of my parents, not to speak of my grandparents. Aunt Korzea who raised me said I was sucking Mother's breast when they killed her. Father died in the Battle of Reeds in which men slaughtered one another with sharpened sticks. Auntie's husband Benda Kpalapili was a huge man and great warrior—always patrolled round wherever we hid. When I was old enough to carry a sword, I accompanied him on several incursions. I remember killing a man once and falling ill for two weeks—I couldn't eat or leave my bed. Kpalapili told me to go right back to the battlefield, the only way I would feel better—and he was right! Then we discovered this tall mountain in the middle of the forest. An expert warrior and hunter called Kpakilah Zowulo (distorted as Zulo) settled on its summit. He wanted a place well secured from surprise attacks because he had a large family. Then another warrior called Gweseh Dobli built his town in Dingshu. The hilltop enabled one to see the enemy from afar but it wasn't safe enough. Who dares venture to an island surrounded by a deep river infested with fierce crocodiles? I wandered to Golaland where I lived with a friendly Gola man who took me as his own son. But the call came irresistibly, persistently, urgently: 'Go where you're planted.' Did I tell you that I lost my aunt and her husband in the war?

50. Puzzle.

"It's been a long and difficult road but a sweet journey because I survived all my battles with honor. No witch, poison, or secret weapon cut me down. I wish you the same. Hold nobody responsible for my death. God's own time he allotted me on earth has now expired. I'm going to him with a pure heart and gratitude." Handing me an old, rusty cutlass he took from under the *gbegbeh*, he said, "Live by this. Never let your mother or any offspring of yours cry or die of hunger. As I go to The Place of Truth, I forbid you to shed a tear. Respect everyone but fear no man! Be strong, brave, and wise! Trust in God." Mother cried loudly, for it was now certain that Father wouldn't make it. "May the sun shine before you wherever you go," he continued after a long pause.

Though I made the effort, my lips couldn't form the four simple words, "Let it be so."

"May your dreams go to the eastern world," Father was saying. "May whatever you plant in the Land grow abundantly. May God protect you from all dangers. Goodbye, Son. Take the first pickup tomorrow morning for Salayea and don't come back, even for my funeral, until you graduate."

"Joe, since you visited your sick father last February, you've never been the same person," Daddy told me with concern in his office during recess one morning. My head bowed, I stood rooted by his desk, uncertain how to account for my absences from class, church, and sporting activities. "We'd thought you would become OK in a few days. It's normal to be thrown off balance a little by such misfortune, but you've been despondent for months!"

He rose from the wooden armchair behind the metal desk, crammed with files and books, and touched me by the shoulder.

"Did your father die?" he asked.

"No, sir," I replied.

"Was he seriously sick?" I nodded.

"I'll get in touch with Pastor Gbada to see if the plane could take him to Curran Memorial Hospital in Zorzor."

"He's dying of old age," I said. "I don't think there's much you can do for him."

Taking his seat, Daddy sighed deeply and said with severity, "You people consider anyone with a strand of gray hair too old and ready to die. Perhaps your father could live ten more years! Cheer up, boy! You're too young to be sad. Your life is still before you! Get busy. We have the library. Read as much as you can. You seem to have a keen mind, which you must keep busy. Keep a diary; a brief account of whatever you experience each day. If the most important event you observed during the day is a football game, write about it. Who won the game? Who lost it and why? Who was the best player or the worst? Right now, you're grieving over your father's illness. Write down any thought that occurs to you about him. In two weeks, you'll feel better. I'll still call Pastor Gbada to see what we could do to help."

After the final exams, Daddy called me to his office to see what progress I was making with the diary. He riffled through the scanty document, scowled, and said:

"Your best bet is a full-length article. Amazing how you think so well! You'll become comfortable with writing if you do it regularly. Get a bigger copybook—By the way," he said, giving me the copybook, "what are your plans like after graduation?"

"Continue with the work in Zamei."

"Good! A worthwhile decision! Your people badly need you. When their own son bears witness of the light among them, they'll put aside the works of darkness and follow Christ." Looking at my face pathetically, a look that spelled foreboding in my mind, he asked:

"Joe, what do you think of death?"

"A long and peaceful sleep," I said. Puzzled, I wondered why he asked me such a question.

"Good answer," he said. "Shows you understand your catechism. We Christians consider death a mere slumber from which you rouse to find yourself in God's arms. When I was a kid, I used to insist on sleeping with my parents. I would sack in with them but find myself in my own room and bed the next morning. That's the story of man—he insists on making this world his permanent home, although he's a stranger here—one book you should read is John Bunyan's *Pilgrim's Progress*—but one day he awakes to find himself where he ought to be—in heaven. With God! Where there's no pain or hunger or hate or disappointment or dying. Only perfect peace, loving-kindness, joy—Was your father ever baptized?"

"Yes, Pastor."

He glanced at my misty eyes and continued: "Good. Now he is in heaven with our Lord and Savior Jesus Christ! You'll meet him at the general resurrection. What a happy reunion it will be! Wipe those tears and listen:

"Several months ago, I received a letter from Pastor Gbada concerning the death of your father. It was written with a heavy heart because he knew how you were deeply attached to him. The pastor said your dear father passed away shortly after you left him. Your mother said it'd be risky to call you to the funeral, for you might not return to school. Pastor Gbada wished that you attend the funeral to learn to face reality. However, he agreed to your mother's suggestion. She also requested that I convey the sad news to you only after you had taken your final exams. I understand that you did well in the exams and got clearance for graduation. Congratulations! You should be happy and proud of your achievement. I have good news for you! Each year, my congregation in Milwaukee provides scholarship for one of our students with good standing in the Church to pursue further education in the United States after high school, and I recommend that student. I've recommended you for the next scholarship because you have the necessary qualifications.

"Our records show that you're not mixed up with those aspects of your culture the Church condemns such as trial marriage, fornication, joining the Poro and other secret societies, worshiping your ancestors' spirits, and so on.

You don't smoke, you don't drink. Yes—you ran into problems with some of your teachers because you never took their opinions as foregone conclusions. You wanted proof, you wanted to do your own thinking and draw your own conclusions. I see nothing wrong with original thinking though it involves making many mistakes, questioning everything, and irritating people. Isn't the whole purpose of education to make you think for yourself? Besides, you have a mind for progress: You built an airstrip in Zamei almost single-handedly. Our plane lands there now, and we'll soon construct a school and a clinic there.

"We missionaries often make the sad mistake of demanding that all those we educate become pastors, evangelists, or doctors. But nothing is achieved if you don't become *what you have to be.* If you make use of this opportunity, you'll bring great progress to your people. And so, put grief aside, for you have an important responsibility to carry out.

"In case you want to visit your mother before graduation, I'll help you with transport fare."

"I'll go home after graduation. That was Father's instruction."

Diving into his pocket, he handed me a ten-dollar note.

"If you happen to change your mind and decide to go home anyway, use this for transportation." Then he asked me to kneel. Placing his warm, smooth palms firmly on my head, he said:

"The Lord bless you and keep you; the Lord make his face to shine upon you and be gracious unto you; the Lord lift up his countenance upon you and give you peace."

Unaccountable joy filled my heart as I left the pastor's office. Indeed, the power of God wasn't limited to finding a healing stone, driving witches away, or helping you get an education. It gives you the assurance that nothing is terrible—not even death. I had never imagined that life could continue without Father until the moment I received that benediction. Hitherto, I had considered prayers and benedictions nothing but words; now I knew they were sources of strength.

BETRAYED

All Haindi welcomed me, dancing to the tunes of *samkpa, gbongbon*, and a joyful Gola song. Mother, Molley, and Sianeh led the dance. I had expected Mother to greet me with the customary uncontrollable wailing, tousled hair, and dusty clothes, the town watching her with pity. Instead, she hugged me, a broad smile on her face, chanting that The Poor One had forbidden tears at his funeral.

"Dance! Dance! Dance!" Sianeh shouted at me as she capered with exultation, a bright smile on her face. She took my box; someone whisked it from her and took it to our house. "They'll fine you ten pounds and a bull if you cry or refuse to dance," she whispered in my ear. "Don't put us in trouble, my friend. Smile and shake your body!"

Two girls with bobbing bare breasts standing at my sides, smilingly swung their hips and wiped the dust off my face, hair, and neck with their headties. Then they threw my arms to their shoulders and held them tight, watching my feet. When my foot movements fell into step with theirs, there was a rousing cheer from the crowd, which never expected a *kwii* to do a tribal dance. Life and death had become one great celebration; anyone drawing a line of demarcation between the two was senseless.

We marched in a gentle wave towards the grassy cemetery lying in the shade of kola trees. The music and the dance became frantic when we reached a fresh grave in a clearing. There was a sudden gun salute that reverberated in Dobangay Forest. Then another. Two more as we circled the grave. A man in red T-shirt who called himself Benda Dualu stepped forward and said he was the "nephew" of our family. Waving the play to a stop with a shriveled arm, he pointed at the grave and, looking in my face, said, "This is your father's grave—the grave of Dougba Senfenui." Surrounded with slabs of red rock and covered with sand, it resembled NanMolaa's grave.

Holding back the tears with great difficulty, I called for my box as the players resumed the singing and the dance, took out my diploma, and placed that symbol of Father's hopes and aspirations on his grave. I made the unusual announcement that I was no longer Joseph Dennis but Dougba Senfenui Jr. I offered the players four silver dollars in appreciation for their honor and consolation. The *samkpa* exploded wild, and the celebration resumed with animation.

That night Sianeh slept with me in my father's house, which I had now taken over. I told her my plans to marry her and take over Zamei mission. I praised her for her long suffering, patience, and faithfulness. She had been brave beyond belief. She said she was prepared to die for me if necessary. Her only fear was that we might run into problem with the Church once the authorities found out that we had had a child out of wedlock. Since I was now qualified to teach in any elementary school in Liberia, I could teach in Kakata, Firestone, Bomi Hills, or even Monrovia. I argued that once we married and I took responsibility for her and the child, the question of our premarital offspring would not arise. She still had some misgivings, but she agreed with me.

Pastor Gbada considered our plans reasonable, although he would have us postpone marriage until I completed my education. "Don't you want to go to college?" he asked me. "What about the scholarship Daddy offered you?" I expressed my impatience to begin serving the Land in keeping with Father's wishes. I could take advantage of the scholarship in the future since it was never too late to learn.

The pastor conducted the wedding the following Sunday. I wore Father's black- and white-striped, flamboyant homespun gown he used to wear on the most important occasions. Sianeh dressed in a beautiful lappa suit. Nearly everyone in Haindi and Zuakpoisu poured into Trinity Lutheran Church in Haindi to witness the event, the first of its kind to occur in Fuama Chiefdom. Our mothers showered us with rice, muttering blessings and dancing delightfully. Well dressed in his pastoral outfit, Pastor Gbada looked impressive in the pulpit. Gesturing forcefully with his arms, he first commended his own father whose support, he said, accounted for his success.

"I implore you parents to send your children to school," he told the quiet assembly. "Maybe you might live to see them become what Dougbalon[51] and I are today; or maybe not. But remember that you're obliged to make life a little better for them than it has been for you. When I see Dougbalon, I see the children of Fuama, well prepared to serve the Land. Making this vision a reality depends on you parents. Don't shirk it by saying that you're poor—was Senfenui rich? Or that you're illiterate—did Senfenui know book? But he loved the Land and selflessly gave all he had to make this day possible not only for his son but also for all of us—"

After talking at length, he asked if I had something to say. As I walked through the narrow passage with scores of anxious eyes flanking me, there was an explosion of nerve-racking wailing. My heart missed a beat, my limbs shook, but I managed to stand straight before the congregation and say between pauses in the wailing that the honor we could render the memory of my father wasn't crying but sending every child of the Land to school as the pastor had urged. "Father's chief purpose in life was serving the Land he loved," I said. "He believed that it is only through education that we can carry out this all-important task. Through his unflinching support, I learned something about book, but the most important knowledge I ever gained came from him. Book taught me how to think, but he taught me how to live. Now I'm ready to serve you, my people—" At this point my voice broke. The people wailed loudly. Pastor Gbada signed to me with a nod to take my seat.

After the wedding, the pastor threw an elaborate party for us at his house and permitted us to invite our relatives and friends. Then he communicated with Daddy by radio (radios were now available at the various missions) concerning my desire to head the mission at Zamei. Daddy, who supervised the

51. Dougba Jr.

parishes of the Western Province, not only approved my request; he invited me and my wife to spend a week with him and his family before taking up the assignment. He sent the airplane for us. Nearly the whole of Haindi and Zuakpoisu was on the airfield to bid us goodbye. People commented openly that book works wonders.

During our visit in their home, Daddy and his pretty wife proved most hospitable.

"Call me Jack," he told me with raillery at supper one evening. "A married man now, you've become my equal. I admire your love for your people. Most fellows of your caliber would rather live in the city or go to America on the first opportunity, caring less how their people fared. It takes courage to go back to the bush to serve."

I appealed to Daddy to permit me to employ at least one assistant of my choice.

"Certainly," he agreed. "You need someone you know and trust to work with you. We want Zamei to be a focal point for the work of the Church in the Western Province, so we're fully prepared to give you every possible support and encouragement."

I made a quick trip to Gbanoimu to find Jacob whom I wanted as my assistant in appreciation for risking his life for me. Most regrettably, his father said that a ruffian partner of his had killed him in Weasua Forest while they scuffled over a piece of four-cornered diamond. The ruffian had won the fight, which left Jacob almost dead; then he searched Jacob's pockets and mouth for the diamond but didn't find it on him. Believing that Jacob had swallowed it, he split his gut open to get it out, but he didn't find it there either. Much later, he saw it in the grass. The Old Man, who was suffering from gout, lay in his hammock as he spoke; he looked thoroughly broken. He said Jacob's mother had gone crazy ever since she heard of their son's death. She ran about the bushes crying, "They're coming! They're coming!" Who are coming and for what purpose, nobody knew. Old Man Sensireh wiped his face and said, "We locked her foot in *kpornoh*[52], but she cried so much that we had to set her free. You chose the right road, my son, the road of hard work and common sense." Sitting up, he cast a forlorn stare at the distant sky and continued: "Some people depend on luck, friends, and relatives for success, but you depend on God and yourself. Many people I know got valuable stones in Weasua Forest and became rich, but, for each of these lucky miners, there were scores of others who died there—like my son." He stopped speaking abruptly and wept bitterly.

My next choice was General. I was certain he wouldn't mind occupying a prestigious position with a good salary in the service of the Church. I had no idea where he lived in Monrovia, but I supposed he attended St. Peter's Lutheran Church in Sinkor. The missionary pastor and his staff didn't know where he lived either. I left a note urging him to join me for us to complete the job we had begun in Zamei, but I never heard from him.

---

52. A log in which a prisoner or crazy person's foot is trapped to prevent escape.

With the people's support, my wife and I began making dirt blocks for the school building and the teachers' quarters. When they saw the plane bringing in bundles of zinc, planks, boxes of nails, and bags of cement every week, the people promised to work with us until all the construction was done. As time was against us, we managed to complete only one teacher house and a house for ourselves. We thus conducted the Primer Class in the palaver house in town. Sianeh taught songs in the morning while I taught reading and writing in the afternoon. In appreciation for our service, parents brought us rice, cassava, palm oil, meat, fish, and vegetables. Much to my surprise, the villagers had either forgotten or forgiven the dramatic clash I had with them when I conducted my evangelism mission in Zamei.

The school building was completed and dedicated at the beginning of our second year in Zamei. Encouraged by the people's cooperation and support, Daddy, who did the dedication, gave me two male teachers and promised to appeal to Christian friends in America for funds during his next furlough to strengthen and expand the work of the Church not only in Zamei but throughout the entire Western Province. In gratitude for his support, the Chief and Elders of Zamei gowned Daddy honorary Paramount Chief of the Kpelle tribe and presented him a white sheep as a token of the town's love and gratitude.

Our evangelistic mission was just as successful. Nearly every adult and child in the town attended the evening service and eagerly learned to read the *Kpelle New Testament.* We conducted service in outlying villages such as Fenpolu, Kologbanei, and Gilingasiaisu. I took care to avoid preaching against the people's culture. I noted that the chances of changing lives increased when you preach about what people ought to do with their lives rather than what they ought not to do—exactly Jesus' approach to preaching. Pastor Gbada baptized more than a hundred new converts in Zamei at the end of our second year of evangelism.

Meanwhile, I went home for my aging mother to take care of her. Sianeh's parents and Pastor Gbada had been her mainstay of support. I told her of my plan to go for two of Uncle Gonoh's children for schooling. She couldn't understand the bother. "The man was mean and dishonest," she said. "He thought of only today and not of tomorrow. You extended the invitation to all your relatives, but none of them honored it except Molaa, who is dead. God and the Ancestors won't blame you if you forget about their children.

"Settle down before helping somebody else," Mother advised. "Don't think that the mission you're building in Zamei belongs to you. One day you'll retire and go home—not to this old, broken house but to a decent *kwii* one. Start building it now."

Recalling Kewalai's suicide, I conceded that Mother was right, but The Poor One had given me a mandate I must carry out. Thus I made a quick trip to Gbangei where I discovered that Gormah was married to a widower, and they lived in the deep forest. Because he couldn't endure the sight of the house in which he and his deceased wife had lived in Gbangei, Old Man Kerkula and his two grown sons and three married daughters had built this secluded *kpanang*[53]. He and Gormah had met shortly after the death of Uncle Gonoh.

Gormah wept when she saw me. The witches had dealt her a severe blow, she said. Her teenage daughter had also died—in childbirth. She was happy when I took two of her children, a boy of nine and another of five, to educate.

When I returned home with the children, Mother greeted me in a somber mood. Taking me aside, she whispered that some people from Monrovia had been to Haindi to arrest me for a crime I had reportedly committed there; she had misinformed them about my whereabouts, and they had returned. Extremely shocked, I sat down to keep from collapsing. She didn't know the details of the case, but I should go quickly to Pastor Gbada who would see to everything.

"Don't be afraid," she said. "Look up to God. Has he not been your guardian and helper? He won't let shame and disgrace befall the family. We'll live to walk over the graves of our enemies." Then she informed me that a girl friend of mine in Zulotaa had also died in childbirth; her parents had brought me the child, a ten-year old boy, after learning that I had become a great kwii. Nuwoo was swimming with his friends in the river.

Wasting no time, I ran to Pastor Gbada who deferred a meeting he was holding in his office to see me. The pastor ordered me to kneel by his desk and receive the Last Sacrament. Astonished, I stared at him with surprise. I wasn't sick, Mother wasn't sick, and I couldn't recall any outrageous sin I had committed against God or the Church that required expiation. But I obediently ate the thin, unleavened bread and washed it down with a locally brewed cherry wine.

"Well, my son, it's fortunate you came to see me," the pastor said as we sat astride each other. There was a tremor in his voice. "This may well be the end of your earthly sojourn, for you have been dismissed from your post and could be hanged for murder!" I thought I was either dreaming or my ears were deceiving me. Watching me selfconsciously, he continued, "During my last visit to Germany and the United States, the Executive Council recommended your dismissal for living an immoral life. With profound regrets and the utmost reluctance, I endorsed their recommendation.

"My son, trust no friend but God alone. It was your good friend General who betrayed you." He pronounced "good friend" with distaste as if the words were bitter. "He told the Council that you worship ancestral spirits and wear a charm on your body for protection against witches; he also said you had fathered a child out of wedlock—the worst crime a Christian can commit. As you know, the punishment for fornication is summary expulsion from the Church. Your marriage to the girl makes no difference. General went on to tell the Council that you had joined the Poro Society, which the Church considers evil and un-Christian. Had you joined it before knowing

53. A small village, usually comprising one family.

Christ—"

"But I'm not a member of the Poro!" I cried. "You may inspect my back." I took off my shirt and turned my back to him.

"Put on your clothes," he said. "Were that the only thing, you wouldn't have been in trouble. General also said that you killed one old man called Emmanuel Dennis in Monrovia and ran away from justice. The police, who said you once accused them of robbery, believed him, and they invaded Zamei, that poor, secluded outstation, to find you. The villagers who appreciate your hard work, refused to betray you. Consequently, the police burned the mission down and arrested your dear wife who died of a broken heart as they carried her to Monrovia. Is this the kind of justice we want our children to practice? This nation is doomed, my son—doomed to extinction.

"Believing that it was the missionaries who had schemed all this, the people of Zamei dug craters on the airfield and covered them with twigs, leaves, and dirt. At the time, the Council dispatched two of its members by air to Zamei for a full assessment of the damage done to the mission. General accompanied them to prove his accusations against you in your presence. The fellow is in league with some disgruntled villagers who hate you for trying to destroy their old culture, but they have no case. The old way does them no good. We expect opposition as we try to open our people's eyes. As fortune would have it, the mission plane crash-landed on Zamei Airport. General was the only survivor; he escaped with minor injuries and was taken to JFK for treatment. You can be sure the people of Zamei are in big trouble—" The pastor stopped talking abruptly and hung his head, his fingers hooked in an attitude of prayer. Resuming his incredible story in a measured tone, he said, "General wanted your job; that's why he betrayed you. Unable to find work in Monrovia, he pimped on a certain bigshot's wife. As you know, most of the bigshots in this country neglect their wives in their old age for teenage girls. And their neglected wives support young boys for satisfaction of the flesh. It didn't work well for General. He was often caught with a girl in the room, which this rich woman was renting for him. She threw him out. General tried to get government scholarship to continue his schooling, but he was no Cooper or Dennis. He couldn't get a job because he has no profession. Hearing of your successes in Zamei, he decided to betray you and take over that mission. 'Vengeance is mine, says the Lord.' Now there's no mission in Zamei for him to take over. Unless the government apologizes to the Church and makes amends for the savage act of its police, I won't open Zamei mission. And as long as I'm president of the Lutheran Church in Liberia, General will never work for this Church."

It was when the pastor had finished telling his appalling tale and stared in my face with perplexity that I roused from my grim nightmare.

"General!" I exclaimed bitterly, turning blind with insane rage, my voice resounding in the ancient palm grove behind the house. Boiling over with fury, I pounded the wooden desk with my fists and declared, "That bewitched son of the devil will be a corpse before sundown tomorrow! I'll throttle him to death with my bare hands! I'll stab him in the chest with a dagger."

Bewildered, the pastor looked at me with horror, tapped my shoulder with a trembling hand, and said in a quavering voice, "No, you can't do that. It's un-Christian and contrary to our tradition. We Kpelle—I consider myself a Kpelle man now—don't kill our enemies. We let them live to see us prosper, thereby putting them to shame. Shame is worse than death! You have climbed many mountains before. This trouble is just one more mountain to climb. Don't risk eternal damnation by committing another murder. The body and blood of Christ have absolved you of whatever sins you might have committed."

Disregarding the familiar admonition with another frantic pounce on the desk, I declared, "General must die!" I started planning the strategy to kill him. No time for scruples of conscience or utopian speculation but practical action! I now understood why Kewalai had said that death is better than disgrace, but he foolishly killed himself rather than his enemy.

Borrowing pen and paper from the pastor, I sat at his well-polished mahogany desk and wrote the following letter to my father:

Dear Father:

I can't save my people or myself. Only God can do that. You'll agree that a farmer doesn't always reap the fruit of every seed he sows, and that life and death contend for dominion over us, with death always winning the victory. Our only obligation to life, therefore, is doing the best we can to take our exit with honor. This may be my last battle. I'll fight it with all my strength and resolve. If I don't survive—and what is wrong with coming to you and our Ancestors?—may you and the Ancestors graciously receive my spirit in The Place of Truth.

Your loving son,
Dougba Senfenui Jr.

Looking over my shoulder, Pastor Gbada read the script with his mouth open. Tapping my back, he said:

"Don't communicate with the dead, Dougba! It's un-Christian! Let's take a walk in the palm grove and listen to the beautiful songs of the birds to get appetite for dinner. I understand that you love nature. Sleep here tonight and calm down before deciding what step to take in this matter. Actions taken in anger are often regretted."

A LONELY AFFAIR

The beautiful guestroom was spacious, airy, and comfortable. The black and white checkerboard ceiling and blue walls shone with fresh, redolent paints. The wide, screened, double window with a blue curtain containing a white center piece commanded the view of a lovely palm grove set in blooming flowery bushes. Below it stood a glossy mahogany table and a chair with cushion encased in brown leather. On the table were a green hurricane lantern, a Bible, a writing pad, and a ballpoint pen. Against the western wall just behind the yellow plywood door, was a wide spring bed with a thick mattress wrapped in a pair of white linen, two pillows in white cases with floral designs and a quilt carefully folded and placed at the head of the bed. The blue tiled floor was gleaming. But my night in the beautiful modern bedroom was restless.

After a delicious dinner of fine-grain swamp rice and chicken gravy, which I hardly ate, and a brief devotion the pastor and his wife held for me, I retired at seven. Sleepless, I tossed in bed nearly all night thinking only of how to stab or throttle General to death. Pastor Gbada's prudent advice was reasonable but completely unacceptable. Human beings have the ability to employ arguments that are equally plausible in defense of, or in objection to, any action they take. Some people give up life for honor while others affirm it despite defeat, disgrace, betrayal, or humiliation. All these are acts of courage. The Bible has been used to oppress people and to liberate people. Who then but God is qualified to determine right action? I must therefore forget the pastor's well meaning advice and make General bear the consequences of his malicious betrayal. After all, justice demands that we take responsibility for our actions. It had been a long and costly struggle. God knew that my parents and I did not shrink from its demanding sacrifices and dangers. Thus, anyone depriving me of my just reward must die.

Deciding to take somebody's life is a lonely affair. Only the decision-maker can understand the regrettable necessity.

We don't kill our enemies, but let them live to make a mockery of us! What entitles them to such a privilege? Your father was unrealistic in investing you with his unfulfilled dreams and aspirations. Salvation comes from a Messiah.

At dawn, the luxurious room grew unbearably hot. The mattress stung my tossing body; perspiration poured copiously all over me, and my heart throbbed fiercely. Dazed, I sat up, then stood up, then paced the room, breathing in a gust of fresh air suffused with the heady fragrance of wild flowers each time I passed by the open window. After calming down somewhat, I sat at the table, toyed with the pen and the paper, then stood at the window mulling over a welter of possible schemes to kill General. For some unexplained reason my arms trembled and my head ached. When the room began closing in on me, I quickly unlocked the door without making a sound and walked on tiptoe to the dark lounge. The night was deathly quiet, except for the noise of crickets and *shansaro* in the palm grove.

Obviously perceiving that I might escape in the night, Pastor Gbada or his wife had locked the front door and removed the key. They were terrified when I woke them up and said I wanted to go home. Raising a hurricane lantern to my face, the pastor who was in pyjamas watched my unkempt, agitated condition with horror. Her head tied with a red bandeau and a deep-blue lappa wrapped above her fat breasts, Mrs. Gbada stared at me with astonished eyes and parted lips; her arms were trembling.

"Go to the bathroom and bathe," the pastor advised me. "You'll feel better. At sunrise, we'll have breakfast and pray for you before you go."

"Thank you, sir," I told him. "I'll bathe at home—in the river. I'm not hungry. I've already said my morning prayer."

"Look, don't frighten your old mother with that horrible look!" said Mrs. Gbada. "Go bathe to get in a better shape before going home. You're disturbed! And don't you tamper with the river!"

"Ma'am," I said urgently, "something strange is happening to me. I have to see my mother right away or I'll die!"

Reluctantly the pastor retraced his steps to the master bedroom, brought back a bunch of keys, found the right one, and opened the door. While walking out, I overheard him telling his wife, "Perhaps he shares the same double with his mother. In that case, only she can help him—still steeped in traditional life—such a brilliant fellow! True, you can't take the country from the man."

As I walked through the silent village in the dawn, I envied its residents who were enjoying their morning sleep. Had I not gone to school, I too would have been enjoying my sleep. Stopping by the cemetery, I stood at the head of Father's grave, overgrown with grass, and reminded him that he never taught me to be a coward. Now he should stand by me in this decisive battle. I buried his letter exactly where I stood and went down to the Deyn.

The lukewarm water calmed my palpitating heart; a lofty feeling of peace and vitality, which had eluded me so long, now filled my heart after I dived to the bottom of the river, swam across it twice. Strengthened and composed, I could now act without fear, hesitation, or compunction. My mother, having played her part in the desolate drama with unspeakable courage, I decided not to bother her with it anymore. Jogging to Tulaytaa, I boarded a pickup for Kakata, making sure to avoid unnecessary conversation on the way. I bought a dagger in Kakata, tied it on my left leg, pulled my pant over it, and boarded another pickup for Monrovia.

It was a busy day at the government hospital with its beautiful frontage of flower garden. Cars bearing patients filled the yard. Women with babies strapped to their backs and carried in the crooks of their arms streamed up several tiled steps onto a tiled floor and through a sliding glass door to the receptionist's desk. Malaria patients, wrapped in blankets and held by the arms, walked with difficulty to the wide waiting hall. Just before I entered the hospital, a six-door, black Mercedes Benz with a fluttering flag arrived. Cars literally fled the yard to make room for the enormous vehicle. Everybody at the receptionist's counter withdrew to the western end of the waiting hall. Smartly dressed in blue uniform, a police officer jumped out of the car and opened a back door. A skinny old man with a close-cropped gray head, dressed in an expensive suit, staggered out and waddled up the steps. They said he was a Senator of Montserrado County and brother of the president. The police opened the glass door and the Senator limped to one of two large elevators without saying even a word of greetings to the receptionist.

I walked with confident steps to the receptionist, greeted her cordially, and asked her if I could see a friend who was a plane-crash victim.

"You din see de Honorable goin' in?" the girl yelled at me. "You see people round here? You stranger in Monrovia? You betta go come back tomorror! Da man na leavin' here jesna."

Regarding her with a surly grin, I walked through the crowded room and entered a wide hall where I met a janitor mopping the floor. In response to my query, the fellow lifted his head, leaned on the handle of the mop, stared in my face askance, and asked me if he was the receptionist.

"She couldn't help me because one Honorable just arrived at the hospital," I said.

"Every crook in dis country a honorable," the janitor murmured with an enigmatic smile. "Go fourth floor and ask for de men general war'."

On the fourth floor I met an old woman sitting at a desk; she directed me with a pen down a wide hallway. The nurse at the door of the men's ward asked which plane crash I meant.

"The one that occurred in Zamei two weeks ago," I told her.

"When dey bring hin here de doctor say he war DOA. A bin long time ago. Where you from?"

"Zamei," I said. "What is DOA?"

The old woman scoffed quietly and said, "When dey tell you boys go to school you follow woman plava. The man die before dey bring hin here."

"I learned that he escaped with only minor wounds!" I tried to sound conversational.

"The person who tol' you da lie to you."

My heart sank. So General was gone! Gone forever! Nothing more could be done to him.

Noticing my disappointment, the unknowing woman told me, "Sorry for da. Accident is part of life; it can happen to anyone anytime. But one girl from Zamei here. You wan' see her? She sufferin' from heart trouber. Maybe she way tell you more 'bout hin. Makey and go before I geh in trouber. The Senior Senator is still around." Not satisfied with the instruction, she herself led me to the women's general ward. A thousand pairs of curious eyes accompanied us to an empty bed in the middle of a row stretching far into the distance.

"Dis her bay. Sit down and wait for her. She gone toiley," the woman said in one breath and hurried away.

Deranged with smothering rage, I sat on a tall stool and stared round the cramped ward reeking with nauseating odor. After seeing this Zamei woman, I would challenge the police to prove their murder charge against me. Sooner or later, that drama would unfold, anyway. No. Let them earn their pay. Before getting me, at least one of them would get the punishment General had escaped!

After waiting in anxiety for ages, I saw Sianeh limping along the narrow passage between the two rows of metal beds, coming in my direction. I ran to her, held her in my arms, and kissed her on her full lips. Caught unawares, she first stared in my face with perplexity, then exclaimed delightfully:

"Dougba! I can't believe it! No, I can't!"

"Sianeh!" I declared, holding her by the shoulders. All eyes turned to us inquisitively.

Tears of joy streamed down Sianeh's cheeks. Recovering quickly, she led me to a large porch facing the Atlantic Ocean. Observing our somber mood, several patients and visitors who lolled on the porch left one by one until we were alone.

"Let us pray," Sianeh said. After thanking God for protecting us, she asked him to help us start life anew and take care of our poor parents who were greatly distressed. Cupping her cheek in her hand and staring at me with a tear-strewn face, she tried to speak, but the words couldn't come.

"Don't cry, darling," I said, putting my arm around her. "Once we're together again, all our troubles are over."

"Dougba, what will we do?" She straightened up, gazed in my eyes soberly, and wiped her face with the back of her hand.

"Return to Haindi," I said.

"Good. Not to Zamei by any means."

"No. Not to Zamei. We can't live there again even if we want to. I've been dismissed. All because of that ill-begotten witch, General!" I chewed the name to bits, pounding my thighs with clenched fists, wishing it were General I was hitting.

"Take it easy, my dear," Sianeh said calmly, holding my hand. "In this country, people never care to give the right information—too anxious to see others' downfall, though they don't profit by it." She looked at the floor meditatively.

"What happened to Guladia? Where's he? How you got here?"

"He's in Zamei with NeKaney who kindly took him from me. That woman is a mother to me."

"They told me that the police killed you. Had they done that, I'd have stabbed at least two of them to death before I die. I'd have waged war on them in broad daylight at their headquarters."

"Well," she pressed my hand hard with one hand and laid the other in her lap, "the jealousy and wickedness of people know no limit. Some enemy of ours gave Pastor Gbada a distorted account of what happened—magnified your trouble to ensure his approval of your dismissal. He too joined the conspiracy because you might train in the future as a pastor and take over the Church. He knows that the missionaries love you, so they might encourage you to be a pastor! Now you can understand my fears about working for the Church."

"General is responsible for all this!" I cried. "He was lucky I didn't meet him. Well, he's dead and I'm alive. That's a great difference between us. Once there is life, there is hope. Who knows what God has in store for us?"

"And why this desire to kill? Joe, every disappointment is a blessing. I think you drove yourself too hard. You lit the candle at both ends! Let's take some time to make better plans."

Sianeh was right. In trying to make life work, I lost sight of it. True, a goal should be pursued with unwavering commitment and sacrifice, but it must be tempered with patience and prudence. Using to the fullest any opportunity the moment presented is all mortal man can do. It was what Father had meant—and not to conquer or save the world as I had supposed.

"I learned that the townspeople dug craters on the airfield, making the plane to crash," I told Sianeh.

"No," she said. "The crash was the pilot's fault. It was his first time landing on Zamei Airfield. He ran into a *beleh* tree. Only General survived, but he died on the way as they brought him down here. Investigators of the Liberian National Airways went to Zamei on foot to find out how the accident happened. The policeman who accompanied them to represent the government carelessly dropped a cigarette butt in your office. The building caught fire and burned down. That's all I learned, for I had fled with Guladia to NeKaney. They said they arrested you in Haindi and imprisoned you on South Beach. When I came down and did not see you, I thought they had killed you. That's how I developed heart trouble—Dougba, what are we going to do?"

"Plant coffee. Darling, the land will not fail us. In five years, our coffee will be ready for harvest, and we'll get more than enough money to build our own school. We can do it! I'm sorry for putting you through all this trouble."

"Five years." Sianeh sighed deeply and gazed into space. "A long time to wait. What about a job in Firestone, Monrovia, Bomi—"

"Sianeh," I interrupted, "unless you do a government job which permits you to steal—something I'll never do—whatever job you do in this country can only preserve your life. I want to work for myself. Be out of everybody's way."

With her bright, angelic eyes, Sianeh looked steadily at the ocean shimmering in the noonday sun, completely lost in thoughts. Dressing close to her, I hugged her hungrily. We never needed each other so urgently.

"When do they discharge you?" I said.

"I'll ask the doctor to turn me loose tomorrow. I'm all right now."

I kissed her passionately and wished to tell her about Kulubah's son, but such staggering news required the intervention of Elders to assuage the shock. That case would be settled at some future time.

After spending a restless afternoon and a night in the cold waiting room of the hospital, I walked to the beach shortly before dawn to stretch my legs. Several guards inquired about my mission. I told them that I was waiting for a patient to be discharged.

Not believing me and probably thinking I wanted to drown myself, one of them advised me seriously:

"Take it easy, my friend. Life belongs to God, so nobody has the right to destroy it. That relative of yours might live for ages to come."

The cold, gentle breeze fluttered my clothes; the foaming tidal wave dashed rhythmically against the beach like Sande graduates dancing in a square. Far in the distance, I saw specks of light on the ocean. Doubtless, a ship was heading for the Freeport of Monrovia. My eyes followed the lights as they drifted slowly steadily towards their inevitable destination. Suddenly captured by a mighty force I couldn't comprehend or resist, I stood still, pulled the dagger off my leg, took a deliberate aim, and threw it into the ocean with all the force I could command. Though a patch of dark cloud tried to dim them, the early stars appeared with uncommon brightness.

MANY THANKS

Throwing that dagger into the sea lifted a burden from my shoulders—I felt liberated, confident, and ready to fulfill my mission. Of course, being on your own can be intimidating when you note that your success or failure depends on you alone, but it has its compensations. You become your own boss and you engage life on your own terms. This means hard work and faith in your resources and goal. Experience soon proved this admission correct.

When I broached our project to some villagers, they said we were biting more than we could chew. Without the backing of the government or missionaries, we would only be risking frustration and disappointment. Sianeh and I had to reassure ourselves constantly that the project was no mistake; that it was feasible within the limits of available resources. Had Ma Miller not built her mission with sticks, thatch, rattan, and mud, which we had in plenty? Indeed, our goal would remain secret until we constructed the first building.

It occurred to me that our impoverishment wasn't due to lack of resources but the belief that only foreign governments, churches, and humanitarian agencies should solve our problems. Ironically, some of the countries we begged for help didn't have a fraction of the immense wealth we possessed—

Initially, I enjoyed the simple, unassuming village life and the ready sympathy and support of the people. A son of theirs had sacrificially acquired education and returned home. What young man of his caliber could afford such humility? With their help, we re-roofed our home, my father's house, and recoated it with fresh clay. Each day we accompanied a family to their farm in search of food, which they gave us generously. But the honeymoon soon ended.

My presence among the villagers, especially the men, became embarrassing. Because I wasn't a *kenamu* and had joined forces with a world beyond their reach, there was a serious communication barrier between us. They talked to me with caution; in their company I was always the only subject of the conversation. What had I been looking for in the "dangerous, cruel *kwii* world"? Why did I treat my old parents with callous indifference? Now that my father had died before his time, and my mother was halfway in her grave! My friends who had wisely left school, were thriving well. Bhea had become an overseer in Firestone; he had three wives and ten children. Bopaa, who lived in Zulotaa, was a great hunter and farmer and a father of five children. Zina was now our Town Chief. They warned me not to tamper with the river and the forest for my own safety. I could drown, get lost, or run into The Bush Thing.

Refusing to yield to intimidation or fear, I renewed my acquaintance with the river and the forest, for they no longer posed a threat to me as they had in my childhood. I now saw them as a mainstay of support for the mission and a source of wellbeing and reawakening. Farming and fishing would generate substantial income to operate the mission. The salubrious air of the forest and the liquid music of the river rejuvenated my spirit. In an indefinable way, they awakened in me the lust for life and the faith that, with resolve and perseverance, my goal would be achieved.

As land was available at no cost to anyone wishing to make a farm or build a house, I had no problem selecting a site for the mission. Remembering my long morning walks to Kpolopele, I chose Mbelleimu, my parents' last farming spot, for the project. Mbelleimu lay within a stone's throw behind Gbonkpotoli Creek, which flows threw Haindi to the Deyn. Though the choice may seem selfish, the locality was ideal for our purpose. An elevated plateau of some hundred acres of fallow land, Mbelleimu was large enough for farming and for erecting an average mission. In addition, it had easy access to the icy creek water, Haindi, and the Deyn.

For the first year, we made a large cassava patch in Mbelleimu and only a small rice farm on Gbonkpotoli's swampy bank. No one could detect that it was the beginning of a mission project. We sold half the cassava harvest to market women from Kakata and even Monrovia, and saved most of the money to build the school. We planted coffee on the old patch. Finding the venture profitable, we continued cassava farming and planting coffee on each old patch from year to year. In four years, we had planted three quarters of the land with coffee.

No one ever took us to task for refraining from making upland rice farms, for cassava became a major cash crop for the village. Every household planted it in large quantities on their rice farms and some people even made patches in addition. Soon, Haindi had its own market day, Tuesday of each week, and the market was always flooded with the tuber. However, the suspicion we feared arose one night when Chief Zina paid me a surprise visit.

It was midnight. Although the moon still lingered, the village was asleep. The Chief placed a gourd of palm wine at our feet on the porch. He drank a cupful and turned the white enameled cup over to me.

As if pampering a child, he said, "Drink, Seporlor, drink. It's all yours. I've had more than enough." Clearing his throat, he said, "Be sure what I've come to tell you is very important. Have I ever visited you at this time of night? Were you a *kenamu*, we would be meeting under a wine tree some afternoon. Why not join the Poro?" He smiled companionably.

"What happened?" I asked him as I drained a cup of wine. The village swirled in my eyes; the sensation was exhilarating, but I strained to keep steady.

"You're strong and brave," the Chief said. "I don't blame you for refusing to join the Poro. You've spent too many years with missionaries who despise our way of life—Promise me you'll keep secret what I'm about to tell you." Chief Zina looked in my face and pursed his lips as if his life depended on the answer I would give.

"I don't betray secrets though I'm not a member of the Poro," I assured him. The strain left his face.

"*Kwii* people know how to think but not how to live, as you yourself once said openly." As I drank my second cup of wine, he continued, carefully choosing his words: "You intend to build a mission here. Your keeping it a secret fools no one. It's no small task for a single man to undertake; besides, the people will thwart it or eliminate you. Who are you to aspire for things beyond their reach? Not that puny little child who played in the sand just yesterday, naked, dirty, with his ten toes on the ground. I recommend Kankarantaa, Willietaa, Zulotaa, or Digei for this worthy project."

"Fire burns where you set it before spreading around," I said. "I can't take progress to other villages while mine languishes in darkness."

"Well," he said, "I only came to give you the benefit of my advice. If you think—"

"No! No! No! I'm not offended. Zina, we grew up together. Fate sent me to school, but education doesn't make anyone better than others. I'm learning from you what no teacher has ever taught me."

"Kwii people have failed to open our eyes because they want us to think the way they do. They refuse to understand us. Our people are not as grateful as you suppose. The fact that you're working in their interest makes no difference."

"Perhaps when they get something to be grateful about, their attitude will change."

"'Grateful' isn't the right word, but whatever it is, don't make a difference here! Live like us." The Chief bobbed his head vigorously with each word he spoke; he looked serious.

"When they see the benefits the school will bring, they'll likely support me. Their children will attend school right under their eyes, and they'll earn much money building and caring for the school."

"I admire your courage," the Chief said in a conciliatory tone. "I too want to see better life round here. We have to pay the price that progress demands. Count on me as your supporter. I'll try to persuade other people to support you, too."

"I'm happy the most important man in town supports me. But I'll give serious consideration to your advice."

"Finally, I advise you to eat from no woman but your wife; keep secret any belief you value; talk less in conversation—do more listening; avoid fishing in the river or hunting in the forest, alone."

"Goodnight, Chief," I said, sleep having overtaken me. "Please inform the town that I want a tree felling *kuu* the day after next market."

Deeply touched by my man-to-man talk with Chief Zina, I pondered over his earnest concern about my safety. His prudence impressed me. His being illiterate had not marred his ability to reflect. The lessons I had learned from him were vital—probably injunctions of the Poro Society.

Although I conceded the Chief's advice, I had my own convictions about my security. First, too much concern about personal safety breeds insecurity. You become afraid of everything including your own shadow. Second, no matter what you do, life has to go; only make sure it goes for a good cause.

Third, as son of the soil I was entitled to the tribe's protection; so, nobody's witchcraft, malice, or conceit could do me any harm. Fourth, when I thought of the miracles God had wrought in my life, I believed that I was under divine protection. Fifth, once I dealt rightly with people and asked the forgiveness of those I offended unwittingly, I had nothing to fear. Sixth, the future belonged to "book people", and the people wanted their children to be part of that future; so, it was in their interest to protect me until the project was completed. With these assurances, I went to bed and slept sound.

Contrary to the Chief's fears, I enjoyed the cooperation and support of the village when the project began. The men responded favorably to my *kuu* summons. They said they were happy Haindi would have its own school. Of course, the rich foods and wages we gave them partly inspired their support.

The school was indeed a duplicate of Ma Miller's mission: a large rectangular hall centrally located for class, assembly, and chapel; four houses for teachers, and a football field on the southern tip of the campus. With the bushes gone, we had a lovely view of Haindi, the Deyn, and even Bo Mountain. No other location for the school would have been more ideal.

Equipping and staffing the school posed our greatest problem. I had used our savings for the construction; now we needed money to meet monthly payrolls and maintain adequate supplies of chalks, slates, dusters, pencils, and other materials. The funding required was by far in excess of our ability to generate. Sianeh suggested that I apply to the Ministry of Education for subsidy. Prior to that we should register the school to prove to the Ministry that we meant business. After all, private schools were entitled to some measure of support from the government.

Sianeh's suggestion was quite in place, for civil servants were not getting their pay, so employees of the Education Ministry were on the hunt for anyone operating school without permit. Once you were caught in their trap, there would be no end to their harassment of you for money to pocket rather than put into government coffers. As for the subsidy, I knew that nothing would come of it, but it was worth pursuing. Wasn't education the government's greatest priority?

Going to the Ministry of Education one Monday morning, I called by the office of the Minister whose secretary directed me to the Deputy Minister for Administration whose secretary, in turn, sent me to the Assistant Minister for Administration. The go-around signaled the possible failure of my effort and the insensitivity of our educational authorities to education. But I was curious to know how things would turn out.

The Assistant Minister's office, like that of the Deputy Minister, was shabby, while their boss' office dazzled with luxurious imported furniture. The walls of the Assistant Minister's office were unpainted, the windowpanes broken, the chairs and rugs dilapidated. Two boys stood in opposite corners and another two sat near the secretary's old wooden desk, chortling about last night's carousals—how many girls they had bedded, how much liquor they had drunk, the Ghanaian hightlife they had enjoyed, and so on.

I sat in a broken chair before the secretary's desk, which nearly threw me over. Thanks to the messenger who had accompanied me from the Deputy Minister's office for giving me a hand.

"Wait for the secretary," he told me after making sure I had sat properly. "Where Kula?" he asked the boys.

"Way de Minister," they replied in a chorus.

In half an hour, a beautiful girl wearing a strikingly yellow dress, her shiny black hair shimmering, opened a creaking door and sat behind the desk.

"What you wan?" she asked me angrily.

"Dis man build new school," one of the boys told her amiably. "Minister sent hin to register."

"I hope you come good. Any you know what to pay? Five hundred dala."

I had expected to pay the money at the National Bank and only do the paper work at the Education Ministry. I had also expected people handling the nation's educational affairs to speak correct English. Noticing the surprise look on my face, Kula became angrier.

"Go come tomorror," she dismissed me brusquely.

"I live out of town," I told her, "and I don't know anyone to spend the night with here." I was hoping the girl would be polite; after all, she and I had never met before.

"My man," she said, laying her head on her folded arm on the desk, "I told you my hay hurting! Man like you can't tell me you ain' know somebody in Monrovia."

"Go come tomorror," one of the boys told me in a friendly tone. They all looked embarrassed. "She way gay you your paper."

I slept in a dilapidated motel swarming with flies and mosquitoes down in Slipway. Here you walked with caution, for neighbors, lacking toilettes in their houses, relieved themselves in plastic bags and threw them out their windows. The stench made me breathless. Grateful for the dawn, I hurriedly passed water in a zinc shack outdoors, dressed in clean clothes, paid my five dollars, and left for the Ministry.

The secretary claimed that the money I had given her was one hundred dollars short.

"I din even checky because Kpelle people can't steal," she told me. "I trusted you but you leh me down. Dese boys dem was here." She waved an all-inclusive arm that took in the four boys.

"Da true! Da true!" cried the boys.

She summoned me into the Minister's plushy office. The furniture was evidently of foreign origin. A General Electric air-conditioner, stuck in the wall behind the large chestnut desk, cooled the office. Behind the desk sat a lanky middle-aged man dressed in a gray suit, white arrow shirt, and red tie. I wondered why the secretary's office was shabby.

In response to my greetings, the Minister told me, "My man, I busy. De secretary will give your certificate. You hundred dala short. Next time you coming, brinkey. See you later."

Before he finished talking, a girl with big breasts and hips swung into the office with a broad smile and sat in his lap, put an arm round his neck and toyed with his tie.

"Lock the door!" he called. I was hardly out of the office when a messenger shut the door with a bang and locked it.

After the secretary gave me the certificate of registration, I handed her my letter of application for subsidy. She skimmed it and told me to follow her.

"You din put de money you wan in you letter," she whispered when we entered the conference room. "Write 'nother wan and put in five tasin dala. To geh dis money, you ga to fine one tasin dala for de Minister. Den five hundred dala for the Deputy Minister and three hundred for the Assistant Minister. Da leave you way two tasin eight hundred dala. Da plenty money for poor boy like you! A you know you way in Finance, you gan geh dis money before end of dis month. You like you can go enjoy youself in America."

Running behind the voucher at Finance would call for another thousand eight hundred dollars or more. No, I would have nothing further to do with subsidy. On my way out, one of the office boys tapped me on the shoulder. Tall and better dressed than his friends, he followed me to the street. I feared that he would rob me.

"My friend," he said in Kpelle, "I have something to tell you. I'm Kpelle, so I can't be here while people cheat my own brother." He kept quiet until we reached an alley across Randall Street. Walking several yards down the alley, we stood face to face. Speaking in a low voice and glancing sideways anxiously, he said:

"Write the president for your subsidy. Unless he gives them a directive, they won't serve you. They'll eat your money for nothing. These rascals have paralyzed the Ministry. They haven't paid teachers for many months. Not even the office staff. Mind you, the Budget Bureau always allots enough funds for teachers' pay, but the Minister, like all the others, does what they call 'budgetary transfer.' When the budget passes, they use any appropriation for whatever they want. They have used over half the year's budget to buy cars, travel, conduct useless seminars and workshops, build fabulous houses for girl friends, buy houses in America and Europe—I see nothing but doom for our country. I too attended mission schools. We learn the right thing on these missions only to find people doing everything the wrong way in the government. Look, the first opportunity I get I'm going to America. Why are we encouraged to go to school simply to have the country run by blind, selfish people?"

"What is your name, my friend?" I said.

"Jeremiah Foday. LTI graduate!" the fellow said, his face frowned with bitterness. "I heard much about you in LTI. They say you're clever."

"Thanks for the information. I too will go abroad, but I want to see about this school first. Tell me why the secretary was angry with me."

"She has too many competitions," Foday said. "Just before you came, a girl had visited the Minister, and while you were there another one came. By no means would she get what she expects from him—I'll make sure your school's name gets on the list. You don't have to do anything for me. Remember to write the president."

I got no reply to my letter to the president despite the many reminders I wrote and the personal visits I paid to the mansion. Again, I met another Kpelle man at the mansion, a soldier this time, who felt sorry for me after I had made numerous unsuccessful attempts to see the president or his special assistant. The fellow took me to the beach behind the mansion when the office closed and told me:

"My friend, stop wasting your time; you'll never see head or tail to that subsidy business. This empty headed winebibber George Dennis our present Minister of Education—"

"Oh! I know the fellow!" I cried. "I once lived with his family."

"George went to America on a drinking spree but returned with documents qualifying him as doctor of education. The Senate approves any candidate the president recommends for any office once they're getting their share of the elephant meat—as Liberia's called nowadays. We must say for George, though, he wanted to be honest. When he took office, he asked the president to lend him money to furnish the house GSA gave him—and buy a car. I was present in the office that day. 'Hi! Hi! Hi! ' the president laughed a prolonged laugh as if the Minister was joking. The Chief Executive was drunk! He had just drained another bottle of champagne. Then growing sober, he cast stern eyes at George and said, 'I made you Minister of Education and you're asking me for money? What a fool you are!' After getting the hint, George waged war on the Ministry's budget. He took all the gas allowance and the teachers' salary allotments for himself as well as funds allocated for school construction, every cent in the bookstore's account, and so on. My friend, the Ministry of Education is broke while the Minister lives in luxury. George has bought a house in America, where his family lives; he visits them once every month. Like the children of most legislators, cabinet ministers, ambassadors—by the way, I learned that our ambassador in London has sold our Embassy there and is now a millionaire with houses all over Europe and America—his children and many of his relatives now live in London and America. Sometimes I wonder why our ancestors founded Liberia when their descendants don't even consider it their home."

"Why does the president permit corruption?"

"For the people to fear him! Since most educated people are government employees, one way to stop them from wishing for his office is let them be corrupt. Should a government official criticize him, not to speak of opposing him, he is dismissed and audited immediately. And which of them won't be found wanting?"

"And what is annoying about the whole affair," I couldn't help remarking, "is when a corrupt official is dismissed, he's given another position in government, by far greasier than the one he lost."

"You know the problem, then. Do your best with the school and not depend on these crooks. Your students could make farm and pay fees."

Fortunately, the coffee would be ready for harvesting in half a year. I never thought it'd take ten long years for this to happen. I first did business with LPMC, a public corporation that purchased farmers' cash crops for export, but when it began failing to pay farmers their money, I found a Lebanese customer in Kakata who paid ready cash for produce. Meanwhile, I continued the cassava business. With the substantial income I now generated, I employed six teachers who had been teaching in government schools on the Haindi-Kakata highway. They were more than happy to give up their jobs because they were seldom paid.

The Dougba Senfenui Academy, which ran up to the sixth grade, had more students than it could handle. They came from Haindi and many outlying villages. Their number sharply increased when Kpolopele closed down the year after we opened the school. No reason was ever given for the school's unexpected closure except that Ma Miller had retired from the mission field, while Pastor Gbada was shepherding the flock of St. Peter's Lutheran Church in Monrovia.

"The Lutheran Church in America has withheld support to the Lutheran Church in Liberia," a former KP teacher informed me, "because they're tired caring for a child that refuses to grow up."

Parents were happy when we absorbed most of their disappointed children, some two hundred of them. We had to build dormitories for the upper students—grade four to six—who lived too far away to walk the long distance twice a day. On their own initiative, the older students built the dormitories, harvested the coffee, made large cassava and rice farms, and fished in the Deyn. To increase their catch, I hired two Fanti fishermen from Monrovia to teach them how to use canoes and nets. Thus, they fed themselves and provided income for the school; therefore, they were not required to pay school fees. After equipping the school with slates and chalks I bought in Kakata, I ordered a small portable generator from my Lebanese customer to enable the students study at night and help secure the campus; and a used Toyota pickup to take our football team around and convey our cassava to Kakata for better price.

Now I was prepared to establish a school in some other parts of the Chiefdom. To do that, I needed the support of the Land. What day was more appropriate to invite them to hang head on the matter than Independence Day?

Nearly all the Chiefs and Elders responded favorably to my invitation. Senator Bheipu Loryii couldn't come due to "previous official engagements", although we learned that he was marrying his fiftieth wife that day. But he sent ten dollars for the school. Our guests brought us goats, sheep, palm oil, rum, money, chickens, and so forth.

It was an impressive day. Joy surged my heart on seeing our students and faculty dressed in their best and staging an excellent program. A senior student was the orator for the day. Speaking in Kpelle, he welcomed the honored guests, thanked them for their support, and hoped that the fire I had lit in Haindi would soon spread all over the Chiefdom. He said the building of Liberia was the responsibility of Liberians, and the only way Liberians could perform this great task was by educating the youth. Posterity wouldn't forgive them if they failed to meet this obligation.

The highest moment of the program was the singing of a hymn in Kpelle the students had composed and practiced for weeks:

We thank thee for the sun
We thank thee for the rain
We thank thee for the air
We thank thee for the Land
That gives us food to eat
Life to all that lives

We thank thee for our fathers
We thank thee for our mothers
We thank thee for our brothers
We thank thee for our sisters
We thank thee for our teachers
We thank thee for the light of day

Forgive our foolish ways, O Lord
The blind of hate and darkness
The past that would not go away
Your mercies and salvation
From the glory of your kingdom
With love and peace our hearts renew

The guests, parents, and spectators from neighboring villages applauded most heartily, stamping their feet, shouting, and throwing coins at the children. Moved to tears, some of them wanted the song sung many times.

Clan Chief Borlormee Lonmeni of Lorla, speaking on behalf of his colleagues, said:

"Our children have said everything in their song and remarks. If we don't send them to school, they, like us, will be the *kwii* people's slaves. I thank God to live to see this day when a native son undertakes the education of his own people. Seporlor, we thank you for your courage. You have proved that we can do anything for ourselves once we're determined. We hope you'll build schools in other parts of the Chiefdom. We support you, and you have our blessing."

In the closing remarks, I thanked the Land for permitting me to build the school. With their encouragement and support, the citizens of Fuama Chiefdom could feed themselves and build their own roads, schools, and clinics. We shouldn't wait for the government or missionaries to do everything for us. For a hundred years and more, the government had not helped us significantly. I didn't think they would help us now. If we wanted a better future, we must work hard. Too many children died from preventable diseases, from hunger and poverty. Why should we be born in suffering and died in suffering? As Chief Lonmeni had said, we were nothing but slaves for *kwii* people. To own the land wasn't only a matter of being born in it, but taking part in running its affairs and having property. With good education we could become Deecees, superintendents, and ministers—even president, vice president, senators, or representatives—we would enjoy the wealth and authority of the land and have control of our destiny. Now that I had the full support and cooperation of the Land, I would shortly begin building schools in other parts of the Chiefdom.

After the program, rumor spread around that I had grown too big for my pants by considering myself the most important man in Fuama Chiefdom. Members of the faculty and student body constantly advised me to leave the area for some time for my own security. I perceived that explaining to the Senator what happened at the program would resolve the crisis.

Taking a goat to him as my white heart, I assured him of my love and respect, and clarified that I had no political ambition; I only wanted to help my people lead a better life in keeping with my father's mandate. Any negative rumor he might be hearing about me came from enemies who didn't want to see progress in the District. Accepting the gift and my explanation, the Senator said I shouldn't worry. He was fully acquainted with Liberian politics; it was wicked, malicious, and selfish. Nothing would happen to me. Was I not his son?

"We need schools in this District," he remarked. "Now that the missionaries have closed Kpolopele, suppose you hadn't built that school? Look, I'll ask the president to give you a big job. You'll be in charge of all schools in Bong County. I'm more interested in people who get things done than in people who only spread false rumor."

NOT MADE WITH HAND

As I inspected students on line at seven one morning, my janitor told me that, at daybreak, he had seen a man he knew sprinkling black powder out of a small black gourd round my house. He would arrest "the witch" and bring him to me for appropriate action.

"The only solution to the problem is that you leave the area," Moses told me. "Too many enemies are after you."

"Moses," I said, "forget that man. God will take care of me."

The witch turned out to be Water Zoe Deynpolu Kollie, who confessed that Senator Loryii had hired him to send me crazy or infect me with an incurably paralyzing disease. I told the boys to set him free. I didn't want to take responsibility for the death of someone who was halfway in the grave. I organized two shifts of vigilantes, the toughest boys I found, to guard the mission day and night. But the Senator employed another strategy that almost succeeded in destroying the mission.

He had The Devil visit the school one Saturday night. Of course, we non-members of the Poro had to stay behind closed doors until he left. Next day, we discovered that all the animals, the chickens, the pickup, and the generator had disappeared, half the coffee farm hewn down.

While I inspected the damage done to the coffee farm, Sianeh came running to me breathlessly, looking unkempt and agitated.

"All the students and teachers have run away," she said. "Suppose you run away, too? They're sending soldiers to arrest you! They'll kill you!"

"Running away won't solve the problem, Sianeh," I said, overtaking her on the way back to campus. "Go to your people for now. You're pregnant!"

Sianeh obediently packed what she and the children could carry and set off for Zuakpoisu. I accompanied them. Her people were still on their farms when we arrived in town. Her eldest sister was the first to arrive at sundown, a baby tied to her back, a toddler at her feet, and a basket on her head. After we exchanged greetings, she said her husband and the Old Man had remained behind to check traps.

"Mapu, we have come to spend some time here," Sianeh told her when she took the basket and the baby down and sat with us on the porch. "You know our problem."

"We know of your trouble," Mapu admitted with a nervous sigh. "It has gripped this town, too. Many townspeople including Brother Gbeasaa and his family have fled. They said the government will kill you people, all your families, and your fellow town-mates, but the Old Man said he would remain here no matter what. We can't afford to turn our back on him. 'If they're going to kill all of us,' he said, 'they're welcome. Once we're not dying for stealing, murder, or witchcraft, all will be well with us.'"

"You people should hide in the forest," I told Mapu. Sianeh bobbed her head in agreement. "They'll surely come here to look for chickens, cattle, and money, but from Sianeh's family only. I don't know why everybody is running away." I gave Sianeh some money to help take care of our large family. We had acquired ten children, including four of our own. Sianeh had made no fuss about Kulubah's son, especially when she learned that she had died.

"Dougba, stay here," she told me. "Our soldiers are not trained or disciplined. They don't hesitate to kill their own people. I advise you to remain here."

"Sianeh, I must go back, or they'll loot the little property remaining with us. I can take care of myself. Every man is a soldier. I don't think they'll do me any harm. You people take care of the children. I must fight this battle to the end. Fight it alone." The assurance wasn't good enough. When Sianeh began weeping, I left immediately.

I met a delegation of four men headed by Chief Zina waiting for me in the school building. They advised me to give up the struggle. It was foolish for one person to fight a whole Chiefdom. The Land had decided that I leave the town for my own safety. The government would run the school; people would remember me as its founder and first principal. This decision was final. Not even the Senator could overrule it. "Had he been here," Chief Zina said emphatically, "he'd be chairing this meeting in Gbekei, telling you the same thing."

Exhausted and not inclined to bother with long talks, I asked the delegation to give me a week to confer with the Ministry of Education because the school was duly registered. I must inform the education authorities of any disruption of its operation beyond my control.

Like a mighty blow, my request made the men spring from their seats, dart their eyes at each other, and walk into the bush. After a long time, they returned and Chief Zina told me:

"Son, you're our own blood. Don't put us in trouble. Should the government learn that The Devil destroyed your school, they'll arrest all the men round here."

Taking advantage of their discomfiture, I said, "I built this school for you people. Why did you destroy it? Who will take you from the darkness apart from your own children? I could have found a job in Monrovia, Bomi Hills, or Firestone with good pay and no headache, but I preferred coming home to help you. Is this my crime? Well, there's nothing I'll get from reporting you people to the government, but you must urge my students and teachers to come back. Otherwise, I'll have no choice but tell the authorities what you people have done."

The following day a few students returned. Upon my request, they went from village to village to urge their friends to return, too.

Every night as I lay sleepless in bed, I pondered whether it wasn't better to abandon the school project, get a fat job, and raise my family as others were doing. But missionaries had taught me that the value of life doesn't consist in living for yourself but in serving others. If you squandered the knowledge you gained in school for selfish interests, it becomes worthless like the salt that loses its savor.

During the tribulation, I found strength in visiting my father's grave, though the cemetery had become a market ground upon the Senator's orders. As if someone challenged his sacrilegious act while workers cleared the hallowed ground upon his orders, he reportedly announced, "Once you die, you have no more part to play in life. What matters is your soul which goes to heaven."

I knew Father's grave site, anyway. At dawn each morning I stood there, faced east, expressed grievances for the malicious obstacles that prevented my fulfilling his mandate, asked his blessings, and then plunged into the lukewarm waters of the Deyn, enjoyed its balm and cleansing. Instantly, my troubled heart would calm down; refreshed and optimistic, I would begin my day's work.

I spent much of my time reading and working the coffee farm. Truly, time and the resilience of youth are great healers. In two weeks I regained my vitality and was ready to engage my job with renewed vigor and commitment. The coffee trees began growing new limbs, and more students and teachers returned daily. They helped clean the coffee farm, make cassava patches, and recondition the campus. I decided to open the school in February, which was three months in the offing.

One afternoon as I sat reading the Acts of the Apostles in the school building, a man of medium height walked through the open gate, a bag in his hand. When he came close enough, I deciphered Jeremiah Foday after searching my memory. His visit was a total surprise.

"What brought you here, my man!" I exclaimed as I embraced him.

"Good luck," he said with a brilliant smile. A student took his bag to my house. "You were born under a lucky star, my man! Look, George Dennis has died. Some people said it was due to heart failure; others said *porlortor* mutinied on him upcountry. I believe the latter account which I got from market women."

"And what was he doing with *porlortor* upcountry?" I said. Before Foday could reply, I told him, "Let's go to the river for a swim. As you can see, the mission is in complete ruin. The Devil visited here one Saturday night and hewed down half the coffee trees, stole all our live-stock, cattle, and the generator. Everybody ran away. It's just a month ago the students and their teachers started returning."

"I know," Foday said, looking at the river as we walked in the tall grasses. "Reports about your misdeeds, or 'insolence' as they call it, come to the Ministry daily. They have reached the president's ears. They say you said unfavorable things about the government on last Independence Day."

"What good luck you brought?"

"I've placed your school on the subsidy list. I did it because I admire your courage. As far as I know, you're the first educated native man to return home to help our people. You deserve encouragement. Besides, we're one family, Dougba! I'm the grandson of your brother Zokpooh. His son Saki was my father. He divorced my mother and sent her home—to Sanoyea where I grew up. I took my stepfather's surname because he sent me to school. I got my education in Lutheran schools. It was after your departure that I learned of our relationship."

"It's a small world, really," I said and snapped his fingers again warmly.

"I fell in love with Kula for her to include your school on the subsidy list, which her boss signed one evening when he was dead drunk. He had just returned from the Minister's office where he had had more than enough to eat and drink. It was the Minister's birthday. No work, so everybody was there, feasting. When Kula prevailed on him to sign overdue letters, he asked her, 'Have you gone through them?' 'Yes, Minister,' she lied, 'very carefully.' Then he signed the documents hurriedly and left. The Minister proper dropped your school from the list. His successor, who knows you very well, signed them. He said you people were once classmates in Kpolopele."

"Could it be Caesar Dennis?"

"Yes. Caesar is George's brother. The Americo-Liberians are not like us. While we fight among ourselves killing each other, they help one another succeed in life. One gets promotion or dies in office—and they find the next of kin to fill his post."

"How did George die?"

"When the president assigned your case to him, George made a national issue of the problem to profit by it. He told the president that the Education Ministry would close your school permanently, and the president consented to it. These people, as you know, don't care much for education because they're afraid if the natives are educated, they'll take the country from them or possibly expel them. Besides, they send their children abroad for school. To me, it'd be in their interest to educate the people and develop the country. Then, they'll get humane treatment during the coming civil war. It might not even come."

"Today, if anyone will get inhumane treatment during this war," I said, "it won't be the Congo people but us. Watch my words."

"George convinced the president for the Ministry of Education to conduct a nationwide survey to know the number of large towns we have in order to build a school in each one, the only practical solution he saw to the problem. But, as you know, that was just empty talk. He had other plans in mind. He began his first tour in Sanoyea to come down to Monrovia through Fuama and Bopolu Districts. When a Cabinet Minister is on tour, as you know, he eats government money recklessly. Then too, he collects all the cattle, chickens, servants, and money he can in his wake—what they call 'gratuity.' In Sanoyea, the Lutherans already had a school. He only collected a little gratuity (a dozen sheep and goats plus two girls) and continued his tour to Fuama. Where there's no motor road, as you know, people carry government officials in hammocks. When they reached a large creek on the way, the hammock men advised the Minister to cross the bridge on foot, for it comprised only a single log which couldn't accommodate four men carrying a hammock on their heads, two abreast in front and two abreast behind.

"'I'm not getting down from this hammock,' the Minister said. 'All I want is cross over. I don't care how you people do it.' Well, the men did the only thing possible. Halfway across the creek, they dumped the Minister in the creek and ran away. Drunk and unable to swim, he drowned instantly. No one attempted to rescue him. The government dispatched a whole battalion to the area and arrested dozens of men including chiefs—people who knew nothing about the incident! They collected the Minister's body many miles downstream and took it to Monrovia for burial."

"And what happened to the people they arrested?"

"They crucified some and used others for *juju*!"

"That's sad," I said. "A major root cause of our problems is lack of education. I Dougba Senfenui Jr. believe that we'll stand a better chance of living in freedom, friendship, and prosperity if we're all educated."

"Dougba, you're certainly correct. Education is our only hope," Foday said. "I'll make sure you get the cash for your subsidy. Education will soon be a respectable and profitable venture. The pressure is building up on the president to have only educated people assume leadership positions in this country. The next Senator of Fuama District could be you."

"Not all the educated citizens of a country must be government employees, Foday," I said. "Unfortunately, people here don't think much of the private sector, even though it's the pillar of any thriving society. Some people have been feeling my pulse to see if I want to join government service, but I'd rather work in the private sector. Once you're meeting some pressing need of the nation, you're a valuable asset to the society."

"Write an article to help the process. You have a good mind. Newspaper publishers in Monrovia are tired of the government's mismanagement of the nation's affairs. They want to publish articles that inform and educate the people. As you know, the pen is mightier than the sword."

It took me a whole week to write the article. With everything to say, where could one begin? The Liberian conundrum is peculiar. Nobody loves Liberia, and Liberians don't love themselves. Our resources develop and enrich other countries. In such a situation, not even the pen can help us, but miracles happen.

In summary, I stated that we as a nation must hold together in order to steer our Ship of State to a safe harbor. We have permitted petty jealousies; ethnic, sectional, and selfish interests plus an accident of history to jeopardize our Ship of State. We undermine one another for jobs we're often unable to do. We accommodate and promote corruption in public administration. In fact, there is no accountability in government. Thus, the wealth of the nation is increasingly misused or shipped abroad, while poverty, disease, and ignorance take inestimable toll of the people's lives. Heinous crimes against the people go unpunished. We ignore the merit system in our employment policy. You're sure of getting a government job once you know some "big-shot" in the government. You don't have to know or do anything.

Perhaps the greatest obstacle to progress in Liberia is the historical accident that some of our people were sold into slavery hundreds of years ago. This tragic legacy has created outright hate and mistrust between descendants of the so-called immigrants and the natives. But ancestors of the natives experienced slavery, too, although they were never sold to Europeans. This preoccupation with a phenomenon beyond our control is self-destructive. Are we then to live in the past rather than confront the problems of today? No people can undo their past. They can only use its lessons to build for a better tomorrow.

We cannot absolve ourselves of responsibility for this shameful betrayal of our country by killing one another. To build a society responsive to our needs and aspirations, the educated sons and daughters of Liberia should run the government. I am not talking about people who have only been to school, but people who, in addition, aspire for excellence in all undertakings, people who have respect for truth and justice, people who put their country first in all circumstances, and people who take an educated approach to problems. Finally, we should always remember that only Liberians will build Liberia.

After reading the draft, Foday made several suggestions. He added that law enforcement should be paramount in the country; otherwise, we would have nothing but chaos on our hands and the nation would never develop. Should the government dismiss any of its officials for corruption, for example, it should recover what was stolen and never give the official in question another job and that official should go to jail. Only those born in Liberia, their roots firmly planted there, should be president or vice president. The legislature should program all administrations for the modernization of the state. Those that fail to meet up with their schedules of development should be discredited, the president impeached. He mentioned something about accountability, freedom of speech, the merit system, economic development, and so on.

"Foday, they'll imprison me for treason if we publish this article," I cried when I read the final draft.

"Not at all," he assured me, laughing. "A wind of change is now blowing over the country. The old order is giving way to a new one. The president himself supports the new order. Now that his days are numbered, he wants to do the right thing. All you have to do is write the article in simple English because the average educated Liberian is a sixth grade graduate. They will publish this article."

When Foday published the article, it caused quite a stir in Monrovia. While some people accused me of treason, a vast majority of my readers said I was farsighted. In a matter of months, a bill barring illiterate people from holding elected positions in the government was passed by both houses of the legislature and signed by the president. All chiefs, district commissioners, and superintendents were henceforth to come to office through the ballot box, not by presidential appointment. The president would only commission elected officials.

These unprecedented developments made me glad. The government was beginning to foster progress. More progress would come once we told our leaders what we wanted in a plain, polite language.

I opened the school in February as planned. Enough students and teachers had returned. Foday was able to secure the subsidy cash as he had promised. Thus, finance was the least of our worries. I asked him to join the staff to help me run the school, but he said it would be to my advantage for him to be in Monrovia. I appointed a former Kpolopele teacher Jaa Motimer as my deputy. The school flourished as never before. We began receiving girls!

During the ensuing elections in November, only candidates who had completed at least the eighth grade could run. Consequently, the Elections Commissioner dropped Senator Loryii's name from his list. The last official duty the Senator performed before leaving office was send me to Camp Belle Yallah, a maximum prison for hardened criminals.

It was a Saturday morning. From behind a dark cloud interspersed with blades of crimson light, the tropical sun came in a hurry. The morning pulsated with cries of animals, murmured greetings of people, and songs of birds. Obeying by instinct a habit I had found too hard to break, I took soap and towel and headed for the Small Cataract to bathe. The women and children were going to their farms, the men having gone ahead to visit traps, hooks, and fish baskets. As usual, sorrow tugged at my heart on seeing the little children going to farms rather than to school: boys carrying chicken baskets on their backs with the basket ropes strapped to their foreheads; girls carrying baskets of foodstuffs and cooking utensils on their heads. Would these precious ones be condemned, like their parents, to fight a profitless, dissipating, interminable battle for mere survival? The women spied me with gloomy faces and greeted me with dour, solemn voices, but I felt no feeling of dread or anxiety. I hurried to the river. As usual, it roared fiercely, foaming and challenging anyone with a passion to swim. I took a bath quietly and returned home to confront four soldiers with M-1 rifles and dressed in khaki short pants and short-sleeved shirts and red caps. Nobody was around except Sianeh who lay before the school building, her hands tied behind her back.

The highest ranking soldier, a Master Sergeant I suppose—if the insignia on his torn shirtsleeve was telling the truth—gave me a casual salute and said in Kpelle that Senator Loryii had ordered them to take me to Belle Yallah. He handed me a letter, dog-eared, which, he said, contained details of my crime. As I read it, they untied Sianeh.

"We're sorry," the Master Sergeant apologized as he helped Sianeh to her feet. "We wanted to know your whereabouts, but she refused to tell us, so we had to detain her until we found you."

Well written, doubtless by some journalist, the letter, which came from the Senator rather than from the Justice Minister, was clear and succinct, the grammar faultless, and the diction impeccable, although the facts were all wrong. It said that under the guise of running a school, I was gathering support to overthrow the government. The matter had reached the president's attention; since it involved a citizen in his District, the president wanted him to handle it. My sentence was life imprisonment in Camp Belle Yallah with hard labor.

Though they looked militant, the soldiers rendered me every courtesy. Sianeh and I went into our house where I turned over to her the cash I had on hand. She told me that all the students and teachers had fled the campus again. Some were kind enough to take our children with them. Her voice was steady. I had not expected her to exhibit so much courage. She mentioned nothing about her detention and maltreatment.

Nothing could we tell each other. You make plans and promises only when you have control of your destiny. After I dressed for the journey, we only knelt and appealed to the Creator for his mercy and deliverance. Then I hurried out to the soldiers.

"I'm ready to go," I told them.

I felt relief as we commenced our long journey, for the sinister, erratic drama had ended. Like a tropical shower, Bible verses Ma Miller taught us poured on me without any recollection on my part:

"Though I walk through the valley of the shadow of death, I will fear no evil, for Thou art with me."

"For to me to live is Christ; to die is gain."

"I'm the resurrection and the life—"

"We have a building from God, a house not made with hand, eternal in the heavens."

"Blessed are ye when men shall persecute you and say all manner of evil against you—"

BELLE YALLAH

The white-wing, red-belly, twin-engine propeller plane swooped down from the cumulus sky like a mighty eagle, twice circled the five acres of black thatched roofs in the ancient forest, alerting its haggard residents to another bright moment of their life. Growing sober, a dozen off-duty soldiers in mufti, who were lounging in the prison's spacious palaver house drinking sharp palm wine and prattling, hustled outside. They trained inquisitive eyes on the booming aircraft as it regained altitude, shot through a patch of black cloud, and emerged with its crimson belly merged with the sunset, then gently descended on the wide, grassy field.

All Belle Yallah scrambled to the barracks and glued their eyes on "the white man's witchcraft." Four soldiers in faded khaki uniforms, M-1 rifles hooked to their shoulders, and a prisoner leaped out of the plane. Two pulled the prisoner along by the arms while the other two kept the crowd at bay with gun butts as they fought to catch a glimpse of yet another "enemy" of the government.

Unable to join the crowd because of the heavy chains on my wrists and ankles, I stood before my prison hut watching the familiar commotion with resignation, the fiftieth in my five years of incarceration at Camp Belle Yallah.

To my amazement, the new "convict" was the well-motivated and learned Pastor Gbada. Handcuffed and stripped to the waist, he staggered between the soldiers who held him firmly while their friends now walked backwards, holding their weapons horizontally to keep the rowdy crowd at a respectful distance. The crowd jeered and denounced the pastor and all educated Liberians who, "consumed with greed for power and wealth, undermine the peace, stability, and economy of the nation." Shrieked in Pidgin English, Kpelle, and Loma, the cynical comments maintained that it was better for the nation to languish in ignorance, poverty, and disease than be under the intolerable yoke of corrupt, inept, and dissolute book people who lacked all moral scruple and thrived on the blood and tears of their own people. Put any of these "arm-chair liberators and defenders of the people's rights" in the Executive Mansion, and you see the worst catastrophe of any nation's history. Can more than one person occupy one chair at the same time? Why don't these "scoundrels", for sake of peace, leave the Old Man alone until he either died or became tired of the Chair?

"We have only one chief in each of our chiefdoms, clans, and villages," mumbled a Kpelle old man in ragged *gbalen*[54] as he hopped along with an old cane past me, "while they who claim to be educated and civilized want a thousand presidents to run this tiny country at the same time!" Pausing for breath, he asked whether it was what they meant by democracy, adding, "These wolves in sheep clothing have betrayed their country. But God

---

54. Shirt made in the form of a gown; fits the body neat and made of homespun.

will reveal them one by one for them to get the punishment they justly deserve."

Frankly, I couldn't understand how a people so poor and blind could be so ingenious in accumulating so many grievances and articulating them so well. Perhaps these innocents were only parroting what the pack of "gravy seekers" surrounding the power that be had taught them. The longer the Old Man stayed in power the longer they were sure of their jobs.

When they brought the pastor at a close range, I retched at his squeamish appearance. Barefoot, his ebony body riddled with swollen whip welts, blood spewed profusely from his everted lips and trailed down his pallid jaw, hairy chest, and potbelly. His face was knotty and shockingly distorted. His reddish eyes gazed at the evening sky with a vacant, forlorn look bereft of hope—a decidedly withdrawn look that seemed to search for peace above. Slowly sweeping the radiant sky, the wistful eyes closed in peaceful repose as the soldiers catapulted him into the hut I shared with a former county superintendent who had fallen from grace for declaring in a commencement address that justice in the country was for auction, and belonged to the highest bidder.

As if that wasn't felony enough, the former superintendent had gone on to say that corruption, immorality, indolence, and sheer mischief had ruined the spiritual, moral, and economic fabrics of the nation. He couldn't forecast the arrival of Doomsday, but he was sure it was somewhere round the corner. Unless Liberians repented and asked God's forgiveness, the nation would vanish from the face of the earth. A few minutes after his "unpatriotic speech", they whisked him to Camp Belle Yallah for life imprisonment with hard labor. Severe beatings had left him half-paralyzed and mute.

As they walked away with an air of satisfaction for a job well done, one soldier said glibly as an afterthought, "Dade place for you book people." They all guffawed. The shockwave soon ran through the lugubrious compound with its scores of harried inmates sitting immobile before their shanties.

Despite my repeated promptings, the pastor refused to speak to me. All night he lay speechless on the dusty floor, facing the mud wall, his cuffed hands tucked between his thighs and his swollen ankles manacled with heavy chains. By noon the following day, Capin Dragon, the chief warder, a short Loma man sodden with palm wine, stumbled into our prison for the regular inspection. Looking at the mangled, seemingly lifeless pastor, he ordered that his grave be dug. It was only then that Pastor Gbada crawled out of his coma and muttered that he was still alive. Capin Dragon removed his handcuffs but not his ankle chains because "book people are quick to run away," he croaked in Loma. "A year ago," he recalled, "seven journalists and three university professors serving life sentence fled this prison. They were guilty of sedition for calling on the Old Man to resign because he had stayed in office too long! Listen to that! What is twenty-five years in the life of a country!" The fellow puffed with anger, his red eyes rolling in their sockets maliciously. "Thinking that educated people were honorable, we never bothered to bind their hands or feet nor have armed guards watch over them whenever they did their token hard labor such as whipping grass and lopping bushes round the airstrip. After their third working day, they never returned to prison!" Then he told the story of an ungrateful county superintendent who had formed a party to run against the Old Man "that election year." Continuing with righteous indignation, he said, "This irresponsible native man forgot that the Old Man selects his own opponent during election." Usually this token opponent was some nonentity with nothing besides the bedraggled rags on his back. At the height of the election, he'd turn his supporters over to the Old Man for a purse, the practice of true democracy. "We brought the reprobate here after we unearthed his wicked plot. Last week he disappeared mysteriously." Many an unmarked grave round the barracks accounted for most of these mysterious disappearances.

For two full weeks, Pastor Gbada maintained silence. He would bathe each morning in the palm thatched enclosure behind our prison hut under the watchful eyes of armed warders, then sit quietly against the mud wall behind the hut all day, staring in the sky with a bleak face, killing tsetse flies on his naked trunk, and wiping beads of perspiration off his pale face. Everyone believed that Jesus had unburdened him of hunger, pain, and the fear of death. He replied queries in monosyllables only:

"How are you?" someone would ask him.

"Fine," would be his curt response.

"You're sure?"

"Yes."

"Ready to eat?"

"No."

"You haven't eaten for three days!"

I thought the pastor had gone on hunger strike in protest to his maltreatment, for what else could make a man, otherwise sanguine and gregarious, so moody and depressed? Convinced he couldn't muster the energy to run away, the warders bothered with him no more. I believed, however, that time would retrieve him. While going through my own apprenticeship at the maximum prison, notorious for its torture and secret killings, I never thought life in bondage could be endured.

For the better part of each day for two weeks, I sat with the pastor to bolster his courage with advice and biblical teachings about suffering, only to find myself engaged in monologue:

"No need telling you to accept not only the good but also the bad from God," I would begin on a familiar note. "You often preached that God does everything for the best." He would listen attentively, his head bowed and his hands clasped between his knees. Sometimes he seared my ragged frame and checkerboard haircut distastefully, giving me the impression that I was making a nuisance of myself. Then he would stare apathetically in the distance. "Remember the Master's bidding that we expect suffering," I would insist. "He had no liking for the *cup*, but he drank it in compliance with God's will. I don't think we sinners can ever be saviors, but God doesn't hesitate to use even the lowly and the weak to do great things. Maybe God wants us to go on this cross to save our people."

As the days passed, the pastor became more and more reticent and morose. If persuasion couldn't work, I thought, threat might.

"You know what?" I told him harshly one morning. "Poverty, disappointment, sickness, death, and all conceivable afflictions don't turn us against life. Our people kill abnormal people, you know, because they believe that such people are possessed. Don't be surprised if they come for you one night, never to be seen again." The pastor only stared away as if I was talking nonsense. Now I believed that we had lost him. Crestfallen, my own fatalness confronted me. I was pretending that all was well while my life had gone to pieces.

Pastor Gbada's recovery came as a great surprise to everyone. It gave hope to many a prisoner. With his theological training, he didn't need much urging to attend the Sunday morning service in the palaver house. His very first time worshiping with us he sat brokenly by me, his wearied eyes focused on the obese chaplain in a homespun gown. The reassuring Scripture reading lit his listless eyes and enlivened his jaded spirit, if his disposition meant anything. When the chaplain, a failed medical practitioner turned evangelist, began haranguing us with his usual pompous pronouncements, Pastor Gbada bowed his head and frowned his face.

"The Bible says," the chaplain began his sermon on a vague note, his English lathered with Loma, "that the endurance we are sustaining is the maternity of emancipation. Therefore, when the glorification is not in our favor and our pendulum can't run, we shouldn't repine. What I'm asseverating is no platitudinous sponterosity. The stupendous malignance that ungracious predestination has made our benevolence is a passage to magnificence—"

As if the chaplain had insulted him, Pastor Gbada leaped to his feet and took over the lectern. Shocked by the impertinence, the chaplain only watched his interloper with amazement while the congregation observed the farce with frozen smiles, for disgust had no place at a church service, but the episode was quite disturbing. Anyone moved by the spirit in church had the liberty to speak in tongue, sing, shout, or stage a fit of convulsion. Pastor Gbada first opened his lips and closed them wordlessly; after a brief pause, he managed to say in clear, simple words that God loved us and had a purpose for our suffering. If we repented of whatever sins we might have committed, God, whose mercy is unlimited, would forgive and save us. We should pray for our persecutors and ourselves—The sermon took no more than fifteen minutes. The chief warder made Pastor Gbada our chaplain over the protest of Pastor Gbada's predecessor, and freed him of his manacles, saying that such a preacher of no mean ability couldn't run away. The pastor appointed me his assistant and, with his influence, freed me of my chains, too.

We preached to the prisoners on Sundays and taught them the Bible each Wednesday night by the saffron light of a hurricane lantern. Our hard work yielded much fruit. Cantankerous arguments (which were often settled with fisticuffs and knives) no longer occurred, and nobody ran away. Grateful that we had made their job easier, the guards gave us better food and lodgings and promised to do everything possible to set us free. After all, we had neither stolen nor killed.

For a whole month after Pastor Gbada's depression was lifted, I tried unsuccessfully to engage him in a discussion of our plight. Where had we gone wrong? He told me repeatedly that the best way of bearing our suffering was to forget it, or it'd only become more painful. Clearly, the reverend had forgotten his psychology, I thought. Nothing is forgettable, and analyzing and assessing a tragic experience is the only way to cope with it.

During my first year in Camp Belle Yallah, when my depression bordered on suicide, my anxieties eased and the urge to take my life went away when I recorded, analyzed, and reflected on the events which had shaped my life. Since our lives had practically followed the same course, I had been hoping that the pastor's view on our common experience would complement mine, making it clearer and more bearable, but his reluctance to discuss our predicament seemed unshakable. Perhaps the bridge might come down if I looked at the problem from his point of view.

"I think you're right, Pastor," I told him one afternoon as we sat in the shade of a palm tree near the airstrip. "Recounting our tragedy accomplishes nothing but more suffering. The mere thought of it is alarming. After losing my mother and everything I earned with my sweat, I've left my fate in God's hand. Should Sianeh remarry, I won't blame her. What I want to know now is the reason for the African's unabated suffering."

The pastor watched me smilingly and chuckled.

"You're quite a clever fellow," he said. "When the front door closes before you, you take the back door. No doubt, you have a point. It's bad our culture doesn't permit the analysis and assessment of issues. We believe that whatever happens to us is the will of God and the Ancestors. That saves us the trouble of doing something about our problems." Looking at me grimly, he said, "Dougba, fifty years from now we'll be exactly where we're today, and our children will kill us for failing them. We pride ourselves on founding the first African Republic but refuse to develop it. Colonialists took over two-thirds of Liberian territory—some 117,000 square miles of it—unknown to us. Had they not told us of their own encroachment we wouldn't have known about it at all. Indeed, we're not the most patriotic people on earth." The pastor sighed, cupped his chin in his hand, and looked into space.

"We still have hope, Pastor," I said. "You used to tell me, 'As long as there's life, there is hope.' Once we identify what is holding us back and root it out, we'll overcome our many difficulties."

"You're right, my son, but we already know what is holding us back: fear of change, petty jealousies, squabbles—and outright laziness. The basest of these is fear of change. Why do we live the same way our ancestors lived thousands of years ago despite the incredible progress the world is making in science and technology?"

"Because we're afraid of change, as you said. Change is risky."

"Dougba, the white man has made great strides in progress not because he has all the answers but because he acts. But even when we see solutions to our problems, we ignore them and prefer living with the problems. Do you know that the white man is still looking for better means of transportation although he has invented vehicles for traveling by land, air, and sea with great facility?"

"Yes, Pastor."

"I'm beginning to believe in the theory I've often heard, that Africans are backward because nature is too kind to them, and white people are progressive because nature is too mean to them."

"In what respect is nature kind to us and mean to white people?"

"We don't suffer from flood, drought, earthquake, forest fire, hurricane, tornado, winter, but white people contend with all these. Since winter takes half the year, they invent machines to make their farms on a grand scale. We have the whole year to make farms. We can even survive without farming. We have enough wild fruits, tubers, animals, and fish to live on without sweat. The weather permits us to do without much clothing. Had nature not been so good to us, we'd have made much progress."

"I beg to differ, Pastor," I said. "Progress is possible anywhere to any extent regardless of circumstances. Go to Nairobi, Johannesburg, Dakar, Abidjan, and Harare, where the white man made his homes until we drove him away—you would think you're in Europe or America. Our backwardness needs a different explanation."

"Had the white man not enslaved and colonized us—"

"The white man too has been enslaved and colonized, Dougba. The Greeks who received the brunt of slavery in the ancient world are the champions of modern civilization. You can't enslave or colonize a people's minds, or their hearts or spirits."

"Then what is our problem?"

Looking far away the pastor said, "We used to deceive ourselves by thinking that Christianity and education would solve our problems because they have done wonders in the West, but they've only created disaster in Africa. The most dangerous criminals are the educated ones. Unless we produce our own philosophers, theologians, historians, anthropologists, scientists, writers, musicians, artisans, and the like—whose works are not mere reproductions of Western thought and culture—we'll never take our rightful place in world community. Indeed, we are divorced from our roots."

"That—we'll find difficult to do, for truth is the same everywhere for all ages," I said. "But this question of our roots is quite correct. We used to think that independence would solve our problems, but all it has done for us is replace white imperialism with black mediocrity. If I may revise my diction, I think 'idiocy' is the right word."

"Even colonialism has its benefits," the pastor said. "What would have Africa been like had the white man never come here?"

"An immensely dark continent," I was quick to reply. "What Joseph Conrad calls 'The heart of darkness.' Well, the white man has come and gone, and we're still in darkness."

"What progress you see in Africa is found mostly where the white man settled. Turn this country over to him, and it becomes like Europe or America in five years."

"Our leaders are responsible for this. When they get into power, they first enrich themselves at our expense instead of tackling any of our many problems. With a few exceptions, they cling onto power until they either die in office or are overthrown. They don't hesitate to give our hard won independence back to the white man for morsels of bread and banknotes."

"If I may say something in defense of some of our leaders," the pastor said, "—many of them went astray because we made them little gods. When we stop making a cult of the leadership of Africa, we'll get somewhere with development. The leader a people get is the leader they make."

The pastor laughed briefly and looked at the evening sun somberly. Speaking quietly, slowly, with an earnestness I had never suspected of him, he said:

"Dougba, let's come home. We in this country deceive ourselves into believing that we have made great achievement merely because we have a locality, a flag, an anthem, a constitution. These things don't build a nation. Nation building requires patriotism, honesty, discipline, a sense of mission, unity of purpose, and a burning desire to excel in all undertakings. All these we lack!" He stopped for a long time, apparently to mobilize his wisdom. "Perhaps our greatest need is unity of purpose," he continued. "How can we make progress when we're pulling in opposite directions? The tribesman worries only about his ancient traditions and rituals, while the so-called civilized man is only concerned with what goes into his belly and his pocket. We have no consideration for each other or the nation; consequently, we live in fear and suspicion."

"European history teaches us that progress is never plain sailing," I said. "You take a step forward and two backward. With determination, one day you take a giant step ahead and there's no turning back. Courage, prudence, and patience are the rules of the game, my friend. The founding fathers might have made a thousand mistakes, but they passed onto us a piece of Africa's map. We can make something of it if we like."

"And only if we know our history—history that highlights our strengths and other resources. But the true history of Liberia is yet to be written. All we have is a jumble of journals, reports, and memos which tell us when Liberia was founded, who have been its presidents—what parties have been in power—what nations have aided us—Dougba, we're thriving on chaos and mistrust because we don't know our true history."

"That's true—"

Before I could say another word, a huge gorilla of a man mysteriously loomed over our heads, pointing a rifle at us.

"What have you fellows been discussing?" the gorilla cried. "How to overthrow the government?" We rose and confronted him.

"No!" Pastor Gbada said fearlessly. I exchanged anxious glances with him, and then stared at the strange man with blinking eyes.

The intruder bobbed his head towards the prison without comment. We preceded him. As we entered our dark, stifled shed, now furnished with palm thatch mattresses, I told him that the pastor and I were old friends. We had been only renewing acquaintance and praying.

"A likely tale," he said. "You fellows didn't talk about blind people leading this country? Look, I wasn't born yesterday. Beginning tomorrow, I don't want to see you two together. And keep quiet in your hut! Understand?"

Early the following morning as I entered notes in a copybook by dull light filtering through openings in the thatched roof, the padlock on our door clicked. A uniformed warder entered breezily and asked for the pastor. I had a premonition of danger. In a while, all may be over for him. The Superintendent and I watched the dismal drama helplessly. Outside, the pastor squealed, screamed, howled, pleading that they kill him once and for all. When his pandemonium lapsed into groans, they came for me. The warder who pulled me along said they were gashing all prisoners' soles as a precaution. They had just received orders from the Minister of Defense for nearly all prison guards to go to Monrovia and help put down a riot. Student organizations, trade unions, and marketers were demanding their rights. With our feet sore, we wouldn't be able to use the opportunity to run away.

Many of those who had gone through the ordeal hopped and ambled round the compound, groaning; a handful came our way to watch our "initiation".

"We thought you'd die," Pastor Gbada told me after my ordeal. He and the Superintendent were nursing their wounds. "You fainted! But God is with you."

"He's with you people, too," I said weakly.

Having no appetite for the tasteless rice and palm oil supper, we slept on empty stomach. Since our encounter with the strange rifleman, the pastor and I hadn't put a grain of rice in our mouths. The Superintendent joined us in empathy.

A week later, we learned that most of the soldiers that had been dispatched to Monrovia fled into the bushes on the way when they heard that the protesters had guns. Those who remained in the camp took off their uniforms; many of them ran away. Hitherto, the army had perceived its mission to be guarding the homes of VIPs, arresting unarmed civilians for petty crimes, and harassing innocent citizens for their livelihood. The prison guards were therefore surprised to learn that they would engage in an armed conflict.

In two weeks our sores healed considerably. The pastor and I dragged ourselves each afternoon to the shade of a palm tree on the edge of the airstrip and continued our discussion. We were frank and forthright in expressing our thoughts but careful to avoid mentioning our dramatic entry into Camp Belle Yallah. One day I felt obliged to know why a man of God with good education, whom the country needed so urgently, should be condemned to rot in a jungle prison.

"What brought you here?" I asked the pastor.

"Because I had the misfortune of telling the truth in the pulpit," he told me right away as if he had been waiting for the question. "I said then, and I still maintain my position, that there will be no progress in this country as long as old illiterates represent us in the legislature. What is the point in sending our children to school if running the country remains in the hands of people who can't read or write? When these innocents accede to power, their only concern is pomp and pageantry and the spoils of office. The elite use them to legitimize their corruption. I also condemned cannibalism, ritual killing, and stealing—vices which run through all fabrics of our life and keep the country poor and undeveloped. Nowhere in the world will you find the perfect society, but when a nation considers evil acceptable, that nation is in trouble." He raked beads of perspiration off his brows with a forefinger. The pastor had clearly deserted me and was preaching from an imaginary pulpit.

"I see why you're here," I said, restraining a smile. "I had thought that by forgetting politics and concerning myself with practical matters such as farming and education, I would be in nobody's way. But I was wrong."

"I also denounced the government, the church, and all our institutions for failing to develop the economy and give our children the kind of education that can prepare them for life," the pastor was saying. "People who are perpetually poor, perpetually sick, perpetually ignorant can't make good citizens or Christians. The government and the church should build enough roads, enough schools, enough hospitals, and enough industries—make electricity and potable water available in every town and village—to make life possible for the people. Only then will we have peace and security. The peace and security we're 'enjoying' is dissatisfaction and resentment under compression. It's not mine to tell when the conflagration will occur, but it will occur!"

"Pastor," I said mildly, "why are we Africans—we Liberians, for that matter—against ourselves? We have all the needed resources to modernize our country, and we have independence. What's holding us back?"

"You're taking us where we began, Dougba. It's fear of change holding us back. We fear change because it entails risk, but stability is also risky. Nature demands that we go either forward or backward."

"Pastor, don't you think we're in trouble because we're trying to do in one lifetime what took the white man thousands of lifetimes to do? If you neglect school until you're forty-five, you can't start with college. That's what we're doing—starting with college. Have I told you how I got here?"

"With the opportunities we have, Dougba, we can accomplish much more in one lifetime than the white man was able to accomplish in a thousand lifetimes. We don't have to invent ships or cars or tractors or airplanes or telephones or chloroquine or insecticide. Why should we wait for a thousand years to do what we can do today?

"Your troubles appeared in the papers in Monrovia, as I'm sure mine have. You worsened your case by publishing an article critical of the government. They say you insulted Honorable Loryii by saying that he isn't qualified to be Senator because he is illiterate."

"Pastor, I sincerely believe that our illiterate brothers and sisters are morally superior to our so-called civilized people. But having them run a modern state is intellectually dishonest. Only those who want Africa to remain in perpetual darkness to exploit will support such a policy. I never belittled the Senator, Pastor. I was only challenging him and others like him to go to school. As you know, it's never too late to learn—

"When the Church fired me, I took to farming and education, for missionaries taught us that opening our people's eyes is our greatest responsibility. I believed them, but I ended up being a target of the tribe's hate for doing just that. The many parents of Fuama Chiefdom whose children had either failed in school or abandoned it, couldn't stomach my success. Senator Loryii thought I posed a threat to him because I was becoming 'just too, too popular!' But I had no political ambition. They would have made no protest had I become a Deecee going about the countryside with soldiers collecting their children, money, and foodstuffs for my own use.

"Some enemies of mine told Senator Loryii that I had said that the true owner of the land was the person with education and much money. Thoroughly enraged, he went straight to the president without even asking me a question, and told him that I said I had done far more for Liberia than what he had done for the country in his two decades of leadership. I had built and electrified a school in the heart of the country. Had I been president, I would have done much, much more. Listen to that! The president, who became acutely worried about his insecurity since he staged that fake coup to get rid of his opponents, told him to handle the problem in his own way. Like Pontius Pilate, he washed his hands of the whole matter, but Senator Loryii knew what he wanted. That's how I got to this miserable place, and why I'll never leave here alive."

The pastor said, "Dougba, we need heroes, true heroes, to save Liberia. No nation can make progress without real heroes. We have heroes of corruption, heroes of mismanagement, heroes of immorality, heroes of indolence, heroes of lawlessness—"

"It's regrettable they destroyed the coffee farm and the school," I continued ruefully, "which cost me so many years of hard work. Since they had no use for me, they could have let somebody else operate them for the children to continue with their education."

"Then your name would have continued ringing," the pastor said. "Too bitter a pill for them to swallow."

"Why are we this way?"

"Only God knows, my son. Change will come because no condition is permanent, but it will come through individuals and not institutions. It will come through heroes of faith and courage—men and women of love and vision—people whose only concern is what to do for others. When our leaders talk about developing Liberia, they're really talking about enriching themselves at the nation's expense. No—development won't come through the state or the church but through people who put Liberia first in all they think and do—true patriots who are prepared to offer their very lives for their country."

"I agree with you," I told the pastor.

It was now twilight. We retired to our prison, ate our ill-prepared supper, and went to bed. Although our weeklong discussion got us nowhere, it relieved our fears and anxieties substantially. I slept well that night and woke up long after sunrise.

My heart sank and my eyes grew dim when I noted that the Pastor and the Superintendent were absent! It was unusual for both men to be away at the same time. Paralyzed with fear, I called them frantically, but only my own call echoed back to me. I searched the bath fence and everywhere my eyes could see, calling them loudly, but they were nowhere around, and nobody had the mouth to advise me of their whereabouts. Late in the evening, a Kpelle warder took me to the outskirts of the barracks and pointed at two fresh, oblong mounds of ruddy earth lying parallel to each other in the shrubs.

"These are the graves of your Pastor and your Superintendent," he told me pointedly.

"And why should they kill a man of God and a public servant for only speaking their mind?" I asked him with alarm.

"Prisoners are not killed here, my friend!" the fellow said in anger. "There's no capital punishment in Liberia! People guilty of capital offense either die of natural causes or go for water or firewood. So these former friends of yours never told you the great crimes they committed?" the warder asked me. "These wicked men denounced the president and all leaders of this country for what they called 'corruption and maladministration'. They refused to recant their misguided impudence and kiss the president's shoes for his mercy! So they had to go for firewood."

"What will happen to me?" I asked the fellow anxiously as we sauntered back to the camp.

"The president doesn't even know you're here," he informed me. "What I suspect is that they'll let you languish here until you die, and if you refuse to die, they'll give you *black diet*[55] to make sure you die. You'll never be pardoned because your case involves treason."

I sat up all night putting finishing touches on these memoirs by candlelight, hoping Sumoiwuo, a former student of mine and my warder now, would conceal the rather bulky document and give it to Foday for it to see the light of day. Lying prostrate on the dusty floor at dawn, I prayed for Pastor Gbada, for the Superintendent, for myself, and for my country. When the blue spears of dawn, riddled with dancing motes, invaded the puny, stifled room through the porous thatched roof, a rooster crowed and the choral songs of birds in kola trees poured softly on the slumbering compound.

---

55. Withhold food and sometimes water.

The prayers relieved me of all fears and anxieties, and filled my heart with unaccountable joy and the assurance that He whose mercies are boundless had taken over my paddle, and I had become only a passenger in the canoe.